THE
BLACKBIRD
SEASON

Center Point
Large Print

Books are
produced in the
United States
using U.S.-based
materials

Books are printed
using a revolutionary
new process called
THINKtech™ that
lowers energy usage
by 70% and increases
overall quality

Books are
durable and
flexible
because of
smythe-sewing

Paper is
sourced using
environmentally
responsible
foresting methods
and the
paper is acid-free

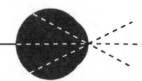

**This Large Print Book carries the
Seal of Approval of N.A.V.H.**

THE BLACKBIRD SEASON

KATE MORETTI

CENTER POINT LARGE PRINT
THORNDIKE, MAINE

This Center Point Large Print edition
is published in the year 2018 by arrangement with
Atria Books, a division of Simon & Schuster, Inc.

The text of this Large Print edition is unabridged.
In other aspects, this book may vary
from the original edition.
Printed in the United States of America
on permanent paper.
Set in 16-point Times New Roman type.

ISBN: 978-1-68324-637-4

Library of Congress Cataloging-in-Publication Data

Names: Moretti, Kate, author.
Title: The blackbird season / Kate Moretti.
Description: Center Point Large Print edition. | Thorndike, Maine :
    Center Point Large Print, 2018.
Identifiers: LCCN 2017046262 | ISBN 9781683246374
    (hardcover : alk. paper)
Subjects: LCSH: Missing persons—Investigation—Fiction. |
    City and town life—Fiction. | Teenage girls—Fiction. | Psychological
    fiction. | Large type books. | BISAC: FICTION / Suspense. |
    FICTION / Contemporary Women. | GSAFD: Suspense fiction.
Classification: LCC PS3613.O7185 B58 2018 | DDC 813/.6—dc23
LC record available at https://lccn.loc.gov/2017046262

For Chip

The river is moving.
The blackbird must be flying.

—from *Thirteen Ways of Looking at a Blackbird,* Wallace Stevens

The day the birds fell, I dealt the tower card. Everyone always said to never read your own cards, but who the hell was gonna read mine?

People believe, though. I don't, but other people do. I was more interested in the idea that there was magic in the world at all. I found a book in the library and I've been reading my own cards every morning since. But two things happened at once, two days in a row, and you should know about them. First, I found a blackbird, just like the others. Perfect. Smooth. Soft. Like it had just stopped breathing. Except, this one had a hole where its left eye should have been. I've never seen that before. The next day, I did a reading and dealt the tower card, the one with that one-eyed raven on it. And then, just when I thought the world was mocking me, it rained starlings.

I try not to believe in signs. But some-times they're just so goddamn obvious.

CHAPTER 1

Nate, Monday, May 4, 2015:
Two weeks after the birds fell

The rain came in sheets, like a wall, forming wide rivulets down the windshield. The wipers swished and couldn't keep up. They were old, needed to be replaced, and left streaks across the glass. But this was Alecia's car and she hadn't told him. His job was the maintenance, sure, but he wasn't a mind reader. He smacked the lever up a notch.

He squinted against any oncoming headlights, the few there were. Winding pavement and black towering pines combined with the lack of streetlights made this stretch of road, up into the Pocono Mountains, a hazard regardless of the season. The Lackawaxen River rushed by to his right, a mere fifty feet over a guardrail, engorged with the deluge of rain, more than typical for spring in Pennsylvania. He slowed to thirty miles an hour and leaned forward, his headlights bouncing off the white line, the yellow centerline almost invisible, faded with age.

His phone rang, the display flashing. He

ignored it. Could be Tripp, but he'd gotten into it with Alecia and she likely wanted to keep it going. He'd been so distracted he'd forgotten his pillow and would be stuck sleeping with a throw pillow on Tripp's sofa, mildewed and lumpy. He wasn't even sure the bag perched next to him on the passenger seat had enough to get him through the week. He'd been unfocused, just shoving things in: jeans, socks, underwear, shirts. Things you need when you have no job, no wife to go home to.

The phone rang again and he took his eyes away from the road for a split second. *Alecia.* He almost picked up, but tightened his hands on the wheel. Pick it up, don't pick it up? Her pecking and pulling at the threads of their marriage wasn't new; it was as old as anything he could remember. She just had so much more to pull at now. Not just Gabe, although always, *always* Gabe.

His headlights caught on a figure in the distance, a hand waving in the air, panicked. He slowed the car, pulled over, until he was next to her, hair plastered to pale cheeks, black clothing rendering her almost invisible in the night, had it not been for her gleaming white hair. He felt the cord of muscle up his arms tighten in a spasm. He rolled down the passenger-side window, but just a crack. Maybe two inches. He'd be damned if he was letting *her* into this car.

"You're going to get yourself killed. What the hell are you doing?"

"I need help." Her eyes were wild, wide and doll-like against her face, and her hands, red chipped fingernails, cupped her cheeks, pushing her hair back. Fingers wound up into that bright white hair at her temples and she shook her head back and forth and back and forth, like a dog shaking off water. That *hair,* a regular topic of conversation with the students, impossibly exotic but just so weird. Teenagers these days aimed to stand out, and that bright whiteness still gave them all pause.

"I can't help you. You know that." There it was. He was finally, *finally* angry. Everyone had been asking him, *are you angry?* In an accusatory way, a way that really meant *why aren't you angry?* As though this alone was proof of his guilt. He wanted to capture the moment, record his voice *right now,* because seeing her, finally, he realized he was really, *really* angry. "Get out of here, Lucia. Go home. Where you belong."

She leaned against the car so her mouth was even with the window opening, her body pushed against the window so he couldn't see her eyes. Only that mouth, that lying little mouth. She wore a white T-shirt, soaked through, and he could see the outline of her nipples, pressed against the glass. Where was her jacket? It had to be fifty-five degrees. Not his problem. He looked away.

"I don't belong anywhere." And when she leaned her forehead against the door trim, he could finally see her eyes. They were bloodshot and her pupils dilated like black Frisbees against a cerulean sky. Fear could dilate your eyes, he knew that for sure. Or was she on something? Pilfered from that brother of hers?

He didn't care.

He picked up his phone. Pressed the numbers 911.

"I can't help you, Lucia. I'm calling the police and I won't leave until they get here, but you cannot get in my car. I can't do anything for you." His voice was gentler than he'd intended. He'd always had a soft spot for her and those like her: the damaged, pretty girls. The smart girls with no guidance. The lost girls. There had been others; Robin Hendricks came to mind, but none who'd gotten him to this place before.

He hit send. *Ring. Ring.* "Pike County Police Department."

"Hi. This is Nate Winters. I need help on Route Six."

"Sure, Mr. Winters, what appears to be the problem?"

"I'm here with a Lucia Hamm. I was driving and I found her walking along the road. She might be on something but I can't drive her any-where. Just send someone, please."

She stared at him, her mouth twisting. She

14

backed up slowly, away from the white line, her eyes narrowed at him, the side of her face illuminated by the headlights.

"Lucia!" He called through the slight window opening. "Don't you dare go anywhere. Stay right there."

She stepped around the front of the car, his hazard lights blinking red against her face. Her mouth curved up in a wicked smile and his insides coiled. She leaned forward, palms flat against the hood of his car, eyebrows arched seductively.

"Mr. Winters?" The voice on the other end was deep and slow. "Is everything all right?"

She blew him a kiss.

He rolled his window down all the way and leaned out. "Lucia!" He called again, his voice dying in the wind.

She turned and walked away, along the white line, the headlights of the car flanking her retreating figure. She wore a short, black skirt and knee-high boots, and her hips swayed.

"Shit." He ran his hand through his hair.

"Mr. Winters? Are you still there?"

She turned, then, maybe ten feet from the front of his car, braced her feet on either side of the white line and gave him two middle fingers. Then she cut right and ran into the woods.

"*Mr. Winters.*" The man on the phone was stern now, angry about having his time wasted.

"Are you still there? Do you still need someone to come out?"

"I don't know." He felt sick. No matter what happened now, everything had just gotten worse. All the pieces he'd been clinging to had flown apart, scattering what was left of his life in a million directions. He was in trouble, he'd *been* in trouble, but now he was more than in trouble, he was as dead as a person could be while still being alive. In one heartbeat, he envisioned Alecia and Gabe huddled together on the couch, himself in prison, a *20/20* special. His dinner rose in his chest and he took a deep breath to quell the panic.

He had no way of knowing that this moment would become the linchpin, the moment that all the moments after would hinge upon. The papers would call him a murderer; the police would come to him; his ex-friends, his gym buddies, the guys who *knew him for God's sake;* and say, *Nate was the last one to see her alive, right?* The last one is always the guilty one.

He couldn't know all this. But he could still feel it, like something physical chasing him and gaining ground, his heart beating wildly, a skittering pulse up the back of his neck. It was more than a feeling. It was a portent, something tangible, almost corporeal.

"She's gone," he said quickly, and hung up, dropping the phone on the seat. He should have just driven away. Everything in his body told him to just drive away.

He opened the car door and stepped into the rain.

CHAPTER 2

Alecia, Tuesday, April 21, 2015

A month before Nate was fired, nearly a thousand starlings fell from the sky. Not fluttering to the earth like snowflakes, but plummeting, like quarter-pound raindrops. They fell hard and fast in the middle of the third inning of opening day at Mt. Oanoke High field. The first one Alecia saw bounced off Marnie Evans's shoulder and hit the gravel with nothing more than a soft rustle. She screamed, her fingers threaded through her hair, *get it out! Get it out! Get it out!* Like it was a trapped bat. Alecia didn't mind watching Marnie Evans freak out; in fact she kind of enjoyed it, so she just covered her mouth with her palm. Marnie Evans treated minor hiccups—missing basket bingo cards and off-color varsity jacket orders—like national disasters all while chewing Xanax like Pez.

But adversity builds muscle, and since Alecia chipped and clawed her way through every day, it took so much more to rattle her than the Marnie Evanses of the world, and a few little birds weren't going to do it. So she didn't mind watching Marnie at all. She hadn't even expected to be at the game. Nate had asked her out of the blue. It felt nice to be so spontaneous. The day had a fresh-air, college-kid-out-on-the-green feel to it, summer break looming, with all its newness.

It was just a regular Tuesday, except that it was a *good day*. And all of Alecia's days were divided clean down the middle, it seemed. Good Days (capital G, capital D) and Bad Days. The deciding factors were variations on a theme: whether they were able to get through a grocery trip, whether Gabe got through his therapy without freaking out, whether she got a call from a bill collector.

Gabe actually did remarkably okay with change, perhaps because Alecia didn't fight against every wrong turn, every slight schedule adjustment, like some of the women in her special-needs-moms' group. But it was always easier when things went according to plan. Today there had been no tantrum, no horrific trip to the store, no bill collector. When the phone rang at two, after Gabe's nap (a record thirty minutes), she picked it up, sort of excited and breathless.

"Hey." She thought it was amazing that her heart still skipped when she saw Nate's name come up on caller ID, and on a Good Day, she might count herself as belonging to the apparently few happy marriages left.

On a Bad Day, she thought about packing

19

a bag, leaving Nate to deal with Gabe, to let him see, for once, how it really was. To fully recognize Gabe and all his cracks and scrapes and bruises and bumps and imperfections. No more *I'm sure you're overreacting, hon,* or, *He's just his own person, that's great!* To understand her frustration when everyone, including Nate, said, *but he looks normal!* Or *are you sure kids aren't just kids?* To live with autism in a way that wasn't a blue T-shirt or a charity walk or a foundation, but to live with the ugly. On a Bad Day, she wished all the ugliness on her husband and nothing but windblown freedom for herself.

"Hi!" Nate exclaimed, both happy and surprised that she was happy.

Alecia pulled the phone away from her ear and adjusted the volume.

"Good day?" Nate asked, a note of caution in his tone that lit a quick fire under Alecia's skin and then settled. The answer to that question would dictate the rest of the conversation: whether Nate would stay on the line and chat, or scamper off with some well-thought-out excuse.

"Yep, so far. He's just waking up." She could hear Gabe, his too-heavy-for-a-five-year-old stomps around his bedroom.

"Come to my game this afternoon? Please?" He pleaded with an unusual edge of desperation. Nate asked so little of her, always wanting to be mindful of her time, of her energies, worried about her stress levels and how *he* could make *her* happy, to the point of dancing on eggshells. She knew that she couldn't say no, this one time, even if it meant dragging Gabe into unfamiliar territory. He'd know some of the people but not all. In Mt. Oanoke, people never change: the baseball crowd, the dressed-to-the-nines gym moms, the coaches' wives, the athletic association groupies. Nate's mother would probably be there, too.

Maybe Bridget would go. It had been months. Bridget Peterson was one of Alecia's only friends who didn't stem from a support network. She was a teacher, with Nate. She wasn't a special-needs mom, or even a regular-needs mom. She wasn't a therapist or a sympathetic nurse or a doctor. She was just a person, and sometimes Alecia forgot what that was like, to have friends who were just people.

Years ago, before Gabe, when she and Nate first got married and moved to Mt. Oanoke, Bridget and Holden Peterson were Nate and Alecia's first real couple friends. They'd spent long, boozy nights at local pubs, laughing till their sides hurt, drunk on cheap rum and Cokes and the golden, sparkly potential of their infant marriages. Before infertility (for Bridget) and special needs (for Alecia) and then, later, the unspeakable.

"We'll see how it goes," Alecia said to Nate, noncommittal, because anything could and sometimes did happen at the last minute. *We'll see* was a standard translation of *yes, unless I let you down.*

"That's a no." Nate huffed into the phone.

"That's a maybe." Alecia sighed, her annoyance creeping in. A crash from upstairs, followed by a quick, air-stabbing wail. "I gotta go." She hung up the phone and took the steps two at a time.

Gabe stood at the foot of his bed, his lamp cockeyed in front of him on the floor. He turned to Alecia and pointed to the mess, the shattered bulb and fragmented plastic lampshade. The lamp was a gift from Violet; "Vi" everyone called her. Nate's Mom. Over half of what they owned was a gift from Vi and most of it had been broken by an energetic, well-meaning Gabe. While Vi loved her grandson, Alecia dreaded the quick flicker of disappointment in her eyes when she inevitably asked where the lamp went.

"Oh honey, what happened?" She bent to pick up the pieces, shards of plastic interspersed with razor-sharp glass. "Back up!" She pointed to the doorway and Gabe scampered in bare feet. He sulked, hands over his ears. Her sharp tone, even a hint of it, could send him reeling, and she took two deep, calming breaths. He hummed to soothe himself.

Still, it was just a lamp, and a fairly cheap one. Vi had picked it because Gabe liked the colors, the red, yellow, and blue fluted plastic splaying bright light on the ceiling and the walls, and also because it was hardy, but no matter. They could get a new one. Maybe next month with what was left of the first baseball check.

"Hey, buddy." Alecia pushed the hair out of her eyes with the back of her wrist, the broken glass and plastic pinched between her fingers. Gabe hummed louder, covering his ears, so Alecia said it again, a bit more forcefully, this time meeting his eyes. She smiled. "Hey, buddy."

He stopped humming. Smiled back at her, his eyes crinkling at the corners and for a brief second, worry-free. She pantomimed a deep breath and he took one, too. Their little inside joke, *breathe, Mama. Breathe, Gabey. It's just breathing, easy peasy.*

"Do you wanna go see Daddy? He has a baseball game. Remember?"

His eyes flicked away, uninterested.

She tried again. "Gabe, let's go see Daddy." He brightened. She tried again. "On the way we can stop at the construction site. We can't go in, but we can look."

"Yes!" He jumped up and ran to her.

Alecia yelped, pointing to the spot with possible shards of glass. "I have to vacuum! You'll cut yourself!"

Instead, Gabe lifted off, jumping over the fallen lamp and landing heavily on the bed, where he bounced crisscross-applesauce and whooped.

23

He recoiled off the far edge of the bed, making a big show to avoid the mess and giving Alecia a pointed look. She laughed. Gabe made her laugh every day, not so much with his words, which sometimes were few and far between, but his wry sense of humor. The way he outright *mocked* her. No one else could see it. In many ways, Gabe was textbook: standard comedy failed him, TV shows were filled with nuance he neither got nor appreciated, humor in any regular way went over his head, or more likely, he just didn't care. But to Alecia, he was funny and warm and she walked that frustrating tightrope, stretched taut between content and flailing every minute of every day.

With her free hand, she leaned over and plucked a small metal toy front-end loader off the ground and waggled it in his field of vision. "Sneakers on. Right there." She pointed to where he stood and he looked down at his Velcro Nikes. He sat, working the Velcro straps, his eyes on the toy in her hand. When he was done, he stood with his arms out and his back straight. Alecia tossed the toy gently and it landed softly on his comforter. He snatched it up, rubbed it against his cheek, and stuck it into his pocket.

"Go, Mama." He gave her a big toothy grin. The vacuuming could wait.

So they went.

And everything was just fine. Gabe was fine.

Alecia was fine. She watched her husband, leaning against the wood frame of the dugout, his thumbs hooked into the pocket in his navy blue athletic pants, his hat low on his brow, looking no older than any of his boys, his eyes only on the batter, and flicking periodically to two men in the upper corner of the bleachers. Recruiters. They came around to one of the first games every year and made Nate pace. *His boys.* His seniors being shunted away to major colleges, maybe, one day, major leagues. He'd always hoped, anyway.

He hadn't even looked up to see her there before the birds started.

As they fell, dead or barely alive, two small ones landed between second and third base, four on the infield, one between home plate and the pitcher's mound, and more than a smattering of black bodies against the green grass of the outfield. Alecia shielded her eyes against the sun and surveyed the sky. A cloud of black birds, thousands and thousands of them, swarmed like mosquitoes. The whole cloud seemed to hover, suspended on some invisible air current while the crowd murmured. The pitcher, Andrew Evans, paused, his hand clutching the ball high in the air and then sort of wilting as a starling hit his feet, his face tipped up to the sky, wondering *what the hell?*

Then, pandemonium. Everyone tumbled, panicked and screeching, running for the small overhang under the concession stand, or the dugout, or their cars. Even the players ran, as strong and tough as they liked to pretend they were. Everyone pressed together. Parents and coaches and players and teachers, people who sometimes could hardly stand to be in the same room together, stood next to the open concession window, the smell of hot grease and pretzels thick, and all you could hear was the *thunk, thunk, thunk* of starlings as they hit the dirt, their wings twitching.

Alecia had the sensation of watching something huge, momentous, but on television. Removed and staticky, a broken broadcasting voice through the haze. She looked around, and even the recruiters—men in sports jackets or windbreakers, with clipboards, their radar guns tapping nervously against their thighs— watched the sky with an open-mouthed, gaping wonderment.

The whole thing lasted no more than three minutes; three whole minutes during which even Gabe was quiet, pulled in against her hip, although Alecia knew he had no real grasp of the situation. He wasn't scared, he wasn't picking up on the cues of everyone else, and she barely had time to be grateful for that before it was all over.

Everyone looked up and started talking again,

whispering, really, stunned and reverent, blinking back into the light, as though they'd weathered a real storm, and surveyed the damage. Hundreds of small black forms, crumpled and fluttering in the wind, like wrinkled carbon paper.

Someone called 911 and a few people scurried away, gathering up their sons and hustling them to their minivans away from some presumed noxious invisible gas cloud. Alecia stayed and waited for Nate, watching Marnie Evans sweep two small carcasses from the front hood of her Pathfinder with her peep-toe sandal, hopping around on one foot. It would almost be comical if Alecia's stomach wasn't so twisted, or she didn't feel like crying, or the back of her tongue didn't taste metallic and bitter.

They were small birds and could have fit in the scoop of her hands had she desired to pick one up. She imagined that—cupping its small, broken wings underneath its still warm body, its eyes shocked open in fright. Where did they come from? Why did they fall? The question would be asked a thousand times over the course of the next month.

Until, of course, more important questions arose, at which time everyone promptly forgot a thousand birds fell on the town of Mt. Oanoke at all.

CHAPTER 3

Bridget, Wednesday, March 25, 2015

The comforting thing about high schoolers was they never changed. Every day they were as self-absorbed as the day before, their phones perpetually inches from their faces, fingers flying over the screens, sending Snapchats and text messages and tweets. Drama over boyfriends and best friends and boyfriends-slash-best friends. Bridget kept her ear to the ground: she knew who were BFFs and baes and whose mom was popping pills and whose dad was sleeping with the biology teacher who wore the short skirts.

Even when Bridget had bad days, really, *really* bad days, when she missed Holden with every breath in her body, when her very cells seemed to vibrate with missing him, with the way his flat, wide thumb used to slide up her arm with a smooth, gentle pressure. It was the little gestures that popped into her mind and stole the air from her lungs in the middle of class, in the middle of a sentence half the time. She swore the kids thought she'd lost her ever-loving mind. Maybe she had. But even then, on those days when she could barely string two sentences together and they all looked at her, mouths agape like catfish, they never let her down. They concerned themselves with her for about one hot minute before they kept on keeping on with their oh-so-gripping soap opera lives.

It was too cold for March. Sneaking up on spring break and still hovering around the thirties and forties. Her Georgia blood wasn't used to this nonsense, and she wondered for about the billionth time why she didn't go back, now that Holden wasn't keeping her here anymore. Maybe because it still *felt* like he was here, only nine months later. Hardly any time at all, and she could still sense him in the bare, crackling trees in the front yard, their leaves scattered and killing what was left of his precious lawn. She could, what? Feel his aura? Oh, if her mother could hear her thoughts. *Ain't got the good sense God gave a rock,* that's what she'd say.

"Earth to Bridge." Nate Winters stood in the door to her empty classroom, only three minutes after the bell, but long enough into her prep period to catch her sitting, hands folded in her lap, staring at the far wall of chipped and peeling cinder block.

She gave him a big smile, shaking her head to clear it. "I'm here. I was . . . thinking."

Nate crossed the room in two easy lopes, turned

29

a chair backward, and sat. "You? Nah." He rolled his eyes and she swatted at him.

They used to joke about that, Bridget's hamster-wheeled brain, the thing that never stopped. Even when she was drinking, she'd stand up suddenly, her whiskey and Coke sloshing over the edge onto Alecia's new carpet (and you could tell she had a small heart attack about it), and proclaim to have an idea. This was back when they thought they could *do things*. Nate and Bridget were teachers. Holden was a doctor. Alecia was in public relations. They were a dream team for some not-yet-established charity that helped children and bought them shoes or taught them to read or gave impoverished girls tampons. They had potential, dammit.

Bridget straightened the papers on her desk, just for something to do, her mind slipping dangerously on the thin ice of the past, the way it sometimes did. Some days she never really found her footing. But Nate made it more bearable. He touched her arm.

"How's Alecia?" She brushed her hair back off her shoulders, sat up straighter, and gave Nate another bright smile. "Gabe?"

"Oh, you know. Ups and downs." He shrugged, and Bridget wondered how many of the downs Nate really got to see up close.

"Give them my love."

He nodded and pulled out a folded index card.

"I stopped by because I wanted your advice on this." He pushed it across the desk at her.

> The ravens came in sets of three
> One for each sword, drawn down, unfreed
> Fearless
> Until nightfall when he'd cower
> Washed with the blood of a thousand kings

Bridget read it twice, three times. It made very little sense; it wasn't even symmetrical, poetically speaking. The rhythm was wrong. But something about it crawled around in her brain, skittering across her unfocused thoughts.

"Who wrote this?" She flipped it over, not expecting a name.

"I'm not sure, but I found it on the floor, near my desk after last period." He leaned back, pulling on the chair back. Nate was a fidgeter, not much different from the long-legged boys in her classes, their knees bopping, cracking their knuckles. "It weirded me out. You don't think it's weird?"

She raised an eyebrow at him. "I'm a creative writing teacher. You should see the shit I read. They're kids. Some of them truly think that what they're going through on any given day is the worst pain they'll ever have in their lives."

Nate gave her a sad smile. "Aw, Bridge."

"No. You don't get to feel sorry for me. That's

not your job." She waved her hand at him. She studied the card again. Something in the last line, the thousand-kings part, jumped out at her. She snapped her fingers and flipped through the journals on her desk.

She'd made them keep a handwritten journal. Some days it was classwork, some days it was homework, but it couldn't be typed. In her view, journals were meant to be taken to bed, scrawled in while tucked under the blankets, a private enclave of thoughts.

Their handwriting was atrocious and they whined incessantly about the assignment. Most of them wrote about what they did, which was boring as all get-out, even documenting what they'd eaten for breakfast. The girls often confessed their weight, a long-held secret, bursting out of them like jelly from a doughnut. They turned them in on Fridays, and Bridget might check to see that they were complete, but didn't grade what they wrote. Sometimes she gave them topics in class, sometimes it was open-ended.

She grabbed the black leather one; she knew which one it was by heart. Lucia Hamm wrote about death and dying—a lot of them did. But most of them glossed over it, or mused about what it was like to die, what happened or how it would happen to them. Some of them were scared. But Lucia Hamm seemed to fly toward

32

the subject, undeterred by her teacher losing her husband almost a year before to cancer. Lucia tackled pain and death clinically, a biology lab dissection. As if Bridget's hurt could be pulled apart like little frog's legs, pinned back to the wax, sliced clean down the middle, and simply exorcised. Bridget had seen it before, a death fascination; that's not what bothered her. It was almost mundane to be Goth. But Lucia got under her skin.

She flipped through until she found the page. A drawing, three blackbirds along the top, feathered over a wire, three swords pierced through a beating heart. No kings. Huh. She flipped it around to show Nate. He studied it.

"Gotta be, right?"

"I've given up trying to figure her out." She shrugged. "She sees birds."

Nate cocked his head, moved his hand in a circle, like *go on.*

She sighed, the idea exhausting her. "She finds dead birds, she says. She's written about it. She says they come to her and she knows bad things will happen."

Lucia, on the fringe, but exotically, unsettlingly beautiful. Crazy white hair, black-rimmed eyes and bloodred lips. She'd been held back in kindergarten, something about emotional and social readiness, so she was a full year older than the other seniors. She had a way of speaking, clipped and certain, her gaze level and steady, like she was humoring you. Bridget always looked away first, couldn't take the directness. Every conversation felt like a confrontation.

She handed the card back to Nate.

"I think there's something going on. Lately her grades have been tanking. She comes in, looks like shit. No makeup. Haven't you noticed?" He tapped the card against his knuckles and twisted his mouth. "She's got that godawful brother, you know?" Bridget vaguely knew. Her brother, Lenny, a dropout, and her father, Jimmy, had skipped town.

Bridget eyed the journal, suddenly ashamed. She hadn't really been paying attention. This was her job, not just the teaching, but to observe them. In that way, Nate took it more seriously than she did.

Nate had anonymous social media accounts. He never posted anything, just scrolled through the newsfeeds. He followed his students and they followed back, not knowing who he was. So stupid, Bridget thought. Didn't they know the creeps who were out there? But Nate knew who was fighting whom, where to be, when to be there, who was getting bullied, who was doing the bullying. It made him a better teacher, he defended. He'd never abuse it, she knew that, but still. She told him she didn't want to know anything. Leave her out of it. She wondered if

Alecia knew that when she lay in bed next to her husband at night, he scrolled through his phone, spying on the lives of his students like they were his own personal miniseries. It was a moral gray area, she admitted, but Nate did it for the all the right reasons. In the drama that played out at school each day, the stage was set online the night before.

"I just don't have it in me. Not this year. Other years, I've been with you. Fighting *for* them. Against the administration, against their parents, against themselves half the time. Not this year. I'm barely hanging in." She opened Lucia's journal, fanned through the pages, and realized for the first time how many of the entries were drawings. Half of them, at least. She'd have to talk to her about that. This wasn't art class.

Then, a glimmer of recognition as she turned the book one way, then the other. She'd known once what it all meant, although her skills felt rusty. Aunt Nadine had taught her how to do a reading when she was barely ten, perched on her lap while a cigarette snaked down to the butt. But that was a long time ago.

The last reading she did nearly ended her marriage.

She pushed the book across the desk and pointed.

"Nate. They're tarot cards."

• • •

Bridget had a cat. A petite gray-and-white stray that she adopted a month after Holden died, an ill-advised decision. She named her Sunny, after the prostitute in *Catcher in the Rye*. It was her own simple, obtuse memorial to her husband, but also she loved irony. The cat was both gray and grumpy. So, Sunny she was, or more likely, she wasn't. No one ever got the joke, but then again, most people didn't get Bridget's jokes, with the exception of Holden.

Lord, how she missed him.

It had been less than a year since his death. Two years since his diagnosis, and ten since they married. Bridget liked to imagine her life in timeline form, and sometimes, if she'd had enough to drink and it was late enough at night, she envisioned it hovering there above her head. A single line with dots, like a subway map, green up to the fall of 2012, red and bloody for that year between 2012 and 2013, and muddy-water brown thereafter with a blinking red You Are Here somewhere along the interminable brown. She couldn't see anything past today.

There was a tiny bit of freedom in being alone. She popped a frozen dinner into the microwave, waited the requisite two minutes, and pulled it out with two fingers, dropping it onto a paper plate. She poured white zinfandel into a red Solo cup because she hated doing dishes, and took her dinner to the living room. Holden would have died, had he been alive. He liked expensive cabernet, from certain regions in France—she had no idea which ones. He was also a particular eater and had specific, bizarre notions of what could and should not be eaten together. *Steak and potatoes. Pasta and pork. Chicken and rice.* Only in those two combinations. In restaurants, she'd feel endlessly irritated at his requests: *whole potatoes, not mashed, no garlic, extra pepper.*

Now she could eat whatever she wanted. Strange how she'd welcome back in a heartbeat all the things she used to wish away. When she talked to him, which she did sometimes, not enough to be called *often,* she didn't look at his picture or up to the ceiling. She talked as though he was right there next to her.

"Tomorrow I'll cook something, H. I promise. Maybe."

You never make promises to the dead that you don't intend to keep. She wasn't religious, but Mama's voice often floated up from the swamps of Georgia just to smack her in the head.

Sunny kneaded at her leg, bucking his head under Bridget's chin. She ran her nails down the cat's back, scratching just above his tail. She popped the last bite of gluey mashed potatoes into her mouth, took a deep drink of wine, and reached across the sofa cushions for the journal.

It was black; many of them were. They could

pick their own, a request they'd all initially groaned at. But later they'd come in with leather-bound notebooks that reflected their personalities, handing them in shyly as if a glitter-pink cover or gilded pages revealed something otherwise unknown about their souls. They were teenagers; black and angsty was their jam. The class, creative writing, held both juniors and seniors as an elective. The seniors were edging toward college, the sweet lick of freedom bittersweet on their lips, so they weren't as moody as the juniors who were stuck in Mt. Oanoke for another eighteen months. The seniors were coming full bloom, all the things that had seemed so confining starting to take on the rosy glow of nostalgia. High school was in their rearview mirror.

She flipped the pages. Lucia's journal was erratic, with changing handwriting, drawings, and block letters filled in with pen. She didn't read all the entries in anyone's diary. The exercise was more for the idea of journaling, writing down their brainy, brilliant thoughts, just to get them on paper. She didn't care about the content, just if they were done on time. They'd ask her, *did you read mine?* For all their complaining, they seemed to crave the approval.

I'm not a virgin. That's a joke, right? No one thinks that. I'm a slut. A skank.

A witch. A fetish. Never a real person. Except to you. And maybe Taylor, although she's been flaky. Cares more about Kelsey and Riana and, depending on the day, Andrew.

I couldn't care less about any of them. I care about you, though, so there's that.

Bridget closed the journal. She'd never heard anyone call Lucia a whore, a slut. Most of the girls steered clear of her with her sharp, red mouth and sharper tongue. She was more likely to be the one flinging names around. The boys mostly avoided her, but some hung around a bit, too. She clung to the edge of the right crowd—Andrew Evans and Josh Tempest—Taylor clicking up behind them, double step to keep up, and Lucia hanging back. Andrew always watching her, his eyes sliding around, his mouth with that sideways smirk that the girls fell all over themselves for.

A lesson from science class: in nature, the prettiest things are poisonous.

Bridget was tired. It was only seven thirty, but she was always tired. Sleep was both an escape from the everyday weight on her chest and a possible chance to see him again. Touch his soft stubbled cheek, if only in a dream. It was worth the crushing moment in the morning when she realized none of it was real. Maybe it was worth it.

The old house brayed and whistled in the wind. She'd moved in hating this house—an inheritance from Holden's great-aunt—everything it represented, the cold, unforgiving north, the life she'd left behind. They moved, ostensibly to fix it up, sell it. Move back south. *Give it one year. If you want to leave in one year, we'll go. I promise, back to the swamps and the bogs and the heat and the y'all. We'll go.* Then she'd gotten a job as a teacher and they stayed. They met Nate and Alecia and she made the house her own and the year came and went with hardly a whisper. That was almost eight years ago.

The house sat back from the road, the original farmhouse for the land that had since been developed. Three-acre lots with three-thousand-square-foot McMansion developments on either side. Commuter families, driving to North Jersey or New York City, coming in late in the evening but with hefty paychecks. Unlike when they'd first moved in, when the town was still reeling from the closure of the paper mill. Now they had neighborhoods with kids and bikes and winding cul-de-sacs and neighborhood barbecues. Mommy nights out and golf games and Super Bowl parties and first birthdays.

There Bridget sat, high above them all. Keeping vigilant watch over a life that wasn't hers to have.

CHAPTER 4

Alecia, Saturday, April 25, 2015

School was canceled for the rest of the week. The EPA vans came, testing air and water. The Pennsylvania Department of Health collected little black birds in Ziploc bags all over town, mostly from around the baseball diamond—437 at the field alone. People stayed inside, not in any official way—there was no curfew, no police or health official directive—but the eeriness of it all kept people peeking through their curtains rather than sitting on their front porches. The bikes lay in empty lawns, their wheels spinning in the wind.

Alecia's phone rang like crazy. Libby Locking, whom she'd met briefly when Gabe attempted preschool and who'd stuck to her like a bur ever since, wanted to know what Nate thought killed the birds.

"Libby, how would Nate know?" Alecia asked, pushing her hair off her forehead with the back of her dry hand. She was cutting chicken, her fingertips coated slick, and she kept the phone pressed between her cheek and her shoulder as she sliced.

"Because he's smart. Ask Nate."

"Nate, what killed the birds?" Alecia called into the living room, where Nate was easily on his third hour of *SportsCenter*.

"How would I know?" His eyes never left the television.

"He doesn't know, Libby."

"You know the Marshalls? Earl put plastic on their windows. They think it's the mill. That the air is poisoned. Isn't that nuts?"

"That's crazy. But Earl's crazy." Alecia, distracted, scooped the chicken into a pan of oil and watched it sizzle. She washed her hands, the water burning, turning her knuckles red and pulsing.

"This whole town is crazy." Libby clucked her tongue, a soft click across the line.

After they hung up, Alecia tucked the phone into her back pocket with the ringer turned down.

She should have been glad Nate was home. On paper, it seemed easier. She had another set of hands, someone to occupy Gabe, and Gabe's hero to boot. She could have had a nap, maybe a long shower, gotten a manicure. Except half the town was closed, so forget the manicure.

But Nate was stressed. School being closed for a week, the first week of baseball, made him batty, pacing around like a caged animal. His phone rang off the hook, and Alecia could hear the panicked squeal of parents through the speaker. With games being rescheduled, even outright canceled, Marnie Evans called almost daily.

"He can throw eighty-five as a goddamn junior, Alecia. This kid, I've never had one like him."

She could swear Nate loved Andrew Evans more than Gabe most days.

Linda, Gabe's therapist, came every day from nine to noon. Every. Damn. Day. In her house, in their space. Rain, shine, snow, but not ice; Linda never drove in the ice. She'd announce this in singsong because Linda announced a lot of things in singsong. She blew in with bags of stuff, odds and ends, toys and string and plastic figurines and blocks and letters and numbers. She carried it all in giant gingham-checked plastic laundry totes she'd gotten from Argentina (Alecia knew an awful lot about Linda's life; she talked more than anyone Alecia had ever met).

Gabe loved Linda. Alecia, on most days, loved Linda. Linda was extraordinarily tall, over six feet, with a loud booming voice and long blond braid down her back that Gabe liked to touch. Sometimes Linda let Gabe touch her braid, tap it to his cheeks, even, grossly, kiss it—truly Alecia almost protested this one—as a reward. Linda could stand to erect a few boundaries.

Instead of staying or watching or learning, Nate would go upstairs. Away from Linda, away from her singing, her relentless talking, her bubbling theories about Gabe. Maybe it was her sheer enthusiasm, for which Alecia felt profoundly grateful most of the time. Nate seemed to want nothing more than to flee from it. The patter of all the things that would burn his paycheck and maybe only marginally fix his son.

But today, Linda had come and gone and Gabe was theoretically napping. Alecia stomped around the kitchen as she listened to him pace. *Step, step, step, step,* a heavy boom at the end where his hand slapped at the wall. *Step, step, step, step, boom. Step, step, step, step, boom. Step, step, step, step, boom.* For fun, she matched her steps to his, wallowing.

"Why isn't he napping? He was up half the night." Nate was suddenly behind her. She wasn't sure if he'd crept up on purpose or if she'd just zoned out and didn't hear him over the patterned racket above their heads.

"He never really naps. I put him up there to get a break. Sometimes he actually does fall asleep." Alecia pushed back her shoulders and chewed on her lip.

"Well, that's ridiculous. Maybe he's too old for naps. He's five." Nate put his hands on his hips and eyed her. "Should I go take care of him? Maybe he needs more discipline. Tell him if he doesn't lie down, you'll take away his toys."

Oh my God. "Discipline? Are you crazy?" If he didn't understand that Gabe wasn't like other

44

kids, that grounding and punishment and taking away his front-end loaders wasn't going get him to lie down compliantly and *sleep,* for the simple fact that he really didn't seem to know *how* to sleep unless he was thoroughly exhausted, then she didn't know what else to do. *Step, step, step, step, boom.*

"You're so soft on him. Too easy. You let him get away with everything." Nate was getting warmed up; Alecia could hear it in his tone. Saying things he'd been thinking for a while, but hadn't known how to broach. Then he thought better of it and softened his voice. "Look, I know that Gabe isn't . . . *normal.*" God, that got under her skin, even from Gabe's own father. She could think it, even say it, but no one else, not even Nate. She opened her mouth to cut him off, but he put his hand up. "I know, you hate that. I get it. What I'm trying to say is, I'm not stupid. I know how Gabe is. But what if all he needs is someone tougher? Instead of these hugely expensive, all-consuming therapies you try?" *Step, step, step, step, boom.* She was getting mad now.

"Someone tougher than me? Like who?" Alecia started to laugh; she couldn't help it. Who would that be? Another someone to take care of their son? *Who?* Nate? Sure. Have at it. She couldn't stop laughing. "Someone else? Who, Nate? You?" Her eyes were watering and she hiccupped. "You want to take care of Gabe? Leave your precious

45

school and your kids and your stupid Facebook account—I know all about that—and all the drama you think is real but you don't realize real life is going on three miles away, *here,* while Gabe shits himself accidentally because he's so wrapped up with his toys. He's five years old and he's so busy playing with toy construction equipment that he shits his pants, which by the way, the size of a shit of a five-year-old is pretty much the same as an adult. And he doesn't really care if I have to clean it up, because he struggles with empathy. And I have to not *get mad at him,* because he cares very much about *that,* because to him, he couldn't help it, so getting mad would be counterproductive and would push him into silence and the therapist is coming in an hour and I have to be sort-of-kind-of together, because she suggested last time that maybe my shrillness was causing his mild regression?" Alecia could feel her voice climbing, screeching really, until she looked down and her hands were balled into fists. When she unfurled her fingers, she saw half-moons of purple carved into her palms. She took a deep breath.

Nate thought she was losing her mind, or maybe that she'd already lost it. Alecia could see it in the way his eyes had grown wider during her tirade. It was her fault, really; she'd had a tendency to keep the small details from Nate. The "shitting day," as she'd come to call it in her

46

mind, wasn't all that worse than a lot of other days, although many days were much better. The day of the baseball game had been a good one until all those birds. He'd surely asked her how she was and she probably said "eh" and told him the broad strokes, something vaguely innocuous like *Gabe had an accident.*

Or perhaps she was suppressing things. Admittedly, as she scrubbed adult-size shit out of Mutant Turtle underwear, she was checked out. In the throes of a bad day, she was elsewhere: a beach, somewhere far away with a drink in her hand and nothing but the sound of the rolling, whooshing waves and the tinkling of ice. Sometimes she'd remember being a child, when her mother would bring her tea and soup in bed, tucking her into the soft folds of a hand-knitted afghan. She'd remember the feel of her mother's cheek on her forehead or the way her small, agile fingers brushed hair back from her eyes and tucked it behind her ears. Then she'd think about how she should call her mother and she'd come to, on her hands and knees scrubbing at something on the kitchen floor with Gabe pacing in front of her saying *sorry, sorry, sorry, sorry, sorry* for whatever she was cleaning up. He didn't say sorry because he was, he said sorry because it made her better, less mad, and also sometimes he just got stuck on the word and she'd have to say hours later, *Gabey, it's okay, you can stop saying sorry* until she wanted to pull her hair out but couldn't act even a little annoyed because then it would get worse before it got better.

Nate touched her elbow. "I'm sorry. I know it's hard. I know you're alone a lot. I'm sorry." Alecia cocked her head, waited for the *but.* "Why do you keep things from me?"

"You don't want the details, Nate. You don't. Your eyes glaze over. I see it all the time." Tears pricked at her eyelids and she squeezed her eyes tight.

"Mama! Look!" Gabe stood in the doorway, a configuration of wood in his outstretched hands. Alecia hadn't even noticed the pacing had stopped.

"Gabey!" She took the thing from his hand and studied it. "You did it! You finished it!" She turned the wooden crane one way, then the other, and she couldn't believe it, it was perfect. A little wobbly while the glue set, but darn near perfect. She handed it back to him. "Show Daddy."

He handed it to Nate, who took it reluctantly. "This is cool!" He exclaimed with forced enthusiasm. Alecia resisted the urge to snatch it away from him.

"Gabe, tell Daddy. We found model kits for construction equipment. I don't know the names of everything. Tell him." That was a lie, she could rattle off construction equipment in her sleep, but this way, Gabe was forced to talk.

"A crane, a front-end loader, a lorry, a road roller, and an excavator." He rattled them off quickly, the words mushing into each other. The first kit she bought him had been manufactured in the UK, so he now he defaulted to the British terms for construction equipment.

"Slower, Gabe, say it again. We don't know as much as you do."

He beamed. "A crane. A front-end loader. A lorry. A road roller and an excavator. That one is last." His tongue found each syllable, proud of himself.

"How come?" Alecia prompted.

"My favorite." His eyes slid sideways but he gave her a smile.

"Gabe, we've been trying to figure out that crane for a week. Does it move?" She went to tap the bucket on the end but he snatched it away.

"When it dries." He maneuvered a slipped wooden dowel back into place with surprising light grace. "Don't touch." He wandered away, back upstairs to put the crane in its rightful place, wherever that might be.

Alecia shook her head at Nate in wonder. "Seriously, that thing was so hard. I barely understood it. I've been thinking all week it might have been a mistake. He was getting frustrated with me hovering over him, directing him."

"I'm not in your club, Alecia." Nate said it simply, but his voice was quiet. Lost. "You and

Gabe, you have a little club. I show up once in a while, do a little song and dance, but mostly, I don't fit in here. I don't know what's going on."

"Maybe that's not my fault," Alecia said.

"Maybe not. Do you think it's enough that I want to be in your club? I want to know more about what goes on here." He spread his hands wide, as though "here" were someplace grand: a castle, a vast garden, somewhere other than their small, cramped, barely together kitchen.

"Then you need to stay checked in." Alecia held up her hand as he started to protest. "Don't deny it. When things get hard, you find a way to check out: a pile of tests to grade, a parent to call, a baseball meeting, the bathroom for God's sake." She took a deep breath, calmer. "I'll tell you more if you stay here. In the muck, with us."

"Maybe I'm jealous. You should have seen your face when he walked in here holding that model. He couldn't have cared less about showing me. He wanted your pride, not mine." Nate looked into the living room and shoved his fists into his jeans pockets.

"Are you jealous of me? Or Gabe?"

Nate took a step back and shook his head. "I really have no idea."

She went shopping, leaving Nate with Gabe-related checklists. *Shopping!* It seemed as unfathomable as a Caribbean cruise and just as exotic. Not food shopping, but clothes shopping. For herself!

She wanted new yoga pants, maybe a T-shirt. She wandered the department store, the heady scent of perfume sample sprays hanging on her clothes, her hair, as she aimlessly picked through racks of blouses. She remembered blouses; she used to own zillions of them. All dry-clean only, soft and silky, in rich colors that pinked her cheeks or sparkled her eyes or brightened her highlights. She remembered pencil skirts and skinny belts, three-inch heels and tights with boots. She ran her hand along a sheer, blowy sleeve. The blouse was coral, with silver, sparkling buttons. Would look perfect with the gray tweed skirt. On a whim, she pulled both off the rack, size eight. In the dressing room, she dressed quickly. Everything fit, her body had bounced back, seemingly with no effort after Gabe, although it had taken awhile. Sometimes she blamed the anxiety, the way she'd stand over a stove, stirring and simmering, scrambling to fix the perfect dinner for Nate. For Gabe. Then she'd sit down, stare at the food that somehow turned to slime on her plate. If anything, she was thinner now than she'd been before she had Gabe. She was lucky; everyone said so.

She pulled the tags off and tucked them into her palm.

She wandered into the lingerie department, lace

and padding, or sheer with silk ribbons. Garters and thongs, push-up bras and fishnets. She remembered this, too. She had a drawer filled with satin at home. She never touched it; most nights she was asleep before Nate even came home. But she remembered. She remembered lighting candles, Nate's first baseball season, when she was pregnant but barely, only the tiny swell of belly over red lace where it used to be flat. The feeling when she splayed out, waiting, of her back against silky sheets, a lethally high red heel on each foot. His footsteps in the hall, the look in his eyes as he stood at the foot of the bed, the weight of him between her thighs, his hands hot on her hard belly, a pulse of life beneath his palm. How fast it was over.

She stood in the middle of Macy's, wearing a two-hundred-dollar outfit she had no use for, holding a black-and-red lace teddy she'd never stay awake long enough to wear. Even if her eyes would cooperate, her body wouldn't. Alecia couldn't remember her last orgasm.

She felt an unwelcome stab of pity for Nate. He was stuck with them, her and Gabe, a lousy lot in life. Guilt filled her throat and her face flushed with shame. He was *lucky* to have Gabe. But Nate still had her as a wife, and lately she'd been falling apart, which admittedly made no sense. Gabe was getting better, inasmuch as someone with autism can "get better." They'd figured out therapy most days. His medicine cocktail (mostly) kept all the tics at bay. His meltdowns had gone from three or four a day to only one every other day, if that. And those were minor. She should have been sailing into the prime of her life, Gabe in elementary school, days free, maybe going back to work. But instead she'd felt precariously balanced on the edge of a cliff, one foot off.

She thought about how she used to be somebody: ran meetings and took minutes, used buzzwords like *synergy* and *influencer* and *marquee client.* She commuted to North Jersey, outside the city, an hour and fifteen minutes each way, sometimes even taking a train into New York for a meeting. Those were long, exhausting days, but days she felt good about later, taking off her heels and letting Nate run his thumbs along the arches of her feet while she told him stories about clients with bad hair and he told her stories about students with bad tests and they laughed at all the badness of the world, while theirs felt like such goodness. And when Gabe came, she took a hiatus, *just a year* she promised both Nate and herself. When the year was up and Gabe still wasn't walking or talking or doing any of the things the books said he should, of course she couldn't go back to work if there was something *wrong.*

One year turned to the next, turned to the next

like a slow, lazy river, so blended she hardly noticed it until one day in the shower, she realized with a start she could hardly remember all those buzzwords. She'd repeat them to herself—*dynamic, paradigm, deliverables*—her vocabulary her last tether to the corporate world she belonged in, not this messy, dirty, vomit and shit and therapy and meltdown world she actually lived.

On a Good Day, though, she could hold it all together. Today, she was unmoored, her thoughts black. There would *be* no prime of her life. There would be no empty nest, no golden years, no *deep-breath-get-through-it,* no reward at the end, no prize from the game. The interminability of it got to her. She was Sisyphus on a forever-climbing mountain. When she gave in to self-pity, which wasn't often, she could wallow better than anyone. Wallowing was a skill, really. Some did it with drinking, or drugs, even chocolate or soap operas. Before Gabe, Alecia wallowed at the mall.

She wound her way to the register, plucking a pair of gray pumps along the way. The tags were bent and damp from her hand, and she handed them to the clerk who thankfully rang them up without any patter. In the mall, Alecia stopped at a kiosk. Bright lipsticks and blushes and powders and creams.

"You like?" The attendant smiled, a flash

of white teeth against creamy red lips. Alecia nodded and sat in the chair, the leather cool under her thighs. If she closed her eyes, she could pretend she was on her lunch break. That Rick wanted a balance sheet for last quarter for the Smithfield account, that she had to hurry up so she could work some creative accounting with the rest of her lunch hour. That she had to pick up a birthday card for Tanya from marketing and get it circulating. And maybe a cake.

When the attendant was done, Alecia opened her eyes, and all she saw was her own reflection, unrecognizable.

"I look happy," she blurted.

"It's not magic. You must *be* happy." The other woman laughed and pushed small jars into Alecia's palm. Alecia held out her credit card and watched her swipe it. She felt sick. What was she doing? She added it all up in her head. Over four hundred dollars. That was a half a month's worth of copays for Gabe's medication. A week of yoga therapy. Three days of horse therapy at a hundred bucks a pop.

In the parking lot, she sat in her car with the door open. The air was hot for April, too hot, but the parking lot was empty. All those fucking birds had scared everyone away. She sat in the driver's seat with her head between her knees and vomited onto the pavement. She moved her feet, keeping her new gray heels out of the mess. When she was done, she turned on the car, blasted the air conditioner right into her face.

She picked up her phone and dialed. "Hi. I miss you and I might be cracking up. Can I come over?"

Bridget's house was a home. A sweeping wrap-around porch that enveloped everyone inside like a hug, drooping wisteria framing the door, filling the air with a sweet, flowery perfume. Painted a sunny yellow, the house had twin turrets, a rickety second-floor balcony, and wide stained-glass windows. While Alecia had always struggled with decorating, Bridget seemed to embrace it like some kind of goddamn earth mother.

Alecia and Nate's small townhouse sat in a busy development, picked as a starter home when, with her burgeoning belly, she thought a neighborhood kid was in her future. She envisioned her son, at ten years old, taking off on his bike till the twilight hours, circling the endless cul-de-sacs, while the parents drank margaritas and grilled steak.

When it was obvious that Alecia wasn't going to become the suburban housewife she'd always dreamed about, she stopped caring about their home. No, that's not right. She still cared. It was clean. It was reasonably put together. The furniture was mostly of the Target and Walmart variety, the Pottery Barn catalogs collecting dust in the corner until they found their way to the trash can. It was hard to justify spending a thousand dollars on a coffee table when Gabe would probably just break it anyway.

Bridget tackled homemaking like a hobby, collecting unique, expensive antique steamer trunks and butter churners. An entire wall in her kitchen was hung with nineteenth-century small appliances: whisks and egg beaters and salt boxes and bread peels. Little clanky metal things that Alecia didn't know the names for. The wide-plank floors were covered in braided rugs and every flat surface held a knickknack. The house always smelled like freshly baked muffins, even though Bridget swore she couldn't bake a premade cookie.

Alecia rapped twice on the front glass and let herself in. She met Bridget in the hall and they hugged, Bridget's bone-thin arms strong. Alecia felt the tears in her eyes and blinked them back.

"Are you okay?" Bridget asked, not letting go, whispering it into her hair. Bridget gave long hugs, without discomfort. She'd strong-arm you in a hug, swaying side to side. Then she'd pull you inside her cocoon of a house and make you tea and serve you store-bought baked goods.

"Yes. No. Yes." Alecia took a deep breath. "I should be fine."

"No one should be fine. That's a stupid thing to

say." Bridget waved her hand around and rolled her eyes. She led Alecia through the living room and into the kitchen. A tea kettle was whistling and she busied herself with two mugs while Alecia pulled a stool out from under the heavy wooden island. Bridget sat down opposite Alecia and plunked a tissue box in front of her on the counter.

"You've lost weight," Alecia said. She hadn't seen Bridget for a while.

"What stage of grief is it where all food looks disgusting?" Bridget wrapped the string around a spoon and squeezed the teabag.

"Aw, Bridge, I'm sorry."

"It feels never ending, that's all. Some days, it's like Holden died yesterday. I didn't expect that, for it to go on forever." She shrugged. "Mama said time heals all wounds. I'm waitin' around, that's all."

Alecia felt stupid with her petty problems, with her son, who despite all his issues, still existed and her husband, despite his shortcomings, was still alive. She shouldn't have come. She stirred more sugar than necessary into her tea and blew across the top.

Bridget broke the silence first. "I saw news vans the other day! ABC and WKLP both at the ball field. Crazy, right?"

"What the hell is going on?" Alecia was grateful for the change of topic. "I saw them, too.

58

And the EPA and Department of Environmental Protection. Everyone is staying inside with their windows shut. Well, except you." A breeze lifted the curtains through the open screen above the sink. "It's like the whole town doesn't know what to think."

"I don't know. Everyone is talking. Some people think it was some kind of air poisoning from the old paper mill, but that thing hasn't been operational in ten years. What, does a building suddenly belch toxic gas?"

Alecia giggled. "When is school opening again? It's been a tough week." In some ways, she couldn't wait for Nate to go back to work and yet, at the same time, she dreaded it.

"They say Monday, that by then the air and water testing will be done." Bridget shook her head, no nonsense. "Maybe the birds all ate something? Could it be that?"

"I'm sure they'll figure it out. They have a thousand bodies to autopsy. If it's poisoning of some kind, we'll know."

"What does Nate think?" Bridget asked.

"Hell if I know."

Bridget appraised her. "You look nice." She took in Alecia's new outfit, her shoes, her fancy makeup. "Job interview?"

"Nope. Just your everyday four-hundred-dollar nervous breakdown, that's all." Alecia's cheeks flamed red under Bridget's gaze.

"Everyone loses their shit, darling. There's no shame in it. I almost wish I could, some days." Bridget grasped her hand across the island, her long, bony fingers entwined with Alecia's. "Do you want me to say something to Nate?"

They'd done it before, years ago, run interference with each other's husbands during fights or in-law disagreements. Theirs was a friendship of ease, almost too close, in each other's lives and houses, sometimes without knocking, the kind where you can open each other's fridge or mix yourself a drink. Then Alecia was consumed with Gabe and Holden died and Nate closed up and they scattered like pool balls hit with the cue.

"No." Alecia toyed with her spoon, passing it between her fingers. Outside the window, a woodpecker worked a tree trunk with a *rap rap rap rap* like machine gunfire. She smiled at Bridget. "This was nice. I think I just needed this. To sit, to be with someone, talking about something other than . . . medical records or whatever." She gave a hollow laugh. "I'm not feeling sorry for myself, swear. Let's do this again. Like on a monthly basis. I'll come over after school. I can get a sitter for Gabe."

"What about Nate?" Bridget raised one eyebrow at her.

"Or Nate. Whatever." Alecia stood. "It's four o'clock. I have to go. Gabe has ABA tonight," she said. ABA was applied behavior analysis, a specialized therapy for autism spectrum disorder. "Nate . . . he doesn't really know what to do. It bugs him. He thinks they treat Gabe like a dog . . ." She even cringed occasionally at the parallels, waving a marshmallow or a magic marker in front of Gabe's face until he complied with the smallest command. *Point to the circle.*

Bridget stood with her. "Come back. Next month. We'll have tea. You can wear your pajamas if you want."

They hugged and Bridget's hair smelled like the coconut oil she used as shampoo. Alecia opened the front door and stepped out onto the sidewalk. A woman stood alone, leaning against the door of her car.

"Can I help you?" asked Alecia, thinking about the birds, those fluttering little bodies.

"Maybe. Are you Mrs. Winters?" the woman asked. She was tall, black hair cut in a bob. She looked severe, perhaps a scientist here to ask about the birds. Alecia was a witness at the ball field that day. Maybe they were talking to everyone?

"Yes." Alecia stood straighter, her jaw clicked.

"Mrs. Winters who is married to Nate Winters?"

Alecia narrowed her eyes. Strangers called him Nathan. Nate felt friendly, intimate. "Yesss," she drew the word out, cocking her head. She realized that maybe this woman was no scientist.

In her hand she held a small digital recorder. A reporter? How would she have found her here? At Bridget's?

"Would you be willing to talk to me about your husband, Mrs. Winters?"

Alecia was confused. "Sure, but he doesn't know anything. He's a math teacher, not a science teacher." She felt like maybe she and this woman were speaking different languages. "Wait, who are you again?"

"I'm Rowena White with the *Harrisburg Courier*." She touched a button on the digital recorder and it turned red.

"Nate doesn't know anything," Alecia repeated. "About the birds?" When she looked back at the house, Bridget stood at the screen door, watching them, her hand splayed flat against the mesh.

"I'm not here about the birds, Mrs. Winters."

"Oh. Did they find anything out?" Alecia asked, her mind churning.

"Mrs. Winters, I was hoping to talk to you about your husband's affair." The woman inched closer; the digital recorder hovered around Alecia's shoulder.

Alecia's arms and legs went ice cold. "What? What are you talking about?" There was no affair. Nate was home, with Gabe, watching *SportsCenter*. "He's been home all week, with me and my son. The school was closed."

"I just need five minutes of your time." Rowena

62

held up her right hand, her fingers spread wide. Her nails were long and deep red. Almost black.

"I don't understand, you're a reporter?" Alecia felt thick in the skull, her tongue tangled. Her thoughts finally came together, clear as glass. "Nate isn't having an affair, but even if he was, how would this concern you? Affairs aren't news." She started to push past the woman, her hand on the car door. She'd just drive away, that's all. People had affairs all the time, they didn't make the paper.

"Mrs. Winters, please stop. Just talk to me." She sighed, resigned, and clicked off that red button. Tucked the recorder back into her purse. "This affair? It's with a student."

You,

We are linked, you and I, tethered together in transient world. Where everyone is so connected with their phones, texting and instagram and twitter and facebook and yikyak and snapchat, but we are all lost.

You are my comfort. You have no idea.

CHAPTER 5

Bridget, Sunday, April 26, 2015

Bridget was dead asleep when the phone rang, the kind of heavy, dreamless state where you wake up and can't place the day. She loved that sleep; it was her favorite. There was no crushing blow once she opened her eyes and realized the Holden of her dreams was just that, a fantasy. There was no quick gasp for breath, clutch at the bedspread, no stab behind her eyes. Just a peaceful wakening, followed by the cloudy sadness that she didn't get to see him last night. Or the night before, come to think of it. The dreams were getting further and further apart now and maybe one day they'd stop altogether. The idea left Bridget a little dizzy.

" 'Ello," she mumbled into her phone, not sure who would be calling at this hour of the night. Her clock blinked 11:13, which seemed irrationally late unless there'd been an accident.

"Bridget, honey?" Petra Peterson's voice was smooth as honey. Holden's mother was made of sugar and just as cloying.

Bridget shot up in bed. "What's wrong?"

Bridget looked around, the white light slanting in through room-darkening shades, and she realized with a sort of sickening thud that maybe it was actually eleven in the morning. Her mind skittered past thoughts of school and her classes and landed neatly on the word *Sunday*. She sighed.

"I'm calling to see if you're up for lunch." Her words tilted up insecurely, and Bridget could envision her baring her teeth in the rearview mirror looking for lipstick smudges or maybe a wayward speck of spinach from her morning veggie egg-white goat cheese omelet. She could see her coral pantsuit with the buttons matching her bracelets, matching her earrings. "I haven't seen you and I'm in the neighborhood."

That was a lie. Petra lived more than an hour away in Bucks County, in a suburb of Philadelphia where Holden grew up, ensconced in the tight, beating womb of private school, music lessons, and theater camp on the Main Line. Bridget could hear the roar of the highway in the distance. There was nothing here, the outskirts of a sleepy bedroom town on the edge of the crumbling paper mill industry, not so depressed that the people themselves seemed gray and daunted, but still. This town had never been anything but a repellent to Petra. No, she was in the neighborhood for no discernible reason other than Bridget.

When Holden had told his mother he'd found a job at Wayne Memorial Hospital as a cardiologist, Petra had balked. He'd thrown a fully paid medical education in her face. She'd wanted Children's Hospital of Philadelphia (CHOP), Thomas Jefferson, even St. Christopher's, where one could be philanthropic (but with dignity) because *think of the children.*

"Petra, I'm not even up yet." As soon as the words were out of her mouth, she squeezed her eyes shut. It was eleven o'clock in the morning; nothing said basket case more than a grown woman sleeping well into the afternoon, which she surely would have done if not for the phone call.

"Oh, no worries," Petra said gaily. "You have an hour. Let's meet at that charming little coffee shop where we went for lunch that time?"

There was only one charming little coffee shop, which Bridget did not go to because each cup of coffee smelled like Holden on a Sunday morning, sleepy, slightly sweaty, with the distinct air of newspaper ink, and she could see him there, with his glasses resting on the bridge of his nose and last week's *New York Times* Sunday puzzle while he asked her for a five-letter word for *smidgen* (answer: skosh).

But now Petra would be there, pinked and cheerful, talking about their latest donation to Jefferson in pancreatic cancer research, or maybe the tree they planted (cherry for the blooms but it was just a guess), and maybe the one-year memorial could be at Penn, where Holden had gone to school. Bridget wasn't ready yet, she wasn't there. Petra buried her son and cried appropriately, dabbing her eyes with a wet, milky Kleenex and mascara that never ran. Bridget had made a scene, snot on her forearm, clinging to the edge of the casket, an avert-your-eyes kind of scene. A real showstopper. Petra had looked at her with pity, edged in a thin veneer of fear that a person could split so wide open. She'd patted her arm, soft and quick, like maybe Bridget's grief could spill out, stain her buttercup suit. But Petra had three other sons (three!) who had all done what she'd expected, two lawyers and a doctor (although one of them had gone off the rails into environmental law, so who knows if she even counted poor Thad). Only Holden had gone and married himself a southern hippie schoolteacher.

Bridget would rather do anything than have coffee with Petra. Anything. She thought about telling her that the stores were still closed on account of the birds and all, but it was too late. She was coming, zooming toward Bridget in a midnight-blue Mercedes to talk about God knows what, and all Bridget wanted to do was sleep. Dreamless, empty sleep.

Instead, she wound her little Toyota to the Bean Café, fifteen minutes late, and found Petra waiting patiently at a table in the far corner, tucked away and private. The pantsuit was cornflower blue. But the earrings and the bracelet were just as Bridget imagined, and they'd hardly bitten into their biscotti before Petra cleared her throat and took Bridget's hand in hers.

"How are you doing really, dear?" Petra examined Bridget's face. Bridget could picture Petra using this exact tone of voice while inspecting a fellow Junior Leaguer's neck lift. Petra wore her grief like a Girl Scout badge, the sash of Most Grieving Mother draped across her chest, her *I'm doing just fine, thank you so much for your kind words* voice practiced. Nothing as pornographic as Bridget.

Petra turned Holden into a cause, a champion for the fight against an incurable and relentless disease. She made his death glamorous, erasing the six months of urine and vomit and shit and ugly that Bridget couldn't forget no matter how hard she tried.

"I'm fine, Petra. Truly." She set the cookie down delicately on the china plate and blew across her cup of coffee. Her gaze wandered to the walls of the cafe, stacked floor to ceiling with old sepia-toned photos of Mt. Oanoke back in its turn-of-the-last-century heyday. Petra cleared her throat again and the two women avoided eye contact until finally Bridget got sick of wasting her day like this and said, "Why are you here?"

She didn't mean for it to come out sour, and Petra sank back against the chair. Her face sagged and she looked ten years older than she had a minute ago. Bridget sighed; when it came to Petra, why was she always the bad guy?

"We have to talk about Holden's memorial. I can do it without you but I don't want to. A year is coming and you weren't returning my calls." Her voice softened. "I know you're hurting, darling, we all are. But it's expected that we'll have a one-year memorial of his death. We can do it in the summer, if that's more comfortable. It doesn't have to be an exact year. We want to plant a tree. Not now of course, but we should start thinking about it now. Finding the site, planning the event."

"What kind?" Bridget asked, only a tiny bit curious.

"An oak maybe?" Petra twirled her spoon around in her hands. "He was so strong. He always seemed immovable to me." A tear escaped the corner of her eye, singly delicate as it traversed her cheek. Bridget studied her perfect hair, her lined lips, her spidery made-up eyelashes, and couldn't help but wonder how she did it. How she got up every day, made salon and nail appointments. Why didn't it all feel pointless and stupid? The only possible conclusion was that Bridget loved Holden more than Petra did.

"Plant a maple tree," Bridget said wearily.

Petra looked surprised because she was. She had no idea that once Bridget and Holden stayed at some bed-and-breakfast in Vermont, the home of maple syrup. Holden, in his infinite enthusiasm for almost everything to the point of annoyance, bubbled over the way maple syrup, *real* maple syrup, tasted different from any syrup he'd ever had in his entire life. Bridget hadn't thought about that trip in a while, but nothing was more classic Holden than his ridiculous excitement over nothing more than a breakfast condiment. And it was just a thing, a small thing in the grand scheme of all things, but it suddenly felt incredibly important that they plant a maple tree that could be tapped. There were probably different kinds of maple trees, but Bridget didn't know, so she'd have to do research. Or someone would.

Petra regarded her with one eyebrow and a dubious look. "This is Pennsylvania."

"If you plant a maple tree that can make syrup, I will come to your memorial."

"I was hoping we could plan it together, dear," Petra said quietly.

Everyone grieved differently, of course. Bridget realized that Petra's grief looked like fund-raisers, ribbon cuttings, golf-clapping crowds, and planted trees. It was an admirable grief. Bridget knew that people in Mt. Oanoke thought she held too tightly to her sadness,

73

wrapped herself in it like a security blanket, hot and sweating.

"Tell me what you want me to do." Bridget sighed and Petra smiled, leaned forward, and patted her hand.

School was opened again, teachers and kids shuttling between classes like nothing had happened. Bridget told Nate about the tree and the memorial on Monday during their break period. He'd popped in, a few days a week, to chat, catch up, stretched out in the front-row desk, his feet resting up on the desk next to him, crossed at the ankles. Sometimes he gave her leftover bagels, hard from the morning but still soft and doughy in the middle. They'd tear them apart while they talked, her elbows resting on half-graded tests scattered all over her desk.

Nate bought bagels from the bakery on the corner to keep on his desk. When she asked why, he gave her a funny look, his head turned sideways, his mouth twisting. "Half these kids don't eat breakfast, Bridge. The rich parents are gone by 5 a.m., trying to beat the bridge and tunnel traffic. The old mill families, well, half of them can't even afford the weekly groceries." Nate believed he could rescue the whole bright world.

He had long legs and big feet, awkward as an adolescent but with thick thighs and a burgeoning middle that Bridget thought was adorable, but mostly in the way he was newly aware of it, his palms perpetually smoothing the front of his shirt down. She'd always thought it strange that she and Nate were friends first, instantly, the way kids are in elementary school because you both like banana fluff sandwiches or wear matching purple socks, but she'd never felt a thing for him outside of friendship. Once, Holden had asked her in his easy, open way if she'd ever fantasized about Nate and she'd burst out laughing because the idea was so out there, so ludicrous. Holden defended him at the time: *he's a good-looking guy, charming, funny.* These things were all true, but Nate was firmly slotted in the brother or close cousin category. Even in her most private moments, Bridget couldn't imagine kissing him. Holden thought she was lying, covering up for any seedling attraction because *men and women cannot be friends,* and nothing Bridget could say seemed to assuage him. *It would be natural,* he insisted, *people fantasize, that's what they do.* Until Bridget had narrowed her eyes at him and asked him point blank if he had a thing for Alecia. Blond, organized, angular, type-A Alecia, and Holden snorted a laugh through his nose. There were no two women further apart than Bridget and Alecia.

Women can tell these things, too. Bridget strongly suspected that Nate held no spark for her, either. He liked his women gangly, and Bridget was all soft curves and curls. Or at least, she used to be.

"I think a tree is a great idea. Holden loved being outside." Nate clasped his fingers behind his head and leaned back.

This was true; he was a hiker, a woods walker, and the twenty-five hundred square miles of state game lands surrounding Mt. Oanoke more than scratched his itch to commune with nature. She told Nate about the maple tree idea and he laughed. "He even gave us one of those small bottles. He gave one to everyone, remember? Nurses, other doctors. He must have bought, what, fifty of them?"

The real answer was thirty-seven, because it was all they had in the store, and they were four dollars apiece.

Bridget feigned laughter because she couldn't do this thing that seemed to come so easily to Nate and Petra, this talking about Holden, remembering him, with a faraway look and crinkled eyes. He still felt too alive. Nate stood up, came behind her, and rested a heavy hand on her shoulder.

"It gets better, Bridge. I miss him, too."

Bridget wanted to say *not like me,* where the sadness felt interminable and resolute, like a living, breathing person had moved in and made himself comfortable, an overstayed houseguest.

Instead, she did what she always did when people offered their "advice": she nodded and gave a smile, an *I can put on a brave face* smile, because people want you to rally. They want to think they're the ones who talked you out of grief, as if grief were something you could be talked out of like a bad pantsuit in a discount dressing room.

The bell rang and Nate stood aside, his hand still resting between her shoulder blades while students shuffled in. Lucia halted in the doorway, staring hard at Nate and Bridget, shifting her backpack from one shoulder to the other while Nate gave Bridget a quick smile and headed to the door.

"What are you doing here?" Lucia smiled, but her eyes were narrowed, and Bridget stopped shuffling papers long enough to watch the exchange.

"Are you in creative writing this period, Lucia?" Nate's voice was friendly, teacherlike, almost condescending.

"Of course." Lucia stepped toward the rows of desks, her back straight with feigned formality. She cocked her head mockingly and Nate rolled his eyes slightly, his chin jutting out. He shook his head a little, laughed, and looked back at Bridget. "Watch that one," he teased, bringing Bridget in on the joke. Lucia watched him leave; her hand shot out to grab his sleeve, a quick tease for fun. He swatted her hand away, laughing.

As the students filled into their chairs, Bridget passed out last week's graded exams. She gave only a few exams a year; the point was to get the students writing, thinking, imagining, not to quiz them on the particulars of grammar and sentence structure. She did, however, instruct them on the craft of storytelling: inciting incident, rising action, subplots, climax, denouement. The tests were easy, for the most part. She paused at Lucia's chair, setting the D paper flat in front of her, her fingertips tented, pressing down on the desk until her knuckles whitened. She leaned close to Lucia's ear, "Stay after a bit, okay?"

"Why?" Lucia's voice was loud, confrontational, and Bridget faltered, surprised. Not that students didn't challenge the teachers. They did. But they didn't usually challenge Bridget. She was too nice, too sad.

Bridget kept her voice soft. "Because you don't usually do this poorly, and this test was fairly easy. Let's just talk." She hesitated, and against her better judgment added, "See if there's a way you can bring it up."

"Not interested," Lucia said, her voice cut with acid, and Bridget stepped away, to the next student, the next test fluttering in her fingertips. But she paused.

"That's your choice," Bridget said nonchalantly, but her voice wobbled, and Lucia raised an eyebrow.

78

Bridget took her usual spot, on a stool in the front of the classroom, the vibe being that of a poetry slam or an improv class. It had always been successful, but today the air in the room crackled, hot with electricity. The students shifted in their seats. She smiled, a quick bright beat, a nervous twitch to her lips. "Today's topic? Anyone?"

The students always suggested the topics for a twenty-minute writing session. Some would then read their entries out loud followed by a discussion, and that was the class, three days a week. The other two days were craft. Bridget liked the flexibility of her days. It was fluid and she felt the palpable relief of the overachievers, allowed for once to slump their shoulders. Close their eyes. Daydream.

"How about change?" Ashlee Williams raised her hand in the back of class. "I've been thinking about this, because we're graduating soon . . ." Her voice drifted off, hesitant. Ashlee was quiet, a good girl. Her journals were all about her boyfriend and fumbling attempts at sex in the dark while her parents watched *Wheel of Fortune* a floor below.

"I like that, anyone else?" Bridget shifted, crossing her feet at her ankles. Her crinkle skirt made a whoosh sound and it seemed unreasonably loud. The kids thought she was a fuddy-duddy with her long dresses, but with bare legs, she'd felt so exposed, so raw, a purplish spider vein winding around the hot crook of her knee.

"What about family?" Josh Tempest, a senior, piped up. Josh was baseball jock with a surprising interest in poetry—Bridget knew so many of their secret sides. "We haven't done something on family in a while."

Bridget nodded. The seniors were starting to lose their adolescence, staring down the barrel of college and independence, both exhilarating and terrifying. Their future stood, shiny as a beacon, but far in the black, fuzzy distance, and they looked at their parents with a new measure of humanity.

"What about reincarnation?" The room got very quiet; even the fidgeters stopped and Bridget felt the hair on her neck stand up.

Lucia chewed on the end of her pen, the black plastic between her teeth reminding Bridget of a cat with a bird. Her smile was sideways, her eyes narrowed.

"Interesting suggestion, Lucia. Care to elaborate?" Bridget picked imaginary lint off her skirt and waited. Someone in the back coughed and tittered nervously.

"When you die, what will *you* come back as?" Lucia challenged her, never wavering, never blinking, those black-rimmed eyes, flat and dry, outlined with that bright blue eyeshadow. And that hair, wild around her face. Her lips, painted with foundation, moved slightly, as if she was whispering.

"Do you think you have a choice?" Bridget asked, clasping her trembling fingers together. It's not that she was unable to think about death, she just seemed unable to do it objectively anymore, and Lucia seemed to enjoy prodding the wound with a hot poker. The idea that her student, this eighteen-year-old girl, could so casually exploit her weaknesses and *enjoy it* made her sick and slightly sweaty. Everyone waited, Ashlee smiling kindly and Josh Tempest averting his eyes, feigning interest in something out the window.

"I'll come back as a blackbird. I already know that." Lucia shrugged, and Bridget thought of her tarot card drawings and her poem. From the back, Josh coughed the word *witch.* A titter went through the room. Lucia ignored them, her eyes narrowed. "Not everyone comes back. I'm sure you have nothing to worry about." Her voice lowered to a whisper, a hoarse rumble. "Good people come back. Teachers, nurses . . . *doctors.*"

Bridget felt hot, then cold. She cleared her throat. "I think," her voice came out strangled, and she tried again. "I think we should do the family one." Everyone began to open their journals, but Lucia just stared that blank stare, her lips moving ever so slightly.

Bridget stood up, dusting her hands off on her knees, official and businesslike, and avoided Lucia, who hadn't moved. Bridget wrote on the whiteboard: Free Writing Topic: Family, 20 minutes. Some of the kids stared off out the window or into the hallway, looking for the words that Bridget always hoped would come— although sometimes they didn't—while others hunkered down, furiously scribbling. Out of the corner of her eye, she could see Lucia watching her. She didn't open her journal, never took that pen out of her mouth; she just stared. Bridget avoided eye contact and sat at her desk, clicking through emails and pretending to read but watching the clock.

Lucia never moved.

When the bell finally rang and all the students filed out, Lucia stayed. Bridget followed the group out the door, leaving Lucia there in the classroom, feigning a bathroom break, scrolling distractedly through her phone, just to leave.

Just to get away from that girl.

CHAPTER 6

Alecia, Saturday, April 25, 2015

The breakdown of a marriage happens in phases, almost imperceptibly, Alecia had discovered.

Alecia charged in the house, a bull seeing red, ready for a fight. Ready for the goring. She gave little thought to Gabe, who would witness the whole thing. All this information was ready to burst out of her mouth, her chest full, her stomach roiling. *A student?* Which student? Alecia's mind spun with the Rolodex of girls she'd seen at baseball games or in the hallways the few times she'd gone to school events. Cute, bubbly blondes and perky brunettes. Long, tan legs. Smooth, sun-kissed faces. Which student? She didn't even know their names. Kaylee or Kilee or Brenna. Something New Age and invented.

Instead, the house was empty. She panted in the kitchen, looking for Nate and seeing only the note: *Took Gabe to therapy. This will be good for all of us. Relax.*

The note was pinned under an ice bucket, a bottle of pinot grigio sweating in the middle, a single stemless glass turned upside down next to it. Alecia would have been gooey at the gesture a week ago. Hell, a few hours ago. Now it just felt suspicious, a deliberate attempt to derail or distract her.

It was a good thing, she realized. She needed to mull this over, decide what to do with everything she'd been told. The idea that a reporter would break the story before she could confront Nate herself left a slick, oily taste in her mouth.

In the bedroom, she sat on the bed, and everything looked different to her. The thin layer of dust on the wooden dressers looked negligent, the fingerprint smudges on the pictures looked grubby. Yesterday she might have called it all *lived in.* Small piles of clothes that needed to be put away, mended, or dry-cleaned sat on the chaise longue, untouched for months. Nate's clothes. Hems that needed stitching. Had she neglected him? Where does a person start to deconstruct their life? Is it possible to isolate a single point in time and say *here is where I lost him?*

Almost three weeks ago, she knew the date exactly, April 2; she'd sat around a long table in the elementary school's guidance counselor's office with the special-education director, the guidance counselor, the principal, the reading specialist, and the math specialist. Their names slid around her tongue, familiar but not yet known. Alecia had taken Gabe for testing two weeks prior. They called it kindergarten readiness testing: cognitive, emotional, social, and intellectual assessments. Long days where Gabe became exhausted, retreating into himself to the point of being mute. She'd had to cancel therapy that week, which would set him back. He'd started to control the tics, the stims, the knee slapping and jaw popping, and now they were skipping therapy and it would all come back, but he was just so damn tired. He fell asleep during the car ride home.

During the testing days, Nate would pop in and out with a quick smack of a kiss on Alecia's forehead. Except for the day of the big meeting, the result meeting, the one where everyone got together and talked about Gabe, like he wasn't a person. Like they knew everything there was to know about him because he could finally put the red ball in the red box. Alecia sat on the edge of her plastic chair, her nails digging into the curve, ready for a fight. The clock ticked as they waited for Nate.

The school-affiliated psychologist avoided her eyes, picking at her cuticles as the seconds turned into minutes. Alecia grew restless. Gabe was home with the neighbor. Mandy was eighteen, still living with her parents, doing a year at community college. She could handle Gabe, could even sometimes reach him when it seemed like Alecia could not. But even she had her limits.

At six fifteen, the principal kindly asked, "Should we just proceed without your husband, Mrs. Winters?"

"He's probably held up at the school. You understand," Alecia offered lamely, and texted Nate one more time to be sure. Still no response. When she had called him an hour before, it had gone straight to voice mail.

The principal cleared his throat at the same moment the psychologist started to talk and everyone laughed nervously.

"We think Gabe would be best served in a special-needs school."

Alecia had been expecting a buildup, a review of the tests and their outcomes. Analytics, discussion, *something*. He was only five, he had a full year before he was required to start school. She'd expected them to say things like *we have time, we can revisit this next spring*. The authoritative finality of the words threw her. They said it like there was no hope for Gabe to "become normal." They didn't use those words, they used words like neurotypical and test-in, but it all meant to "become like other kids." They weren't the first people to insinuate such a thing: therapists and preschool teachers and social workers had all shunted Gabe along, someone else's responsibility. Alecia would always feel wild, flinging anger at this: both at the people who wanted to "normalize" Gabe and then, horribly, at Gabe himself for refusing to comply. Just once, she'd wanted him to comply, but he never could, not even for the smallest thing.

Mainstreaming felt right to Alecia because unlike these suited, tired men and women, she knew her son. She'd seen it now that he was in intensive five-day-a-week therapy. His self-awareness was new, in its infancy. She knew what he could do if he was only challenged, even just a little. She also knew the risk. Gabe was big for his age. His meltdowns had grown rarer, but they were mighty and unintentionally violent. She had nightmares about him throwing chairs, hurting kids, getting expelled.

Nate had lobbied hard for special-needs schools in the past. Now he would get his way and he wasn't even there. Sometimes it seemed like it was Alecia and Gabe against the whole world.

"Mrs. Winters, you should prepare yourself for Gabe's life. I feel like you might be denying the depth of his issues. Or overestimating him. Both are unfair." The psychologist rummaged casually in her purse as she spoke, as though for a lipstick. She pushed a shiny black card across the table with a manicured finger. Learning Support Services was lettered on the front. "Do you have support?" Her brows knitted in concern.

Alecia shook her head. Everyone else exchanged glances. "What?" she asked, uncomprehending in the pregnant moment.

"Mrs. Winters." The reading specialist reached across the table for Alecia's hand and stopped halfway. "You do realize that Gabe is not likely to graduate a mainstream public high school, right?"

The words were icy knives to her heart. High school was *thirteen years* away.

"There are lots of options. We have other schools, there is home schooling, and there is an autism school in Scranton," the psychologist said. Scranton. Close to thirty miles away. She tried to imagine a thirty-mile drive, twice a day with Gabe, his feet kicking relentlessly against the seat in front of him.

Alecia left the meeting, dusk settling over the parking lot, and drove home. She paid Mandy and went through their nightly routine. Bath and bed. Gabe was, for once, calm. Compliant. After all this, he was compliant, finally.

She called Nate and his phone went straight to voice mail. She texted him: *Should I call the police? Where are you? You missed Gabe's kindergarten meeting.* No response.

Later, when he crawled into bed next to her, his arm snaking around her waist, she murmured, "Where were you? I've been calling you."

He sighed into her hair, his palm flat against her stomach. "I've had a hellish day. A student, I'm sorry. I'm so sorry. It was life and death. I forgot about the meeting." His voice came in fervent whispers, huffs of air, and when Alecia turned her head, she thought she smelled cigarette smoke.

"I wouldn't have missed it if it wasn't urgent." He massaged the tops of her thighs, kissed the back of her head. "Do you believe me?"

When she didn't answer, he asked again. "Do you believe me?"

Now her mind skipped back to that night. The smell of cigarettes on his hands. The roughness of his fingertips across her midsection. The coldness of his sweatshirt, like he'd brought the outside early spring chill in with him.

When she had questioned him about it the next morning, he would only tell her in vague terms a student needed his help. If she pressed him on it, he grew impatient.

"Do you trust me, Alecia?" He had put his hands on his hips, staring her down. Of course she did.

Alecia picked up her phone and looked through her calendar. Highlighted April, right swiped till she found the date, right there: *April 2. Kindergarten readiness meeting, 6 p.m.*

Her heart pounding, she opened the laptop, opened Nate's email. She knew his passwords; his commonly used ones anyway. He'd never tried to keep any of it a secret. It took her two tries: Gabe2009. Of course. Nate wasn't secretive, he wasn't even very good at subterfuge; any truth was evident on his face, in his voice. Nothing about any of this felt true deep down true. When she thought of Nate, she thought of that affable laugh, the way he touched her shoulder when he talked. The way he'd stand, a hand clapped on Coach Berkit's back as they discussed players, or an arm slung over Bridget's and Alecia's shoulders while they made dinner in Alecia's kitchen. *My two girls now,* he'd said. They'd laughed.

A student?

Emails from Coach Berkit, another teacher she didn't really know; one from Tripp Harris; two Dick's Sporting Goods flyers. One from Bridget on April 2. Alecia hesitated, then double clicked.

Hey, found a sweatshirt of H's, want it? It's UNC. Let me know, I'll bring it in. PS. Tried wasabi chips, are you nuts?

Alecia almost laughed. Emails about potato chips and here she was clicking through them, quick and suspicious, pounding heart. She closed the window and navigated to their shared bank account. No activity on April 2. She flipped the laptop lid shut and sat for a moment, stumped. She had to know; she could just ask, right? Tell Nate about the reporter, the accusation, the date she couldn't get out of her mind.

Without thinking, she clicked open the computer again and typed an address in the navigation bar. She opened her wallet and typed in all sixteen digits off their single credit card, mostly maxed out. Nate had argued for an additional credit card: *we have no safety net at all, Alecia.* She'd been firm. They lived *so* close to the line every month, she had to be careful when she paid specific bills. She remembers what it was like when they were *dinks.* They'd laughed about it then: dual income, no kids. Swank restaurants in the city, bar tabs she signed her name to, and the only reason she looked at the total was to drunkenly calculate a decent tip. She'd kill for that freedom again.

She never looked at the credit card balance, just paid her two hundred bucks a month, which may or may not have been covering the minimum. It was like gas, right? Why did anyone ever look at the price of gas? You needed your car, you'd put gas in it no matter the price. Her eyes scanned the statement, skipping over the total. Gabe needed his therapy, every blessed one. Knowing the cost would only keep her awake at night.

She scrolled through the charges in April, her finger tracing down the screen: Whispering Pines (horse therapy), The Balance Center (Gabe's yoga), A&P (sadly, charged groceries, not an uncommon occurrence, but one Alecia avoided dwelling on). Deannie's MH, $125. Her finger paused there. She searched her memory for a therapy or maybe a lunch at someplace called Deannie's.

In another tab, she opened Google and typed it in and clicked enter. When she scanned the results, she knew she'd found it and tugged on the ends of her hair, the roots aching.

Deannie's Motel Honesdale.

I saw a blackbird yesterday, right on the sidewalk in front of the house, stuck between the concrete and the weeds. He was dead, and weirdly perfect, but they always are. I always know that something bad will happen on the day I see one. And then you came home, you see?

You're so stupid, ugly, skinny. I tend to believe I'm the only one afraid of you. Who would be? You think smack makes you do bad things, but really, you're just a bad person. If I said that, you'd kill me. I really think that, that someday you'll kill me. Jimmy would hate what you've become. I'm almost done with you, only a few more months.

CHAPTER 7

Bridget, April 2, 2015:
Three weeks before the birds fell

Lord, Bridget missed Georgia. April already and just still so damn cold, some nights you could hardly inhale, your lungs seemed to freeze midbreath.

Bridget sat at her desk long after the final bell, distracted, thinking about her mama. She'd spent the week south, in Colquitt, Georgia. They'd had off Monday and Tuesday, some slim semblance of a spring break, although to Bridget that had always coincided with Easter. She guessed they didn't do that anymore, separation of church and school and what have you.

So she'd taken a personal day and made it a five-day weekend and flown south, like a snowbird. Down to Mama, her mobile home propped up on a poured foundation on thirty acres of land. Aunt Nadine in a unit behind Mama, on the same plot, the path between their homes worn thin from the sisters traversing the lawn in the dark. Bridget sat outside with them on the nights that it spiked up into the seventies, legs thrown over lawn chairs while they played canasta at a card table on the in-between dusty grass. Aunt Nadine surrounded the table with buckets of citronella candles to keep the skeeters away, and they sang loud as anything because who cared, they hadn't any neighbors. The air was sticky wet, even in winter, the swamp behind the trailer vaporizing into the air and hanging there like a thick fog.

She hadn't seen Mama since Christmas, when she'd barely managed to get the tree up, a spindly teetering thing, propped up in the corner, strung with big colorful outdoor lights and only a handful of ornaments. When Bridget had asked her about it, Mama only muttered and waved her hand around in a circle, *it's good enough, bebe.* Mama wasn't Cajun French, but she claimed she spent a summer on the bayou as a teenager. With Mama it was hard to tell what was real and what only existed in her mind.

Mama's crazy seemed to keep getting a little crazier and Nadine had gotten a little more watchful, but Mama took her pills and Nadine set limits on her wine and it all seemed to be working. Nadine, the spinster, took care of Mama, the widow. Sometimes Bridget couldn't believe she'd followed in her Mama's footsteps, a widow at thirty-seven. Sometimes she wondered when Mama's crazy would get her, too.

Bridget left as tired as she'd come, but for drastically different reasons.

She'd gotten so lost in her own brain, thinking that it had been too long since she'd been down there, that she needed to make more time, more often. Thinking about how Nadine would cope when Mama went first, which she surely would, lifelong bipolar medication eating away at her liver like a Georgia swamp parasite.

"Mrs. Peterson?" Taylor Lawson stood in Bridget's doorway, her messenger bag slung across her body, her shoulders hunched forward with the weight of it.

"Hi, Taylor," Bridget said with a smile, but she was tired. She wanted to go home to her sandwich and her tea and Sunny the cat.

"Um, can I talk to you?"

"Sure." A dark green plastic and metal chair was pushed against the whiteboard and she pulled it to her desk with her foot. Bridget motioned for her to sit. "What's up?"

"I'm worried about Lucia." She pushed her bangs away from her face with her hand. "I know you don't like her."

"That's not true, Taylor. I don't dislike her. I think . . ." Bridget paused, because her feelings seemed irrelevant, but then also because Taylor was Lucia's unlikely best friend, inasmuch as Lucia could have a friend. Taylor, dark and petite, friendly but a bit of a follower, trailed by Lucia like a pet. She gave Lucia what little social credibility she had, got the duo invited to parties and events. People mostly liked Taylor and tolerated Lucia's strangeness. Or were at least fascinated by it, until she became some kind of oddball fetish: *where's the weirdo?* Then later: *where's the witch?*

Bridget thought it odd, these mixing of classes. When she was in school, the juniors and seniors stuck to their own like cattle in a chute. These days, everyone was all mixed up in some kind of bubblegum soup.

But Lucia and Taylor had been added to the right table in the cafeteria, between Andrew Evans—King Evans—and Porter Max, vying for the attention of Riana Yardley. Josh Tempest, with his arms thrown around Kelsey Minnow, protective and needful, his face in her hair while she chewed iceberg lettuce from between two fingers. Lucia perched on the end, her legs thrown to the side, as though ready to bolt at any time. She rarely saw them talk to her. If Bridget had to guess, she'd wager most kids were afraid of her.

"I think Lucia needs attention. Everyone is looking for the same thing, to feel loved. Lucia's no different," Bridget finally said.

"I just don't know who else to talk to. It's weird, because she's eighteen."

"What's weird?"

"Lucia said she ran away. She said she's been living at the old paper mill." Taylor ran her fingernail along a ridge in the wood top of the desk. Bridget felt her heart speed up. Oanoke Paper stood on the edge of town right before a thick impenetrable woods, part of the twenty-two thousand square acres of preserved game lands in northern Pennsylvania. While some well-traveled areas contained winding but clear trails, most of the forest was left untamed, dense and disorienting.

"Taylor, that's not possible. The nights are still pretty cold. In the thirties sometimes."

"She says she has a fire. And some kind of oil heater? I don't know where she'd get that."

Every other person in this county was a hunter. Schools were closed for opening day of buck season. Camping equipment wasn't hard to come by.

"Plus, I think she skipped work. She never does that." Taylor kicked the leg of the desk, a quiet, steady thump vibrating up Bridget's arms.

"She works?"

"At the Goodwill. A few nights a week," Taylor said, but with an air of confusion like a girl who'd never had a job might say.

"What do you know about her family?" Bridget asked, her tongue thick. Taylor shifted the binder in her hand and stared at the wall behind Bridget's head.

"Enough. I don't go there much. Her dad left, but I don't know when. He's a drunk. Her brother is Lenny Hamm. He was supposed to graduate like three years ago but he dropped out." She shrugged like this was no big deal. "Heroin."

"Heroin?" Bridget blanched.

"A lot of kids use," Taylor said.

Bridget sighed. She thought of her tea. Her cat. She stood, grabbed her purse. "Come on, Taylor. You're in it now."

Taylor stood but hung back. "I should get home, Mrs. Peterson . . ."

"I'll take you home," Bridget said. "After."

Bridget had never been to a student's home. That was more Nate's thing; he'd been invited for dinners with the baseball players, steaming plates of homemade meat loaf and mashed potatoes. Comfort food as thanks. Bridget kept a nice air of distance and she'd wanted it to stay that way.

Lucia's house sat outside of town, away from the developments and square streets that formed "downtown" Mt. Oanoke. It stood alone, beyond the trailer park on the outskirts, over the railroad tracks, literally the wrong side. It was asphalt sided, broken in places, and the shingles were hanging. The house was grayish-brown, a noncolor, and the porch was sunken as though supporting the weight of some invisible giant. The upstairs window was broken, splintered out like a spiderweb.

Bridget stared at that window, halted at the end of a broken sidewalk, one arm outstretched protectively in front of Taylor.

"What's wrong?" Taylor asked.

"That curtain," Bridget pointed to the broken window. "I think it moved?"

"I've been here before, it's no big deal." Taylor shrugged. "It's just a mess. Her family is a fucking mess." Her hand went to her mouth and she let out a little whoop. "Sorry."

"Should we have called first? Lucia, I mean," Bridget asked.

"She doesn't answer her phone much anymore, anyway. Just text, and only sometimes."

Bridget navigated the upended concrete. The porch groaned under their combined weight. She knocked. Waited. Knocked again.

Finally, the interior door slid open, wide enough for a face, a pair of gray eyes.

"Yeah?" The boy looked like Lucia, skinny with that same shock of white hair. Lenny, Bridget guessed.

"Is Lucia here?" Bridget asked, and Lenny looked past her to Taylor, regarding her with a nod.

"No." He started to close the door.

"Lenny, wait." Taylor reached out, her hand on the screen door handle. "When did you see her last?"

"Uh, I don't know. Awhile ago." Lenny

shrugged, and in doing so the door inched open. Bridget could see the living room beyond, dark and brownish. Trash on the floor. A smell wafted out the door, ripe and sour, like beer and body odor.

"Is your father here, Lenny?" Bridget asked, hiking her purse up on her shoulder, reflexively crossing her arm across her chest.

"No. Who are you?" Lenny finally asked, his eyes narrowed.

"I'm Mrs. Peterson, Lucia's teacher. If she's not here, have you reported her missing?"

"Uh, is she missing?" Lenny scratched his head. "Has she been in school?"

She had, of course, but Lenny didn't know that.

"Where is she staying, Lenny, if she's not here?" Taylor pushed past Lenny into the house and Bridget followed her, impotent.

On the inside, the smell was worse. Greasy, cloying. Bridget held her breath, looked around. The place was sparsely furnished, a couch and a television propped up on wooden crates. She craned her neck to look to the kitchen, piled high with pots and pans. As far as she could tell, the garbage had been accumulating for months.

"God, I haven't been here in forever. What the hell happened?" Taylor turned in place, a slow pirouette. "Where's Jimmy?"

"Who's Jimmy?" Bridget asked.

"Lucia and Lenny's dad." Taylor said. "This place has always been a shithole, but not like this." She didn't even apologize for the curse this time.

"Jesus, Taylor," Lenny said, coming into the living room behind them.

"Lucia said she ran away. She's been staying in the old paper mill. When was she here last?" It seemed irrelevant. They would just go there. Bridget hung back, trying to gauge their intimacy. They knew each other, but how well? How often had Taylor been here? Were things in Lucia's life ever normal? Happy? She tried to envision a mother. None came to mind.

"Lenny, where is your father?" Bridget pressed. She got the feeling Lenny was avoiding the question.

"I don't know," Lenny grumbled, sinking down onto the plaid couch.

"You don't know?" Bridget asked. He was probably twenty years old. Lucia was eighteen, it was hardly a concern if they lived alone. But to *not know?*

"He left here, drunk, months ago. I ain't seen him since. We had a fight. I figured he skipped town. Listen, this ain't that weird, you know. He done it before."

"He has? When?"

"I don't know! He don't like what I say, so he leaves. We're all adults."

"What happened to your mother?" Bridget asked, and wondered about the invasiveness of the question.

Lenny laughed. "That bitch? Well, gee, now y'all go digging and y'all don't stop. I ain't seen her in prolly ten years. The mill closed and then she left same as him. Took him a little longer, but I guess she's smarter. Now Lucia. Only me in this house."

"Did you call the cops about Jimmy?" Taylor asked.

"Sure. You know what they told me? They'd put out an APB." He let out a *pffffttt*. "Do you think they care about the town drunk and his druggie kid? They ne'er found his car but I guaran-damn-tee they ne'er looked."

"So you're telling me that Jimmy's gone and now Lucia's gone and you never called the police about her?" Bridget asked, her voice slow and deliberate.

"I just figured she ran off to find him or something." He made it sound illicit.

Bridget shivered.

"Why would she do that?" Taylor asked.

"Oh, 'cause she took care of his drunk ass. Waited hand and foot on him." Lenny wiped a line of grease from his forehead, up into his hair, glinting and wet. "Ne'er gave a fuck about me, though. 'Cept to beat my ass."

• • •

"Let me take you home, Taylor." Bridget's offer was halfhearted.

Taylor shook her head. Hard. "If you're going to the mill, I'm going with you." She hesitated a beat. "Even if you're not, I'd probably go myself. I'm worried about her. There's been something off with her. I can't tell what." She looked out the window. "Lenny's bad. I've never seen him like that."

"How long have you been friends?" Bridget asked softly.

"Since kindergarten. They had a mom then, though."

"What happened to her?"

"I don't know. She just . . . left. After the mill closed, when Lenny was still normal. I guess we were ten or so. She sent letters for a while, but Lucia was pretty pissed about it. I don't think she ever wrote her back. My mom takes care of Lucia a lot, feels bad for her. We had a séance once." Taylor traced a pattern in her jeans with an index finger, avoiding Bridget's gaze. "Maybe sixth grade? We burned everything. Her mom's clothes, her letters, her pictures. Jimmy found us. He said he was mad, but there was no conviction behind it. I got the feeling . . ." She took a deep breath. "He was proud of her for it. Listen, she's never been normal, I know that. She pushes into people, gets under their skin. She flies in people's faces. Sometimes I think it's all she has. This . . . persona. But deep down, I think she's more like everyone else than she wants to believe."

Bridget considered this, Taylor with her Seven jeans and her Free People boots. Lucia with her black secondhand clothes. Taylor gave Lucia social credibility. Lucia gave Taylor's bubble gum an edge.

"Okay, you can come with me, but we're not going alone."

Tripp Harris didn't look comfortable. They met in the dusty parking lot of the paper mill, their cars meeting nose to nose, hers blue, his black. The redbrick facade of the mill was crumbling and the roar of the dam in the back made it hard to hear.

"Bridget." Tripp smiled uneasily. "Nice to see you again. Although, this . . ." He spread his arm out wide. "You should let me call this in."

"We will. If it's anything. I promise." She pulled her hair back from her face and lifted one shoulder. "It's a student. If I can avoid the police, I'd like to."

"You know, I *am* the police." Tripp smiled and leaned down to peck Bridget's cheek. "What's the urgency?"

"I think a student of mine is living in here." Bridget stomped her feet to get the cold out, her breath coming in puffs.

"Okay. And you are . . ." Tripp looked at Taylor.

"Taylor Lawson. Lucia's best friend." Taylor dipped her chin, shy.

"Another student," Bridget said.

"Aw, Bridge, let me call it in. Take Taylor home," Tripp said again softly. His teeth gleamed white in the purple twilight. He put his hand on Bridget's elbow and she was reminded of the last time she saw Tripp, at Holden's funeral, standing with the rest of the bar league softball team. Tripp had been a periodic fifth to their four-some, single and flaunting a string of girlfriends at cookouts and barbecues. Girls, not women, merely twenty-five, perky breasted, and lean legged. A man-child with a badge.

Bridget ignored his request. "How do we even start to look?" It was four o'clock; the sun would be setting, the sky streaked bright red, plunging the mill into darkness. Close to nine hundred thousand square feet, the mill stretched out for what seemed like miles of broken windows and crumbling brick. The interior was likely to be treacherous. Bridget realized at once how stupid this was. Lucia could be anywhere. She looked at Taylor. If something happened to the girl, Bridget could lose her job, maybe her license.

"Let's just do a quick perimeter search. If we don't find her, we'll call it in," Tripp said, eyeing the pinkish sky. "But keep in mind, she's eighteen. As long as she's coming to school, they might not invest the time. They're taking regular OD calls. It's getting worse, you know? We're a small force."

They picked their way around the side of the mill and Tripp retrieved a mini magnum flashlight from his back pocket. He shone the light in the side windows and the beam bounced off giant spools and tables, the detritus of a decrepit industry. Aside from words scrawled on the walls in haphazard spray paint (Whore, Bitch), the place looked appropriately abandoned.

Bridget kicked a Miller Lite can and everyone jumped.

Tripp moved to the next window, then the next. He shone the light up to the second floor, then the third, but unless Lucia was crouched near a window, they'd never see her.

In the fourth set of windows, there was a crumpled red shirt in the corner, covered in dust. Been there awhile.

They moved on, Tripp leading the way, Bridget close behind. She held Taylor's hand with one hand while gripping the back of Tripp's jacket with the other, the slick nylon sliding between her fingertips. He smelled of cologne, and she wondered if he had a date later.

"Bridge, I see something." Tripp stopped short and Bridget ran into the back of him, pulling

Taylor with her. The light from the flashlight glinted off something metallic.

A kerosene heater.

Taylor dropped Bridget's hand and ran. Toward the water, the dam, that loud rush. In a panic, she yelled, "Lucia! Lucia!"

Tripp chased her. "Taylor! Come back, she won't hear you!"

One side of the double-door entrance to the mill had been kicked down years ago. Only one door hung creakily from a twenty-four-inch hinge.

Tripp stopped and swung the light between the interior and the outside, where Taylor had run, indecisive. The lure of Lucia won out, and he turned into the corridor of the concrete building.

"Lucia!" called Bridget, her skin alive, crawling. "She's not out there. She wouldn't hear you anyway."

Taylor stopped, her back to the mill, staring in the direction of the dam, the mist collecting in her hair. She shrugged and turned back, pushing past Bridget and inside, after Tripp. Bridget followed.

Dust and beer cans, garbage and plastic bags, clothes, the makings of a campfire littered every room. It was a teenage party haven.

They got to the room with the heater, which was off. There was a small black backpack, the zipper tied with a rainbow braid, that Bridget recognized as Lucia's. A journal, the pen between the pages like a bulbous bookmark.

Taylor came up behind them, breathing hard, her face red and sheened with sweat.

"Any luck?" Bridget asked, but Tripp already had his cell phone in hand, dialing.

"Nothing," Taylor said.

Lucia was gone.

CHAPTER 8

Alecia, Saturday, April 25, 2015

"Do you think an affair with a student is something to laugh about?" Alecia stood in the living room, her hands on her hips. Gabe was in bed, finally asleep, and the story of the day came out fast and jumbled. She'd never had a poker face, never could play her cards close to the vest. The truth spewed out.

"It's so ludicrous, that's all." He cocked his head. "You can't believe it?"

"Tell me why I shouldn't." Alecia shook the single sheet of paper—the bank statement with Deannie's Motel—in front of his face. He cupped his forehead and stared at it.

"I did buy a hotel room for a student. Do you know Lucia Hamm? Have I talked about her?" He sat in the chair, choosing to avoid the couch where Alecia perched on the edge, brittle and nervous. "She's troubled. I don't know much about her home life, but she called me a month ago for God's sake. Said she was sleeping in the paper mill. It was forty degrees at night. But she'd run to Honesdale and asked if I could meet her."

"That was the day of Gabe's kindergarten meeting." Alecia tried to keep her voice calm. "You couldn't just *tell me*?"

"Why? You'd flip shit, Alecia. You count every penny in this goddamn house, every single thing is budgeted, we eat generic oatmeal, like I can't even have Quaker Oats, and you want me to tell you that I'm spending an hour's worth of Reiki therapy on a random girl's hotel room for one night?" His voice edged up; he was getting pissed now. "If I told you I spent that, I'd have heard about it forever."

"Why there? Why Honesdale?" It felt illicit, like a tryst kept away from the community.

"I don't know why!" Nate palmed both knees, the printout fluttering to the ground. He leaned forward, puffed out his cheeks and blew, like blowing out candles. "I didn't ask many questions. I tried to keep her calm. She was crying, hysterical. I told her I'd help her for one night, and then told her I would call Tripp to get her the number of a shelter. She's not a minor. The foster care system is useless to her."

"How'd she have your number?" She yelped then, an *aha, caught you.*

"All the kids have my number. I give it to them." He said this dismissively, waved his hand in her direction.

She ignored it. "So then what? Did you go back?" Her questions were a freight train, ramming into the front of her skull. She couldn't ask them fast enough.

"No. She freaked out. Said that Tripp was looking for her. Officer Harris, she called him. That for some reason, Taylor and Officer Harris were together at the paper mill, going through her stuff. She was afraid of getting arrested."

"Arrested? For what?" The entire story felt made up; nothing made sense.

"I don't know! She just said she ran away, that she couldn't trust anyone anymore, and would I help her? I said I would for one night, then she needed to go to a shelter. I asked her what happened at home but she wouldn't talk about it. Only that she couldn't live with her brother anymore." Nate cleared his throat, his foot tapping. "This is stupid, Alecia. You can't believe any of this. It's like . . ." He searched for an analogy and came up empty.

"Aren't you worried? This reporter is spreading this story, you could lose your *job*. Don't you care?" Her voice pitched into a screech. He'd put their whole family at risk for a girl and a motel room. For what? What would happen to them if Nate got fired? "An affair with a student is a big deal. People get fired on the accusation alone. It's *rape,* Nate."

"Alecia!" He barked, looked around like someone could have heard her say the word. "If the story is about Lucia, she's eighteen, it's not rape."

113

"Oh my God, that's your thought? That makes it better?" Alecia tangled her fingers in her hair, almost laughing, and stopped. "This was almost month ago," Alecia said. "Why now? What is this reporter talking about, then? Who else knows about your motel room?"

"It's not *my* motel room, Alecia. Knock it off." He stood up, walked into the kitchen, opened the fridge. Alecia heard the pop of a beer, the last indulgence she'd let him keep. His case-a-week habit was getting expensive, though.

"We can't afford to buy this much beer all the time." She stood up, followed him into the kitchen. She knew it wasn't the time or place, but the words popped out of her mouth before she could stop them. She stopped herself from continuing, *if we're going to also be subsidizing runaways. If no one around here is going to have a job.* They'd fought about her nasty fighting for years, her acerbic tongue, quick as a snake's.

"Goddamn it, Alecia, just shut the hell up. For once." He slammed the beer bottle down on the counter and it shattered, the glass slicing through the palm of his hand. His anger seemed so sudden, so intense, Alecia wondered if she'd said what she was thinking out loud by accident. "Fuck!" Nate grabbed a dish towel and wrapped it around his palm until it stained red. He panted hard and stared at her, his face pinched and twisted.

He'd never been mean before. Told her to shut up, called her a bitch, called her any names at all. She was the nasty one. He was mostly apathetic, intent on keeping the peace, willing to go along to get along. Didn't he ever get sick of it? She wanted to push him; her anger flashed, hot and quick under her skin.

"Fuck you, Nate," Alecia said quietly, something she'd never said before, either. The blood dripped on the brown linoleum. The colors blended together and she couldn't tell where the circular, dirty-water pattern ended and his blood began.

He laughed again. "Fuck me?" He shook his head, flicked the bloody towel at her feet, and pushed past her. "Nah, that's not a thing you do anymore."

No matter how brutal their fights, Nate always dropped off to sleep like falling off the side of a building, hard and fast. Alecia lay in bed and listened to his even breathing, her heart pounding. By the time she'd shoved the bloody towel into the garbage, collected herself, and found her way upstairs, Nate was out. It felt like a deliberate affront.

His phone blinked on the nightstand, splaying blue and green on their ceiling, waiting notifications, text messages, or emails. His phone was a constant, always buzzing and binging. It felt like a living thing in his hand, between them. She'd successfully banished it from the table, but it still blinked and beeped from its nested spot in the basket on the counter. Someone always calling him, needing him, wanting him, to make a decision, or just simply make him laugh. She'd be lucky to have so many friends. Nate's friends were her friends by default. Even Bridget was Nate's friend first; how could you not be?

Alecia remembered a time when Nate's popularity was a draw. The blond boy with the smiling eyes had picked *her* in the hazy North Carolina sunshine. His rich, northern roots, his baseball uniform blue and shiny like the cloudless sky. He'd plucked her, like peach off a tree, right out of the baseball crowd, surrounded by her sorority sisters, friends she'd paid for because she was too angular, too type A, too held together to make friends on her own. She'd never had the nerve to ask where the good parties were. Greek life seemed easier. But she sat on the grass watching the game and he'd picked her. A lean and mean second baseman with a quick mind and an even quicker heart. She'd hardly met anyone who didn't love Nate, even back in college. She got used to his flirtation, the way he touched other women, just a shoulder here, the tender square on the spine, the tingly place that men touch when they want to get laid. She tried to tell him women love that, be careful. He'd always laughed at her and shrugged, like it didn't matter.

His heart was as wide open as his laughing mouth. He fed stray cats; they collected at the back door of the baseball house, meowing all hours of the night until the guys threatened to kick him out. Tucked bills into beggars' caps. Volunteered for United Way school campaigns. He wooed her with his goodness, his round face wholesome like a chocolate chip cookie. Alecia had never known such virtue, like the universe had delivered her own private Boy Scout. Her mother and father would have never put themselves out for anyone. Not that they were unkind, they just weren't *giving* people.

They went to a wedding once, for a distant cousin of Alecia's. They were all distant. Hers was a holiday, wedding, and funeral family: polite and thin lipped. A woman at their table, maybe a cousin, Alecia couldn't remember, held a red, angry infant, screaming and punching into the air. Beads of sweat rolled down the mother's forehead as she longingly eyed the door. Nate had laughed, taken the infant from her arms, and walked the baby around the perimeter of the room, patting his diapered end, whispering and smiling. Alecia watched him in awe, because who takes a stranger's baby away? The mother never even looked to see where he went.

Alecia found him outside, the baby's eyes wide

and blinking under the fluorescent parking lot lights, quiet and not quite cooing, but calm. Nate was pointing at the stars, talking, his voice low, about Orion and the Seven Sisters, the moons of Jupiter, the rings of Saturn, all things Alecia had no idea about. She'd called him a good politician and he laughed, not understanding what she meant.

"Kissing babies?" she asked. "You never heard that expression? Shaking hands and kissing babies?"

"Like I'm doing it for show?" His eyes crinkled up.

"Maybe?" She traced the top of the baby's head, the soft triangular fontanel pulsing like a heart under her fingertip. "Because you can't be for real."

"You think I'm trying to trick you into something?" With his free hand, he yanked on her hair softly. "Ah, you'll marry me anyway."

She was shocked then; they'd never talked about marriage. They'd only been dating for six months, still in college. Still spending Saturday nights at keg parties in dank basements, draped across wet plastic beanbag chairs.

"Are you proposing?" She covered her discomfort with coyness.

"Not yet. But I will, you can count on it." He kissed her forehead and slapped her bottom with his free hand, walked away laughing, to take the baby back to his mother now that it was calm and gurgling. She followed him in, found the mother at the table, her hair tucked back into place, smiling, nursing a glass of wine. The woman fawned all over Nate and he let her, winking at Alecia the whole time. "See?" He whispered later as they danced, his arms crushing her against him, stealing the air from her lungs until she felt like she would burst. "Everyone loves me."

Even ten years later, she wondered how much of Nate's smile, his seemingly wide-open heart, was real. She would have thought she'd know by now.

Alecia pulled back the covers and quietly crept from the bed. There was no reason to take such care to be quiet. Nate slept hard, his breathing slow and even, often waking in the same position he'd fallen asleep in. On his side of the bed, she detached his phone from the cord with a quick flick of her thumb and took it into the bathroom. Sitting on the closed toilet seat, she clicked through his Facebook. She'd resisted social media—who had the time?—until a year or so ago. When Alecia had first joined, she was assaulted by pictures from high school friends: kids with gap teeth, climbing onto school buses for the first time, shopping, eating at restaurants, gourmet meals they made at home, stylized with photo filters. All the glossy facade breaking her heart slowly, immeasurably, a hairline crack at a time. She unfollowed all of them and her feed had become a carefully culled collection of parenting websites, autism communities, special-needs moms groups.

Nate's newsfeed was old college buddies, colleagues from the high school, students, coaches, parents, his cousins. It was loud, like a virtual fraternity party. So little of it represented his actual life. One slightly grainy, blurry picture of Gabe that she had tagged him in a few months ago.

She clicked on his messages and scrolled through quickly. Parents, coaches, a few students here and there asking homework questions. His Twitter was all Philadelphia sports. Alecia knew that Nate used social media to keep an eye on the students. The drama that played out in school was set up the night before, he always said. He knew where to be to break up a fight, when to intervene, and when to let it play out.

She opened Snapchat but he had no stories, no pictures. His account looked vacant. Which seemed weird. Why have the account?

She clicked the Instagram icon and scrolled through the feed. Stylized perfection seemed so far out of reach, so unattainable, that even thinking about it made Alecia tired. The girls were oversexualized, tinted yellow or blue or with the right amount of blur to appear "artsy," all this manufactured beauty in a perfectly cropped pixelated square. Long legs and newly painted toenails (#pedi!) announced the excitement of spring; girls trying on prom dresses (#prom, #spring, #seniors) and taking diagonal selfies in dressing room mirrors; kissing photos, the boys appropriately stubbled and the girls heavy lidded with half-parted lips (#bae, #love!). Out of curiosity, she clicked on Andrew Evans's profile. A few unsmiling selfies; him and a tall, bony boy she recognized as a Tempest at a baseball game; a group shot: Andrew, two boys she didn't know, smiling, glossy girls, thrown together on a couch, their legs intertwined. One of the girls was Jennifer Lawson's daughter. Taylor, was it?

She barely understood what it all meant, her mouth woolly and dry. What did Nate think about when he looked through these pictures? These girls, barely eighteen, some even younger, with their big glossy mouths and long hair, edited and cropped and filtered to perfection. Tan and tight squares of flat tummies (#abworkout!), perfect little bodies, twisting around each other, tangles of arms and legs. How could anyone live up to this? How could Alecia?

Alecia studied the feed, a dark black heart under each picture to indicate likes (117 likes for the blonde with the gauzy cleavage in a meadow (a meadow!). She wondered if Nate interacted, if he commented or hashtagged (#teacher4life!) or even liked any of his students' pictures. She wondered how she could know so little about his online world, thriving and thick with life. Alecia tapped the heart under a picture, an innocuous cup of coffee. She watched it turn red, tapped it again, and it returned to white.

Alecia opened his account settings and saw it: Posts You've Liked. She clicked it. There was nothing, only a blank screen, white. Innocent.

She clicked to his profile. No pictures. Nothing posted of his own.

She closed his apps, absently opened his photo gallery, scrolled through his pictures. Nothing but baseball images: games, a cracked bench in the dugout, practical, economical things. She imagined him texting the cracked bench to the athletic director, angry, demanding repairs.

She opened his Facebook account. Nothing posted on his own profile. No profile pictures, just the white outline of a man, like a ghost. This is how he watched them: ethereal and fleeting.

In his gallery, something caught her eye: Screenshots. It was a folder, the Instagram logo barely visible, but a glimmery flash of peach and cream. She opened it, her hands clammy.

The girl with the white hair, the girl he helped. The troubled girl. Red lace, bursting cleavage, blur to cover the rest. Her white hair cascading down over even whiter breasts. Her face turned down, her lips dark as blood. What was her name? Lucia.

And Nate's solid red heart, stuck there, long after it was undone, frozen in time.

When I think of childhood, it's shiny, like a new penny. When Jimmy still worked at the mill. We were seven? Eight maybe? Everything was good. Not perfect, but not terrible. You were there, remember? We rode our bikes from my house to Mr. Tibbs's store, all our quarters weighing down the pockets of our jeans. If you got there on a Friday afternoon, you could snag those giant deli pickles just as they replaced the jar. We used all our quarters for that, right? You were still hungry, so you, you idiot, tried to get away with stealing chips, like a whole bag. All that crinkly foil. Mrs. Tibbs knew right away and she grabbed your arm so fast. No one stole from Mrs. Tibbs. *You got all the money in the world,* she said. Remember? She was right. That was so stupid. You could have just run home, asked your mom and rode back. Easy peasy. But no. You spit at her! *Spit at her.* Do you remember this? Who does that? Anyway, she was such a bitchy old hen. She said, *I'll tell your mama, I know just who you are!* You said, *Then who are we?* Did you really think she was lying? She called you out so fast. *Taylor Lawson,* she said, and then she looked at me, like she'd never seen me before. *Lulu something,* she said. You nearly died laughing.

You've called me that ever since. Sometimes I still think about that.

CHAPTER 9

Bridget, April 3, 2015:
Three weeks before the birds fell

In the beginning of spring, sixth period, immediately after lunch, always dragged on forever. Something about the last of the melting snow from a late winter storm, the rising temperature combined with the rain. Everyone yawned, huddled deeper into their sweatshirts, their heads popping out like turtles. No one listened. Teachers gave quizzes just to keep everyone awake.

Bridget had gone to the office in the morning, her fingers scanning the attendance sheets until she saw the name Lucia Hamm in the absent column. The girl was inches away from truancy and no one seemed to care.

Bridget cleared her throat at the administrative assistant, a dandelion-puff head of a woman, who grumbled and grouched at Bridget no matter what she did anyway. "Did anyone call Lucia's house?"

Bridget studied the small flower arrangement on the desk in front of her. A coffee mug, a ball of daisies and carnations like a scoop of strawberry ice cream. Nate's scrawled handwriting on a rectangular card. *To Ginny, Happy Birthday. We'd all be lost without you! Nate.*

Bridget forgot her name was Ginny. To be fair, Ginny had started last year, right before Bridget's leave.

Ginny reached out, her long red fingernails snatching the coffee mug back, out of Bridget's reach and tucked it behind the desk. "We haven't had a phone number for that girl since she started high school and her father disappeared."

"I don't understand, how does a student just skate through the system like this?" Bridget slapped the attendance sheet on the counter and Ginny rolled her eyes.

"She's eighteen now." As if this negated the need for help, as if seventeen was a world away from eighteen. As if overnight, they were no longer children.

Bridget still held out hope that Lucia would show up to seventh-period creative writing. Ask for help, admit to needing someone, anything. She'd never known her to.

Bridget texted Tripp. *She's not in school today.*

If you can't find her by 6 p.m., we'll file a report. I'll go back to the mill today. Tripp's reply was immediate, like he'd had his phone in his hand, waiting. Then another quick buzz. *Are you ok?*

Bridget was so used to people asking her this question, or subtle variations of it: *Are you ok? How are you doing? Do you need anything?* Often the question was accompanied by a casserole, a bottle of wine, an edible arrangement delivery. Bridget was grateful, but sometimes being on the receiving end of everyone's pity was grating. Today, the question, framed by a new situation, felt fresh, almost thrilling.

Fine. She hit send, then texted a smile emoticon. He didn't write back.

At least now, she had a purpose, something to keep her busy besides her frozen dinner and her red Solo cup of cabernet.

Seventh period passed, as did eighth, and then the final bell. Bridget closed the door to her classroom and waited for the commotion in the halls to die down. Her feet bounced as she sat, restless, and her heart pattered irregularly.

She checked her phone a hundred times between four and five o'clock; nothing from Tripp. The minute hand inched toward the twelve as she waited for the buzz of an incoming text, Tripp telling her he found Lucia or, alternately, to meet him and they'd file a report together, but nothing came. She'd stayed late to read journals; she'd fallen behind with the craziness of the past few days. They weren't hard to keep up with, just a check to make sure the students were doing them—class topic assignments and a few sentences, at least three days a week. Generally, they wrote much, much more.

The one black-and-gold-trimmed journal flashed at her from the bottom of the pile. She pulled it out and fanned the pages, the smell of smoke and must wafting up. Bridget's thumb ran along the edge of the pages until she found the latest:

> I can't ever go back to that hell. He is such a useless prick, a fucking tool. He's so high he doesn't know I'm his sister or he doesn't care and now all I can think of his breath that smells like garbage close to my face, so close I can't breathe, and he's so heavy. I'll have a scar forever, on my neck for the whole world to see. I hate it here. I hate this town. I hate everyone.
>
> I will never go back there, no one can make me. I have nowhere else to go.

Underneath the entry was a drawing, a delicate, finely drawn wrist, with a lotus flower tattoo. A black raven resting in the outstretched hand, the feathers black and wispy, its head turned. One exquisite eye seemed to watch her from the page. A large disembodied hand clamped down over the forearm, above the tattoo but below the elbow. The knuckles were knotted and the fingernails ratted and torn. The smaller hand, delicate and drawn with a pencil, the fingertips curved up gracefully, cupping the bird under the tail feathers, its claws hidden from view. The fingernails were shaded in, but not black, and they were elegant, manicured. The large hand looked quickly sketched with charcoal, the lines thick and smudged, like maybe it was drawn later. Underneath, quickly scrawled: *wrist to floor, hand like an ape.*

There was no date at the top, but it was the last entry in the journal, handed in two days ago. Bridget thought of Lenny, his hair slick with grease, those dark marbled teeth, and felt her stomach turn. She wondered what it all meant. Did her brother abuse her? Hit her? She fought back, got away. And then went where, to the mill?

She stood, reaching her hands high above her head, raising her chin to the ceiling in a long-forgotten yoga pose. When Holden was alive, she used to go to class late in the afternoon, stretching her muscles, her long legs to the sides, up to the ceiling, feeling the expansion of big breaths in her chest. Sometimes she thought the only time she could breathe was in that class.

The clock above her desk clicked to six fifteen.

A trip to the bathroom, then she'd leave. If Tripp didn't call her before then, she'd decide what to do. Her stomach rumbled and she clicked her dry tongue against the roof of her mouth.

The halls were silent, only a faint hum of pipes working underneath her feet and up the walls. A distant squeak of a janitor's wheeled bucket. Even the bathroom lights were dimmed and every soft thump, squeak, and bump echoed in the dark building. She rarely stayed this late.

She looked down the hall. The science wing ran perpendicular to the English wing, the building shaped like an H, with the English Department dominating the connecting hall between everything else—language and math—and science.

Nate's classroom spilled light to the empty hallway.

Bridget immediately turned toward it. She'd been withholding the mill adventure from him, just until she was sure what was going on, but Nate always had a unique perspective. Thoughtful. Maybe he'd even heard from Lucia; he'd been worried about her, too. Bridget knew that Lucia talked to Nate, at least more than she talked to anyone else. He'd had her as a junior and again as a senior, repeating algebra and electing a statistics class. Not that Lucia was dumb, far from it. Bridget couldn't imagine her home life lent itself to any kind of study habit.

If nothing else, Nate might listen. Plus, she wanted to rib him about the flowers for Ginny. What a suck up.

His door was partly closed and she silently

nudged it open with one hand. She almost walked right in but stopped and hovered in the doorway, blinking.

She saw Lucia first, the fine, downy hair the first thing she noticed. Nate sitting in his desk chair, and Lucia leaning against his desk. His hand resting on her shoulder and her hair, covering her face, fanning out, spilling over Nate's outstretched arm.

Bridget stood frozen in the doorway, dumbfounded, but exposed. If either had looked up, they would have seen her.

Lucia leaned forward and pulled at a handful of Nate's shirt, hovering over him, his knee between her legs, her hair covering both of their faces.

Then she kissed him.

CHAPTER 10

Lucia, March 31, 2015

Her Goodwill shift ended at nine and she stuck around with Randy for a while, just shooting the shit and smoking cigarettes on the stoop after they closed.

Randy was twenty-two, almost as poor as her, lived with his mom in a trailer. They'd taken to going to his place while his mom worked. He'd roll a joint with his thick fingers and seal the paper with his tongue. They'd play Xbox, stupid war games she didn't care about. Sometimes she let him do things to her, his hand between her legs, his fingers sliding around inside her, his tongue in her ear, licking, his stubble scratching her cheek. Once she climbed on top of him, his jeans pulled tight across his thighs, boxers bunched up under the buttoned waistband. She lifted her skirt and took him in, just for a second until he pushed her off, rough, and came all over the brown velvet couch, the wet spot combining with all the other stains to form a pattern.

This time, she shoved him off, and he blinked, hurt and rejected. When he dropped her off later he gave her a half wave. She could tell he wanted to come in, but she eyed her house, never knowing if Lenny was inside or not.

Lenny.

The hitting started not all that long ago. Shortly after Jimmy left, long after their mother left. Their house—owned by Jimmy's father, then Jimmy, and now, apparently, Lenny—stood, slowly biodegrading into the dirt, like paper in a landfill.

She tried not to come home until late, after Lenny had retreated to his room. She tried to not turn on any lights. Because of this, she could tell by the smell the house was growing things: mold, fungus. She could hear the scrabblings of mice late at night. Squirrels in the ceiling. Coming for the food rotting in the kitchen sink.

It was only ten o'clock.

She opened the door, the smell hitting her in the face like a wall. Goddamn it.

In the kitchen, Lucia flicked on the light to the audible skittering of cockroaches. Her father would have died. Before he became a drunk, when she was a kid and the mill was still open and her father had a job, he was a decent father. Not a great one. But he was there. He kept them fed.

This would have appalled him.

She dumped half the dishes straight into the trash can. Under the sink, behind crusted bottles of cleaning solution, she found rubber gloves and donned them. She hadn't eaten here in weeks, instead grabbing on the go, out of her own paycheck, stealing food from the caf, and sometimes Randy even bought her McDonald's. She didn't need to eat a lot, so she didn't.

When the garbage was cleared out, she ran hot water in the sink. Found an old rag and some dish detergent and let the water scald her skin red, her arms zinging with the burn. Things weren't always this bad. This was neglectful and disgusting and she couldn't live like this. This was squalor. Worse than Randy's trailer.

Lucia closed her eyes. She envisioned Andrew's bedroom, that warm vanilla candle smell. Taylor's family room, the softness of the sofa beneath her bare thighs, exposed by silky track shorts. She imagined Mr. Winters's home, his cozy townhouse living room. She'd never seen it, of course, but she saw the outside once, drawn there like a magnet, driving by in Lenny's truck. A row of townhomes, mums on the stoop, in a cul-de-sac filled with kids. Quaint.

When she opened her eyes, she was still there, in her kitchen, the garbage stinging her nose. She pulled a plate up out of the sink and at first she thought it was rice. Then the rice moved.

She screamed, threw the plate, which shattered against the wall.

"What the fuck is going on?" Lenny stood

behind her, for how long she didn't know. When she turned to look at him, she knew.

She wasn't an idiot. Lenny was a drug addict. Heroin, mostly, she thought, but she steered so clear of him she could never be sure. His usual high was dopey, slow, falling asleep so hard and fast she thought he'd died. Sometimes she'd hoped he'd died. Lately, it had been something else. Something up, jumpy and angry, a flashing behind his eyes and in his voice that scared her. A new kind of violence. Him hitting her, only a few short months ago had been new.

"This is disgusting. How can you live like this? How did I let it get like this?" She lived here, too. How long had it been since she'd even entered the kitchen? Weeks?

"Shut the fuck up. You're never here, what do you care?" His voice was gravelly, broken, and his eyes darted around at the sink, the garbage, the maggots on the plate, then at her face. He sucked a cigarette and blew smoke at her.

Without thinking, she smacked it out of his hand and it rolled to the linoleum. She dropped the garbage bag.

He closed the distance between them, his palm striking her cheek, quick and biting. It wasn't a hard hit—he was too messed up for that—but it still stung. Brought tears to her eyes and a pulse to her face. She covered the spot instinctively with her hand and took a step back.

"Fuck you." She spat, unable to tame the anger that crested in her throat, her head. She had to get out of there, not just for the night, but permanently, but how? He came at her and she pushed him away, hard. When they fell to the ground, her on top, she punched at his chest.

The fight was slow, almost childish. She, weak from lack of solid sustenance and exercise, and he, feeble with the chemicals in his blood. Her hands around his neck, a rapid pulse beneath her thumb. Too rapid for heroin. Was it coke? Meth?

His hand shot out across the floor and the cigarette was there, suddenly in his hand. She felt the sear against her neck, the smell of burning skin.

She let go, cried out, jumped back. She clutched her neck, the boil bubbling beneath her fingertips.

From the floor, Lenny laughed.

She left, the screen door slamming behind her. Standing on the broken sidewalk, the weeds tickling her ankles, she could still hear him laughing, a loose, maniacal sound, and she knew she'd never go back.

CHAPTER 11

Nate, Tuesday, April 28, 2015:
A week after the birds fell

"You have to understand where I'm coming from, Nate." Tad Bachman crossed and uncrossed his legs, settled finally with his ankle resting on his knee, his body pitched forward as if any moment he might dart for the door.

Nate studied the degrees behind his desk. Mounted in gilded frames, the glass glinting with a hint of Nate's own reflection.

"Suspended? No, I really don't. I didn't do anything with this girl. I bought her a hotel room to get her away from her abusive brother." His mind flashed briefly on her fingertips brushing his bare skin, a feather touch between the buttons of his shirt. He took a breath, took a gamble. "Bring her in, ask her. The reporters are here looking for a story. There's no story in the birds. There won't be for weeks. They know that. They've all gone home, except for one. Why? She's looking to take something back to her editor. She dug up this little gem; who cares if it's not real?" He was protesting too much, going on about it too long. He could see the doubt in Tad's wrinkled forehead, his face almost a wince.

"I made the same argument to the super-intendent. I did." He paused then, picked up a pen, flicked it between his fingertips. "But we did bring her in, Nate."

"What?"

"This isn't about what the paper says anymore. It's what she says." Tad's voice dropped and he looked off to the side, a bare expanse of wall that held no interest. Nothing to look at, except it wasn't Nate's face.

"What the fuck are you talking about? Lucia wouldn't say that. We're friends."

Tad's face snapped back, his eyes widening. "Friends? How so?"

"Don't pull this shit on me, Bachman. The same way I'm 'friends' with all my other students. I teach them algebra, precalc, statistics, yes. But you know as well as I do they come to me. I'm the coach. I pay attention. Which is more than some of their parents do."

"You're on dangerous ground, Winters."

"Again, what the fuck does that even mean? I'm not doing anything differently than you've known about for years. And now you're high and mighty on me? Come off it." Nate stood, his legs shaking, his blood pumping in his throat. He gripped the edge of Tad's desk, an easy three feet between them.

"I never thought you'd abuse it." Tad's voice was loud, almost a shout. Nate pictured Ginny on the other side of the door, her fingers working at her blueish hair, a nervous twitch, her hand hovering over the phone. To call whom?

"I'm not abusing anything!" Nate slapped at the desk, his hand stinging, and Tad jumped back, took a breath.

"Look." Tad lowered his voice. "Let me just do my job, Nate. If you weren't involved," his voice broke on the word, "it'll come out in the wash, okay?"

"She really said that? That we were involved?" Nate's mind spun, thinking back to all their twilight conversations in his classroom, after the halls fell silent, that veered toward too intimate, too close, the ones that made his heart thud in his chest like a drum.

"She called it . . . love." Bachman flexed his fingers against the glass top of his desk, his eyes darting at the word *love.*

"I need to know, Tad, exactly what she said," Nate said, a scratch in his throat. He tried to clear it, but couldn't. He could hardly breathe.

"I can't tell you that. It's an ongoing investigation," Tad said. He held his hands out, plaintive. "It's my job, you get that right?"

"She called it love?" The idea seemed unfathomable. They'd never uttered those words, the very idea of it ridiculous.

Tad stood, crossed the room, put his hand on the doorknob. A dismissal. Nate's job, then, suspended. A continued paycheck, but for how long? Tad half turned, his head down, eyes studying the carpet, a red-and-black square pattern that looked like a maze.

"She said you loved her."

CHAPTER 12

Alecia, Tuesday, April 28, 2015:
A week after the birds fell

The story first hit the *Harrisburg Courier*, a second-rate paper with day-old news. The byline said Rowena White, the reporter who cornered Alecia outside Bridget's house the day of the shopping spree (was it only Saturday?).

"Teacher Accused of Student Affair" was the headline, but Alecia could hardly bring herself to read the story. She read it in bits and pieces on the computer, scrolling up then down again, the text flying by making her dizzy. The whole story rested on anonymous sources; it was horrible reporting, really. Irresponsible. The reporter corroborated that Nate and Lucia were seen together at Deannie's Motel. She found the desk clerk: "I thought she looked young, but not like a student. I'd never seen either of 'em before in my life." You could hear the gum smack through the print.

The story named no one on record.

The school had no comment. Nate, of course, had no comment. Alecia had no comment. Alecia suddenly wanted to punch something, a surge of anger blooming bright hot in her chest.

The article itself was short, only a few paragraphs. The only pictures included were Nate's yearbook photo and Lucia's senior pictures. Her long hair looked more blond than white, and her makeup was minimal. She looked almost girl-next-door, save for the glittering piercing in the soft skin between her lip and her nose.

Nate came home at two, before the last bell, and he stood in the hallway, his backpack hanging impotently in one hand. "I think I was fired."

Alecia could only nod, the bile rising in her throat.

Now that it was in print, it all felt so much worse. Even if she had believed Nate before, when he begged her to and got mad and broke the beer bottle and cut his hand that night in the kitchen (Was it only three nights ago? Saturday? How was it possible?), how could she believe him now?

She could ask him about the picture, the girl's ivory skin, her bursting cleavage. Alecia wanted to ask him if Lucia felt younger, tighter, smoother. She bit back the words. He might lie. She wasn't sure if she could bear it, the way his eyes would skip around the room, his tongue finding the words slowly. She needed more first, she needed something concrete.

She stared at him, his hair ragged and disheveled, and felt angry, like she wanted to punch his chest, and profoundly sad. What had they done to each other here? If she couldn't even be sure he was telling the truth, what did they have?

"Alecia, I didn't do this. You have to know that."

"Do I? Do I have to know anything?" His reasoning seemed sound, his actions explainable. Except that picture. The red bra, the pale expanse of skin. She couldn't unsee it.

Gabe was coloring at the dining room table, mostly arranging the colored pencils to comply with some internal need. He loved markers, crayons, colored pencils. He rolled them around his hands and smiled. He pressed the sharpened tips against the pads of his fingers and threw them across the room when they weren't sharp enough. He peeled the wrappers off the crayons and then got furious when they broke. They spent half of Nate's paycheck on new crayons alone. Oh God, Nate's paycheck.

"Fired?" Alecia repeated, feeling slow, late on the response. "As in . . . ?"

"Temporary leave. Until 'we get the mess sorted out.' Bachman's words." Tad Bachman, Mt. Oanoke school principal, a young guy, not much older than Alecia. Nate's racquetball buddy, of course.

"I'll have to go back to work." Alecia said automatically, her brain spinning. She said it like it could be a sacrifice, and she flashed on the new outfit hanging in her closet. Shoes she hadn't even shown Nate. Expensive, creamy makeup. It didn't feel like a sacrifice, it felt slippery and decadent and freeing.

"No. It's temporary. I'll still get paid. I'll just be . . . here." Nate looked around then caught Alecia's eyes. "I didn't do this thing. Never."

"Why do they think you did, then? What did you actually do?" Alecia pulled her arms around her waist. She was shivering. Their townhouse had a shoddy air-conditioning system; it needed maintenance, maybe replacement. It rambled and groaned and they spent April through September sweating through the thinnest T-shirts. But Alecia couldn't get warm, and her back teeth clanged together.

"I let a student get too close. I wanted to help her. Her family—it's awful. You can't even understand the nightmare. I've done this before, you know. Gotten too close, tried to help too much. It's never backfired like this, and it's never . . ." Nate looked around the room, avoiding Alecia's eyes. "Sexual. It wasn't this time, either. God, this is impossible. Someone is saying it is, that I *slept with her.* That's just crazy."

"Who is saying that?"

"Bachman said that *she admitted it.* Those were his exact words. I said, *admitted what?* You can't admit a lie." He toed the chair, like a caught toddler, and shook his head. "I asked what's ten years of friendship mean to him? He said it's more complicated than that."

"I don't know what to believe anymore, Nate." Alecia remembered the Instagram picture, the flush swell of breast up close to the camera lens. She imagined Nate thumbing the image, his breath hitching. She imagined that girl straddling her husband's body, her long skinny, teenage legs wrapped around his middle-aged naked bottom, her white hair splayed on a white pillowcase.

"Look, I'll tell you the same thing I told Tad. I paid for her hotel room. I met her at that motel; she said she needed help and I helped her. The reporter took a picture of me hugging her. I was comforting her. Do you see that?" Nate said slowly, annunciating each syllable, like they often did to Gabe, but with more patience.

"I know this is what you *say*. But you lied about it. You lied to me. How do I believe you now?" Alecia knew that Nate often believed she was unreasonable. That her opinions on mostly everything, to him, seemed unfounded. The difference between them was that he blindly trusted: people, fate, goodness. And she, largely, did not.

"I explained all that. I've *been* explaining all of that. For days now, but like everything else, you can't let it go."

Alecia said nothing because she knew he was

lying about at least one thing: that picture. A lie by omission is still a lie.

She imagined saying it now, *I know you liked her picture.* She imagined his reaction. Would he laugh? It was just the Internet. Nothing real, not tangible. It seemed undignified to divorce her husband because of something that may or may not have happened on *social media,* like they were sinking to the level of his students.

His student.

But no, it was real. It was tangible. The affair, if it happened, was with a *student,* for the love of God. Were they divorcing? Is that what was happening?

She wondered if, at fifty, she'd look back here at this moment and think *oh, this is how it ended.* And then maybe later, *of course it did.*

"Whoever is saying all of this is lying," Nate insisted, still holding that backpack, still standing in the same spot. "Alecia, I don't know why, but I swear I'm going to find out. I just need you to believe in me."

When she didn't answer, he said, for the first time, "You know I love you, right?" But his voice quavered a little and caught on the *love* and the first words that flitted into Alecia's mind weren't yes or no, but *do I? Do I know that?*

He dropped the backpack and stepped forward, toward Alecia. He gripped her arms, his fingers digging into the soft, bare flesh, his thumbs sliding under the sleeves of her white T-shirt, his eyes wild. His chin wobbled. "Do you believe me?" He brought his hands up to cup her face, his fingers sliding around her neck to thread through her hair. She could smell the desperate musk of sweat on his skin. "Do you?" He whispered again, his voice hoarse and shaky.

Alecia couldn't do this, she couldn't look into his eyes and break his heart, no matter how many ways he broke hers. She needed time to figure it all out, to be alone, to think.

"Yes." She gripped his wrists and sagged against him, her weight pulling against his arms. He crushed her to his chest, her face pushed into the solid muscle, his breathing ragged. He stroked her hair, her face, and all she could think about was the day ten years ago at her cousin's wedding, the same feeling of having all the air pushed from her lungs. She whispered back, "I believe you." It could have even been the truth.

She remembers after that wedding in the parking lot they looked at the sky before driving home. They saw three shooting stars, right in a row. *A shooting star isn't really a star,* he'd said. *It's the dust from a comet's tail, burning up in the earth's atmosphere.*

So the thing everyone wishes on? It's both the end of everything and actually nothing at all.

The phone rang all day and Alecia left it for Nate to answer, a kind of penance. Libby Locking called the house, then Alecia's cell phone, alternating until finally Alecia answered.

"Is it true?" She demanded, then her voice softened. "Are you okay? Do you need a . . . safe house?" Her voice dropped to a whisper.

"For God's sake, Libby, you know Nate. Do *you* think it's true?" Alecia pushed her thumb into her eye socket. "And a safe house? Are you kidding me?" She regretted taking the phone call. Bridget had called, twice, but Alecia declined both. Bridget was too close to it; she didn't want to listen to her either defend Nate or bash him. She just needed the day. Just to think.

"No. I don't know. You should hear what people are saying." She coughed into the phone. "What do you need? Are you staying with him?"

"Yes, of course I'm staying. Libby, it's a lie. Do people *really* believe that Nate would sleep with a student?" From downstairs, Alecia could hear the sounds of lunch being prepared. Their second day home together, after having a week together only the week before, and she thought about driving up to Motel Deannie's herself, just to see it. Gabe wailed in protest at something Nate did, and Nate responded, his voice muffled but loud, frustrated. Nate didn't know there were only certain plates—sectioned so his food

150

wouldn't touch— that Gabe would tolerate. There was so much Nate didn't know. Alecia drummed her fingertips against the phone, anxious. "Libby, listen to me. Nate didn't do this, okay? Tell everyone that. I mean, even Bachman believes him, he just has to do the full investigation. The truth will come out. Okay?"

There was a pulse of silence. Alecia pulled at a thread in the pillowcase and all the stitching zipped out with a single pop, the hem opening up in her palm like a flower.

Libby said, "People are worried. About their . . . own kids. This is a really small town, not like Philly." Libby had a daughter, a junior, not in Nate's class.

"I'm from Doylestown, Libby," Alecia snapped back. The implication had grown old: Nate, born and raised in Honesdale, was one of them. Alecia was bright lights, big city, sleek and blond and missing that rural twang from the back of her throat, that Pennsyl-tucky drawl.

"The parents are calling a meeting later. At the park. Supposedly Bachman will answer questions, but he's said he can't say much, it's an ongoing investigation."

"A meeting? About *Nate?*" The idea was alien. Three weeks ago Nate was some kind of hometown hero. "Libby, what are people saying happened? Who supposedly discovered the affair and why or how did it get into the paper?"

151

"Oh, you didn't know? That reporter saw them together at a motel, last week I think."

"Last week? Not a month ago?" Alecia felt her hands go cold, palms and fingertips numbed, the blood coursing through her body seeming to skip her hands entirely.

"No, a week ago. Maybe less? Not more than that. Not in Mt. Oanoke, though, I forget where."

"Honesdale," she whispered.

"Yeah! That's it. How'd you know?" Libby's voice sounded tinny, far away.

Alecia felt her heart unfurl, like the hem in her hand.

I never give her any thought at all. You asked why and I don't know. I just don't think of her. She never thinks about me. You said how do you know? She's your mother. And the truth is that I just know. You said you'd help me find her, if I ever wanted, which is maybe the funniest fucking thing I've ever heard in my whole entire life. Everyone I've ever known has one thing in common. They don't want to be found.

I shouldn't come to you every day. I know this. I'm not an idiot. You don't send me away, though. I can see your eyes drifting. I can see your smile when I knock on the door. I can see you. You just don't know it.

CHAPTER 13

Bridget, Thursday, April 30, 2015

Bridget watched from her car. All the parents—
mostly she knew them all—trudged across the
parking lot toward the pavilion, their hands
clutched, their faces white and blank. Blinking
eyes and open fish mouths, a sort of soulless
wandering.

To talk about Nate. Was there anything crazier?

Bridget stayed in the back. The last picnic table
under the pavilion, far in the corner.

About forty people milled around, waiting for
someone to take charge. Tad Bachman tapped
his foot against the picnic table bench, his hands
tented under his chin, like in prayer. Tad was
young, smart, attractive with a soft wave of
chestnut hair that fell over green eyes. It was no
secret that he and Nate were friends. Until two
days ago, everyone and Nate were friends. Tad's
pink polo shirt was tucked into khaki pants and
he gave every parent an encouraging smile, a
soft, mild-mannered hello.

After a while, the din died down.

Jennifer Lawson, Taylor Lawson's mother,

stood, smoothed her palms down the front of her Under Armour running jacket and spoke first. Her voice was high and her jaw shook.

"I wanted everyone to meet today to discuss Nate Winters. I know we all have girls in the high school. I just wanted this to be a . . . *safe space.*" She splayed her hands out, moved them around in a circle. "To see if anyone had information that could aid Mr. Bachman and the school board in the investigation." Her lipstick was bright red, her eyes rimmed in black. She had dark brown hair that fell in glossy waves down her back, and her clothes fit her like a second skin. She was barely five feet tall, and at five foot eight, Bridget always felt like a towering giant when Jennifer was around.

Jennifer was an interesting choice to lead the meeting. She had a reputation for sleeping with married men herself. Husbands on the PTA, fathers of classmates. None of it was substantiated, but she was divorced and dressed the part, and people talked. It was Mt. Oanoke; sometimes there was nothing to do *but* talk.

Jennifer stood, ironically sanctimonious, on the picnic table in front. Sweatpantsed stay-at-home moms—who just last week would have rolled their eyes at her tight Lycra shirt, her lululemon leggings, her French-manicured nails—now watched her rapt and nodded along. They were all suddenly teammates, united for the same noble cause.

Jennifer took a deep breath, her breasts heaving. Tad looked away.

She dabbed at her eyes. "I also wanted a *safe space* to ask questions. We all have . . . so many questions. Our *girls.*"

Oh brother. They acted like Nate was convicted, abusive. Bridget wished she'd stop saying *safe space* as though the school was a danger zone.

Bridget was here because she told Nate she'd come. He'd called her, whispering from his car. *Alecia said there was a parents' meeting at the park about me. Tonight. Can you go?*

Bridget wanted to ask Nate what did Alecia believe?

Tad Bachman stood.

"I can answer a few questions, but not many. We are doing everything we can to get to the bottom of this. To understand what happened, and most important, *why and how.* We are cooperating with the police, with the school board, while trying to be sensitive to the young lady involved as well as Nate Winters." The crowed murmured and Bachman held up his hand. "We do not live in a guilty-until-proven-innocent society. Nate Winters has been an exemplary teacher up to this point, going above and beyond for his students."

"Yeah, I'll bet," Kelsey Minnow's father grumbled loudly.

"And," Bachman continued, "the school and the board are not defending him, but everyone has a right to due process. We are trying to understand all the pieces. When we do, we'll issue a public statement and figure out next steps. Right now, we're all in flux. I understand it's uncomfortable. I'll answer any question I can, but right here, tonight, most of my answers are going to be *no comment.*"

The crowd hummed. A smattering of hands went up.

"Are there other girls involved? Has Mr. Winters had relationships with other girls?" Mrs. Minnow asked, her voice tired.

"There is no reason to believe that and no one has insinuated that. No," Bachman said.

"Will Mr. Winters be allowed back at school?" Jennifer asked.

"We can't comment on his employment at this time."

And on it went. For twenty minutes, parents fired questions, most of which Bachman was unable or unwilling to respond to, and the crowd grew weary. Bridget watched the whole thing with growing anger, a pulsing in her core that inched up into her throat.

She promised she'd just watch, not speak. But she couldn't help it.

"Does anyone here believe that Mr. Winters, one of our beloved teachers and our baseball coach, is innocent?" Bridget finally asked. She looked around. Jennifer picked at her fingernails. Kelsey Minnow's mother and father whispered to each other. Ashlee Williams's mother untied and retied her shoe. Josh Tempest's father stood up, his hands on his hips, and glared at Bridget but said nothing. In the distance, a dog barked.

In the back, the Evanses stood, holding on to each other, their arms entwined. They nodded, but said nothing. Andrew Evans. Nate's star baseball player, his favorite student. He'd written letters of recommendation for Andrew, on the verge of acceptance into University of Texas's baseball program, one of the most competitive programs in the country, and only as a junior. Half the major league teams recruited from the Longhorns, and in two years, Andrew would be there, in no small part because of Nate. Yet his parents stood, nodding at her, silent and pinched.

"We know you're *friends*," Jennifer said finally, clearing her throat on the word *friends*. "Maybe it's not appropriate for you to be here?" Her voice tilted up, sweet and syrupy.

Bridget stood, dusted off her long skirt, took her time. "This isn't easy for anyone," she said, and made her way through the picnic tables, her back straight. As she passed Bachman, she gave him a small smile. "Thanks, Tad."

She sat in her car, in the far corner of the lot, watching from a distance, while the parents asked questions. Some stood, their arms waving around as they gave their impassioned pleas. Finally, Bachman stood, gave a final statement, and headed toward the lot. She lowered the window and he stopped a few feet from her car.

"Do you believe Nate?" Bridget asked, and Bachman shook his head.

"Bridget, I can't tell you any more than I tell them. I'm stuck in a shit spot, okay?" He looked back at the throng of parents, still talking, an hour and a half into the meeting, a father pacing in the back. They both watched in silence, unable to hear any words. "The Nate I know wouldn't do this. I can tell you that." The sun was starting to set, a sailor's delight, as Bridget's mother would say. "Do you believe him?" Bachman finally asked.

"I do," Bridget said with less hesitation than she felt.

Tad touched his fingertips to the top of her car and gave her a nod. Then he left. She wondered how much of what she'd said to Tad was true. How much she believed.

Two days ago, when it all came out, Nate had come to her room, his eyes wild.

"Someone is telling lies about me. They're

going to ruin my life. *My life, Bridget.* This is my whole life. Alecia, Gabe, baseball, teaching. This is my entire life."

She'd read the paper, of course. She'd tried to text him and call him all day.

"Nate." She'd closed the door behind him, wondering how it would look if they were discovered. Everything was suspect now. Nothing could be innocent, trusted. "Why now? All this with Lucia happened weeks ago."

"I don't *know why* now." He leaned forward. "You're the only one who believes me. I think even Alecia thinks I'm guilty."

"I called her. She won't take my calls."

"She won't talk to anyone. Not even me." He raked a hand through his hair, then his palm scraped against the rough of his cheek. His eyes, bloodshot and red rimmed, looked around the room searching. "Lucia called last week, Thursday. I couldn't take the call, I was on the field. But she emailed me. It said, *meet me at our hotel. I need you.*"

"Christ on a cracker, Nate. You went?" Bridget flattened her palms against her desk. I mean, how *stupid.*

He nodded his head. "The last time I went there, the girl was beat up, purple bruises. I think Lenny hit her. She had no money, sleeping in the paper mill with a kerosene heater. To me, *I need you* meant I need help. I thought she needed

161

me to pay for another night. That something happened at the shelter or that she went home to her brother. I had no idea."

"*I need you* didn't sound sexual to you? Suspicious?"

"No. It didn't. It sounded like she needed help, *just like the last time,*" Nate said.

"God, you're stupid," Bridget said, shaking her head.

"In retrospect, maybe, but think about it. I had no reason to think any differently. I wasn't actually having an affair with her. I've done nothing but help her."

"So you went."

"I did. I met her. She came out of her motel room and hugged me. She was crying. Thanking me. Said it was the last time, she just needed to hide out. Get some space and figure out where to go. I didn't know what she meant and I didn't ask. I calmed her down. Paid for her room and left. I was home before dinner."

"What'd you do with the email?" Bridget had asked.

"I deleted it. This was before the news story, but I knew Alecia'd have a bird. That's two hundred dollars I spent on this girl. Gabe needs that money. *We* need that money. She'd be furious." Nate stomped his foot, like he was trying to shake feeling back into his toes. "It's the same reason I didn't tell her the first time."

162

"So does Alecia know about this last time? At the hotel?"

"No." Nate shook his head, adamant.

"You are a dumb twit, do you know that? She's going to find out. The whole town is crazy. You have to come clean."

"Bridget, you don't understand." He pinched the bridge of his nose and breathed through his mouth. "Pretty sure my marriage is over either way."

The thing she should have said to Nate, but didn't, was *yeah, but you kissed her.* She did say it, right after it happened, but that was before it became the thing they didn't talk about. They'd had one conversation, one confrontation, and that was it.

Right after the kiss, Bridget had waited for Nate, on the other side of his door, so when it swung open it nearly hit her in the face. Would have broken her nose, too. Then Lucia ran out and Nate called after her, but Lucia didn't even slow down, her hair flying behind her like a cape. She thought maybe Lucia was crying, but it was possible she imagined it.

Nate was slow to come to the door and he looked left before he looked right.

"You are a dumb, dumb shit, Nate Winters."

When he whipped around, they were practically nose to nose. Bridget could see the faint sweat curling the hair on his neck. The way his pupils were dilated. The quiver in his chin.

"Jesus Christ, Bridget. You gave me a heart attack."

"You should be so goddamn lucky. What did I just see? With my own eyes, please Lord, tell me I just didn't see what I think I did." Bridget clenched her fists, her nails cutting into the flesh on her palms.

"She kissed me. I stopped her. She ran away. It was *nothing*."

"Bless your heart." She wanted to slap him, she really, really did. He took a step backward like he sensed it. He'd never seen Bridget mad, not at him anyway.

She'd been plenty mad in her life, especially at Holden. Years ago, Bridget threw the biggest temper tantrum of her adult life. Mama would have been proud. They'd all been drinking. Playing cards. The one and only time Bridget had ever seen Holden even *look* at another woman. Nate had invited another teacher, Carla something, a substitute gym teacher, as tight and toned as Bridget was soft curves. From the moment she got to the Winters', she set her eye on Holden, touching his arm, laughing at his jokes. Bridget could see it in his eyes, he was taken with her. Charmed the pants off him, or at least almost. They played euchre, a game Bridget mostly stunk at, having never heard of it, so she sat and watched, at first curious about this new Holden, the one who noticed women and was charmed by them. It was almost a turn-on. Until he stopped looking at Bridget entirely, didn't even notice when she went a whole hour without saying a word. When Carla left, with a sweet little waggle of her pin-painted fingertips, Bridget lost her shit and Holden had the nerve to *laugh*. He laughed at her. In front of their friends. Bridget left him there, got into the car, and drove home. The next morning, early, before school, he showed up with his tail between his legs. She let him simmer for a day before she forgave him.

So Nate had seen Bridget mad. But never at *him*.

Nate had pulled her into his classroom, closed the door so the latch rested against the doorframe, not fully shut. He sat backward on a chair, his thumbs driving into his eye sockets. Bridget stood in front of him, her arms crossed. Waiting. "I've been helping her, Bridget. Her dad is MIA, her brother is abusive. He *hits* her. Maybe worse. She's cagey about it." He leaned forward, pushed his palms into his knees. He looked out the window, his breath puffing out. "I don't know what's true anymore, but I think she's being bullied pretty badly."

"Bullied? Lucia? She's more likely to be the bully, Nate." Bridget saw Lenny, had seen her house, the filth she lived in. Still, at school, she remained untouchable. Kids had whispered for years about her being a witch, her sharp tongue knowing instinctively the weakest points of her classmates. "If she says she's being bullied at school, I think she's pulling one over on you."

"Not just at school, Bridge. Look, do you know what trichotillomania is?"

"No."

"I didn't, either. She pulls out her hair." Nate tugged on the end of his blond curls to demonstrate.

"Where? It looked fine to me just now." Bridget was trying to be sensitive, but *come on.*

"Underneath. If you look underneath, it's all scabs and bald spots. She was showing me just now. That's what you saw."

"I call bullshit. I saw her kiss you." Bridget wasn't an idiot. That smile, so coy, so chilling. Those big red lips stretched across bright white teeth.

"She did, I'm not denying that. She had her head turned like this." Nate stood up, took his thumb under Bridget's chin, turned her head, just so. Bridget could feel his breath on her neck. The warmth from his body. He lifted up her hair, her neck cool and damp. When he sat again, in the chair one seat closer to her, he let her hair fall back down against her back. When Bridget turned her head, they were eye level. "She was showing me her hair, what she's doing to herself. Then she kissed me."

166

"What did you do?" Bridget breathed out.

"I stopped her. Of course I did." Nate stood up, put his hands on Bridget's shoulders. "She's confused, that's all. Don't make it worse by making this a thing. I'm the only person on earth being nice to her right now. I was comforting her and she got confused."

"Nate! This is a thing, whether you want it to be or not. You could lose your job!" She shimmied away from his grasp. "Mt. Oanoke would fry you in a second. These people . . ." She let her voice drop. *These people* were Nate's people. Bridget and Alecia were outsiders. City folk, southern folk, same difference. Not us folk. Nate, though, he was us folk.

"Trust me; do you trust me?" His face looked so earnest Bridget wanted to cry.

Nate, the Boy Scout, born and bred in the country, his face red and corn-fed round, those bright, long-lashed eyes. He grew up here, the woods hiding a multitude of teenage indiscretions and later, adult ones. His naïveté and arrogance were stunning. Sometimes Bridget thought that the whispers of idle gossip actually powered the town. They'd thrill in stringing up one of their own, maybe even more than an outsider. So much further to fall.

When Bridget didn't answer, Nate continued. "She asked me not to tell anyone this. She doesn't have anyone else."

167

"She has Taylor." Bridget said, then stopped. Maybe, maybe not.

"Do you know they call her a witch?" Nate pressed.

"I've heard that for years now. Since she came in as a freshman. It's the hair, her nastiness." Bridget sighed. She could have done more to stop it. It was never rampant, just whisperings.

Josh Tempest had cackled at her once in class and Lucia whipped around and barked at him like a dog. At the time, Bridget hadn't known what to make of the exchange, but later, she heard in the faculty room that Josh had been caught by Kelsey Minnow's father over the weekend in a particularly damning sex act, and the barking then made sense. Bridget chalked it all up to the language teenagers spoke and she only sometimes understood and promptly dismissed it. If she was being honest, the witch thing had been around for a while. Lucia didn't seem especially bothered by any of it. Sometimes, if you asked Bridget, Lucia seemed to use it to her advantage. She liked her own edges sharp.

"You remember what you told me about the birds, right?" Nate asked.

"Yes." Bridget pressed her fingertips into her thighs, an exasperated sigh in her throat. "It's nonsense, really. I mean, how many dead animals do you see? Birds that fall out of nests, squirrels on the side of the road. Deer, for goodness' sake.

I don't take it as an omen." It was Pennsylvania, deer were more than abundant—they were a destructive force. "You hardly take note of it. It just is."

"I hear you. But listen, a couple years ago, she left one. On Andrew Evans's doorstep."

"Oh God. Why?" Bridget fanned her hair up, her eyes big. Her patience was waning.

"She was angry. Hurt. Rejected maybe? She says she wanted to scare him. They called her a witch, it was like a *fuck you*."

"Nate, they call her a witch because she does things like that. It's not a self-fulfilling prophecy," Bridget said. She thought, then, about Lucia's journals, the entries that called out to Taylor, a desperate sort of grasping, like the slick edge of a cliff. So different from her angry, scribbling entries, so different from her childlike ones, memories and poems. Bridget couldn't know, or even understand how many different sides there were to Lucia, to anyone really, but she could at least acknowledge there were things she couldn't understand.

She was so close to saying all this when Nate spoke, his voice hushed.

"It's so obvious to me, but maybe not to you." Nate swallowed twice, his blue eyes shining, blinking. "We all become what people expect us to be."

CHAPTER 14

Alecia, Thursday, April 30, 2015:
9 days after the birds fell

When Alecia finally did ask Nate to move out—temporarily, she claimed, although she was never sure if she meant it—it was without fanfare. He agreed to it as though he'd been expecting it, which made Alecia want to kick and scream. Nate never made a scene about anything, ever. He'd certainly rarely bucked her or disagreed with her, with the exception of lately where he picked sulky fights at any opportunity. He sighed and packed a single duffel bag and Alecia stood in the doorway to their bedroom watching him, thinking this was someone else's life, out of a movie, certainly not hers.

"Tripp said I could stay there for a while." He stood staring at the closet with his back to her and Alecia wondered what he'd pack now that he didn't have to go to work anymore. She felt like scum, like dirt, making him leave when the whole town was against him and he had no job. But having him there was too disruptive, too awful, the anger burning hot and bright under her skin, making her jumpy. She snapped at Gabe, her patience fried by Nate's shoes in the hallway, his cereal bowl in the sink, his *thereness*.

"I just need you to go away so I can think," she said lamely, and he shrugged like he either understood or didn't care. He packed jeans, sweats, polo shirts, a button-down shirt. Casual, but not what he'd wear to work.

He didn't look at her when he started talking. "Is this it for you? I feel like you've made this decision in your head, that our marriage is over and I have no choice and nothing I could say to you would matter. You think I'm a liar and a cheat."

He folded his shirts, his socks, his underwear he'd pulled from the crumpled clean basket at the foot of the bed. It struck her then that after he'd left, she'd still be folding his blue plaid boxers, putting them away in a drawer that may or may not be his anymore. *Stay.* She mouthed the word but did not say it.

"No. It's not *it for me.* Nothing about this is simple or easy. I don't even think we can afford a divorce and keep Gabe in therapy. But I'm just so . . . I can't even look at you. I'm too mad at you—for lying. For whatever you may have done"—she held up her hand and turned her head away, willingly blind to his open-mouthed protest—"and I just need to think without you here."

They each had gone around and around this so many times it just felt like words now, loose and unattached, clattering buttons in a tin. They'd gone through the yelling and the screaming and the crying the night before, Gabe huddled in his room, his hands cupped over his ears, until Alecia (and only Alecia, she might add) thought to go comfort him.

He finally looked at her, his eyes bluer than Alecia had ever seen them, shiny and wet and blinking.

"You don't let me think, that's all. Every time I turn around you're pleading your case. And then it turns into this fight. Just . . . for a few weeks. Please." Alecia didn't even know what she was saying *please* to.

"It will look bad," Nate said, but he said it blandly, like he didn't care. And then, like he'd just heard it. "Weeks?"

"Who will know?" Alecia whispered. "I won't tell, will you?"

When he didn't answer, she said, "Is it a conflict of interest? For Tripp?" Tripp Harris was Nate's best friend and a Mt. Oanoke police officer. He wasn't assigned to the investigation, but there were only a handful of cops in Mt. Oanoke. Tripp would have access to Nate's case.

"Ah, I don't know. I don't think so." Nate shrugged, relieved to have something official to discuss. "I'll come back at the end of the week. To see Gabe, get more clothes?" His voice tilted up insecurely, even though it wasn't actually a question.

Alecia nodded. She thought it was odd, unexpected, that this is how it would go when your husband was moving out. These desperate words tangled up in the everyday business of ending your marriage. *Maybe* ending your marriage.

He stood in front of her, his bag hanging down at his side, his fist flexing and unflexing. She moved to the side to let him pass and he paused, unsure of what to do. He hadn't left the house in ten years without kissing her good-bye, even when fighting. Sometimes the kiss was so quick, so perfunctory, it felt like steel against her cheek.

He leaned down and brushed the side of her face with his lips. He didn't say good-bye. Neither of them said I love you.

Alecia stood in the upstairs hallway until she heard the downstairs door click open and shut.

Day one and day two didn't feel that different from life before Nate left. Alecia hunkered down, her house a cocoon, only leaving to take Gabe to occupational therapy and then on day three, a doctor's appointment. The only change in her routine was not texting Nate after to tell him that

Gabe lost two pounds and wonder together if they should be worried. She singly decided they should not, and went about her day.

She felt so good she turned right to go to the A&P instead of left to go home. From the back Gabe whimpered, his hand jamming up against the window as he watched his street pass him by. Pushed out of his routine, his distress grew and he flat palmed the window, *slap, slap, slapping.* He rocked forward until he knocked his forehead on the seat in front of him, which happened to be Alecia's seat. Her head thrummed with Gabe's rhythm.

"Gabe. Gabey. Gabe." She said over and over, waiting for him to calm, for the moment to pass. She didn't sense a full-on meltdown coming, but she might have been blinded by her earlier euphoria. Alecia turned up the radio and flipped to a classical station; sometimes the only thing that calmed Gabe down was a little Beethoven. His window slapping and head bobbing slowed and Alecia circled the A&P parking lot with an eye in the rearview mirror. Typically, she'd wait until Nate got home at night to go grocery shopping, but if this is how things were going to be, and she barely dared to think permanently, then she needed to get Gabe used to it. What better day than today, when she felt so damn capable?

With *Moonlight Sonata* blaring in the speakers,

and a Dum Dum lollipop in her hand, she parked and climbed into the back seat.

"Gabey, here. We're just going to the store. I should have told you, but I didn't and we're here now and everything is okay, okay?" Alecia gently pushed his arms down to his sides—sometimes he let her, sometimes he fought back, once even blackening her cheekbone right below her eye— and held him there, rocking him side to side in his booster seat. He fought only once and then melted against her, his body hot and limp. She kissed the sweaty patch above his ear, her hand pressed on his back.

"We're okay. We're okay," Alecia murmured until Gabe finally stopped, his breathing leveling out to a few hiccups. She pulled him back, looked into his dark brown eyes, eyes that seemed as deep and black as the peak of night, and smiled. "We're okay?"

He looked past her out the window and she waved the lollipop in his field of vision, looping it around her head until he made eye contact with her. She nodded once at him and said firmly, "We're okay." He nodded back, his hand outstretched.

God, if anyone knew how many Dum Dums she went through in a day they'd be appalled. All the sugar. The Red Dye Brigade would kill her.

Alecia had already gone through the food allergy phase with Gabe. Lactose? Sure. Red dye?

Not so much. Which meant she'd burn through the whole damn bag if it got Gabe to look at her, *really look at her*. Nate had admonished her once, waving his smartphone in front of her face like he'd invented it. *They linked red dye to autism*, flashing an article he read on Facebook. *It's all those lollipops you give him.* She couldn't do anything but laugh and wave him off. He'd been diagnosed well before she started feeding him lollipops anyway. *Welcome to my life a year ago, Nate.* I mean, really, didn't he ever listen to her? When she kept notebooks of his food, charting his tantrums (and meltdowns, and documenting how tantrums and meltdowns differed), what he ate that day: lactose, milk, sugar, wheat, gluten, red dye, organic, pesticide-free, free-range, I mean, God, didn't he ever *just listen to her?*

If she thought about it, right in the parking lot of the A&P, she'd lose her shit all over again. She herded Gabe toward the "fire truck," a cart with the front painted red that Gabe could ride in. It was huge and had a wide clasping belt. It also had a horn that annoyed everyone in the store, but Gabe was seventy pounds. He no longer fit in a cart.

"Fire truck!" Gabe yelled. Two white-haired ladies turned their heads and smiled at Alecia. One waved to Gabe. He didn't wave back. *"Fire truck fire truck fire truck!"* His voice screeched up, excited. As if the scene in the car had never

happened. Alecia gritted her teeth at how easy it was for him to switch gears when he wanted to. She firmly planted a toy metal construction vehicle in each hand. *Stay busy,* she mentally pleaded.

They got through produce and dairy before Gabe started to fidget, but Alecia fished another Dum Dum out of her pocket and passed it up to him. He happily pawed at it and stuck it in his mouth.

Alecia kept her head low, avoiding the eyes of other shoppers. Everyone knew everyone, and if people were whispering about her, she didn't want to witness it. She wanted to order her pound of Swiss cheese and be done with it.

"Hi, Alecia," said a mild female voice. Alecia tensed as she turned.

Jennifer Lawson. The mother of a student of Nate's, Taylor Lawson. Taylor's brother had played baseball years before, earning a scholarship from it. To say Jennifer loved Nate would have been an understatement. She curled around him like a cat whenever she saw him. She might have done that to everyone, though.

Jennifer was a yoga instructor, her bouncy hair in a perpetual ponytail. The only time she'd ever seen Jennifer out of Lycra was the Tempests' Christmas party three years ago, when she wore a bright red dress cut up to here and down to there. The memory of that night took her breath away, so sudden and unexpected. It was back before Gabe was diagnosed and Alecia and Nate still did those things. Socializing had been Alecia's favorite thing to do, when she was clinging to the idea of being one of them: a future playdate and PTA mom. Whether the exile from the soccer circles was real or self-induced was something Nate liked to debate. But Jennifer Lawson—Jenny, as Nate called her—was the last person Alecia wanted to see.

"How are you holding up?" Jennifer was ballsy, Alecia would give her that. Surely anyone else at this juncture, this close to the scandal, mere days from the article's release, would turn their heads and look away, pretend to be searching for the perfect Brie. Jennifer's voice was honey sweet.

"I'm fine, thank you." Alecia ducked her head, tucking the plastic bag of cheese under the eggs and bracing her fingertips on the cart.

"I heard you kicked Nate out? Good for you." Jennifer leaned forward, her French-manicured nails resting proprietarily on Alecia's cart. Alecia stared at her long, tanned fingers, devoid of rings. Her husband left years ago, a scandal at the time in its own right, involving embezzlement of his company and his secretary. Alecia wondered what happened to Burt Lawson and shook off the urge to text Nate to ask.

"Jennifer, I didn't *kick Nate out*. We're . . . I don't know what. Trying to figure out the truth."

It sounded lame, even to Alecia, and Jennifer's mouth opened in an O, her red lips almost laughing.

"Wait, you don't actually *believe him,* do you? No one does. *No one.*" She whispered the last part, urgently, her breath a hot spearmint, and her hands made a slice in the air.

"I don't know that it's any of your concern." Alecia gripped the cart, blinking. Gabe hummed loudly from the cart and Jennifer shot him a glance.

She stuck a hand on her hip, leaned off to the left, and looked around the store. "Listen, I can't tell you what to believe. You know why *I* believe your husband had a thing with that girl?"

Alecia shook her head, her throat like a tumbleweed.

"Because two years ago, after that Christmas party? The one at the Tempests'? He drove me home, remember?" Jennifer leaned forward her lips brushing Alecia's hair, near her ear. "And your hubby, Saint Nate? He kissed *me.*"

CHAPTER 15

Lucia, forever ago

The mall had used to have fifty-five stores, but only thirty were still open. The Gap, the Orange Julius, the last record store in the history of all malls, ever. The tops of the benches were dust-covered and the air smelled musty, damp like still water.

"I want to get my nose pierced," Taylor said, a Blow Pop spinning and clattering between her teeth. Her dark bangs fringed over her forehead, wispy and childlike.

"Piercing your nose is what good girls do to pretend they're edgy." Lucia thought this was mostly true, and that if you really wanted to be edgy you'd get a tattoo and maybe hepatitis from the needle.

They were sixteen.

The mall was dying. Its deathly black breath wheezed from somewhere deep inside where the fountain used to run. It sat, mostly drained save for a few inches of water and a bottom coated with pennies, unused in front of Bon-Ton. Some-body had thrown bleach into it just to keep it from growing shit and now the water held a thin kind of skin, almost translucent. As if Lucia ran her finger around it, it would come up in her palm like a moss.

Lucia looked into the black depths of an old Hallmark store, the racks black and dirty, still containing cards. *Happy birthday!* She rattled the cage and Taylor swatted her arm. An old couple in the food court looked over and the woman shook her head in their direction, her mouth twisted like a lemon.

Taylor bought a lip gloss, glittery and bubblegum flavored, from Claire's boutique. The cap was crusted on and they had to run it under hot water from the bathroom to open it.

"We have to get out of Mt. Oanoke one day, Lulu." Taylor watched out for Lucia in a way no one else did: when they met in second grade, when Taylor gave Lucia her midday snack every day, because Lucia never had one, or split her book-fair money.

Where was Lucia going to go? No, she was firmly planted in Mt. Oanoke, like a root. Her father certainly wasn't paying for college. Lenny was a druggie. But Lucia had Taylor, always, and sometimes, Taylor's mom. Her mouth shimmered and she made a kissy pout in Lucia's direction. "How's it look?"

"Like someone'll wanna kiss it." Lucia kicked an errant rubber ball down the beige hallway that led from the bathroom back to the mall. Taylor shrieked, her voice echoing. Taylor had a ring on every finger and seventeen bangle bracelets on her wrist. When she ran her hand over the tiled wall, they clattered and clanged. "You'll get out. I won't. That's a fact."

"Oh, I'm a lifer." Taylor smacked her lips again. "If I wasn't before, I am now. Burt made sure of that when he left my mom. College is . . ." She flicked her wrist, quick, like she was waving. "Nope. I'm here now. You and me forever, can you handle it, Lulu?"

"What are you talking about? You're rich as shit."

"Was, dahling. Was. Have you looked at Ms. Jenny lately? Her highlights are do-it-yourself and her Ann Taylor is at least three seasons old. Maybe five."

Lucia stared at Taylor, who never talked about her dad. Never talked about the scandal. Never talked about all that missing money, where he'd run to, or who he'd run with. Lucia could hardly breathe, she felt so close to the sleeping beast, too close. Before she could think, Taylor said, "Think they miss us in seventh period?"

Lucia shook her head. Maybe Taylor, they'd miss. Never her. "If you get caught, you'll be benched for at least one meet. Right?"

"Right. So we won't get caught." Taylor didn't

care about track. Taylor's mom, Jennifer, cared about track. Said it would keep Taylor thin.

It seemed so trite to skip school just to go to the mall. So pathetic. An act of rebellion just because they could, not for any real reason. If they kept doing laps, someone would notice, eventually. Besides, Lucia didn't have any money and she had to be at the Goodwill soon. Her shift started at four. Her stomach turned, slick, and she shivered.

"Look." Taylor wandered away, to the Piercing Pagoda kiosk. She took one bright pink nail and spun a display of earrings. The hair-bunned lady inside rolled her eyes. Taylor plucked something from the ring rack and waved it in front of Bun Lady's eyes rudely. "Yoo-hoo, I wanna buy this?"

She was slow to get to her feet, grumbling, her *Woman's World* magazine sliding down her tan polyestered thighs and crumpling on the floor.

"What are you buying?" Lucia asked, her attention diverted toward a couple making out on a bench. The girl straddled the man; he looked at least ten years older and her feet wrapped behind him, her legs between the seat and back slats. Her feet dangled inches from the slimy water, a black flat ballet slipper hanging on precariously to her toes.

"Look, I got you a present." Taylor produced it with a flourish and dropped to one knee. She held Lucia's fingertips, gazed up at her like an expectant groom.

"Get the fuck up, now. People are looking." Lucia whispered, laughing. Taylor slid the ring on Lucia's pinkie finger. A half-broken heart, a single clasp.

BE FRI

"Say you'll be my friend forever." Taylor inched toward her, on her knees, her mouth in a sticky pout. She showed Lucia the other half, stuck on her own pinkie: ST ENDS

"*Yes,* now get the fuck up."

Bun Lady grunted as she picked up her magazine and Taylor popped to her feet. "We're friend-engaged now. Can't ever take it back." She tapped her lollipop against her two front teeth and Lucia pretended to gag.

"Shut up." Taylor leaned close. She smelled like cotton candy and cherry Blow Pop. Lucia's hair tangled in all the stickiness.

Lucia didn't say anything, she just let Taylor hug her, her arms long and warm, her breasts up against her bicep. Eventually, Lucia hugged her back.

"We need each other and you know it." Taylor whispered. "B-E-S-T F-R-I-E-N-D-S." She waved her pinkie, the fake gold of the broken heart flashing in front of Lucia's face until Lucia swatted at it.

Taylor flicked off her flip-flops and climbed

into the fountain, arms outstretched. She looked up at the skylight and twirled in a circle. She laughed and kicked up the murky water, splashing at her calves. The couple on the bench stopped kissing and stared at her. Bun Lady yelled *Hey!* from halfway down the mall. She laughed, the light glinting off her glossy mouth, shiny teeth.

"Luuuuuu-luuuuuu." Taylor spun and spun and spun, her black hair flying out to the sides like a dress. "Luuuuuu-luuuuuuuu." She spun faster, faster, losing her footing and finding it again, stumbling and righting herself, laughing, until even the Gap clerk came out to see what the commotion was about. That thick, chemical water licked at the bottoms of her shorts; her suntanned thighs glistened.

Everyone watched. And no one tried to stop her.

CHAPTER 16

Nate, Friday, April 3, 2015

Spring hadn't quite found them yet.

It was one of those cold muddling days, a month after the season started, when it still got dark at five thirty and the nights at home afterward dragged on interminably. He had one night off a week if he was lucky, one night that he should have gone home early, eaten dinner with his family. But every night was the same play; it could drive a guy batshit crazy. Alecia catered to Gabe, Gabe stayed locked up in his little world, Nate watched television. Alecia chased Gabe around the house with plastic chickens, or goats, or cows, or something else nonsensical, and tried to get Gabe to repeat his therapy successes for Nate. The bitch of it was, Nate didn't really care. He didn't see leaps-and-bounds progress he thought he was paying for, but he didn't think that torture was a solution, either. Gabe ended up crying, Alecia would cry, and really all Nate wanted was one nice night at home with his son. Maybe catch a spring training game.

Nobody could blame him for mixing it up a

little bit, staying late, grading some tests, reading crap on the Internet. There was no shortage of crap. He needed the escape, the downtime. The quiet, away from the field, away from the chaos of his house. Was that really so bad?

"Mr. Winters?" A soft voice, a knock at the door. Kelsey Minnow stood in the doorway, twirling a lock of hair around her index finger and looking past him at the whiteboard.

"Hi, Kelsey, come on in." She was mad at him. She held a precalculus test in her fingers like a poison, the giant red D flashing back and forth. His rule was, anything less than a C had to have the problems reworked and you could turn the test back in for extra points. He did it in all his math classes, but the precalc kids bucked it the most. Most kids repeated the test, but in the upper levels, some didn't out of laziness or lack of interest or even spite. Kelsey was none of those; she wanted the extra points.

"I finished up the test, I wanted to turn it in." She pushed the paper onto his desk. He picked it up, scanned it, and nodded.

"I'll grade it and get it back to you. Thanks, Kelsey. I'm sure it's fine now, but if not we'll talk about it." He smiled. She rolled her eyes at him and turned to leave.

"You're welcome!" Nate called after her, trying to incite a laugh. She didn't bite.

Lucia Hamm stood off to the side, her arms

crossed over her chest, letting Kelsey flounce away. He couldn't be sure, but he thought Kelsey muttered "witch" under her breath. Lucia shot her a look but Kelsey ran down the hall, shouting at someone to wait.

It was late, almost six o'clock. He didn't remember staying at school until five thirty when he was in high school, and yet every night he seemed to have students hanging around until all hours.

"Lucia. Do you have a test for me?" He asked, not really expecting an answer. She didn't move. He pushed his chair back, folded his ankle over his knee. "Everyone is looking for you, you know. They went to the paper mill, saw your stuff. Where have you been? You weren't in school today."

"You checked?" Her head bobbed up and down, her hair tangled in her face. Her skin was waxy, pale. He waved her in.

"Come in, please. What's going on?"

"I have nowhere to go. Lenny is . . . I just can't go home." She shook her head. "Taylor thinks I'm a liar. That I'm a witch, casting a spell on Porter."

"Porter?" Nate asked, surprised. Porter Max, Andrew's best friend. "What does Porter have to do with anything?"

"You didn't hear anything? About me?"

"Just that they were looking for you. Ms.

Peterson, Taylor, the police." Lucia's head snapped up and her eyes narrowed. Nate stood, put his hand on her arm, tried to guide her to his desk. She stayed, standing in the middle of the room. He dragged up a chair. "Sit? Please?" Nate sat back down. Level playing field, see? He patted the chair again.

She shook her head. "How do I report that I'm being bullied?" She stuck out her jaw.

"Um, I guess you can tell me. We can go talk to Mr. Bachman together tomorrow. Or the guidance counselor. Whatever you want." He couldn't keep the incredulity out of his voice. *She* was being bullied? He knew her brother was an asshole. She didn't have friends, except for Taylor. But the idea of Lucia being bullied didn't jive. Avoided? Yes. Even feared.

Her tongue lapped at her lips, her eyes darting around the room. Nate wondered if she was on something.

She came up to him, close and sudden, smelling like campfire and cotton candy. Nate tried to stand but she put up a hand to keep him where he was.

"I want to show you something. A thing I do." She reached down and took his hand and brought it up to her neck. She leaned back, partially sitting on his desk, and turned her head far to the right, her voice hitching a little mewl, her chest bobbing.

"Lucia—" Nate started.

She shh'd him and pulled her hair off to the side, guiding his hand behind her head. He felt the stubble then, the scab-pocked skin, the uneven tread behind her neck. His breath caught.

"Lucia, what is this, who did this to you?" When he stood and lifted up her mane of hair, her neck was red, bruised purple over brown. Large clumps of hair were missing from the bottom to the middle of her scalp, in various stages of regrowth. His skin bloomed hot. "Really, who did this to you? Was this Lenny? Your brother?"

It looked like it had been violently ripped out. It would have been bloody when it happened.

She turned, her hair dropping from his hands, her fingertips splaying on his chest, her chin dipped until he thought she would put her head on his shoulder, and he wondered if she was crying. He gripped her arms, begging her until he felt like a fucking idiot. "Is there anything else they're doing? Are there other bruises? Lucia, this isn't bullying, this is abuse. Really, tell me, who did this to you?"

She looked up at him, her lip caught between her teeth, her eyes wide, intense.

"Why do you care?" She whispered, her breath hot on his neck, and his body went still. His heart thumped. Twice, then seemed to stop.

"I care, Lucia. I do. I just . . . want to know. Is this your brother?" He all but whispered it.

She gripped his short-sleeved shirt then, her hands cool and small, fingers slipping between the buttons to touch his skin, seeking the soft downy hair of his stomach. Her mouth pressed up against his and her tongue lapped against his closed lips. He opened his mouth to speak, too stunned for the words to come, and her tongue slipped once quickly inside, finding his teeth, darting hot and quick, and he felt his insides pool to liquid, his knees weaken, his throat close. His hands tightened around her arms and the whole room swirled in a whirlpool that centered around her and that hair, like a feather up and down his forearm, and that tongue. Her breasts pushed up against him, braless through the thin cotton of her shirt, the small knot of a nipple against his bare arm and his breath came in wet gasps.

He gripped her arms hard and pushed her away. "Lucia." He turned his head, looked out the window to the horizon, anything to find his bearings. Shocked, then ashamed, at how little control he seemed to have over his fucking body, his mind. "Oh my God." He pushed his mouth against his own shoulder and backed up, to find air. He filled his lungs, once, twice until the room righted itself.

He put the back of his hand over his mouth, his heart slowing from a gallop to a steady rhythm. "That *never* happened. Do you understand? And it never will again."

She cocked her head, her mouth open in surprise.

"You want to know who did that to me? My hair?" She leaned forward, her mouth close to his ear, her breath tickling. "I do this to myself."

CHAPTER 17

Bridget, Friday, May 1, 2015

The faculty lounge was worse than the halls. The students buzzed with the hushed excitement of drama, their faces flushed, skin pinked. The teachers were sullen, drawn in and whispering. They avoided Bridget's eyes, gave her thin smiles, and while they talked to her—subjects like the weather, crazy seventh period, the new administrative assistant—no one asked her about Nate. This, more than anything, gave them away. They talked to each other, but not to Bridget. They asked each other, "Do you think he really slept with that girl?" She heard them whispering and then they'd clam up when they saw Bridget. They coughed and changed the subject when Bridget went to heat her cup of soup up in the microwave.

Bridget thought long and hard about slamming the break-room door shut, standing in front of it, and asking everyone, point-blank: *Do you really think Nate's guilty?* She thought about pointing to Dale Trevor, who taught algebra in Nate's department, who had a daughter with

Down's syndrome in a special school. She wanted to remind him that last year, Dale and Nate chaperoned prom, and Dale brought his seventeen-year-old daughter, his sweet, happy, wonderful daughter in a cotton candy gown because their school didn't hold a prom. Nate brought her a corsage. Nate danced with her, and Dale didn't flinch; in fact, he took a picture. He didn't seem to think Nate was some kind of danger to society. He posted it on Facebook for crying out loud.

Bridget wanted to remind Paula Hortense of the time her car had a flat tire, and Nate stopped on the Owega turnpike because he recognized her car and her vanity plate—LGoM#31, (Let's Go Mets #31)—and helped her change her tire *in the rain,* then followed her to the tire center, over twenty miles away. On a Saturday.

None of it mattered. Nate was now a creep, a scum, slept with a student, sick, practically a pedophile. Bridget kept her mouth shut, thinking of that kiss, and how sometimes the truth is actually right smack dab in the middle between speculation and perception. He was her friend. Alecia was her friend. There was a truth somewhere, and Bridget had no intention of eschewing it simply because it was easier.

The microwave dinged and suddenly Dale was behind her, emanating the smell of oily fast food. His wife must have favored the deep fryer because he always smelled like wet french fries.

He coughed and Bridget stood off to the side while he heated up a frozen dinner. She watched him press the numbers with his pale, shaky fingers. Finally, she couldn't take it anymore, the cup of soup burning hot in her palm.

"Dale," Bridget hissed.

His shoulders hunched like he'd been expecting it.

"Talk to me. You can't think Nate did this . . . thing. Can you?"

"Oh, I don't know, Bridget. It's a serious allegation. You know?" His glasses slid down to the end of his red nose and he twitched, twice, like a mouse. "They're saying *institutional assault* now."

"What does that mean?" Bridget asked.

"It means that Lucia is eighteen but it doesn't matter. He was her teacher, it's still rape."

Bridget balked. "Nate would never *rape* anyone."

Jane Blue, who taught gym (and whom all the boys called "blue balls," although Bridget pretended not to know this), hung behind her, studying the bulletin board, her blond hair threaded into a thick braid. She inched closer.

"I really can't say, Bridget. I can't go out on a limb, though, because what if it is, you know?" Dale shook his head. "It doesn't seem like the Nate I know, but—"

"Have you called him? Emailed him?"

Dale shook his head. "I just want to let the school board and the police do their job. If Nate's innocent, we're all here for him. If he's not . . . well . . ." Dale cleared his throat and pushed his glasses up. Squared his shoulders. Lowered his voice. "Bridge, you know, there've been rumors before, you know that, right?"

"About Nate?" No she did *not* know that, she'd never heard one blessed word about him. He was Saint Nate, the baseball coach with the disabled son, the beautiful wife. These are all the things she'd ever heard about him. Everybody's buddy. What a bunch of stupid hypocrites to say this now, *oh we always knew.* That was the way it went, right? In the paper—*there was always something strange about that guy, he was just too nice.* Is that where this was headed?

"Just a few years ago. You know he's on social media. I mean some of the teachers knew about it, but the administrators don't. It's not an outright rule yet, but it's *highly* frowned upon. So the Nate we know wouldn't necessarily sleep with a student, but he'd cross *that* line?" He shrugged. "He's too close to them, you know? So anyway, it's hard to be sure, that's all."

"Give me a break, Dale." She was about to leave, then stopped and turned around. "What rumors?"

"What's that now?" Dale played dumb.

"You said there have been rumors before? What happened before?"

"It was a few years ago, I don't quite remember. Anyway, it wasn't like this, but another student did lodge a complaint. He favored her, catered to her, that kind of thing. She wasn't well liked, kind of like Lucia. I can't remember her name, though." Dale looked upward, like the answer might be scrawled above on the yellow-stained drop-ceiling tiles.

"Robin Hendricks." Jane said behind them. "Her name was Robin Hendricks."

Bridget turned and Jane smiled, her fingers coiling the end of her braid. "Everyone forgets about that girl. She had a ton of problems: drugs, a bad crowd, you name it. She graduated, though, thanks to her good pal Nate Winters. Pulled some strings, who knows? All I know is, the summer after she graduated, somebody saw them together at the Quarry Bar."

The Quarry Bar sat a few miles off Route Six, dilapidated, its neon signs hardly even lit up anymore. A place for drunks and hookups.

"I never heard this part," Dale interjected.

"Oh sure, dancing to the jukebox. Not acting like teacher and student, that's for sure. I don't spread rumors much, and I don't even know if it's true, but I heard later that his boy took a header down the stairs that night. His poor wife sat in the ER all night long alone. My sister was a nurse on duty, so that part I know for a fact. Shame, really." Jane shook her head, a feigned kind of sadness, and Bridget fisted her fingers in the pocket of her dress, her nails slicing into her palms. Jane was trotting out a dusty old rumor, playing it off as some kind of truth. Bridget remembered now, she'd heard it before, years ago, but it was right after Holden got sick and Gabe was diagnosed and they'd all been consumed, stuck in their own whirlpool lives, and some days it was all Bridget could do to take a breath deep enough to fill her lungs and stave off the starry, wheezy feeling of grief. She'd never known what to make of the rumor, but you couldn't forget the fact that it was at least two and a half years old and Jane had a lot of nerve, that's all.

Across the room, Paula Hortense asked, "Do you smell smoke?"

From out in the hallway, a girl began to scream.

By the time Bridget and the other teachers reached the hallway, a crowd of students had gathered. Bridget pushed her way through to where Lucia faced off against Riana Yardley. Riana, tall, stately, graceful, her black hair pulled tight against her scalp, her black eyes wide with terror, or maybe wonderment. Between them, a thin piece of loose-leaf, its edges browned and curling, a wisp of smoke spiraling to the ceiling.

Lucia's face was whiter than the paper. Bridget put a hand on Riana's back, expecting warmth, but her skin, beneath the sheath of a netted Mt. Oanoke Raiders jersey, was cool to the touch. Bridget eyed the ceiling, the sprinklers, wondering if a the single curl of smoke would set them off.

"What happened here?" Bridget inserted herself, her hand slicing the air, her authority heavier than she actually felt.

"Crazy girl here accused me of planting a *love note* and then *poof!* The whole paper burst into flames. Like she's Carrie from the movie, she's gonna burn this place down." Riana punched the air with a single pointed finger, red acrylic nails glittering in the sunbeam from the lone hallway window. The light filtered behind Lucia and her white hair looked orangey-red, backlit like a haloed angel. She looked on fire.

Bridget glanced at Lucia, who stood shocked, her mouth slack and pale. Bridget realized for the first time that Lucia was wearing no makeup: no black-ringed eyes, no sticky, spokey eyelashes, no red lips. Nothing, just waxy skin shining like a baby's bottom.

"That's impossible," Paula said dumbly from behind Bridget.

"I know. But that's what happened. She opened her locker and turned to me and started screaming at me, that I did this—whatever *this* is—and the girl was pissed off." Riana jutted out her chin, her hips swiveling. Her friends had gathered behind her: Josh Tempest, Kelsey Minnow. Andrew Evans, rawboned and sleepy, tilting to one side, a sly smile on his lips. Taylor huddled on the outside, between them, her eyes darting from Lucia to Riana, her pale pink tongue lapping at her mouth like a nervous cat. "Then, bam, the whole paper exploded like it was a firework."

"Lucia?" Bridget demanded, like this was one of Lucia's tricks, one of her mean-streaked power plays. "You can't have lighters in here."

Lighters. Bridget had seen them as she walked to the parking lot after school: Kelsey and Riana, their bodies languid against the brick side of the athletic building before track practice, the smoke seeping from their lips as they whispered behind cupped hands. The Pall Mall box matching the royal blue of their track shorts, peeking out of the side of Kelsey's black lace bra. Bridget always thought that was backward; they'd run track and then smoke cigarettes, literally grinding all their hard work into the track dirt with the toes of their Adidas. In Mt. Oanoke, aside from the baseball players, nobody really took any sport seriously. It was all just something to do until they got out.

Then Bridget thought of the *flick, flick, flick* of a lighter in class during her third period, when it was too much work to ferret out who the owner was because Bridget was too tired to do anything about it anyway.

Bridget imagined, could envision clear as day, the quick snap of a lighter under Lucia's paper. A spontaneous decision, borne from fear and power hunger, and maybe just a touch of revenge for what she did to Nate. The alliances snapped into place, clicking like a lock's tumblers: Riana and Kelsey and Josh and Andrew. Andrew, Nate's little protégé, his lackey.

Dale sensed her hesitation and took one tenuous step forward, his arm outstretched ineffectually.

"I don't smoke," Lucia finally said, her voice soft, watching the last coil of smoke meander upward toward the ceiling, mesmerized.

"It's just her. A spell or something," Kelsey screeched, her voice high and itchy, scratching at something inside Bridget, but Lucia stayed rooted to the spot. Never looking up, her eyes fixated. Unblinking.

"Dude, that is fucked up." Josh's voice from the back, punctuated by a thick, mucid laugh.

"What spell?" Bridget asked, the back of her brain twitching with the answer. Something Nate had said. *She's being bullied.* Bridget looked at all their faces; they were blank, shiny. "Lucia, who was the note from?"

She looked up into Bridget's face, her eyes glassed over. "It didn't say. Then it started burning." She looked helpless, cheeks rouged with self-doubt.

A love note, though? Kids sent texts now, Facebook messages, Instagram and Twitter DMs. They had a hundred ways to reach each other, during and after school, and none of them involved a pencil and piece of paper.

"This place has been a nightmare ever since those goddamn birds," Kelsey muttered, and elbowed Taylor for backup. Taylor smiled gamely, watched Lucia's face. It never moved. Kelsey continued anyway, toeing the gray tile linoleum like it was dirt. "I bet you did that, too, right? How'd you kill all those little tiny black birds? Poison? Icicles through their brains like the papers say?"

"Enough, Kelsey." Dale finally took charge. They'd all let Kelsey go on longer than they should have, their mouths hanging, and even Jane, usually forceful—she once dragged a sophomore down to Bachman's by his dyed-blue hair because he accidentally-on-purpose grabbed her ass—was stunned silent. "Everyone. Back to lunch. Back to wherever you are supposed to be. The bell rang"—he checked his watch—"four minutes ago. Go. *Now.*" Dale, meek and sort of impotent, his pointy shoulders in his short-sleeved dress shirt, his rimless glasses, and Hush Puppy shoes that squeaked when he walked. But they listened and the hallway emptied. "Riana and Lucia, now, to Bachman's office." He put a hand on Riana's bicep, steering her down the hall and Lucia followed, her gaze still empty and blank.

Bridget couldn't believe Lucia had come right back to school. Nate had only been suspended a few days ago. The rumor mill swirled and churned and spit Lucia back out on the other side, and something about the whole thing nagged at Bridget, pricking at some part of her: the fact that she would come right back to class like nothing happened. The teachers, although seemingly on Lucia's side, made no move to comfort her or walk with her, and she trudged the long hallway, dragging behind Dale and Kelsey, her fingertips aimlessly skimming along the lockers, a faint humming in her throat. The half-charred remnant of a note fluttering between Dale's long white fingers. She hadn't seen him grab it.

Bridget couldn't help but study Taylor, who watched Lucia with a kind of dazed awe, her head pivoting back and forth between Lucia and Riana, but she made no move to catch up with her best friend. When Kelsey whispered something to her, she laughed, her head thrown back, and Andrew turned around, his mouth open.

On instinct, Bridget jogged to catch up, reached out and pinched Riana's elbow, spun her around, and the girl gurgled, sputtered with surprise. Bridget's hand went lightning quick to

Riana's jeans pocket—one, then the other—and plucked out a clear hot-pink lighter, the safety broken off. She snapped it up once in Riana's face with a smirk and Riana barely got out a *hey!* before Bridget fell back, following them down to Bachman's office.

It only made sense: Lucia found the note, started hollering at Riana, and Riana taught her a quick, mean little lesson with the *snap, snap* of her fingers.

Bridget hustled next to Dale and his face whipped around and his eyes narrowed, almost like he wanted to scold her like a student. She snatched the small paper out of his hand, which was burned into a circle, a little slip of a thing.

The writing was in bold, black Sharpie. It could have been written by anyone, intentionally disguised, all capital letters.

It said *everything you touch.*

CHAPTER 18

Alecia, Christmas, 2012

Nothing fit. A mother's lament. Alecia was two years out of pregnancy and her breasts still spilled out of tops, her waist thick and straight. But now, standing in front of the full-length mirror, with Nate downstairs whistling, the air heady with his aftershave and steam from the shower—why couldn't he turn on a vent fan? Anyway, now, finally, the extra weight bothered her. She tugged on her hair, straightening the kinky waves, wondering why it hadn't bothered her before tonight. It was still all relatively new.

Being a mom to a toddler was more work than any book had said it would be. The terrible twos had zapped the energy right out of her: the meltdowns, the tantrums, the sleep regression. Gabe was up all night again like a newborn and Alecia, tired and hungry and angry at Nate who snored comfortably from their bed, had been seeking refuge in 3 a.m. chocolate chip cookies. The days blurred by, Alecia nipping grilled cheese crusts off Gabe's plate, and even once a whole half a sandwich off the floor after he threw it in refusal. She was too tired to make one for herself.

But tonight, there was a party. The Tempests, Peter and Bea (that's it, just Bea, not even short for anything), lived in the neighborhood behind the high school, near Bridget. Their house stood high on the hill, the largest in the development, the biggest pool, brown-and-tan stone, a five-car garage that would hold Alecia's whole townhouse. The invitation was a coup. Even Bridget seemed awestruck when Alecia told her. Maybe awestruck is too strong a word: impressed. The Tempests were impressive. Two strapping teen boys, both baseball players, both blond, both toothy-grinned: Quentin, the eldest one, and Josh, his younger brother, who were left (albeit happily) home alone several weeks a year while Bea and Peter traveled. They had parties, of course, as warm-blooded teenage boys do, but not wild ones that showed up on the newspaper police blotter the next morning.

Behind her, Nate cleared his throat. Alecia met his eyes in the mirror and he gave her a sideways smile that always melted her heart, even when he said, "We have to go, you know. We're going to be more than fashionably late." Nate looked perfect: black pants, a button-down shirt, crisp belt, his hair gelled in soft waves.

"This is a big deal. I don't look right."

"You look beautiful. It's not a big deal. It's

a party." He rubbed his chin with his palm and covered his mouth and Alecia whipped around, swatting at the air. He was laughing at her. "A big deal is the house over by the lake that burned down last week and now four children don't have a home. A big deal is that the polar ice caps are melting. A big deal is pancreatic cancer." He raised his eyebrows at her and Alecia rolled her eyes.

"I know this. I know. You're right. Of course." She tilted her head. "But also, low blow." Because of course Holden was sick and Bridget was a disaster, and in the grand scheme of things, this party did not matter, not even a little bit.

Except that it did. Perspective mattered, but so did acknowledging that the question of importance is personal and not discriminatory.

"Well, I think you look amazing." Nate held her wrist and pulled her toward him, kissed her neck.

"This. Look, I'm a mess." Alecia gestured to her cleavage, a bit more than just cleavage, a bit wobbly and spilling up and over, all the Lycra in the free world holding the rest of her into place, pushing everything up, up, up and over. She didn't look sexy or bombshell. She looked fat. Wiggly, jiggly, uncomfortable and just plain fat. Her black sweater hugged in all the wrong places and the deep neckline was a joke. Her chest looked like a mogul run. "I have to change."

Nate bent down and kissed her chest, the swell of breast then the other. "Don't you dare. I love this sweater." He kissed her mouth, his tongue licked gently at her lips, and Alecia felt her legs wobble. His hands moved down her waist, to the soft bubble of pudge above her waistband.

"Nate. Stop." She pulled away, averting her eyes. "Where's Gabe?"

"Relax, he's in his crib." Nate shook his head, his brows knit in annoyance. "He's fine."

"Nate! He can climb out of his crib. You can't leave him alone this long!"

A crash and a wail from the other room and Alecia threw a pointed glare in Nate's direction before she rushed to Gabe's room. She listened to Nate's heavy footsteps on the stairs; he hadn't even followed her.

In the car, he was quiet. Alecia tried to hold his hand; his fingertips lay in her palm like a dead fish until she gave up and let it rest on the emergency brake between them. Gabe kicked his legs in the back seat, yelping a high pitch over and over, rhythmic and unrelenting on the twenty-minute drive.

"Gabe. Enough. This is a small car, buddy," Nate said. "Don't you think he should be talking by now?"

"He talks, Nate. You just don't pay attention to him." Alecia wriggled in her seat, adjusting her sweater. Nate could be so dense, so rigid in his expectations. It irritated the living shit out of her.

The Tempests' house was lit up from the inside out, bright twinkling lights everywhere, their trees outlined in glittering white. Bing Crosby's "White Christmas" spilled into the driveway and the cars were parked all the way down the street, onto the next block. Alecia, Nate, and Gabe trudged across the front lawn, Gabe's small mittened hand tucked into Alecia's.

Inside, people stood in groups, holding wine and martini glasses, laughing and talking over each other. Nate had told her that kids were invited but Alecia didn't see any other kids.

"The Winterses are here! So glad you could come!" Bea rushed up to them, her long blond hair flying behind her, glittering in a sequined top. Alecia was underdressed. A man in unassuming black pants and black shirt appeared and took their coats as Bea kissed both Alecia's cheeks and squealed at Gabe. "Oh I just love this age, look how stinking cute he is."

He *was* cute: dark haired and fair skinned, he looked like a porcelain doll. He howled when Bea hugged him and she laughed. "Oh, kids." She waved her hand in a circle. " All the other kids are in the basement, or upstairs in the gym. He can go wherever," displaying little understanding of a two-year-old's capabilities. Alecia knelt down, rolling her eyes where Bea couldn't see her, fixed Gabe's hair where she'd ruffled it, and gave him a smile. His gaze fixated on the kitchen.

Bea floated away, on to greet the next guest. "Does she really think he can just wander around unattended?" she asked Nate, annoyed. "He's two."

Nate stared at her, a hard penetrating gaze, without smiling. "Alecia, do you think for one night, you could lighten the hell up? It's a party." He gave her a smile then, a small, forced smile, and Alecia blinked. He'd never talked to her that way before and she felt her insides shrink up. She bit her cheek, wanting to cry and wanting to leave. Gabe flapped his hands, up and down, his new habit that he seemed to adopt whenever he was stressed, which was mostly in public. Alecia, red faced and sweating, pushed down on his hands and between her teeth gritted, "Gabey, calm." Miraculously, he calmed.

A woman in a deep red dress, looking like she'd just come off the runway, approached them and leaned in to kiss Nate's cheek. Alecia eyed her, her deep neckline with not a wobble in sight, a slit up her thigh revealing long, tan legs and a silver, sparkling stiletto. A stiletto! Alecia's toes curled inside her two-inch pumps.

"Alecia, this is Jennifer Lawson. Jenny, this is my wife, Alecia." Nate cleared his throat. Jennifer gave Alecia a smile and smooth handshake, her dark hair glossy as a raven's back. *Jenny?*

"Oh, Nate you'll never guess who actually came. Here, let me show you." She giggled, her fingertips curling around his arm, and pointed.

Nate leaned backward, toward the kitchen, and laughed at their shared inside joke. Alecia almost asked to be let in, asking who was in the kitchen?

She was interrupted by Peter Tempest. He greeted Nate with a firm handshake and a booming voice and said a quick hello with a swift peck in Alecia's direction, never acknowledging Gabe. He was tall, towering even, and positioned himself between Nate and Jennifer.

"Mind if I steal your husband for a moment?" Peter asked, already guiding Nate's elbow away to the media room, where the men stood around the television watching football or something else that Alecia couldn't care less about. Jennifer paused a moment and then wandered away without a word, leaving Alecia alone in the foyer with Gabe.

Gabe gazed up at the looming crystal chandelier, sparkling and throwing rainbows through hanging prisms, fixated. "Come on, Gabe," she whispered to no avail because he was in the zone, as she liked to call it. When he took off toward the formal sitting room, the only empty room where the lights were dimmed low, Alecia chased behind him, breathless.

In under two minutes, she had snatched a glass candy dish, a crystal vase, a set of candlesticks, and an expensive-looking ceramic sculpture that vaguely resembled a vagina from Gabe's thick fists. In five minutes, she'd pulled him off the couch, leaving one slightly damp footprint on the blue suede. In ten minutes, she'd settled him in front of the enormous wooden coffee table, spreading out his wooden number set that she'd stuck in her purse before she left. He arranged them in order, correctly, every time, which was kind of amazing, and Alecia kissed his forehead, damp with perspiration.

"Have you ever had him evaluated?" The woman leaned against the doorway, a stemmed wineglass in one hand, watching them. She gave Alecia a kind smile.

"For what?" Alecia breathed deep, filling her lungs, closing her eyes.

"Autism spectrum disorder?" She raised her eyebrows and Alecia felt the back of her tongue go sour. She'd never considered it.

"No. He's fine. He's just . . . he likes what he likes." She shrugged like it was no big deal. Like she wasn't exhausted by Gabe and his likes and dislikes and his vehemence and enthusiasm for both.

"I'm a psychologist at the middle school. I'd be happy to give you some names. I know some wonderful social workers—"

"He's fine, thank you." Alecia's voice was curt, even though she didn't mean it to be. She watched Gabe pull the wooden numbers and put them in order, one chubby finger after the other, over and over again.

"It's incredible that he knows his numbers like that. He's . . . two?" The woman knelt down in her pencil skirt, delicate and perfect, and removed the number four with a single French-manicured nail. Gabe pounded the table and howled. He moved the four back to its rightful place and held it here, defiant. She then removed the eight and placed it before the one. Gabe sat silent for a pause, and Alecia held her breath, her heart hammering in her throat. He picked up the eight and threw it against the wall, the hard edge of the wood leaving a tiny, almost unnoticeable divot in the drywall.

The woman stood and put a hand to Alecia's arm and Alecia stared at it like it was an alien thing.

Alecia stood abruptly, scooping up Gabe and gathering his numbers into her purse. She gave the woman a thin smile, and tried to say *thank you, thank you,* but she couldn't get the words out and her nose began to run as she bent down and picked up all the debris of *being Gabe,* so she put an elbow to her face and rushed out the room, feeling her cheeks flame red and hot.

Alecia found Nate in the living room, a tumbler

of scotch in his red fist, his Irish complexion glowing ruddy with alcohol. He was laughing with a group, and Alecia tugged on his sleeve like a child.

"Nate, we have to go. I have to go. This isn't working." She talked into his shoulder to hide her tears.

"What? We just got here. Alecia, it's a party. Let Gabe go upstairs for God's sake. Let him play with other kids for once."

Oh God, not here. Not this conversation, not like this, not now.

"Nate, he doesn't *play with other kids*. Have you ever watched him? He's never, not once, interacted with another kid. He just doesn't." Her voice pitched up to a wail; she could hear the high note, even as the crowd quieted around her.

"Alecia." Nate's voice was low, his teeth gritted. "People are starting to stare. We can talk about this at home. We just got here. Come stand here, next to me. Let Gabe play on the floor. Have a glass of wine. Here, have my whiskey." His voice edged up, louder, and he gave a wide smile, to the nervous titter of the women—Alecia suddenly realized it was all women, so typical— around him.

Alecia's eyes searched for Gabe, standing in the brightly lit, noisy living room and found him under the tree, his hands over his ears, rocking.

Alecia watched him, a sense of dread creeping up her spine, her hand to her mouth.

Gabe began to scream.

The car ride home was as quiet as the ride there, with Gabe humming loudly from the back seat. Nate tried to shush him but gave up, and twenty minutes later they parked in their driveway.

"I'll get him to bed. It's late anyway and you know how long it takes," Alecia said, gathering up her purse, her coat. "Sorry about the night."

"Alecia, it's fine. It's not your fault, I just wish . . ." Nate's voice faded in the dark, his fingertips drumming on his knee. "I just wish he didn't upset you so much. I think he feeds off of you, that's all. I think he feels your stress."

She was too tired for this. Maybe he was right, who knows? It was possible. But mostly, this conversation felt old and tired and she felt old and tired and she just wanted to sleep for days.

"I forgot my coat," Nate said suddenly. "My sport coat. I need it for Monday, I've got that baseball luncheon."

"Okay," Alecia said.

"I'll be right back. Just go in, I'll be back in twenty minutes."

"Forty," Alecia corrected, but shook her head and waved her hand.

"I'll be right back, okay? I'm sorry." He hopped over the console to the driver's seat and

Alecia hesitated with the keys for a second. How many whiskies had he had? It might not matter, Gabe's meltdown sobered everyone up quick.

He backed out of the driveway as Alecia ushered a tired Gabe inside, his head drooping under her palm. She changed him into jammies and got him into bed, tonight without protest. His tantrums seemed to exhaust him lately, and for once, Alecia was thankful.

When Gabe was asleep, she flopped facedown on the bed, peeling off her pumps and replaying the night in her mind. The woman in the pencil skirt. Bea's long blond hair and carefree smile. Jennifer Lawson's calculating eyes, her private jokes with Nate. Finally, she thought of Gabe, screaming under the Christmas tree, his hands over his ears, his eyes shut. Her heart twisting for the discomfort of her child and yet, at the same time, hating that he couldn't just be a normal kid for one night. They never seemed to be able to just go places, do things, like other families. It was all so hard, or maybe it just seemed that way and she wasn't doing a very good job. That's how Nate seemed to feel.

Alecia closed her eyes, so tired. She just wanted to sleep, to end the night, to have it be tomorrow; it was bound to be better. She drifted off almost immediately, so fast, so hard that she didn't hear her phone buzz. She didn't see the incoming text until the next morning.

1:42 a.m.: *Took Jenny home. Burt left her at the party, they had a fight. Drama! Will explain tomorrow. On my way back now.*

As she read the message, she looked over at her soundly sleeping husband, wondering what time, exactly, he had gotten home.

CHAPTER 19

Lucia, a year ago

Like everywhere else, there was a hierarchy to baseball games, where the crowd sat. Parents and teachers perched in the bleachers, backs pressed against cool metal, lined up, expectant along the bottom few rows. Coaches' wives sat higher up, showing up all at once, coordinated through text messages. As if there was an unsaid requirement to attend a certain number of games to be supportive, and *they'd fill it by God, but they'd do it together, and are those new shoes?* Most of the kids sat along the fence: they wanted to yell, hoot, and catcall. Whistle and insult. Andrew's crew sat up on the grass hill, behind the dugout, but high enough to watch him, face pinked and shining, his arm like a rocket.

Mt. Oanoke had baseball. The football team limped along in last place, fraught with ligament sprains and concussions, the consequence of too much weight, too little speed, and half-assed training. Basketball did okay, but they hadn't made postseason in as long as Lucia could remember. Most of the kids felt like Taylor did about track: it was something to do.

No one felt passionate about anything. Except baseball.

Lucia watched Coach Winters, his face scrunched and red, as he bounced on the balls of his feet, watching Andrew. Pick his hat up, run his hand through his hair, put it down, resting back on the tuft of his blond-brown curls, the sweat down the back of his neck, and Lucia wanted to dip her finger in it.

She watched the boys in the dugout vie for him, just for a second to feel the heat of his eyes, so intense, cut you right to the center like you weren't fooling anyone, to feel the thrill of being called out on your own bullshit.

Some days she'd trade anything for that, even in a class as boring as statistics. She'd started to hang around after, seeking it, that look in his face, the way he'd say *Lucia! What sort of interesting discussion do you have on probability today?* His eyes twinkling, like something out of the paperback romance novels she saw at the library, where every man's eyes sparkled and twinkled like they were all made of glittery icing or pure goodness, and that's what she started to think about Mr. Winters. That he was made of goodness.

Her eyes darted to Andrew, his arms and legs tangled up, so fast and long, that ball coming like buckshot across the dusty white plate. Batters up, then down. So fast you could hardly count them.

She sat behind them, Porter and Riana whispering. Taylor twining her gum around her finger, her phone in her hand, thumbs flying over the keys, glossy lips laughing. At what?

Lucia had no idea. Taylor had asked her in the hall, an offhand comment, *you coming?* So quiet she almost didn't hear it. Andrew's mouth had smirked at that, Porter elbowing him in the ribs. This is how she got invited to things now: last minute, a guilty sigh, a laugh she didn't understand. Ever since last year.

That fucking bird. She fucked a good thing up with them. Even Taylor had been different, shifting hot and cold with the wind since that bird. Lucia held fast to the denial, but Taylor knew, her eyes flicking around Lucia's face looking for the lie.

Lucia had a temper, Jimmy used to tell her that. She knew they called her a witch. Fuck them, she'd be a witch then. *You become what people expect.* Who said that? Lucia pulled her journal out of her bag, scribbled it on a page, and shoved it back into the front pocket. She'd look it up later.

She glanced up to see Taylor, as if seeing her for the first time. She smirked, leaned over to Josh, a light tickling of his arm, and whispered in his ear.

Lucia didn't know why she kept coming to these things. So desperate to be invited that she'd put up with this kind of shit? Not knowing what to do with her hands and her eyes or even the muscles around her mouth; they felt stiff and like they weren't really hers.

The back of her head tingled and itched and she wound a tendril of hair around her index finger, pulling just to the point of pain, just enough to stop the urge. Taylor watched her and shook her head, a short burst, with a roll of her eyes. *Don't you goddamn dare.*

She stood, too quickly, the pricks of stars dancing in her eyes, her legs swaying, and for a moment she thought she might pass out. *Jesus God do not pass out.*

"Where you going?" Taylor kept her eyes to her phone, her fingers dancing, those French-manicured tips white and bright over the glow of the screen as a smile played at her lips, the kind of smile she used to give Lucia but was now giving the nameless phone person, and Lucia almost, almost slapped that new iPhone right out of her hand. She was this close to it.

"Home."

Her head snapped up and she snorted, a quick burst of air through her nose. "For what?"

The bitch of it was, she didn't have an answer. Lucia looked out onto the field. Mr. Winters was pressing his palms against the ceiling of the dugout now, the hem of his shirt inching up, a soft stripe of skin there. Andrew's face was a sheen, glowing, on fire. The whole crowd was quiet.

"You know he's working on a no-hitter, right?" Porter pointed into the stands, his voice a whisper, the recruits with their radar guns clicking. "They're watching him. He's a sophomore. And they're watching him. Fucking amazing."

Lucia didn't know. She thought of Andrew, that mouth against hers, those big-knuckled hands against her back, in her hair, her scalp tingling. That openness in his face that she never saw again, his eyes closed up tight now, those lids like curtains. It could just make a person so goddamn tired all the time, all this effort.

She looked back at Taylor. Her fingers waggled in her direction, *bye, see ya, go now,* but she didn't look up, and then suddenly she laughed and leaned over, showed Riana her phone and Riana laughed.

Later she'd learn that Andrew finished that no-hitter, the second in Mt. Oanoke history. That later, because of that game, UT Austin would come, watch him try to repeat it and fail, but they'd offer him a full ride anyway. Because he was Andrew, no one expected any less.

But all she'd remember is their laughter at some inside joke. A big fucking mystery. Some inner circle she couldn't understand and she'd never be part of again. She was so sick of wondering what they were talking about, laughing about, and how to figure it out, if she was doing the right thing or the wrong thing, and whether she was everything that was wrong or nothing that mattered at all.

That was the worst part: trying to figure out if she mattered at all.

CHAPTER 20

Nate, Tuesday, May 5, 2015

Tripp's couch might as well have been made of cement. Nate tossed one way, then the other, punching the square, knotty throw pillow in his sleep. In his dream, Lucia came to him, sat on his lap, his head resting on her shoulder. She kissed his cheek, stroked his hair. She held out her closed fist and he took it, kissed her knuckles, cold against his lips, and when she opened her hand, a starling lay half rotted and paper-boned in her palm. When she laughed, the inside of her mouth was black, like fur.

He sat up, his heart hammering inside his chest. The room was dark, only the faintest light peeking out through the curtains, a thin, pink beam. It seemed like morning but the clock read 2 p.m., his brain thick with fog, his mouth tacky.

The night before came back in a rush. First the argument with Alecia. He'd just gone to pick up a few things: a new shirt, a pair of jeans, another pair of sweatpants. To say hi to Gabe.

"Will you stay for dinner?" she asked, her back to him in the kitchen while Gabe played

224

with his toys at the table. He lined up the metal construction vehicles, according to an order in his head, and Nate watched him, fascinated. On the refrigerator stuck his worksheets from the week. His name, painstakingly printed in block letters. He used to write, get frustrated, scribble and tear the paper. The letters had to be exact, which was beyond his capability. These letters were perfect. He was getting better, advancing.

"Gabe, you're doing great, buddy. Look at this!" Nate pulled a thin red-and-blue lined sheet from beneath its magnet. "It's almost perfect."

Gabe hummed but smiled to himself. He'd heard his father and that gave Nate a beam of pride. He crossed the kitchen and hugged Gabe from behind. Gabe liked affection, but mostly only from Alecia and a few select therapists. From Nate, he sought approval.

To Alecia, he said, "Do you want me to stay for dinner?"

She shrugged and stirred something on the stove.

"I shouldn't. I told Tripp I'd meet him." A lie.

"Whatever. Do whatever, you're not obligated to be here." Alecia brushed past him into the living room, picked up the remote, and scrolled through the channels. She was a fidgeter when she was mad. She couldn't sit still, brood like a normal person. He doesn't know how many fights they'd had over the washing machine, or the kitchen mop. She needed to move her body, expend her energy. He loved that about her. Her movement. The way her arms and legs were strong from fifteen years of childhood gymnastics classes, when she filled out after Gabe was born to a soft curve, so new and supple, and then later, when Gabe was diagnosed and she was such a nervous wreck she lost it all, the weight sloughing off of her like a skin. Today, in the living room with the twilight sun across her face, her fingers shaking as she pushed up, up, up on the remote, and cursing under her breath, she looked like a paper doll.

She didn't look real.

"Are you eating?" he asked, knowing immediately it was a mistake.

"What the fuck do you care?" She asked not even looking over at him, her voice wobbling high.

"Jesus, Alecia. I care. Okay? You kicked *me* out." His palms itched, his scalp, his nose. His skin felt tight and hot.

"You slept with your student." Her voice was firm, resolute. She *still* wouldn't look at him, her hair falling in her face, hiding her like a shield.

Nate picked up his duffel bag—he didn't come over here to fight about this, about any of it. "So you believe it now? Before, you weren't sure but now you are?"

She whipped around to face him. "I went

through your phone, you know. A few weeks ago. You liked a picture of hers. That girl with the white hair and the boobs out to here"—she pushed her hands out in front of her chest, her palms shaking—"I saw it. You *liked* this slutty red lingerie picture."

Nate felt his face pale, the blood drain, and his fingertips tingle. He'd forgotten about that.

It had been an accident. Truly. It was months ago.

He'd woken up at night, three, four in the morning. It was a long-standing habit. He'd picked up his phone, scrolled through his Facebook, his Twitter, Instagram. He remembered the picture, the angle, the eyes looking into the camera, they looked so scared. Like someone was making her do it. That was his initial thought, she was being forced to dress up like that, her breasts pushed up almost to her chin, a red satiny V where her legs met, in a blur at the bottom corner that he couldn't seem to stop looking at. He paused, his thumb on the picture. It had been posted an hour prior. She'd been awake at 2 a.m. on a school day. He pictured her, dressing in her room, for herself or someone else? He had no way of knowing. Later, it was all he could think about: Did someone make her take that picture? He pictured a gun against her back, a knife against her throat. For what reason? It seemed irrational. The next morning, he felt stupid for the thought. It had hardly made any sense. But still. Those eyes.

In the moment, though, his thumb caught, tangled up in the fear in her eyes, beneath the wisp of hair across her face. He pinched his fingers together, then apart on the picture, trying to blow it up, and realized that it wasn't possible. Instead, he took a screenshot, the dull vibration of the picture saved to his file. The favorite heart was illuminated red, and underneath, his username appeared. He panicked, his tongue sticky and dry, and without thinking, he double tapped again. The heart changed back to white, his name was gone. *He thought.* He was sure of it, wasn't he?

In his photo gallery, he opened the screenshot, blew it up. Right at her collarbone, next to the ornate lace of her bra strap, was a circular red dot, covered with makeup, the skin an angry pink bubble.

A cigarette burn.

He'd unliked the picture. Right?

Would she still get notified? He didn't know.

A week later, he'd been standing at the door as the kids filed out. He wore a red polo. She'd touched his sleeve. *You like red?* Her fingernails traced a feather touch against his forearm, making all the hair stand up. Her smile was so coy, so obtuse, he jerked his arm away. He stumbled back, knocking over the small metal trash can.

He couldn't deny that she'd gotten under his skin, that girl.

He worried about it for days, the bright bloom of the red heart under his thumb. When nothing came of it, he forgot.

But Alecia knew? How? He realized, a second too late. The screenshot. He'd never deleted it. Initially, he saved it to show her, to ask her about the burn, maybe even to ask her about the picture itself, didn't it look like someone made her do it? But the idea unsettled something in him, a feeling of wrongness, too many lines crossed, and he'd let it go. Even if it was Lenny. Even if the burn was abuse. But he'd never deleted the screenshot. So many stupid decisions, it was almost astounding.

"It was an accident," he said lamely. Jesus Christ, he didn't even believe himself anymore. He heard all his excuses and half lies, piled up on top of each other like playing cards. The only thing he had control over was how he told the truth. "Seriously. It was an accident. She'd told me about her brother, burning her with a cigarette. I saw a mark on her collarbone and I tried to blow the picture up, but Instagram doesn't work that way. I accidentally 'liked' it. I didn't even realize it at first. I was trying to see the mark on her. Her brother . . . You don't have to believe me, but it's the truth."

She laughed, her hair covering her face, and

she pitched forward, her hands on her knees. The remote clattered to the wood floor and she laughed again, covering her mouth with her palm. When she finally stood up straight, her face was splotched red and white at the same time, her hands on her cheeks, shaking her head back and forth, fast like a seizure.

"You must think I'm so stupid, Nate." Voice high and hysterical.

"Alecia." Nate reached out to touch her but she recoiled and shook a finger at him.

"Don't. Just, leave. Leave us." She pushed past him, back into the kitchen, back to Gabe and her dinner and Nate did as she asked. He left.

He could have begged her. He had half a mind to. The thing was, though, why should he have to? She didn't believe him, no matter what he said. He could have gotten down on his knees and fucking begged. Said he loved her until he ran out of breath. He shouldn't *have* to do that. Even if she had doubts—hell who wouldn't?— she should at least believe him a little bit. At least about the biggest part: he didn't sleep with her.

He stopped at the Quarry Bar, a place a guy could get a drink without any hassle. Without any questions or stares. Plus, no one he knew ever went there. The bar smelled like dank basement. Sweat and beer and sex and spit. He drank two tumblers of scotch *(neat, cold),* fast, like a teenager, and then sat at the bar spinning his empty glass between his palms, waiting for the liquor to take hold and calm his nerves. Then he waited for it to leech out, his vision to clear so he could drive. Nobody said a word to him, which worked out just fine.

He drove home in the dark, on the winding stretch of Route Six, the rain pelting his car, reducing his visibility to nothing. Until he'd seen *her,* white and gleaming, her head like an eagle, stark against the black trees. Her bare legs flanking the white line, the smirk that accompanied her middle finger. That red mouth. All of it was a big *fuck you.*

Now he struggled into a sitting position on the couch, rubbing his face, running his hands through his hair. The back of his eyelids scratched from lack of sleep. What time had he gotten in last night? Two? Three? Maybe later.

He checked his phone; a text from Tripp blinked. He looked around the living room. No Tripp, probably at work.

Where r u? Tried to call.

Then another. And another.

Hey, something weird is going on, call my cell.

Did you see Lucia last night? I'm hearing things. Pick up your phone.

Nate's stomach knotted, taking the breath from his lungs.

She'd pressed her body against his window, so

231

thin and frail, chattering in her clothes. He should have helped her. *I don't belong anywhere.*

She was right, though, that was the thing.

After she'd run into the woods, he'd edged the car along the guardrail and flipped the flashers. He sat, rethinking, second-guessing himself. Then he'd gotten out, the rain stinging his face, his shoulders, soaking his jeans and his boots in a matter of seconds. He leaned over the guardrail and called her name into the inky blackness.

He thought about it, those woods. A million and a half acres of state game lands all in total, much of it wild, dense. Thick brush, few footpaths. He stopped, almost didn't do it.

He'd yelled until his head swam and he felt the veins in his neck pop. *Lucia!* Over and over, his voice swallowed whole by the rain. He hitched one leg over the metal rail, then the other, sliding almost immediately down the muddy embankment, his body somersaulting feet over head halfway. At the bottom, the red blinking of his car looked like miles away. He stood; his bones ached and he stretched his legs, his shoulders. He hadn't fallen like that in years; it seemed to be a skill honed in childhood and left to deteriorate with age.

He might have walked for five minutes into the woods, half running, half walking, calling for her before he realized it was hopeless. Stupid, he was so stupid. She didn't really want his help. She didn't want someone to save her. She preferred victimhood. It got her out a myriad of troubles, from late class assignments to skipping work, to getting drunk at parties and sleeping with men. Boys. Except, *except.* Nate's mind skittered around. He had to go back.

Get back to his car, get to Tripp's, change his clothes, call the police. Maybe go to the station. Tripp was working a double, he could ask for help. Advice.

When he turned around, his car was gone. All he could see in any direction was the black outline of trees against a slightly less black sky, his eyes blurred with the rain. He spun one way, then the other, and then looked up, the air wet, and he gurgled, sputtered, choked until his vision exploded with stars. He took ten steps back the way he'd come, nothing in front of him or behind but gnarled brush.

Something scratched at his arm and he jumped.

In his pocket, he fished out his key chain, a small carabineer, with a mini-LED flashlight. He pressed it on, swung it one way, then the other, illuminating mere feet in front of him, and wondered how long it would last. The rain was rhythmic, falling hard, then soft, a pulse that matched the racing of his heart. Nate pushed forward, in the direction he thought he'd come, walking far longer back than he'd been walking *in,* and that's when he realized he'd gotten himself lost. He stepped over a fallen log that he was sure he hadn't stepped over to get here.

He stood with a hand on his hips and brought the other hand to his head in a long-standing habit of men everywhere: lift his baseball cap, scratch his head, put it back. He realized then that his hat was gone, presumably when he'd fallen, tumbled down the hill, caught in the mud.

His Mt. Oanoke Raiders hat, the burgundy COACH on the back. He'd had it since the first year he'd started coaching. Oh well, if he found the embankment, he'd likely find the hat.

He pushed on through the brush and wondered if he was in fact walking *away* from the road. There was a rustle to his right and he called, *Lucia!* Not expecting an answer.

If he was lost, she was likely lost hundreds of feet ahead of him. He pivoted, walking the opposite direction, figuring he'd have to do it for at least twice as long before he hit the road. *If* he hit the road.

He could just keep doing this, quartering off his walk. He was a math teacher but he grew up in the outdoors. If he walked ten minutes in one direction, he should be able to turn and walk twenty in the opposite and maybe hit *something*. Turn ninety degrees, repeat. If he kept going this way, he'd eventually have to find the road he started from. Eventually.

So this is what he did, periodically flicking on

the flashlight to swing in front of him, but keep his feet planted in the direction he was walking, keeping his orientation. The rain let up. The steady falling of his sneakers against the brush, in the mud, sticks poking at his calves, scratching at his arms, his neck. The skin piercing open with a warm flood. It was almost a comfort, the pain. Like Lucia, those dotted patches of scabby skin along her scalp. He could see it now, the relief that came from physical pain. It drowned out the noise in his head.

When he finally saw it, the tall muddy tower of the embankment, the lights of his car still blinking hypnotically, but faintly, draining the battery on the old Honda, he almost whooped. The relief felt like a high.

He clawed in the squelchy mud, coming up a hundred feet down the road from his car. He scampered over the guardrail and jogged back, his energy renewed. In the car, the engine sputtered and turned over and he flipped on the heat as high as it would go. The hot air blew in his face, his eyes red, his neck burning. His skin doughy and pale, like a dead fish.

He looked at the dash clock, which blinked 2:17 a.m.

He'd been lost for three hours.

CHAPTER 21

Lucia, forever ago

It's hard to figure when everything changed. Lucia spent a lot of time thinking about this.

See the thing is, they all used to be friends in pairs: Taylor and Lucia. Kelsey and Riana. Josh and Porter. But then there was Andrew, who didn't need anyone.

Sometimes Taylor said Andrew was stupid, and although Lucia didn't agree, Taylor was far from the only one. He fooled a lot of people with his eyes half lidded and his deepening voice, that sleepy "what?" that was always followed by a laugh. Everyone else always laughed, but Lucia, she saw him. It was an act.

The mill closed when they were all ten, still kids, riding their bikes to Tibb's shoving their pockets full of penny candy and riding back to Taylor's. Before Mr. Lawson left, Taylor's house was the newest, not the biggest, but the friendliest: plush, plaid couches and lit candles, hot cookies and big, sunny windows. You could forget, for a second, you were in Mt. Oanoke in that house; it smelled like a scratch-and-sniff sticker.

Mrs. Lawson would fuss and fidget and do all the things that Lucia never knew a mother should do: cooked them dinner, poured their milk, and once even sliding a pair of flip-flops into Lucia's backpack because she noticed her heels hanging off the backs of her old ones, her ankles dusty from the summer dirt. When Taylor found them later, digging through Lucia's bag for a pen, all she said was *fucking Jesus.*

Then somehow, eighth grade happened, and that was the beginning of the end. Kelsey went from a little bit fat to curvy in the right places, earlier than everyone else, with this long wavy blond hair like in the magazines that Lucia found in Lenny's room. Kelsey and Josh started hooking up, sneaking off alone, leaving Riana the odd girl out. Near as Lucia can tell, this was the tipping point. When Taylor finally realized Lucia wasn't so great, after all, and Riana was there. It was only a matter of time, really.

They all joined track and that first year, in ninth, Mrs. Lawson paid for Lucia to join, too. Bought her track outfit: blue-and-white little shorts and a tank top, running pants that buttoned down the legs and a nice pair of sneakers. Then the year between ninth and tenth, Mr. Lawson lost all their money and left town and Mrs. Lawson never said another word about it. By then Taylor and Riana were already showing up late to practice, smelling like cigarettes and gum, hairspray and perfume from Riana's mother's bathroom.

Lucia wasn't too upset when Mrs. Lawson didn't sign her up again. She wasn't a distance runner and was the slowest sprinter on the team. Coach Blue hardly looked up from her stopwatch, her mouth curled up and her eyes closed, when Lucia crossed the finish line.

She started going with Andrew and Porter, almost accidentally, while Taylor and Riana were at track. They'd invited her off the cuff— *you coming?*—in the hall, as Taylor and Riana ran for the locker rooms. Then every day after, Lucia wondered when it would end. She hung around too long, waiting for Andrew's voice, *you coming?* Terrified for the day it wouldn't come.

They'd end up in Andrew's bedroom, his parents still at work, his house nothing like Taylor's or Josh's, in the smaller development from the eighties, but still warm with plush carpet you could curl your toes into. Andrew and Porter smoked pot, the smoke sweet and thick, listened to something old, Nirvana or Radiohead from Andrew's iPod. Andrew always said that music from after 2000 was beat, shitty. Ate the freshly baked oatmeal raisin cookies Andrew's mom left out for them.

Until the day Porter was sick with strep throat.

Lucia ended up in Andrew's room, alone,

and she felt the pulse of her heart in her neck, a steady thrumming over which she could hardly hear. His big hands, they seemed bigger than only a week ago, flicking through the songs, looking for the perfect one as she sat cross-legged on his beanbag chair, then stretched her legs out, too skinny in ratty jeans that she stole from the Goodwill, where she'd just started to work shifts in the back room, sorting through other people's smelly, unwashed underwear.

She watched Andrew find something, from a band called Screaming Trees, and watched him talk about grunge and how they all missed the greatest musical decade ever, by mere years. How if he could go anywhere he'd go back to 1993 in Seattle. She watched his mouth form the words, slow and easy, and his eyes blink his lazy, measured way and felt something pull, quick and tight low in her belly. She watched him and he smiled at her as he talked, and she felt the room tilt just a little, which was a feeling she'd never had before.

Lucia felt her breath coming then quick and shallow, like she was afraid to breathe, afraid to move to break the spell.

From then on, she was just a little bit in love with Andrew Evans. In hindsight, she should have been a little less obvious about it, but the next day Porter was back, and even with him hanging around, she watched Andrew's mouth, wondering later, at night, what it would feel like on her mouth. Her neck. Her body.

She could feel the buzz, just under her skin, when she accidentally on purpose sat next to him in the cafeteria. He waited once, by her locker, handed her a pen with a slow, sideways smile and those half-open eyes, and said, "You forgot this in my room yesterday." Amy Pinter—the girl whose locker was next to Lucia's—opened her eyes wide and nudged her friend, and for once, Lucia felt like she wasn't merely tagging along.

It could have been her imagination, but she felt the buzz coming back from Andrew, too. That gaze held a little too long, the way he sometimes walked too slow into the cafeteria, like he was orchestrating their seats, and when they ended up next to each other, he'd give her a little nudge and say, "You again?" but he never did that to anyone else.

Sometimes they'd end up at the mill, in the parking lot, chucking stones at the glass, hollering at the loudest breaks, a forty of Colt 45 in a paper bag clutched in Andrew's fist, the girls passing around Mad Dog 20/20, their lips pink and wide like watermelon. They all dared each other to go in alone, and it was on one of those Saturday nights when the air seemed to zing, when their laughter seemed to bounce around them, when even Taylor was being overly nice.

"Here, you need this." She smiled sweetly, slicking glittery lip gloss across Lucia's mouth, and Lucia felt the pull of anticipation, something sweet and swirling in her center, down her legs and into her toes.

Lucia stood up. "I'll do it, I'll go in." She was feeling bold and, newly, like one of them. Andrew's flirting had elevated her: she was no longer Taylor's weird sidekick but a girl in her own right. She walked in through the ajar steel door, the smell of dust and rotting paper stinging her nostrils. Her head pounded, her hands shaky as she pressed them against her belly, pushing the air out of her lungs. She stood in the first room, the biggest room, with the stainless steel pulper and held her breath. Waiting.

It was that kind of magical night, when she knew how things would unfold, where everything seemed inevitable. He came up behind her, like she knew he would. His hand on her back didn't startle her, and she felt the smile on her face before she turned around and he was there, taller than she thought he'd be, but so close. He smelled like Abercrombie cologne and fabric softener and something lemony and soft.

"What are you doing?" It was a stupid question, but the only one she could think to ask, and she breathed it right into his face, laughing.

"I'm saving you. Didn't you scream? I heard you scream." He leaned closer to her, his lips so close to hers, his head dipped. "I came in to save you."

And that's all he said before he kissed her, his hands then around her waist, down her back, her first real kiss, and it was slow, measured, like Andrew himself, his hands finding their way under her filmy top, inching up to her bra, and she let him. He cupped her, unhooking her bra strap and then easing her back against the cinderblock wall.

She let him do anything he wanted, drunk on his Andrew-ness, the newness of belonging. She was still there, in their first kiss, when she started thinking of their couplehood—like Kelsey and Josh—sneaking away from the group, away from Taylor. She would have something, someone, that Taylor wouldn't.

The idea both excited and terrified her.

When Porter started hollering and making noise outside, they broke apart, Andrew laughed a little, and said, "We should go." He walked out ahead of her and Lucia waited for him to take her hand, but he never did.

What she didn't know then, but she knew now, was that sometimes beginnings and endings feel the same.

On Monday, when Taylor and Riana scampered off to track, she waited in the lobby until long after the final bell. Long after all the other students had cleared out, the buses left, the parking lot had emptied, until she finally started the three-mile walk home. Summer was looming, next year they'd be sophomores, starting to think about college and leaving Mt. Oanoke. Not Lucia, though. She'd be working at the Goodwill until she was old and gray.

She pictured Andrew and Porter, stoned and sleepy in his bedroom without her. Would they talk about her?

She felt the fury rise in her chest, a metallic bitter taste on her tongue. She'd only wait once, she hoped he knew that. One time, one chance. Jimmy taught her that. *Fool me twice, shame on me.*

She can't deny that she looked, though, for those two bobbing heads in front of her, one abnormally tall, one short, dark, and blond, thin and round. She saw nothing.

Her toe kicked it before she saw it, its black wings shining in the sunlight. She bent down and knew it was dead, its eyes frozen open, but unscathed, like it had simply dropped out of the sky. They all came to her that way, perfect, unharmed, but utterly still, like the breath had simply left their little lungs and never come back.

She picked it up, the blackbird. It was still soft, like it had died only seconds ago; the feathers were smooth in her palm, and she ran her finger under its silken wing.

In the distance, she saw Andrew's house, out of her way in the cul-de-sac at the end of the street and began to walk. She tucked the bird in the crook of her arm, like a doll, or a real baby.

She heard the music from his room, heard his laughter. Imagined she could smell the smoke. She could taste that cool pop of raisin and the warm sweet oatmeal on her tongue.

She laid the bird down on the welcome mat (the one that said *Wipe Your Paws*) and wondered if they'd think the cat brought it in, but then decided she didn't care. She nudged it with her toe, almost changed her mind, but didn't.

She ran all the way home.

"What'd you do?" Taylor hissed, dragging Lucia into the bathroom the next day.

"What?" Lucia shook her head, her ears buzzing.

"I know it was you. You have the bird thing. What the fuck, Lulu." Taylor pinched her arm, twisting the skin.

"It wasn't me. They have a cat. It was probably the cat." The skin on Lucia's arm started to welt where Taylor's fingers were.

"You can be such a freak sometimes. Why? Was it because he made out with you at the mill?"

Lucia blinked hard. She hadn't told Taylor. Then, reflexively, "No."

"He makes out with everyone. Did he do that thing with his hand?" She motioned down toward her pelvis and fluttered her eyes. She flipped her hair and looked in the mirror, her reflection watching Lucia, her eyes narrowed. She inspected her face, pulled at her nose, mumbled about her pores. "You're lucky, you know."

Lucia's stomach felt hard and heavy, like she'd swallowed a rock.

"You're so moony over him. We all see it. But you didn't really think, did you?" She turned then, her eyes wide, her mouth open in a little O.

Lucia shook her head again, her mouth dry, a film of hot tears she'd never shed against her eyelids. The warning bell clanged. Taylor turned to leave, leaned in close, her hair soft against Lucia's face, her fingertips against Lucia's arm cool and light.

"I'll drop you so fast, Lucia Hamm. I will. This is high school now." She said it like a warning.

And that's when everything changed.

CHAPTER 22

Bridget, Thursday, May 7, 2015

"It was a poisoned berry bush. By the paper mill, arsenic in the soil, and it poisoned the berries." Dale's face was flushed, breathless with the delivery. Bridget was grading journals, her feet propped up on her desk, her chair leaned back. She read every third one, skimming the rest. So tired of teenage angst.

"What?" Bridget asked, distracted.

"The birds. The DEP figured it out. It's all rumor right now, but they're saying it was an arsenic poisoning. From the paper mill." Dale's hands waved toward the window.

"I'm not sure that makes sense. Wouldn't the water be contaminated, then?" Bridget tapped her pen against her teeth, thinking. They'd taken air, water, and plant samples from around the town for days after, their vans and Tyvek suits all anyone could talk about.

Bridget was beginning to think the town itself was a blight. A poison.

It reminded her of something.

"Dale," she said, but he was already halfway

out the door, hot to be the first to spread two-week-old news that no one cared about anymore. Talk of Nate and Lucia had replaced the birds in the halls, in the cafeteria, the faculty lounge. Everywhere. The story of Lucia's "abilities" had spread, well, like wildfire. She even heard that Lucia's eyes glowed red and she mumbled some kind of spell that everyone, even Principal Bachman, had heard. It was all nonsense, but it seemed like only Bridget treated it that way, brushing off the whispers with a wave of her hand, a little burst of air from the back of her throat in disgust.

They'd hired a substitute to replace Nate. She was young, twenty-two, fresh out of college, scrubbed clean and squeaky. It was almost a mockery. She wondered if they did it on purpose. She was blond and wore turtlenecks. The boys elbowed each other when she walked down the hall and the irony hadn't escaped Bridget.

Dale turned back, poking his head back in, his glasses slid so far down his nose she couldn't see his eyes.

"Have you seen Lucia?" Bridget asked. "She hasn't been in school since the paper incident. Today is day four."

"Hmmm, was she suspended?" Dale asked, obtuse. Deliberately, Bridget thought.

"No. Because Riana almost set her on fire? No, Dale. Lucia was not suspended for that."

"Well, not exactly, and we don't know what happened," Dale stammered, then backed out of the room, waving a little, his smile watery.

Bridget sighed. *Because Lucia was clearly capable of setting things on fire with her mind.* The idea that there were teachers playing into this, well, the whole thing was disgusting.

The phone on her desk buzzed. Her mother-in-law's number, but Bridget declined it with a twinge of guilt. *Sorry, Petra.* The voice mail later: *Have you thought more about a location? Please call, Bridget. Time is running out.*

Bridget deleted the voice mail. She had more important things to take care of. Between classes, she snuck into the office and peeked at the attendance sheets for the week. Lucia's name had been on the list Tuesday, Wednesday, and today. She asked the secretary if anyone tried to contact her.

"How?" Bridget had heard it before, only a few weeks ago. The only number they'd had was Jimmy's.

Bridget thought about how a person could just drift away from their life and leave not one ripple behind.

After the last bell, she packed up her bags, quick, at the last moment, throwing Lucia's black leather-bound journal in.

She drove slowly to Lucia's house, the porch sinking like she remembered, a yawning mouth.

The window dormers were like angry eyes and the upper left one with a cardboard patch reminded her of that nursery rhyme.

Cry, baby cry, stick your finger in your eye.

This town was the curse, not Lucia. In the right dormer, the curtain moved and Bridget thought she saw a face. Lenny. Bridget pounded on the door, but no one came.

She sat in her car, in front of the brown ramshackle house, and called Tripp's phone, letting it ring over and over. She gripped the steering wheel, willing her heart to calm. Her skin buzzing, hot and cold. She pressed a hand to her cheek.

Her phone rang in her palm and she almost answered it, assuming Tripp. *Petra.* Again. Her finger hovered over the red button, shaking in midair. She hit decline.

At Tripp's house, Bridget rang the doorbell, a finger pressed and held there.

Tripp finally came to the door, his face pinked with sleep, his eyes heavy lidded. He wore a faded T-shirt and basketball shorts, barefoot. It felt too intimate, somehow.

"I'm sorry. Were you sleeping? I can come back." Bridget felt her face flush.

"Bridge, what's up?" He opened the door wider, yawning, and motioned her in. She slid past him, into the house.

"I think Lucia's missing?" She came right out with it, but it got hung up at the end, like a question.

"Again?" He lifted up the hem of his shirt and wiped his mouth, a boy gesture, something she'd seen Holden do a million times. "This girl runs off a lot."

"I think it's real this time. There was an incident at school and I haven't seen her in four whole days." Bridget's voice hitched up, a shrill squeak.

"Bridget, are you okay?" His face slackened, worried.

"Everyone thinks I'm going to drive my car off the bridge into the Lackawaxen." She lifted her hair up, sweat popping up at her hairline. She'd been having these hot flashes lately, her hair suddenly sticky at the neck, her cheeks bursting red.

"It might be . . . understandable," Tripp said. Like he would know anything about it, his singly focused life. He didn't, as far as Bridget knew, even have a girlfriend. No one to care about but himself. Bridget tried to envision Tripp taking care of anyone else. The kind of shit-piss-vomit end-of-life care. Bridget fanned herself with her fingers.

"Do you have any water or something?"

Tripp got her a glass of water that he filled from the tap, no ice, and when he handed it to her their fingertips brushed. She downed it in one gulp.

"I think I need to fill out a police report." She handed the glass back to him. "Will you come with me?"

Tripp rubbed his chin, looked out the window above the sink, through the yellow gingham curtains. The sun was burning too bright for such a weird day; the air had a circus-music feel to it.

"Yeah, I can come. But, Bridget, why are you the only one doing all this? What about her family? Other teachers?" He looked back into the living room. "You know Nate is staying here, right?"

Bridget nodded. Alecia had told her, perfunctorily, when she'd called the day before. Her voice had been so flat. *Everything is so different now, you don't even know. I found things.*

Bridget flashed back to Lucia kissing Nate, her hand pulling him against her by his shirt. The way he seemed to lean into her, his body seeking it. His words, later, saying a different thing.

She had asked Alecia what *things,* but she just said, *I don't want to talk about it.* Their conversations were so halted now. Formal. *How is Gabe? He's doing great! How's school? Oh, you know, end of the year coming.* They didn't talk much about Nate, neither of them sure where the other's loyalties would lie. That's the trouble with "couple" friends. When there was no longer a couple, was there still a friendship? She'd asked her once *do you believe Nate?* Alecia just snorted into the phone. *Sometimes yes, sometimes no.* Which didn't really answer the question, but Bridget, being southern, didn't press even though she wanted to. *Nate's situation,* as they called it, flowed between them like a wide open river, fast and furious. They didn't cross it, or talk about it, except in roundabout ways *(we should get together soon),* but sometimes, Bridget could hardly hear Alecia over the loudness of the rushing water. They talked louder to cover the noise but it all felt a little bit hollow.

Bridget missed her real friendship, the one before the river. And the past few days, Bridget couldn't breathe and maybe if she talked to someone about it, it would get better. If she could just say *I don't know why but I can't breathe,* maybe she'd be able to breathe again. But Alecia was in the thick of it, and maybe she wasn't the right person to talk to anyway.

"Where is Nate now?" Bridget looked around, seeing no trace of him at all.

Tripp just shrugged. "I haven't talked to him yet today. I got home from work, I worked a double. He was passed out on the couch. I went to bed. He's gone now. Sometimes he leaves a note." He gestured to the empty table.

"Tripp, do you believe him?" Bridget hadn't meant to ask it, didn't even know what she'd hoped to accomplish.

"I do." Tripp straightened and did that thing with his shirt again, lifting it to his mouth. Bridget could see his stomach, muscled and carved in a new way. She wanted to press her palm to the ridges, feel the dew on his skin. Feel how it was different. Holden had been fit, he could run miles and often did, but he was rounded in the belly, soft with age. She used to move her hands around it, holding it like a globe. Tripp was still talking. "Nate is complicated. He wants everyone to like him. I think he was trying, in a weird way, to rescue her. But, he, uh, sometimes goes too far."

Bridget didn't ask what that meant. She didn't want to know.

"I just mean that he tries too hard," Tripp clarified.

"You don't think he slept with Lucia?" Bridget asked.

"He says he didn't. I've never known him to be a liar. I can't ask too many questions, you know?" He shrugged and saw her face. "Because I'm a cop. I'm not on the investigation, but if I knew anything definitive, I'd have to report it, right?"

"Tripp, I think she's missing. I went to her house. It's just that creepy weird brother there. He didn't answer the door." She gulped, her throat thick. Something occurred to her, an awful, clawing feeling. "Do you think . . . ? Do you think it's possible that Nate is with her . . . ?"

Tripp blinked, then puffed out his cheeks. Looked around his kitchen like he'd never seen it before.

"I'll get dressed," he said.

"Tripp, wait," Bridget called to his back, and he stopped, turned his head so she could see his profile. "Do you think we should call Nate?" Where did Tripp's loyalty lie? Would he risk his job for his friend? Would either of them? It really didn't seem possible that Nate and Lucia were together.

Tripp didn't say anything for the longest time and Bridget stared at his back, the broad expanse between his shoulders, the flex of his calf muscles and the whiteness of one heel, then the other, as he shifted his weight, the curve of his ankle.

Finally, he answered her. "No."

Mt. Oanoke police station sat behind a Texaco on Route 543. A wide, flat building, it reminded Bridget of a strip mall with a trailer hanging off the side like an afterthought. Inside, it smelled like fresh paint and new carpeting. The front desk was encased in a glass window, like a doctor's office, and the room behind it boasted open cubicles and bright blue paint. It was such a surprisingly cheerful place, maybe the most uplifting place in all of Mt. Oanoke.

Tripp leaned over the desk and called out to someone in the back. "Is Harper around?" Bridget heard the low murmur of another voice and then the sound of a lock being disengaged. Tripp motioned to follow him through the metal door.

They walked to his desk and Bridget hung back, out of place. Tripp's cube was low and simple, a computer, policy papers thumbtacked to the sides, and a single framed photo of a beautiful Asian woman and a girl about ten years old. Tripp caught her staring.

"That's my daughter and my ex. They live in Jersey, and I, uh, well, had some alcohol issues back then. I see her sometimes, but not as much as I'd like." He tapped the frame. "I'm working on it." As an afterthought, he added. "That's her mother." His voice, as well as his expression, remained unreadable.

Bridget was shocked. She'd never known Tripp to be anything other than a bachelor, but then again, she hadn't known him a decade ago. She didn't ask if they'd been married, but it pulled at her. She wanted to know.

A tall, thin man in khakis and a dress shirt came out of a conference room in the back and walked purposefully toward them.

"Hey, Tim. This is Bridget Peterson. Bridget,

this is Detective Tim Harper." They shook hands; his grip was firm but quick. Tripp explained to Bridget that Detective Harper was investigating Nate's case. Harper led them back to the room he'd emerged from and motioned for them to sit around an oval conference table. He turned the blinds closed and the effect was immediate. The room felt like a closet.

"Bridget, what seems to be the issue?"

"I had a concern over the whereabouts of Lucia Hamm." She pushed at a ridge in the table with her fingernail. "I'm confused about one thing, though. Is Nate being investigated in a criminal case? I was under the impression that Lucia being eighteen would eliminate any criminal wrong-doing." She treaded carefully, playing dumb.

Detective Harper leaned back, folding his hands over his midsection. "Well, I can't out-right comment on an ongoing investigation, but in Pennsylvania it is a violation of the penal code to abuse authority given to a teacher at a public institution. It's called institutional sexual assault."

"So Nate could go to jail?"

"I can't say that, Mrs. Peterson. I can only say the investigation is ongoing."

Tripp shifted in his chair. Bridget wondered how everyone had known about this. It hadn't been in the paper. She thought of Dale, his nose twitching, almost gleeful over the word *rape*.

Detective Harper opened his laptop and eyed her over his bifocals. "You want to fill out a missing-persons report?"

"Yes. I think so. She has a history of running away, so it might be all for nothing." Bridget held her purse in her lap and realized she was gripping the strap, white-knuckled.

"It's okay, just tell me everything you know or think you know and we'll decide what to do with the information from there." The detective furrowed his brow, staring at the screen, and pecked a few keys. "We have to do everything electronically now; you can ask Officer Harris here how much that delights me." He gave a wan little smile and Bridget tried to smile back. He hit a key and then turned to Bridget. "Go on."

Bridget told him about Lucia, the things she'd heard at school, the love note, her home life. She told him about the fight in the hallway, the burning paper, the coiling smoke, the way no one but Bridget seemed to believe her. Then again, no one but Bridget seemed to believe Nate, either, but Bridget didn't mention that to the detective. And she definitely did *not* tell Detective Harper about the kiss; in fact, didn't bring up Nate at all. She told him of the first time Lucia ran away, her campsite at the paper mill. She was careful only to include things she'd seen firsthand.

He quietly typed while she talked, asking few questions. When she was done, he gave her a look. "Do you think this has anything to do with Nate Winters?"

"No. I don't know. I don't think so. I just know that someone should be looking for her. Or at least care that she's missing."

"But have you seen Mr. Winters today?"

"No. Why would I?"

"It was just a question, Ms. Peterson." He smiled, thin without teeth. "Did you report to the school that you believed Ms. Hamm to be missing?"

"I asked the principal. The secretary. The problem is no one knows how to get in touch with her. Her father's cell phone is the only one on file and Jimmy's, well, he's gone." She pushed her palms down on her knees. "I went to Tripp's house to see if he thought I should come to you?" It accidentally came out like a question.

"I see. And neither of you has seen Mr. Winters today, despite him staying with you, Officer Harris?"

Tripp shrugged. "I, uh, actually haven't really talked with him in a few days, but I've been taking all Ratzen's shifts while he's away, you know that. I see him when I come home in the morning. He's still asleep on the couch. The past few days, I wake up, I go back to work. By the afternoon, he's usually gone. Today, Bridget was knocking on the door and he was gone."

"Where does he go?"

"I don't know. I guess the gym. We've had a few text conversations, *there's leftovers in the fridge,* or whatever." Tripp rubbed his hands together.

Detective Harper gave a *hmmmm* and typed a few things on the computer. The clock behind Bridget's head clicked with the seconds and the silence stretched out, long and thin, and Bridget felt her lungs tighten.

"And you last saw Lucia Hamm when, Mrs. Peterson?" Harper had already asked her this, but Bridget answered again.

"Friday. The argument in the hallway when someone set a paper in her hand on fire."

"You said Riana Yardley, correct?"

"That's who the fight was with, yes. Riana claims it caught fire . . . by itself."

Detective Harper raised his eyebrows and shook his head, mumbled *teenagers.* Bridget wanted to grip his forearm. These weren't fifteen-, sixteen-year-olds. They were seventeen, many eighteen. Looking toward the horizon of freedom, Mt. Oanoke already behind them, nipping at their heels. They weren't looking back. Which is why none of the venom against Lucia made sense. In a matter of mere weeks, they could all choose to never see her, think of her again.

Then again, Bridget had experienced firsthand Lucia's personal brand of strangeness, the way she could needle a person, get under their skin.

But then she heard Taylor's voice, *Sometimes I think it's all she has.* Bridget wondered if Taylor was right, that fear and hate were at least better than apathy.

"Well, Ms. Peterson, Officer Harris, we'll look for her. Look into it, go to her house. She's eighteen, so she's free to drop out of school and leave town. But considering the allegations at the moment, this will be taken seriously, I can assure you."

That didn't make Bridget feel any better. It seemed like she was choosing Lucia's safety over the appearance of Nate's innocence, which was never her intention. It seemed as though she was being dismissed.

She stayed, stuck to the chair. Waiting, wanting to say something else.

"We'll call you if we need anything else," Detective Harper said finally. Tripp guided Bridget out, through the maze of cubicles.

As they were leaving, Detective Harper said something to Tripp, which sounded like, *it'll come together.*

They climbed into Tripp's truck in the parking lot, and Tripp put the keys in the ignition and didn't turn the engine over. His hand rested on his knee, flexing and unfurling his fingers, and Bridget watched them. His knee was wide, and even through the denim she could see the thick rope of muscle in his thigh, his knuckles digging into it. She watched his face. He looked at her, his eyes big, his face stricken.

"I have to tell you something, Bridge. I couldn't have said it before, I guess." He shifted up on his thigh a bit to look at her. "I'm in a spot, though. It's kind of terrible."

"I don't understand." Bridget said.

"You know how I said I've been working doubles all week?"

Bridget nodded.

"Monday night, the desk clerk fielded a call from Nate. He said he was on Route Six and he saw Lucia. And she ran into the woods."

"Wait." Bridget shook her head, to clear it. "Nate *saw* her? Why wouldn't you tell me this? I never would have gone to the police." She pressed her back up against the window, the door of the truck, the anger quick and hot beneath her breastbone.

"Bridget," Tripp raked a hand through his hair. "I *am* the police. You came to *me*. I had to let you report a missing person. I couldn't tell you what was already being investigated."

"You set me up," Bridget accused.

"There's no setup. I couldn't tell you what was going on until you talked to the detective. I could lose my job. I'm trying to do the right things here, but this is . . . complicated." Tripp scrubbed at his cheek, the stubble making a scratching sound. "I've barely even seen Nate, talked to

261

Nate. I'm working so much and when I get home, he's gone."

"You're saying that everyone knows that Lucia is missing already?" she asked, her voice sounding far away, underwater.

"No, not really. The call was suspicious, they called him back a few times but he didn't answer. Eventually they sent a squad car out but didn't find anything. They checked attendance records and she had been in school on Monday. She was out on Tuesday, but that's not really a crime. So until now, there wasn't much to investigate. Does that make sense?"

"Until me, you mean."

"We just know that according to your time-table," Tripp's mouth slacked, his voice slow and sluggish. "Nate was the last person to see her."

CHAPTER 23

Alecia, Thursday, May 7, 2015

In another life, Alecia cared about Thursdays. On Thursdays, there used to be happy hours and late nights over Jack and Cokes, cigarettes and boozy, furtive whisperings while her coworker stole kisses from the guy in Content Management, you know the blond one with the cute mole-slash-beauty mark? Followed by slightly embarrassing Friday mornings and furtive, giggling conversations in the ladies' room until it was Thursday night and time to do it all over again, either with the same guy or a different guy, it didn't matter either way. They were young then.

But now, Mondays looked like Thursdays looked like Wednesdays, the only difference between them being what was scheduled for Gabe that day. So sometimes Alecia forgot the days of the week altogether. When the doorbell rang on Thursday and it was Vi, Nate's mom, she didn't think twice about it. She didn't think about how Vi should be working—she was a receptionist at a dental office and worked every day, despite her sixty-four years, because the paper mill killed Bob Winters. Just keeled over one day at work; *it was the fumes,* she'd said to anyone who would listen. Even now, if you got her going, she'd tell you. She had to work, she should have been going into the prime of her life but the mill killed Bob and she had to work.

Had Alecia stopped to really think about it, she would have realized that Vi had a reason for showing up at 9 a.m. on a Thursday.

Violet Winters had been aptly named: in the face of any hardship, she shrank. She wasn't the kind of person to "make a fuss" and waved off even the biggest inconveniences. She had one son, one child, her light and golden life.

"Where's Nate?" Vi asked, standing in the hallway, clutching her purse to her chest. She wore scrubs and nursing clogs, even though all she ever did was answer the phone.

Alecia waved her hand toward the door. "He's out, Vi. Hold on, I'll get Gabe. He'll be happy to see you." Which wasn't really true; Gabe was only ever over-the-moon happy to see one person.

"I came to talk to you."

Alecia had no idea what Vi knew, but it hadn't quite been a week since the paper published Nate's story and only a few days since Nate was "put on leave," so Alecia didn't consider it her responsibility to call her mother-in-law and tell her that her son was sleeping with his student and might be fired. She slotted that in her husband's column of responsibility and moved on with her day. But here Vi stood, worried and uncertain, and somehow this, too, had become her job.

"Oh." Alecia turned and walked away from her. "In that case, I'll make tea."

Alecia really only drank tea around two people: Vi (Lipton) and Bridget (loose-leaf herbal blends that Bridget invented). She boiled the pot and let it whistle, and meanwhile called for Gabe again. He was in his room, oddly quiet, and Alecia was just so tired that she'd sat on the couch maybe a half hour ago and hadn't even gotten up to check on him, even though a half hour is way too long to leave Gabe unchecked.

Vi followed her, her footsteps small and silent.

"How are you holding up?" Vi finally asked, and Alecia felt relieved that she wouldn't have to play detective to figure out what Vi knew.

"Oh you know. Just fine and dandy. I mean it's a fairly common event when a gal finds out her husband has been sleeping with a student." Alecia yanked open the refrigerator door and poured milk into a crystal creamer. When she shut the door with her foot, she could see Vi's face, the way her eyes had widened, horrified, or her mouth hung open, then closed, then open again. Her shoulders had slacked and she leaned against a chair.

"You can't . . . believe her, can you?" Vi shook

her head, but her voice shook, and Alecia almost laughed.

"Of course I can. You can't believe *him* can you?" Alecia said this even as she felt the prick of doubt, the same one she'd been feeling for a week now, even when her mouth was insisting Nate was guilty, to Bridget, now to Vi, a few small cells in her brain were shouting with protest. It was a dissonance she couldn't reconcile, and it was enough to drive her crazy. She'd been wanting someone to prove her wrong, to show her with hard evidence that Nate could not have done these things. But so far, no one had.

Of course Vi would believe her son. Of course she would have gotten the story from him. She looked wildly around the kitchen, craned her thin, veiny neck toward the living room, and Alecia realized that Nate had told her *part* of the truth, but not the whole truth. Not the part where he wasn't living here.

Vi patted her blond hair, a round bowl cut that looked like a helmet, her short, squared fingernails flittering. "He's my son. Of course I believe him. He's always been this way, sticking his neck out for people that don't deserve it."

Alecia gasped, thinking at first that Vi meant her, but realizing too late that Vi meant *her*—Lucia what's-her-name, the sexy weirdo.

"Vi, I can assure you that Nate enjoyed this

particular charity act, whatever it was." She busied herself gathering sugar and spoons and set them up on the kitchen island. All this civility over such an ugly conversation that Alecia had run out of patience for.

"Alecia!" Her lip trembled and her eyes, limned in red, twitched. Alecia realized then how fragile Vi looked, how pale, how shaky.

"Vi, I'm sorry . . ." Although she wasn't really sorry at all. Alecia squared her shoulders, and with her palms on the cold Formica countertop, said, "If you want to find Nate, he's probably at Tripp Harris's house. Remember Tripp? The Mt. Oanoke cop? He's staying there for a while."

"You kicked him out? Now? He needs you, Alecia. He needs you to believe him. He told me that; he cried."

"I believe he cried to you, Vi. I really do believe that." Alecia stirred her tea, blew across the top to cool it, but Vi remained standing, unmoved.

"He didn't tell me he moved out. He just told me what the papers were saying, what that *slut*"—Vi spit the word out, her eyes pinched shut at the violence of it—"was saying. She's lying. You have to realize that." Her voice was edging louder, maybe the loudest Alecia had ever heard it in her and Nate's eight years of marriage.

"Violet, listen to me. Your son might not be guilty of everything they're accusing him of, but he's guilty of some of it. I cannot figure out which parts of his stories are true when he is here in this house. Do you understand? I've found credit card statements and Instagram posts and evidence that *something* was going on, but I can't be alone with my thoughts, my own brain, with him rattling around here pleading his own case twenty-four-seven. Until I know more, he's out. He's staying with Tripp and we can talk in a few weeks when I've got my own head on straight. I have a son with special needs who demands my attention fourteen out of twenty-four hours a day. He comes first."

"That's the trouble, though, with you and Nate," said Violet. "Nate has never come first. Not since Gabe was born. Not one day since he was born." She pointed her finger at Alecia's chest, her mouth pinched, angry. "You can't forsake your own marriage."

"He is your *grandson*. He is not like other boys. He needs more than most kids. He needs his mother—"

"He needs his parents to be married! You are sacrificing your marriage to your child! Can't you see that, Alecia?" Big, fat tears dripped down her cheek, her chin trembling. "You are sacrificing *my boy* for *your boy*."

"Your boy is a liar. And maybe an adulterer. And maybe, in the state of Pennsylvania, a *criminal*." Alecia shouted this last part and felt immediate regret. Violet wilted, her fingertips gripping the countertop. It was too much confrontation, a wintery blast of reality on her velvety cheeks.

A crash, followed by a piercing wail came from upstairs. A second later, the doorbell rang, a long and insistent tone, followed by a sharp rap on the glass pane.

"What the hell?" Alecia put her hand to her forehead, just for a second to calm her buzzing brain. "Violet can you get the door, I have to see what happened to Gabe." The crying had stopped but Alecia hurried past her.

Violet moved through the kitchen, the living room, and the front hall, hot on Alecia's heels. Alecia was halfway up the steps when Violet said, "Oh dear God, Alecia." And the tone in her voice stopped Alecia cold on the seventh step. She turned around and Violet's face was even paler, had that been possible.

Her mouth seemed not to move when she said, "It's the police."

For whatever reason, Gabe had been trying to align his toy construction vehicles along the top of the window molding. He'd balanced himself between the desk and the metal radiator in Alecia's bedroom and it was a wonder he didn't crack his head open when he fell. She calmed him, kissed his cheeks, and led him back downstairs.

Vi stood in the middle of the living room with a rumpled man in khakis. "Alecia, this is Detective Harper." She seemed not to know what to do with her hands and she wrung them in front of her, then crossed them around her middle.

"Hello," Alecia said. Gabe clapped loudly next to her and she attempted to shush him with a gentle hand to his head. "Vi, can you take Gabe back upstairs so we can talk?"

Vi directed Gabe out of the room, under squawking protest, and she heard his heavy clomping on the wooden steps.

"Do you want tea?" Alecia asked, averting her eyes, and started toward the kitchen, motioning for the detective to follow her. He did. "I just boiled a pot."

"Tea would be fine, Mrs. Winters."

She gestured toward the kitchen island and Detective Harper took a seat in one of the metal-backed chairs. While Alecia poured two mugs, she was able to study him out of the corner of her eye. Tall, thin, maybe sixty. He wore wireless framed glasses and an unkempt mustache. He looked like an insurance salesman rather than a detective, but it was the keen blue eyes behind the glass that made her hands shake as she scooped sugar. When she set the ceramic mug in front of him, it clattered on the wooden countertop.

He seemed nice and comfortable with the silence.

Alecia wiped her hands on her jeans. "What can I help you with, Detective?" she finally asked. She remained standing across the island. The other chair would be too close, too intimate.

"I'm here to ask you about your husband, Mrs. Winters. And Lucia Hamm."

Alecia stared into her mug, the surface ringed and rippling from Gabe's heavy running upstairs. She'd gotten so used to it she hardly realized he shook the floor anymore. Detective Harper looked around their small, thin-walled townhouse, the teetering clutter on every flat surface: papers and envelopes and folders and bills and toy trucks and felt markers—always markers everywhere—and felt the apples of her cheeks grow hot.

"What's to ask? I don't know anything." Alecia shrugged.

"You might. Tell me about your husband. Where is he now?"

Alecia felt a stab of annoyance. "He's staying with a friend, Tripp Harris. I assume you know that already."

"Why?"

"Because I'm unsure where our marriage will end up. Because I don't know what happened with that girl."

"Do you believe him?"

"Mostly, yes. But we've been less than perfect

271

for a long time. I need space to think, that's all. It's temporary."

"What kind of troubles?" Detective Harper pulled out a small notebook and a Bic from his shirt pocket.

"I hardly see how or why that matters. Just standard-issue troubles. Are you married, Detective?"

Harper nodded. "Twenty-two years."

"Then you know. It's not all skipping through meadows."

"No." He smoothed the ends of his mustache with his fingers and wrote in his notebook. "But I've never asked her to leave so I could 'think.' "

"Then you're a better man than me. Which is fine."

"Mrs. Winters, where was your husband on Monday night? Did you see him?" His voice was short, the banter was over. Alecia was relieved, she wanted him to just get to the point.

"He came over around six. I was making Gabe dinner and he showed up, no call or anything, to get clothes. It threw me. We had a fight."

"About what?"

"Who knows?" Alecia traced the handle of the mug with her finger. "Our life. Him not being here. The girl."

"What about the girl?"

"He just denies it and I can't make sense of it, that's all."

"I'm going to need you to be more specific," Detective Harper said. He sat up straighter, his patience with her waning.

"I can't be! He came over, I was mad, I picked a fight. He asked me if I believed him and I said I didn't know. It's literally the same argument over and over again." Alecia felt the back of her knees sweat; a bead between her breasts rolled into her bra.

"No new information?" he asked, sounding skeptical.

"No," Alecia lied. She had no intention of helping them arrest her husband, but she flashed on the Instagram picture and Nate's plea, *it was an accident.* It might have been the truth, who was she to decide?

"Mrs. Winters, have you seen Lucia Hamm?"

"God, no. I've never seen her at all in real life. Only pictures."

"What pictures?"

Shit. "I looked her up on social media," Alecia admitted. This part was true. "She's a teenager. You know, bedroom eyes, cleavage, the works. She's got that hair. Crazy blond, it looks white." She bumped her mug with a shaky hand, the tea splashing on the counter. "She's got a look about her, though. Something in her eyes seems off."

Harper was quick, flat with his reply. "How so?"

"Just, I don't know. They're . . . empty.

Soulless. Don't you think?" Alecia searched the detective's face. It remained impassive. "Well, anyway."

"What time did your husband leave here on Monday night?" Harper asked, shifting in his seat.

"I'm not sure. Maybe six thirty? He didn't stay very long. Gabe was happy to see him and mad when he left." Correction, Gabe was inconsolable when he left. For two hours. She didn't add the part where she almost texted Nate not to come over anymore. That she'd bring him his clothes. Anything but throw Gabe into another fit. Her eyes skimmed to the back door, the missing glass panel that she'd duct taped over. Harper followed her gaze.

"Your son do that, ma'am?"

"He . . ." She didn't know how to answer that. He'd thrown an IKEA kitchen chair at it, the leg cracking the glass, splintering it outward until she screamed, the walls shaking with it.

He turned a page in his notebook and this, somehow seemed bad to her. That he would turn a page. *The investigation took an unexpected turn.*

"He's *five*," Alecia said finally, her teeth clenched. "Do you know about autism spectrum disorder? These children can be violent. They are frustrated. That's all I plan to say about my son."

He wrote, a wild, loopy scrawl for a moment

and then flipped the page back and forth.

He gave her a smile, quicksilver. "That's fine, Mrs. Winters. You were home all night?" He thought for a moment, then added, "With your son?"

"Yes of course. I can barely find a sitter for him in the daytime." Alecia felt the hair on the back of her neck rise, a prickling sense that this was not routine. That this was something more, something bigger, darker. "What's going on? I thought you were investigating Nate and this alleged relationship. Why are you really here?"

The detective leaned back against the chair, the cheap metal creaking with the effort to keep him upright. He watched her carefully. "Because the last time anyone saw Lucia Hamm was Monday night. She's missing, Mrs. Winter."

Alecia felt the world tilt just a bit. She gripped the edge of the island for support. "Missing?"

"Not going to school, not at home. A teacher at the school filled out a report."

"Which teacher?" Alecia asked, sharp. She knew before she asked, before Harper said another word.

"Bridget Peterson. You're friends, right?" He raised his mug, slurped loudly on the now-cold tea.

Alecia didn't answer him. Instead, she pressed her palm to her brow bone where a cluster headache started to pound. *Bridget?* She had to know how this would look for Nate. The girl had likely skipped town. *What the fuck?*

Detective Harper wasn't done. "The last *person* to see her alive, that we know of, is your husband, Mrs. Winters."

CHAPTER 24

Bridget, Thursday, May 7, 2015

The mill had ceased production in 2005 and now it stood, forgotten, its exterior failing it in innumerable ways. The brick crumbling and the mortar giving way. The windows were soaped and broken, some fully punched out, some jagged and peaked. A large chemical tank stood rusting, the pipes skewed, uneven, their connections ripped and battered from winters in the mountains. Along the far side, overflowing into the parking lot, was a pile of blackened and rotting pallets, the weeds growing between the cracks, winding around the wood.

Even the air felt dusty in her lungs.

The sky had turned gray, the air warm and rumbling with the soft hint of a distant thunderstorm, and Bridget rolled down her car window. She could hear the dam behind the mill, a loud constant that drowned out birds, insects, other people, leaving behind only a whooshing silence. The parking lot was deserted, which wasn't unusual, but Bridget sat in her car with the windows down, simply listening. If she closed her eyes, she could be anywhere: a beach, a spectacular waterfall in Hawaii (not that she'd ever been), the bank of the Flint River in Georgia, her feet ankle deep in gray-black clay mud. If she closed her eyes, she could be seventeen again, lying down in that muck, her hair tangled in the leaves and the rocks and the mud, her mouth and tongue seeking a boy's. What was his name? Ricky Tomlin. Sweet Ricky Tomlin, a boy himself, but with a man's wants, and those hands—God he knew what he was doing. Bridget could practically feel the mud, cold and chalky on her mouth.

If she closed her eyes, she could remember being seventeen. Eighteen. In love.

Everything now was so different: social media, the Internet, texting. It all sharpened people's edges, made them the opposite of social. Turned them feral.

Bridget got out of the car, shutting the door carefully behind her. She made her way across the parking lot, her sandaled feet crunching on stones and hardened dirt, the dust kicking up when she walked. Today, thankfully, she'd worn jeans to school, and although it was close to five o'clock, the looming summer meant longer days, and the air felt thick, almost viscous. She could taste it.

It was easy to remember being eighteen, that was the thing. It was harder to remember being in love as an adult. Easier to remember Holden the way she'd met him under the blazing southern sun, his Yankee white skin blistering with the heat of it. On the patio of a Mexican chain restaurant, where the waiters slapped a straw sombrero on each of their heads and sang "Happy Birthday" in unison to the two of them, a table apart. He'd bought her a margarita; it had been her twenty-second birthday, his twenty-seventh, but it was *their birthday,* and this above all seemed to mean something hugely profound. Only a few years removed from Aunt Nadine's mysticism, she'd felt so certain that she and Holden had been fated to be together from the moment she saw him.

Remembering the early days of summer love and long nights in wet grass under black skies kissing and kissing and kissing with nowhere to be and no one to answer to. That was easier than remembering later, when love felt like something wet and slick in her hand. When they would fight until 2 a.m. until one of them fell asleep midstonewall, when they didn't even have "real" things to fight about yet. After that she'd felt the early doubts sneak in, that maybe fate isn't what held a marriage together. That sharing the same birthday didn't mean they were destined for each other, that it didn't mean anything at all.

Maybe a month before he was diagnosed, she'd found something. A single broken acrylic fingernail in his car, painted red and sheared angrily from the base. He'd been at a conference the week before and lost in his own head since he'd been back. She prodded him but he blamed it on feeling sick—intermittently nauseous and tired—until he'd snapped back at her. She kept that broken fingernail in the fleece of her bathrobe pocket, waiting for the right time to bring it up, and she'd find herself rubbing the nail between her thumb and forefinger like it was the silk edge of a security blanket for weeks. The right time never seemed to happen.

Then she found something else, a business card in his pocket from a radiology group from somewhere in New York. But that wasn't the interesting part. The interesting part was the writing on the back, a woman's handwriting, and all it said was *Watercress, 6:30*. Which again by itself could have been anything. But the fingernail and the business card together made her skin crawl. The handwriting was loopy but neat and almost fanciful. She kept that, too, and a week later finally looked it up. It was a bar near the medical conference but not one on the charge cards or the bank statement. She supposed he could have not gone to Watercress at 6:30, and that would have been the simplest explanation, but her sixth sense tingled anyway.

So Bridget did the worst thing she could have done and instead of asking him about it, she pulled out Aunt Nadine's tarot and gave herself a reading. When she dealt the lovers card and the chariot reversed, she put the cards away and squared her shoulders and prepared to confront Holden the minute he came home.

Except he came home and sat her down and told her he'd been diagnosed with stage III pancreatic cancer—the worst kind of cancer there was—but that he was going to beat it. She tucked the fingernail and *Watercress 6:30* into the silky bag along with Aunt Nadine's deck, then placed it in the bottom of her underwear drawer. Their life became chemo and radiation and surgery, something called a Whipple procedure, and diet modification. She learned new words like *bilirubin, cachexia, protease.* She forgot (almost) entirely about *Watercress 6:30.* Almost.

Sometimes she wondered if the worst part wasn't that he died, but rather that he died before she knew if he'd stopped loving her.

She cupped her hands around her eyes and peered into the mill through a broken window, searching for remnants of Lucia. Why had she come? What would she say if she found her? She didn't know.

But she did know that Nate was in trouble, more so than before, if that were even possible. It was no accident that it was Detective Harper who took her statement and then followed her out the door. Back at Tripp's, she'd all but run to her car, wanting to avoid any run-in with Nate, but also because Tripp was getting to her. Something had shifted, ever so slightly, and she wasn't sure how to put it all back the way it was. She needed to be away from him and Nate and this whole thing, except she was pulled here, to the mill, *just to check* she kept telling herself. A quick look around and then she'd leave.

She saw the flash of white on the other side, the window to her left, but it was opaque, heavy and gray, and she couldn't get a better look. She moved down the line, the brick crumbling beneath her palm, and looked through the bottom panel, splintered in like it had been hit with a baseball or a stick. She knew the boys threw stones at the windows, accumulating points for a good loud break. The white flashed again, soft and downy, and Bridget's heart skipped. She heard the distant pattering of feet so she called out, "Lucia!" with an overwhelming sense of déjà vu.

The window at the far end was punched all the way in, the wooden lattices splintered at the edges and wide enough for an adult to climb through. Bridget was tentative with her footing, and the jagged glass scratched along her shirt, nearly cutting through to her skin, but she made it in, only a two-foot drop to the floor.

Inside, she called out again, the building blocking out the sounds from the dam, her voice tinny and hollow bouncing against the cement.

The room was darker than she'd thought, the sun having long been hidden behind twilight clouds, and she squinted trying to make out anything. From another room, or maybe the one she was in, she heard a rustling, and she spun one way then the other, convinced already that she'd made a mistake in being here. She followed the rustling, trying to steady her breath, which seemed to be coming in quick bursts, and called, "Lucia!" again, just to make sure. There was no reply.

Bridget navigated around the stainless steel beams positioned every ten feet or so in the enormous concrete room. The floor was littered with cardboard tubing, various diameters, and if she wasn't careful, she'd roll right over one and break a leg.

The next room was filled with stainless steel machinery. Large steel tanks were sunk into the concrete floor, the steel of their caps rusted and thin. Piping, four feet in diameter, connected one tank to the other, a remnant of a mechanical assembly line ending in the pulp room. Bridget ran her flashlight beam into one of the ragged openings, wondering what lay beneath the ground. What lived in those caverns—animals? People?

She shuddered. Behind a beam flashed that white again, quiet and quick. Bridget followed it, whispered "Lucia," the rustling of a soft step guiding her deeper into the mill. The air thickened and she turned the corner, expecting to see the girl, crouching, terrified.

The thing flew at her before she knew what it was, shrieking and wild. Bridget screamed and covered her face.

Someone grabbed her from behind, pulling her down.

"Jesus Christ, Bridget. I can't keep following you all over hell and creation. You're going to get yourself killed." Tripp's hands were on her biceps, his fingers digging into her flesh.

The white thing, the thing that flew at her, toddled away. A goose. Not Lucia. She'd been tracking a goose.

"A snow goose in May?" Bridget asked.

"A loner, maybe." Tripp shrugged, his breath at her ear. "Lost?" The goose bleated in the corner, like them, looking for a way out. They'd come in here in the daylight, ventured in far too deep, and now the exit seemed impossibly far away and cloaked in darkness.

Bridget struggled to calm her racing heart. "I really thought I'd find her here," she said lamely.

"She might be here, but we won't find her tonight."

"What do we do with the goose?" He hadn't let her go, and for a second, Bridget let herself lean back into him. His skin smelled mossy, a waxy, soapy smell.

"We have to leave it, if we stay here any longer,

it'll get dark and we'll be stuck. Don't worry, he got in, he'll get out. He's weeks away from his flock, though." Tripp said into her hair. "The guy is pissed; listen to him. We couldn't get near him if we wanted."

Bridget didn't move and was suddenly tired enough to lie down, right in the dark, in the dust and the steel and the warmth of Tripp's arms and take a nap. He stepped back, putting space between them.

"Come on, Bridge, it's about to get full-blown dark out. We'll be in deep shit then." He took her hand and pulled her gently from the steel machines, rusted stuck in time, to the open room they'd come from. Bridget took one last look in the lost goose's direction, its cry growing more distant as they navigated the mill debris, away from it. She couldn't help but feel sorry for it, wandering among the man-made landscape, with the natural sounds of the dam and other birds close enough to hear and unable to find his way out.

In the parking lot, Tripp turned to her at her car. "Dinner?"

"What?" She'd been thinking of Lucia, and if she was honest, about Nate. Where he was right now, where Lucia was right now, if they were together. If they were *together* together. She hadn't realized how firmly the doubts had taken hold, but now they were there, solid as though they'd always been there, and she found if she was honest, she no longer truly believed in him.

"I said dinner? The *543?*" Tripp repeated as Bridget started to shake her head no. "You have to eat no matter what, right?"

Bridget felt her phone vibrate in her pocket, and without looking at the display, declined the call. Petra had already called three times that day alone.

She followed his truck in her car for the three miles into town. She thought maybe she should call Nate, tell him she was meeting Tripp. In another life, he'd have gotten a kick out of this. Back when Holden was alive, and she and Nate and Alecia and Holden were a foursome, they'd have parties at Nate and Alecia's.

Sometimes he'd come to Nate's without a date and flirt with Bridget and Alecia, vying for their attention, the men oblivious or just not caring or even teasing them all. Holden would say *here comes your boyfriend* and laugh, and Bridget would redden. Or she remembered one of his girlfriends, Aubrey with the perm, who worked nights at the Quarry Bar, who sat incongruously at the living room card table next to Alecia. Alecia with her Seven jeans and her straight blond hair. Aubrey went out to smoke a cigarette and Alecia had hissed across the table, *Jesus, Tripp, are you slumming for women now?* And

Bridget had elbowed her, because honestly, the girl-on-girl trash talk irritated the living shit out of her. Didn't they get enough bullshit from men and now they had to give it to each other? Tripp would say, *Aw, A, you're such a bitch sometimes.* Bridget had laughed, because that, at least, was true. Tripp would put his arm around Bridget, his big hand squeezing her shoulder, and say, *listen, my two favorite women are already taken.* Holden would roll his eyes and later say, *I don't know how anyone can stand that guy.* Bridget would defend him, *he's just kidding around, lighten up.* But lightening up wasn't in Holden's repertoire and he only tolerated Tripp because Nate loved the guy. Their card nights had always seemed like postcollege shenanigans, where the rules of normal society didn't exactly apply and they could all be as ridiculous as they wanted with few consequences.

But now the weird part was, Bridget was available and Holden was dead, and none of them had partied like that in what seemed like years. Since Gabe was diagnosed, at least. Three years felt like a lifetime. Sometimes she asked Nate how Tripp was; he even once told her that Tripp was engaged—maybe to the woman in the picture on his desk. At the time, she'd been oddly sad about it.

And now, Tripp was here. She remembered the way his fingers clutched her arm as she leaned into him at the mill, gentle and firm. It made her wonder what his hands would feel like on her bare skin and then chastise herself for the thought. But truthfully, the idea had been there for a very long time, if only in a boozy afterthought way. If she was *truly* honest about it, she'd always used to put on a little bit more makeup, her shirt a little lower cut, her hair a bit more curled on the nights she thought Tripp might come.

Now he sat across the booth from her at The 543 giving her a grin she'd thrilled at only a few years ago, and the jolt under her skin went up her arms and straight up into her hair, then dissipated, instantly, like static.

She wasn't that same person. She couldn't remember the last time she'd worn lipstick. Her clothes hung on her—she'd been curvy at one point, but a sporadic diet of frozen dinners and red wine for dinner had run the curves right off her body. Now she had no hips, no waist, just a straight blob from her neck to her knees, and had Aunt Nadine seen her now, she would say *girl you gotta stand up twice to cast a shadow.* The jacket Bridget wore had been Holden's spring jacket—a tan canvas, utterly unfashionable with no shape whatsoever. She was a widow now, still having sex dreams about a man who died a year *(nearly a year, must call Petra!)* before, and being content with orgasming in her sleep and calling it a *good night.*

Dating was a laughable proposition. Then again he hadn't asked.

She ran a hand through the ends of her hair.

They both ordered coffee. Tripp suggested pancakes and Bridget went along with it because food didn't have much taste and she truly didn't care. The waitress took away their menus and the pregnant silence was followed by them both speaking at once.

"So, do you think—" Bridget started.

"What do you want—" Tripp said.

They laughed. Tripp motioned for Bridget to talk first.

"I was going to ask you, do you think Lucia and Nate are together?" She shook out a sugar packet and tore the top.

"I don't know. I called Nate just before I saw you at the mill—"

"Did you follow me?" She interrupted him without thinking.

"I did," Tripp conceded, stirring his coffee. "I had a hunch you wouldn't go home. You left my house in such a rush. Tell me, why are you so intent on figuring this all out? It doesn't seem like you believe Nate. You don't believe Lucia, do you?"

Bridget considered this. It was a perfectly fair question, and one she'd been asking herself the entire drive to the mill earlier. Again, because today seemed like a particularly good day for honesty, she had to admit maybe it was the curiosity of the whole affair that pulled at her. I mean, what else did she have? Besides Petra and the perfect maple tree, which seemed pretty stupid now. For God's sake, let Petra find the tree.

"I think I believe Nate. I do. He's not a cheater. I've known him for years."

"Does a cheater have a type?" Tripp asked slowly, unfolding and refolding his napkin.

"Oh, I don't know. I think so." But then Bridget flashed on Holden, on *Watercress 6:30,* on that broken red acrylic fingernail, each so seemingly innocent. Holden—stiff, conservative, predictable Holden drinking one (and only one) bourbon and water on the rocks at the bar after his medical conference—had taken a red-fingernailed radiologist to his bed. He didn't seem the type, either. He'd voted for Bush. "Maybe not," she conceded.

"Alecia cheated on Nate, did you know that?"

Bridget looked up then, stunned. "No. When?"

"Years ago, before they were married maybe? Someone kissed her at a work thing. This is how life happens, though. There's no type for anything. People are just doing their thing, being people, right?"

"Maybe. But with a student?" Bridget tried to figure out if he was defending Nate. It was one thing to explore a kiss at a work function when you had a boyfriend, but it was quite another to hunker down with a student when you had a wife and a disabled son at home who depended on you.

"I don't think so." He moved in his seat, tucking his hands under his legs and leaning forward. "Lucia being missing? This changes things, I think. They'll gun for him. Harper already had a closed case on the guy for institutional assault. I don't know if it would have stuck. He was talking to the DA. But he wanted Nate, for sure."

"Should you be telling me this?" Bridget practically whispered, looking around. The closest occupied table was ten feet away, but still.

"Probably not. I'm basically just a traffic cop; there's no crime in this town. There's drugs, but even those have a larger regional task force. It's no secret I can't stand Harper. He goes after what he thinks the truth is, be damned with what he finds out along the way. I want to be a detective, but not his way."

"Something was going on at school," Bridget admitted slowly. She thought about the witch comments, the burning note. She thought about Lucia's creative writing journal, sitting on her desk, the bizarrely cryptic entries she'd initially attributed to her brother. *Wrist to floor, his hand like an ape.*

She thought about how disengaged she'd been as a teacher in the past year, the past few months.

How life seemed to be happening around her, and if she had to picture it, she felt like an observer. A patron in the monkey house. She realized that maybe all of this was related, that maybe Nate was collateral damage.

She couldn't articulate now how the kids all seemed to slide sideways since Lucia disappeared. How their eyes shifted away from Bridget, away from Bachman, their mouths smirking, whispering behind cupped hands.

There was a missing piece. Something that no one knew.

The waitress brought dinner. Bridget ate and thought about how she'd been turning a blind eye, out of laziness or tiredness or the sensation she was being weighted down. That anything she did was hopeless, that the students at Mt. Oanoke would go on being ruthless or chipper or doing heroin or underage drinking and nothing she did would make a difference. She was simply treading water. For a teacher, apathy was a crime; she used to believe that. Then again, like Tripp said, she was just a person trying to get through it.

"I think I've been stupid. Or at least willfully ignorant." On her plate, a half serving of gluey pancakes remained. She hadn't eaten that much at once in weeks. Months maybe. The hard knot of dough and sugar felt lodged in her esophagus, stuck.

"Well," Tripp cleared his throat and rummaged in the plastic holder for more sugar packs. "You've been through a lot." When he looked up he met her eyes, tilted his head. "Did I ever tell you how sorry I was? I was. I am."

He didn't. At the funeral, he gave her a quick peck, but mostly avoided her. He'd said, *let me know if I can do anything.* Like of all people in the world, when she was at the absolute bottom, when the world seemed black and shot through with silver sharp pain, when getting out of bed or taking a shower seemed like daunting tasks, when she just wanted to *talk* about Holden because all anyone else seemed to want to do was change the subject or bring her macaroni-and-cheese casseroles, she would have called Tripp? No.

"You didn't. But I appreciate it." She was better at accepting condolences, about smiling back instead of crying. To say *Oh, thank you, yes it's so hard, no don't worry, I'm fine.* That in the strange role of widow, people expected her to comfort *them. Oh yes, I know it's terrible, so awful. Yes, he was so young. Oh, I remember that time at community picnic, yes he was very good at softball.*

"I should have said something sooner, but I never knew what. Plus, the guy didn't like me much."

And for once, Bridget laughed. Most people wouldn't have dared to say it. So she smiled at him and spoke the truth, which felt a bit liberating. "No. Not so much."

"I made too many eyes at his wife, I guess." He took a sip of coffee but kept Bridget's gaze until she looked away, out the window to the dimly lit parking lot. To the older couple shuffling to their car, he using a walker, she guiding him with one hand under his elbow. Bridget felt the familiar sting in the back of her throat, the burn in her eyes. "I admit I was jealous of him. Nate, too. Y'all had what I wanted. These happy marriages, a friendly foursome. I wanted that with Melinda, my ex. My daughter. We got engaged for a spell there. It didn't last. She wasn't the cheating type, either. And still, somehow." He gave her a knowing smile and a slight lift of one shoulder and Bridget looked away.

She held her breath, her mind wiped white of words. Tripp played everything so close to the vest and Bridget had never pried. She knew so little about him; any personal inquiry in the past had been laughed off, treated like a joke. The intimacy felt too sudden, too urgent.

"And now?" Bridget asked, because she couldn't think of anything else to say but knew absolutely, positively that she didn't want this conversation to end, although she couldn't have quite pinpointed why.

"Now?"

"Yes, now. With Melinda? Or . . ." Bridget

looked around, her hands out helplessly, her face reddening. "Anyone else?"

"Nah. It's too hard. I'm getting old." He laughed, but silently, his mouth opened and she could see the fillings in his teeth. Silver amalgam; she didn't even know they still did that. "Have you tried dating? It's awful."

"No," she said much too quickly, her voice hitched and her hands flat against the table.

He appraised her then, his tongue moving around in his mouth, his cheek bulging with a wry sort of smile. He picked up the bill, and in a smooth motion, shifted out of the booth to pay. When he came back he held his hand out to help her up, and when she stood, they stayed, just close enough for her to feel his warmth, smell the syrupy pancake on his breath, the soapy, dewy fragrance of his shampoo. "You should, you know."

"I should what?" she asked, flustered.

"Try dating."

CHAPTER 25

Alecia, Friday, May 8, 2015

Search parties on television were a bustling, dazzling affair: efficient and clipped detectives, the buzz drone of walkie-talkies, people coming and going at all hours of the day and night bringing lasagnas in foil pans and tins of homemade cookies. When pregnant wives of suspicious husbands go missing, particularly those who are beautiful and rich, it's a national spectacle with news crews and cameramen shuffling for the spot next to the detectives. There's always more than one detective.

Not so much for the teenage mistress of a married teacher.

They'd put the call out the night before, shoved between the local news and weather and a single headline in Thursday's paper on page three: "Volunteers Needed in Search for Missing Local Teen." People in Mt. Oanoke were rarely motivated to do much of anything; Alecia shouldn't have been as shocked as she was at the desolation.

She hadn't told anyone she was going. It was

all too weird. She expected throngs of people, chaos and confusion. It was depressing to think about how many people a year must just vanish—poof!—and no one looks for them, no search parties, no police reports. No loved ones ceaselessly pushing the media and police. No one hanging missing posters. It was jarring to realize how much of that work was done by a victim's loved ones, that these things just didn't magically happen, and when there was no one to do them, they simply did not get done.

Detective Harper and another plainclothes detective had set up a folding banquet table in the parking lot between Texaco and the police station, handing out grainy photos of Lucia to a growing group of women—all women, no men. An ambulance and a fire truck sat toward the back of the parking lot, a few EMTs and firefighters hanging on the sides of each one, laughing, throwing barbs at each other that Alecia couldn't hear.

Alecia tucked a lock of hair back up into her baseball cap and surveyed the crowd. Familiar faces, but the names all escaped her. No one from Nate's crowd; would they have dared? Did he even have a crowd anymore? The accusation and media seemed to scatter them all; even Tad had vanished.

Alecia had called the neighbor to baby-sit at

9 a.m., even deciding somewhat last minute to forgo Gabe's swimming class and one ABA session that was scheduled for the afternoon. She hadn't stopped to examine why she'd come, just that she felt compelled. She had been counting on the chaos of a crowd to shield her. She hovered near a red Pontiac, feeling exposed and naked in her sunglasses and hat.

"Ms. Winter, here to help?" Harper called to her, and she almost fled. Almost. But she felt trapped, a butterfly pinned to the wax, and it was likely that leaving would have only made her look worse. Alecia tucked the stupid sunglasses into her purse and approached the card table.

"Do you still need volunteers?" she said, her voice low. Harper and the second detective exchanged a glance.

"Sure," Harper said, pushing a glossy photo across the table. Alecia looked away. He tapped his fingers against the plastic table in front of him, his tongue clicking in his mouth. "Seems an odd choice. For you, I mean."

Alecia clutched the strap of her purse tighter and backed up. "I'll just go. This was a mistake. I wanted to . . . help. I don't know."

"No, no. Stay. We have precious little in the way of resources. Hard to find a girl no one cares to find. We're leaving at ten and we're heading up to State Game Lands 214, where your husband claims he saw her run. At this point, we're not sure there's a crime, see? It's easy for a person to get lost in these woods." Harper chewed on a toothpick; Alecia could hear the crackle between his molars. She imagined them yellowed, cigarette-browned spit making the wood soggy.

"I shouldn't have come," Alecia repeated, maybe looking for someone to tell her *it is okay, we're glad you're here, come have a snicker-doodle,* but no one did. A group of ten women were gathered at the edge of the parking lot, a few inexplicably clutching Maglites, in various plain T-shirts and jean capris, sport socks and Nikes, hands smoothing their shirt fronts and looking around, shifting uncomfortably. A few whispered, someone giggled. They didn't invite her over, just watched, one of them chewing, chewing, chewing slowly on a pretzel, like cud, the bag crinkling in her fist. Alecia hated them.

They were there because they were bored, these fiftyish empty nesters or moms of high schoolers who stopped talking to their parents, maybe moms of kids whom Nate had failed, unpopular themselves in high school, resentful of Nate's charm, out to prove he'd done something to *the poor girl.*

The poor girl. People all over town were dividing into two camps: *the poor girl* vs. *let's not be too hasty,* another phrase Alecia had heard in line at the checkout counter, a husband and wife arguing over which camp they were in. She had slunk behind the impulse-gum rack and waited them out.

But now there was nowhere to *slink* and she'd done a stupid thing of making herself visible, or as Vi would have said, *a spectacle.* This would surely be in the paper, and then what would people think? What would Nate think?

"Alecia?"

Bridget stood behind her, her head cocked to the side, waiting for an explanation without asking for one, and even though they hadn't really talked, and the last few times Bridget had called Alecia had pressed decline, Alecia was still so relieved to see her. She held her arms out and Bridget hugged back, patting between her shoulder blades and whispering, "What the actual fuck are you doing here?" and Alecia laughed, a half hiccup really, into her hair.

"I have no idea. I thought it would be busier, that I could feel like I was doing something. I've been so fucking impotent in all of this, I can't even tell you." Bridget tried to pull away but Alecia held tight, just for a moment longer. She finally released her, stepping back, and found herself unable to meet Bridget's eyes. "Don't you have school?"

"In-service day. Kids are out, we're supposed to be in. I played hooky." Bridget shrugged.

"This looks weird you know." She motioned to Alecia and then spread her hand wide toward the Mom Squad, as though Alecia didn't know.

"No shit. Should I leave? I should leave."

"Maybe not?" Bridget raised her chin in the direction of the Texaco, where a white car had just parked, and who got out of the driver's-side door but Rowena White, reporter extraordinaire. Her black hair gleamed in the sunlight, and she hung back writing in a notebook, snapping her own pictures with her cell phone, documenting this sad, pathetic excuse for a search party.

Under the hot May sun, Alecia's arms popped with gooseflesh. Before she could decide to stay or go, Harper stood and flicked his toothpick into a metal trash can, seemingly placed next to the card table for this express purpose. He fished a fresh one out of his shirt pocket and approached the group of women, his hands on his hips.

"We're going to meet a mile past the post office on Route Six, where Lucia Hamm was last seen running into the woods. We're going to walk two miles in and two miles out, twenty feet apart. We are performing a search and rescue, but please keep your eyes open for anything along the way that will provide clues to Ms. Hamm's whereabouts. Two miles in is approximately halfway into SGL 214. There are close to five thousand acres of dense woods and wetlands here. We'll be covering the area by helicopter later this afternoon. We expect everyone to be back here before five o'clock and we'll do an attendance check. Keep your neighbor in sight at all times. It's very easy to get turned around in this forest."

The Mom Squad nodded in unison and Bridget squeezed Alecia's arm. "I think it's good you came."

For the first time, Alecia wondered where the students were. She'd think that at least one student would show up to look for their missing classmate, and it had to mean something that no one did. She turned to Bridget to ask her, but Bridget stared ahead, fixated on Harper. Instead, she leaned in and said, "Stay close to me, will you?"

How much pressure can you put on a friendship before it snaps like a stick under an eighty-dollar pair of Nikes?

"I'm close. I'll stay close," Bridget promised, and who knows, maybe she meant it.

The only reason Alecia owned hiking boots was because of Nate. How ironic then, that her first real hike involved looking for a girl he might have . . . what? Kidnapped? Killed?

The boots were a birthday present when Gabe was two. Right after the Christmas party from hell but before Gabe was diagnosed, that blurry middle time when life still seemed on plan, when the direction of their marriage, while aimless at times, was still a topic of conversation. Nate complained that they'd gotten lost, that they didn't do things together, just the two of them anymore, and Alecia always thought this was staunchly childish. Like Nate and Gabe were on opposing sides, vying for her affection. She'd gotten strangely protective of Gabe's feelings then, at the time just an innocent, babbling toddler, and they'd gotten in a fight about it. Nate had shaken his head at the argument: *I just want us to stay people, as well as parents. To be a couple.* They knew people whose entire coupledom was absorbed by their children, and they called each other Mommy and Daddy even when there were no children around, which was almost never. Suddenly it wasn't about *I like,* or *he likes,* but rather *we like,* as in *We actually really like The Wiggles, you know?* Alecia could picture them, long after the children were tucked into bed, drooling into bowls of vanilla ice cream watching Australian folk singers jump around in rainbow-hued drunkenness sing about fruit salad. No, they were not these people.

But Nate thought they were.

So he bought her hiking boots when she'd never hiked a day in her life, when only Nate seemed to like the outdoors. But it was pretty typical of Nate to get her a gift that reflected only something he wanted to do (even though, admittedly, she hadn't made any gesture at all, so who was worse, her or Nate? It was hard to tell, and one of those recurring rhetorical questions that over time built a marriage). She tried not to show her exasperation with him, and the boots sat in the box untouched. He'd organized a few hikes, only to have her beg off at the last minute: Gabe needing something, or a headache, or once a stomach flu. And no matter how legitimate the reasons—and they were legitimate!—the act of constantly rescheduling left them both a little deflated, until after a while, Alecia (or maybe Nate, she wasn't even sure) stuck them in the back of her closet where they collected dust for almost three years.

Until now. Until she paced off two miles of untrodden woods, dense undergrowth and sticks slapping at her calves, her arms, her cheeks, her feet, new boots and all getting sucked deep into wetland, the beginnings of a blister forming on her big toe.

To her left one of the moms huffed out the first mile, losing her sneaker in the mud only once, her voice reedy, calling *Carol! Carol!* Until the mom to her left stopped. Alecia kept going, not sure her help would be welcomed anyway, and from fifteen feet, gave Bridget a little wave. She couldn't discern from her friend whether Bridget was on team Poor Girl or team Wait and See or maybe on her own team: Team Figure Shit Out. Or Team Avoid Holden's Mother.

"Alecia!" Bridget yelled, her arm waving above her head to get her attention. "Stop! Pass it on!"

Alecia called to the mom next to her, "Stop! They say to stop! Pass it on!" She waved lamely, not really knowing who *they* were. Harper or someone like him, she assumed. It couldn't be time to turn around yet, they'd only walked for about a half hour at a snail's pace.

"They found something," Bridget said.

"They found Lucia?" Alecia asked. Bridget shook her head. "I don't think so."

Alecia closed the distance between herself and Bridget, rubbing a branch scratch on her cheek. Bridget's face was flushed, with either the exertion or the excitement.

"What if they found her?" Alecia asked again, but Bridget shushed her with a hand. A small group had gathered near the base of the embankment and Bridget slowly started picking her way in that direction. Alecia followed.

Harper, an EMT, and one of the firefighters stood in a huddle. When Alecia approached, they turned to stare at her, their faces unreadable. Their mouths forming words Alecia couldn't hear. Bridget called, "What did you find?"

No one replied for a beat, then one of them said, "Show her." And lifted his chin in their direction. Unclear on which *her* he was referring to, Alecia took a step forward, her arms and legs cold, her skin crawling.

Harper extended his hand. A white baseball cap, the burgundy embroidered COACH thumbed over with mud.

She'd know it anywhere.

CHAPTER 26

Nate, Friday, May 8, 2015

There was no shortage of clichés about time: it healed all wounds; it was always a-changing (said with an upward lilt and a soft click of the tongue); it flew when you were having fun. What was lesser known, though, was how elastic it became when you had *only* time and nothing else. The days became evenings became nights became mornings, one blending into the other with graceful slowness and seemingly almost by accident. With no job, few allies, no to-do list—a longtime staple of adulthood—he reverted back to a teenager. Nate spent most of his hours on the couch, avoiding the adults in his life, watching endless hours of daytime television and *SportsCenter*. The only teenage staple missing was his cell phone, often left haphazardly around Tripp's townhouse, the ringer turned down, the notifications off. Social media held nothing but vitriol for him, his texts were sporadic and went unanswered. *How are you doing, buddy?* From a handful of random gym friends, a few baseball dads, one a week ago from Peter Tempest.

He thought more about the people he didn't hear from: Dale Trevor, Tad Bachman, Bridget, Alecia. He could ruminate for hours on the hidden meaning of silence.

He'd never been a perfect husband, he knew that. But he did think he was a *good* husband. A good father. Maybe not a great one. He lost his patience with Gabe too quickly. Alecia said his expectations were too high, which might be true for everyone. Except all he ever wanted from his wife was her attention, which didn't seem like a very high expectation at all. He didn't care if the house was clean or his laundry was done. He didn't say one word about the nights she ordered to go from Ruby Tuesday. He'd rather these shortcuts, preserving her energy for them, for their family, and childishly for him. Instead, she seemed to spin herself out before he'd even gotten in the door most nights. He walked in and she was raised and ready for a fight, picking and pecking until he lashed out, then blaming their argument on his quick temper.

Then again, his temper was quick, always had been.

These things, these *marriage things,* were the hard stuff. He'd take it all if he could just go home.

Nate was used to moving his body, at the gym, running around the baseball field—one of the only coaches to ever join the warm-up jog. He liked it. He got his blood moving, made him part of a team. He'd missed that.

Which is why Saturday he woke up early: 9 a.m. Earlier than he'd gotten up all week, Tripp clomping past him in the living room making no effort to stay quiet anymore. He pulled out his hiking boots. He used to hike all the time; he'd spent his whole childhood in the woods. Alecia didn't like it. The walking itself was boring; it was either too hot or too cold, and she was never interested in the nature aspect. She'd gone a few times, pre-Gabe, and talked the whole time, prattling, really about whatever popped into her head. He'd tried to tell her a walk is for silencing your mind, looking around. The animals fascinated him; as a kid, he'd return to the same spot, two miles from his parents' home and watch a blue heron every day. When he told Alecia this, she asked, *what did it do, though?*

Nate scrawled a note to Tripp: *went for a hike.* He'd drive to Bear Creek, the opposite direction of the forest he'd gotten lost in earlier in the week. The air was perfect, the fish would be rising. There wasn't much to get jazzed up about these days, but the hike came close.

The doorbell rang as he was tying his boots, checking the laces. He answered it absently, without looking through the peephole, wholly unprepared for Detective Harper on the other side of the door. A tall, thin man with a thick knot of a mustache stood behind him, nose like the beak of a hawk.

Nothing about this would be good.

"Going hiking?" Harper asked, an odd delight in his tone that Nate couldn't figure out.

"I was going to, yes," Nate said, and opened the door. They walked past him into the living room and into the kitchen and Nate followed. Tripp was at work, but they surely knew that and they acted like they owned the place. "Can I help you?"

"Sure. We have some questions." Harper was direct and his last round of questioning hadn't been kind, but it wasn't aggressive. He'd collected a statement from Nate about the nature of his relationship with Lucia, prodded with everything they had, from the motel to his cell phone records (two calls from her, incoming or outgoing, two! Both calling for help, he'd told them). They hadn't found much to support the claim, except the photo: a clear close-up of Nate, hugging Lucia, his eyes closed. Her up on her toes, like lovers. In real life, it had been a grateful embrace, almost awkward and fumbling. She had said *no one cares like you do.* He had hugged her, wondering if it was true, thinking about Taylor, wondering if he could call her and get her to come to the dive of a motel. He hated this place, hated that it was the cheapest place in the area, hated the peeling paint, the yellowed lace curtains.

He'd stood inside her little dank room, the air cold and smelling like plastic and cigarettes. The bedspread thin, striped with a large coffee-colored stain in the middle. He wouldn't even sit on it. But he'd left her there, as much as he didn't want to.

"We have a problem, Winters," Harper said. "Your girl is missing."

"Not my girl," Nate said, correcting him, and Harper waved his hand like it didn't matter, but you know, it wasn't a fucking pedantic detail. She wasn't *his* girl.

"Missing how?"

"Either ran away or, well, something happened to her. Hard to say. Hasn't been in school since Friday."

Tripp hadn't said a word. They'd played two-man poker—"heads up"—until Tripp beat him and then wouldn't take his money, like a bitch. It pissed Nate off and he went to bed. That was maybe Tuesday? Wednesday? He'd never said a thing to him.

"I haven't been in school in over a week, Detective. I have no idea what's going on." He hated the whine in his voice, he sounded like the kids in his classes. Defensive, argumentative.

Harper gestured toward the other man, a detective, Nate assumed. "This is Clark Mackey. He's another detective on Lucia's case."

"Her case?"

"She's technically a missing persons case at this time, Mr. Winters." Clark Mackey's voice was low, and rumbled like he had a throat full of sand.

Missing persons.

"You called in a report Monday night. What can you tell me about that?"

"I was driving here from my house and I was going slow and I saw her on the side of the road. She waved me down. I think . . . She might have been on drugs."

"What makes you say that, Mr. Winters?" Mackey's tone was quick, sharp.

"I'm around a lot of kids day in and day out. I can see when they're on something," Nate said. "She was jumpy and wasn't making sense. I told her to stay put. I couldn't let her in my car, I was calling you."

"Why couldn't you let her in your car?" Harper asked, and Nate couldn't tell if he was joking.

"Are you serious, Detective?" When Harper stayed deadpan, Nate shook his head. "Okay, fine, because she and a reporter have accused me—wrongly, I'll add—of an inappropriate relationship. I am currently suspended from my teaching position at Mt. Oanoke High School and I was trying to do the right thing. I called the police. When I said that she took off into the woods."

"What did you do?" Harper asked, and Nate flinched.

"Do?"

"Sure, what did you do next?"

"I came home." Nate felt the bottom drop out of his stomach then, a sick, twisty sensation. He'd never lied to a cop and had a feeling it was a bad time to start. Hell, until this moment, he'd never been questioned by a cop. Cops were poker buddies, racquetball partners. Harper didn't look like he'd seen a gym in twenty years. With his bony hand on one hip, the soft flesh of his arm hung off the bone, a skinny kind of fat.

"Right home? Did you stop anywhere?" Mackey interjected.

"Uh, I stopped over at the QB before I saw Lucia, if that's what you mean."

"Nope it's not what we mean, Winters. Did you go anywhere after you saw Lucia and before you went home?" Harper was losing his patience.

"No. I came right home," Nate repeated, and scratched the back of his neck.

"Did you get out of your car and follow Ms. Hamm?"

Pause. "No."

"You didn't get out of your car at all?"

"Do you think I . . . did something to her?" Nate demanded.

"Why, has something been done to her?" Mackey asked.

"No. Not by me."

"So that's a no then?" Mackey pressed.

Mackey and Harper exchanged a glance.

"That's a no," Nate said.

Harper nodded once and then smiled disarmingly. "Glad we chatted, Mr. Winters. We'll be in touch."

Nate walked them to the door and hesitated. It might be so easy to call them back, tell them he made a mistake. He's nervous, scared, whatever. Any other guy might do the same, right?

He was still thinking about it when they got into their unmarked car, a gray Buick, too new for the taxes in Mt. Oanoke, with doors so heavy they hardly made a sound as they thunked shut. The engine barely hummed as it turned over. Nate was still thinking about it as they pulled away from the curb and he put his hand up in a wave, like a simple idiot.

Only after they made a right, the taillights winking out of sight, did it occur to him that maybe he just really fucked everything up.

CHAPTER 27

Bridget, Monday, May 11, 2015

"You know they found something on Friday," Dale said, his pale fishlike skin shining, spittle at the corners of his mouth.

"How do you know?" Bridget asked. She hadn't told anyone she'd gone to the search and rescue. Even thinking about it made her eyebrows sweat. She hadn't called Nate, told him what they found; she'd been too afraid of what he'd say, that he'd lie to her. She followed Alecia home, both of them shaky and scared. Alecia said very little except, *tell me how it could mean nothing, tell me.* And Bridget said, *he called the police that he saw her. He must have tried to follow her. He's a good person, Alecia. He tried to do the right thing.* Bridget mostly believed it. She left Alecia with Gabe, making dinner, because being alone was preferable to being together, although if pressed, neither could have articulated why.

"This is Mt. Oanoke." He shrugged like this explained everything. "They found Nate's coach hat in the woods where Lucia ran. Do you think he went after her? Have you talked to him? Did he go after her?" Dale was practically panting, his breath hot and warm, the odor of cafeteria gravy. Bridget stepped back, turned her head away, and took a breath.

"I don't know, Dale. I really don't know anything."

"Then where is she, Bridget? Where?" Dale's eyes blinked, rapid-fire, his lips twitching.

"I don't know, Dale. No one does." Bridget shook herself, moved away from him, under the guise of talking to a student, holding her index finger up like she'd be right back, which of course they both knew was a lie.

The cafeteria at Mt. Oanoke operated like a social command center, but not in the typical way, Bridget didn't think. There were cliques, sure, but less so maybe than other schools. There was bullying, sure, but less so than other schools. Bridget had always really believed this, defended it even when Nate had called her a Pollyanna. He was further inside than her, the wolf watching the henhouse, and now Bridget wondered if he was right.

Josh, Riana, Porter, Andrew, and Kelsey sat at the center table, holding court. Taylor sat on the end across from Kelsey. Bridget watched them from the vending machines, laughing, throwing napkins at each other, a single unified, *ew, Josh, you're disgusting,* from Kelsey and Riana. Taylor was quiet, smiling naïvely and head bobbing, in

316

a haphazard and random way. She was mostly ignored except for a periodic whisper from Kelsey. Riana paid her no attention. Andrew held the middle, the king on his throne, tall and lanky, and remained a bit dazed, would chime in once every few minutes and the table would laugh, riotously, overacting, like no one had ever said something so new, so funny before. Kelsey picked at a salad and reapplied lip gloss. Riana ate a cheeseburger, fast, with both hands, while Kelsey watched, her mouth hanging open, her cheeks candy pinked like conversation hearts.

Bridget had never really *watched* them before, the way they interacted, how different they were from each other. She remembered knowing her previous students so much better than this bunch, all their nuances and kindnesses, cruelties and insecurities. But this crew confounded her. Their allegiances seemed to change with the wind. Maybe it was just her energy level this year. But it was May, the year almost over, the students sliding past her almost liquidly, her only knowledge of them what they wrote in their notebooks and turned in, half-truths and scribbled confessions. She hardly ever knew what to believe, and she'd been skimming more than reading.

Bridget walked past their table, saw their heads bent together, whispering. Suddenly, Kelsey's voice, high and shaky, "Witches get hanged."

And then Riana broke up laughing, followed by Josh. Andrew looked around like he lost the thread, a dopey smile stretched between his cheeks. Taylor got up and threw her trash away, left the cafeteria.

Right before the bell, Bridget went to the bathroom. In the stall, she caught her breath, her cheeks pressed between her knees, heels balancing on the lid of the toilet, her skirt lifted up to her thighs and tucked, gathered, between her legs as she drew big, lung-expanding breaths. This had been happening a lot lately, this light-headedness, like she could just drift off to sleep and never wake up.

The doors burst open and Bridget kept her feet up, held her breath. Two giggling girls, loud, swearing, *fucking Jesus, what the fuck was that shit?*

Kelsey and Riana.

"God, Josh's been pissing me off lately. I'm gonna dump him before next year": Kelsey.

"You've been saying that since tenth": Riana. Then, "Dude, Andrew needs to erase that shit before he gets in trouble."

"He's such a whore. Did you see his face?"

"No, I can't look at his face, that big-ass nose." Laughter. Deeper voice, mimicking. *"Uh, what?"*

"I meant in the video. Like he's gonna jizz by just looking at her." Kelsey giggled, high and honking.

"It's his dream come true." They both laughed. Then Riana: "Don't let T hear that."

"Oh, like I care? She don't belong with us."

"Watch yourself. I like her": Riana.

"Oh, now don't go lightin' me on fire." Kelsey's voice went high, singsong, and there was a smack, hand against the bare skin. Bridget held her breath, waiting. Then a laugh.

"Come on, you know Andrew wrote that note. That was some kind of joke."

"Nah, he's too thick for that. I don't know who did it, but it was someone smarter than Evans," Kelsey said. Then, "But you lit it up, right? She did not do that shit with her eyes."

The click of a purse, the smack of lips. Bridget leaned forward, almost touching the metal beige door. *Everything you touch.*

Then, Riana. "Cat or scope?"

"Scope, I think." There was a rustling, and the garbled sound of a video, then a deep, slow voice, dreamlike. *Say you want it, honey. Say yes. Look here and say it. Male laughing, several of them. A garbled hoot.*

"Shhh!" Kelsey said, cutting off the video. "I heard something. Is someone in here?"

"The bell's about to ring, just go. I'll catch you later. If you see him, tell him to take that shit down." Riana, the boss.

"I don't know if you can. It's streamed. I don't have the app, I wouldn't touch that shit with a ten-foot pole. People are crazy." Kelsey, giggling again.

Their feet clattered on the tile, high-heeled wedges and short shorts; Bridget could see their long legs through the crack in the door. They weren't supposed to wear things like that but only the teachers like Dale ever tried to enforce it.

The bell clanged, echoing in the cavernous bathroom, and the door slammed shut. Bridget waited a moment until she was certain she was alone and then left the stall. She had a sixth-period class, Lucia's class, but stood in the empty hallway, uncertain of what she'd heard and what it meant. She couldn't stop hearing Kelsey's voice in her mind, *you lit it up, right?* What did Riana say? Nothing as far as Bridget could hear.

She stopped in the faculty lounge and found a one-sided flyer for this weekend's battle of the bands and a pen. She scribbled some of the things she'd heard: *streaming app? cat, scope, look here, and say it.*

She folded the flyer into her palm, and rushed to class.

After the eighth-period bell, she followed the kids out and rushed to the math wing. Dale was packing up his bag and she knocked a beat— shave and a haircut—on the doorjamb.

"Hey, can I ask you a question? I know you're into tech."

Dale gave her a weary look. A *now you want to talk because you want something* look. After a second, he shrugged, his pointed shoulders lifted up to elfin ears, a sullen gesture.

"What's streaming?" Bridget felt stupid; she should know this by now. He made an incredulous face.

"Like for TV? Netflix, Amazon, YouTube?"

"No," Bridget faltered, because she really didn't know. It could be YouTube. "Like if you were going to stream something yourself?"

"Hmmm, YouTube is static content, mostly. You make a video, you upload it. There are streaming apps, is that what you mean? You can upload a live feed to the Net."

"Yes, I think that's it."

"Okay, right now there's Periscope, which is connected to Twitter and Meerkat."

Cat or scope? Scope, I think.

"Bridget, why, what's up?" Dale cocked his head, legitimately concerned.

"Nothing it's just a conversation I overheard. Thanks, Dale."

She waved and left, the back of her neck tingling. He called after her, *wait Bridget!* But she pretended not to hear him. She grabbed her coat from her classroom and bolted out the front door.

The spring sun beat down, relentlessly cheerful. Kids in the parking lot whooped and hollered, like it was the last day of school. The senioritis was setting in; every day had a jailbreak feel to it.

Bridget climbed into her car and let the heat bake her. She liked this feeling, the greenhouse of her Toyota, heating her from the inside out, warming her blood. She pulled her phone out of her purse and called Tripp.

"Hey, are you working?" She bit her pinkie nail. "Is Nate there?"

He seemed surprised to hear from her. "Uh, no I think he went to the gym. Why?"

"Can I come over?" Her cheeks warmed and she rushed on. "I have a reason, I mean. I think I heard something and I don't know if it's something or nothing."

"You don't really *need* a reason." She could hear his smile.

"Okay."

"Okay." She studied the nail, jagged and ripped at the corner. "I'll be over."

When she hung up, she was smiling.

Bridget parked in front of Tripp's townhouse, the front plain and tan, all the way down the line. Some of them had bright flower pots outside, lining the three cement steps up. Window boxes. Welcome mats. Not Tripp's. Aunt Nadine would have clicked her tongue and said it needed a woman's touch.

She rang the bell and Tripp answered the door in shorts and bare feet, his smile so wide and happy it caught her by surprise. His ankle was encircled by a black, swooping tribal tattoo, the hair on his legs tapering down to smoothness at midcalf. It felt too intimate, his nakedness, that she should know how the hair on his legs grows.

She followed him into the living room and sat on one end of the couch, while he sat on the other.

"What's up now?" he asked after a moment, the silence thick like a fog.

She told him about the conversation in the bathroom, leaving out the most vulgar parts, because while she wasn't a prude, saying the word *jizz* was a bit too fast of an advancement of their friendship.

"Dale said there's an app called Periscope. Riana said, 'Cat or scope?' and Kelsey said 'Scope.'" She pulled her phone out of her purse.

"There's only one way to figure it out," Tripp said, leaning close to look over her shoulder. She navigated to the app store and downloaded Periscope. She created an account and logged in. On the main page, hundreds of broadcasts streamed by and she realized too late that she had no way of finding what the girls were looking at. She clicked the friends icons and tried to look for Josh Tempest, Andrew Evans, but no luck.

"Oh," she said dumbly. "I need their user-names." They wouldn't use their real names, most likely.

"Nate would know," Tripp said as he sat back against the cushion, closer now, his knee on the couch almost touching hers.

She texted Nate, *Do you know Josh or Andrew's Twitter handles?*

She waited for his reply and crossed and uncrossed her legs, her skirt suddenly feeling dowdy, its bright paisley marmish. She pulled at the gauzy sleeves of her peasant blouse.

"I'm out of my element at the school more and more each year," Bridget said. "The technology, it's so . . . invasive."

Tripp ran a palm through his hair. "We had to take a class in it last year. A training on social media. It's probably already out of date."

"This Periscope, this is scary," Bridget said. "I mean, with YouTube at least you have a second to think, *is this a good idea, should I upload this?* This is like, real time." She remembered Dale's words. "A live feed."

Her phone binged in her hand: *@TheKingEvans, @JTemp007.*

The king? She almost laughed. They all thought of him that way, but to think of that yourself? Sitting in the middle of his crew, his arms out like Jesus at the last supper.

Bridget motioned Tripp over and she typed in @TheKingEvans into Periscope. It popped up with ten recent broadcasts. She clicked them and his profile opened. She scrolled through the list until she hit the second one from the bottom, close to three weeks ago: *Temp's party.* She clicked it.

"It's over thirty minutes long," Tripp said, his shoulder touching hers.

"I'll skip a lot of it. I don't know what I'm looking for, but they said he was going to get in trouble."

Say you want it, honey. Say yes.

A shaky, wobbling, pixelated stream of Josh's house, the gourmet kitchen, the fifty-foot foyer, up the steps to the darkened hallway. A bedroom with a mahogany bed, thick carpeting, and clothing strewn everywhere. Still nicer than Bridget's room at home, though. Wide, flat dresser, piled with soda bottles and notebooks.

In the background, Josh's laughter and Andrew's loud commentary, his voice deep and cracking in the background. The camera shaking and then black, a girlish screech from behind, followed by a lot of giggling.

The camera settled on the bed, a girl, half lidded and mouth half open. Her shirt off, a lacy red bra and flat, pale stomach dipping into low-cut jeans. Cascading blond hair. The camera jangled and got closer. *White hair. Lucia.*

"Heyyyyyy, baby. Wake up, babbbbyyyyyy." A guy's voice. Porter's wide mouth, long bulbous nose cut into the frame. "Yo, dude, she's out. Maybe? What'd you give her?"

"Me? Nothing. That's all on her, bro. That's the jungle juice in her veins. Cause she's wild like that."

The camera shuffled and dropped, with a deep *fuck* in the background. When it was picked back up, Andrew's face flashed for a moment. The camera angle was even with Lucia's face, her eyes half open. She mumbled something and waved her hand around, laughing, but she looked asleep.

"Come on, baby, you wanted me up here, now I'm up here."

A girlish voice in the background. *La lalalalalwooooooooooooolalalalala.*

"Is she up?"

"She will be. She told me to come up here. She ain't playin' like this."

A hand reached out, a thick scar across the top, and jostled her chin with his fingertip, gently like a lover.

Bridget knew the scar. In tenth grade, Andrew had sliced his hand with a meat slicer at his father's deli. He wrote about it in his journal.

"Say you want it, honey. Say yes."

Lucia for one second opened her eyes, saw Andrew, and smiled. Her eyes, clear and white-blue, the lightest part of the morning sky. Her teeth white, her lips red stained like Kool-Aid. She laughed, a hysterical hiccup, just once. Her eyes fluttered shut, and she said *okay, yes.*

The girl in the background again, singing, high and tight, *wooooooooowoooolalalalalwoooooo.*

The camera stayed on Lucia's face. Porter's voice in the background, *she said yes, dog.* Followed by laughter. Andrew's hand on her breast, shook it twice, and Lucia didn't open her eyes. The broadcast ended.

Bridget felt sick. She looked over at Tripp, white and stricken.

"Jesus Christ," he said.

"Tripp, oh my God, she was raped." She closed her eyes and shook her head. "By one or both of them."

"That's the most messed-up thing I've ever seen." Tripp sat back against the couch, deflated.

"Can I take this to the police? Can I report them?" Bridget's hands were shaking, her voice squeaked. She felt tears gathering in her eyes. God, she hated teenagers.

"I don't know. She said yes, but this is clearly not consent. Not in any meaningful way. I have no idea what the law would say about this. I mean, yeah, we should. At least Harper should see it." He grabbed his phone from the side table. "Play it again, this is a low-tech way, but right now it's all we got, unless you have a recording app on your phone?" Bridget shook her head. He held his phone above hers. She played the video again, the haunting *wooooooooollaaaaaalallaaa,* the *say you want it, honey. Say yes.* The deep, cracking laughter, the shaky camera. Andrew's hand jiggling Lucia's breast. Bridget couldn't watch it a second time.

She didn't even want to know what happened after the camera was turned off.

CHAPTER 28

Alecia, Monday, May 11, 2015

"Gabe, hi Gabe, Gabey, Gabe." Then, "What's this?"

Alecia, from the kitchen, could hear Gabe's therapist, Linda, but not Gabe.

Alecia shoved the remnants of a gooey bagel into her mouth and chased it with cold, stale coffee. She listened to Linda, plastic farm animals lined up in front of Gabe at the wooden table in the living room. They'd had to move the living room around to accommodate; Alecia remembered mainly the fight about the television. Gabe couldn't be next to a window, he was too distracted. In the kitchen, he'd wander to Alecia's side. In his bedroom, the shades pulled shut, he'd get sleepy. When she and Linda moved the living room around, relocating furniture, adjusting the cable wires, Alecia had been proud of her prowess. Gabe, surprisingly, cared very little about the new furniture placement. They celebrated Gabe's flexibility with Skittles.

Nate had whined about the windows being opposite the flat screen because of the glare.

Alecia had initially been furious, but later, pleaded with him. *You'll see so many improvements in him after this, I swear. I know it's a lot. It's a miracle cure, they say.* He stopped grumbling about the glare on the television after that, and even for a short while got on board. He'd ask her daily about his son's progress, but quickly it became underwhelming.

When the therapy didn't prove to make the kind of strides Nate expected, he went back to grumbling about the television. Gabe was still fundamentally Gabe, and to Nate, this implied some kind of suspicious cash diversion. Besides, he'd insisted, Gabe was fine.

Applied behavior analysis, Nate had scoffed. *It sounds like the pamphlets the religious nuts bring you on Sunday mornings.*

So, research it. It's not. It's proven scientifically to work. Some people even say their autistic children have been cured. Alecia had pushed the brochure across the table at him.

Maybe he doesn't need a cure. Maybe he's fine the way he is? But all this meant was that Nate didn't really know his son. That he didn't really see him the way Alecia did.

It seemed to Alecia at the time like a dream within reach. A cure! For a brief few months, she allowed herself the indulgence. She kept a private Pinterest board that she filled with teachers' gift ideas, fun rewards systems for good behavior, mom hacks, educational field trips. She visited dozens of websites on how to sneak vegetables into macaroni and cheese and homemade ice cream, how to bake the perfect brownie, 101 Valentine's ideas for kids, twenty April Fool's Day jokes. She bought a single plastic sticker: a soccer ball. For the minivan that didn't exist, and the sport Gabe didn't play. She tucked it underneath the lacy underwear in her top drawer.

Her dreams were never big, yet still somehow not quite small enough to accomplish.

Failure to advance. Inconsistent improvement. Struggling. These were the words that came after a year of three- to four-hour therapy sessions a day. He needed more, Linda explained. Nate put his foot down, *do they just want more money? Why would we do more if what we're doing isn't working?*

So here they were. Three to four hours every single day, and progress had stalled with Gabe knowing maybe a hundred to two hundred words. Alecia could see improvement in his communication; he now pointed to things or used his words. There seemed to be fewer breakdowns. The improvement was slushy and gray, too nuanced for Nate to see it, and sometimes Alecia wondered if they were actually just standing still.

"Horse!" Gabe yelled, his chair cracking on the hardwood floor as he jumped up excitedly.

Linda laughed, a honking duck noise. "You always get the horse!"

"What's this?"

Gabe threw is hands in the air now, laughing. "Cow!"

"What's this?"

"Rooster!"

"Alecia, he finally got rooster!" Linda clapped her hands and whooped and Alecia pushed her fingertips against the bridge of her nose. She wanted to yell back, *big fucking deal*. They'd only been working on rooster for two weeks. Two weeks for the word *rooster*. Besides, how was it valuable? They weren't farmers. He'd probably never even see a real, live rooster.

She felt pushed to the brittle edge.

If she could focus on anything but that hat, the muddy COACH, Nate and the vision of him sliding down that embankment, losing his hat and running after the girl with the white hair, to what? To do what? Did he catch her? Kiss her? Kill her? Alecia had no idea. Then there was the way Bridget looked at her, like she was some kind of monster. The idea that they were all this close to their lives falling completely apart.

She did not for one second care about rooster. She didn't have the stamina in her to even summon the enthusiasm for whatever small measure of progress Gabe managed. Following closely behind the fatigue was a crushing guilt that she *should* care. The knowledge that he would only advance *if* she cared, and that maybe the reason he was *struggling* was because she hadn't quite done enough. Felt enough. Tried hard enough. Pushed herself far enough.

Linda appeared in the doorway.

"I read the paper, honey. No one could blame you for being distracted today." Linda helped herself to a glass of water, running the tap and flicking the water stream with her fingertips to test for temperature.

"I'm not distracted," Alecia said, slamming her own glass of iced tea down on the counter so hard it sloshed over the side. "I just don't see the point in all of this. He's not getting better. He's not going to get better."

Linda filled her water glass and took a long drink. She carefully set the glass on the counter next to Alecia's and retrieved a paper towel, mopping up the water spill and discarding the towel before she spoke. "This is not a destination trip, Alecia." She stopped, tapped her index finger against her lips. "He may or may not get 'better,' but I think it's high time you looked at what your definition of 'better' is. Your son is a wonderful little boy, exactly how he is. What we are hoping to unlock is his potential. We are not going to fundamentally change who he is. I think you want the latter, not the former. Until you adjust your expectations, you will always feel like we're standing in still waters." She stepped closer to Alecia, her voice low, towering over her, and placed a large, weathered hand on her shoulder. "You measure his success here, based on three hours a day, with a limited ruler. You define him by whether or not he knows the word *rooster* and how fast he knows it."

"He has less than one year to be ready for kindergarten." Alecia heard the shrill in her voice, the panicky pitch.

"And so what? What if he doesn't make it? What if he's not ready until he's seven?" Linda's hand pushed down.

"He has to be ready when he's six to go to public school. With his friends."

"He doesn't have friends, Alecia."

Alecia winced. She'd meant the kids in their development, the ones who paid Gabe no mind, not even to say hello. The ones who rode bikes in the cul-de-sac and watched Gabe run a cement mixer down their front steps for three hours at a time, up and down, up and down, up and down, never once asking him to play.

Linda sighed. "I think you'll find if you open your narrow view of Gabe's world and really *look at him,* you'll find that you have plenty of options. There are other schools, you know."

"You mean special-needs schools. Autism schools." Alecia shook her head. "No. I just want him to be a normal boy."

Linda shrugged, her palms out, and gave Alecia a sad smile. "It's hard to say; what's so great about normal?"

In the living room, she turned on the stereo, a loud country twang, and Alecia gritted her teeth. Gabe, for some godforsaken reason, adored country music. The guitar, the lament, the soulful crooning. Linda turned the volume up and she and Gabe danced around the living room, singing. Patsy Cline and Willie Nelson and Kenny Rogers and Glen Campbell; the more Nashville, the better.

Alecia texted the baby-sitter next door and got an answer back right away. She called into Linda, "Hey, Mandy is coming over for a bit. I'm going to run to the bank. You okay, buddy?" she asked Gabe, and he waved wildly.

She let herself out the back door, just as Mandy was coming in. Alecia pushed a folded twenty-dollar bill into her palm and raced to the car, where she flipped on the air, the cold blowing in her face. She drove to the end of the block, parking the car in an empty church parking lot, where she closed her eyes and promptly fell asleep.

Avoiding public places seemed like a good idea, but Alecia had an insurance check in her purse pocket for two weeks, and with Nate out of work, they needed the money more than she needed her dignity. The bank seemed like a quick errand, and a decent escape. She rubbed the sleep from her eyes; a quick ten-minute nap had calmed her racing heart considerably. Linda's little acceptance speech felt very far away, and that was a good thing.

She avoided looking at anyone directly, instead studied the check in her hand, as if the signature on it, the logo held her utmost interest. When her teller called out *next!* she shuffled to the window and pushed her signed check across the marble top.

She felt a stare, or maybe heard a giggle, or a whisper—it was hard to pinpoint what made her turn around, but she did. Bea Tempest and Jennifer Lawson stood together, looking her way, by the potted ficus inside the front door. She stiffened her back and pretended not to see, rummaging through her purse for something, anything—gum or candy or a hair tie—anything to look busy. She thought of Jennifer Lawson in that red dress, her green eyes quick and darting, that tongue sweeping the corners of her mouth. *Your hubby, Saint Nate.* No, no, no, no, no.

Alecia was wrung out, the fight clean sapped out of her. She dug through her bag, made a big show of it, shaking her head, mumbling *where is it* under her breath, waiting for the teller to call *next!* For Jennifer and Bea to wave their French-manicured fingers at each other, *byeeeeee,* and go to their respective black SUVs.

She was, in fact, so busy looking busy that she didn't notice the front door open, the little bell above it chime. Alecia didn't pay it any attention until she heard the dragging noise, some kind of huffing behind her. She looked up, and the first thing she saw was gray-white hair, slicked straight with grease. Thick, leathered skin. A mouth open like a gray-green O. Words, garbled and unclear.

"Do you care at all that she's missing?" He asked her, his voice warbling and dense, thick as he coughed.

"Excuse me?" Alecia's head snapped up then, the remnants of the bagel from breakfast slick and rolling in her stomach.

"You all act like it doesn't matter. A girl is missing, maybe dead, and no one cares." His hand rolled around his forehead, dirty fingers pushing his shaggy hair to the side, slicking it against his eyebrows.

Oh my God. It was Jimmy Hamm. Back from God knows where, and judging by the looks of him, nowhere good. Alecia opened her mouth to speak and found she had nothing to say.

"Nonyas care!" Jimmy shouted, and spun around. Bea and Jennifer scurried out the front door, the sun gleaming off Bea's blond hair as they tipped their heads together and watched the scene through the glass door. Bea whipped out her phone and made a call, her hand waving and pointing toward the door.

"Next!" The teller called, oblivious, and Alecia scooted away from Jimmy, who'd started to pace, his foot dragging slightly behind him, step, whoosh, step, whoosh. Alecia closed her eyes. Jimmy reached from behind her and slapped the wooden counter, his hand wizened and black under the fingernails.

"Why is no one looking for Lucia?" he demanded, and Alecia backed up, her hand behind her gripping the counter; she clutched her purse to her chest.

"Hey!" The teller leaned forward, finally realizing Jimmy was there and there was about to be a scene in the bank. "Jimmy Hamm!" she called. "Where you been, honey?" She was older, in her sixties. Everyone looked familiar in Mt. Oanoke, but Alecia couldn't have produced her name.

Jimmy swayed on his feet, his eyes fluttering back then snapping on Alecia's face. Her heart thudded in her neck. "You've seen her, though, eh? I read the paper. I usedta know your husband, back when he'd come to the Quarry Bar. He do something with my little girl?"

Alecia shook her head, her tongue swollen in her throat.

"What do *you* know about it? Or is the wife

always the last to know?" He cackled and inched closer. He smelled like mildew and smoke, whiskey and something fetid, his teeth gray and glistening.

"Hey now, Jimmy," A voice from the door and Jimmy whipped around. A uniformed officer was silhouetted in the doorway. He moved slowly, his hand on his waistband, a deceptively easy smile on his face, and Alecia sagged back, relieved. "Ronnie from the QB called me and said you were in town. That your Chrysler out there?" The cop motioned to the parking lot, where Bea and Jennifer still huddled. Behind them a gray, paint-stripped Chrysler station wagon sat idling, the engine still running, the air thick with diesel.

"I don't want no trouble." Jimmy walked slowly past the cop, toward the door, his hand on the push-bar when the officer stopped him.

"I can't let you leave here, Jimmy. You're drunk as a skunk at ten in the morning. You can't get in your car and roll back out of town as fast as you rolled in. You wanna come with me and sober up in the tank? Just for the day. Have a meal on the county?"

Jimmy thought about it. A decent meal, even one as gluey and greasy as he'd get in the drunk tank, seemed better than what he could scrape together at the QB. Alecia held her breath, praying he'd say yes.

"Nah, I'm okay, man. I'll just walk around."

"Hey, have you seen Lucia around?" the cop asked.

"Not since last year." Jimmy's voice was low, his back against the door blocking the entrance.

"Where you been, Jimmy?"

"Had a job at Fizz's." Jimmy's voice trailed off. Fizz was the soda bottling plant about thirty miles south, in Allentown. Alecia saw, for the first time, what shutting down the paper mill had done to the town and the people in it. She wondered about the Mt. Oanoke of Nate's youth, the one he used to talk about, with a thriving industry, a stable economy, enough jobs for people to stay.

"You still got that job?" he asked softly, and Jimmy shook his head.

"Why'd you come back here?" The officer reached out and gripped Jimmy's elbow gently, and Jimmy let him.

"I read the paper. This town's gone to shit." Jimmy whirled around to Alecia and the teller and said, "I sent them money, you know. Every month until a few months ago. Ever'one thinks I just skipped out on 'em. I sent money. No one knows that."

Alecia thought about Lenny and how that money probably went right into his veins or his lungs and wondered if Lucia had even been aware of it.

"I ain't a shit father," Jimmy yelled again, and

this time the cop guided him out to the waiting car in the lot. "Ever'one thinks I am but I ain't."

The car pulled away, its lights whirling just once, out of the parking lot, and Bea and Jennifer scurried to their cars and drove off. The only people who remained were Alecia and the bank teller, the lobby so silent that Alecia could hear the seconds tick from the clock on the wall.

"Hon, you still want that check cashed?" the teller asked from behind the counter. Her name tag read Yolanda. Alecia realized she still held the check, and with a shaky hand, passed it to her, along with the deposit slip. She counted money, her eyes flicking to Alecia's face every so often, until she handed fifty in cash across the gate.

She pushed the two twenties and a ten into the pocket of her purse and barely mumbled good-bye. Yolanda shook her head, her mouth pursed like a lemon. "That Jimmy," was all she said, but Alecia didn't reply.

She stumbled out of the lobby and into the bright May sun, shining like it was any other day, the rays hot on her skin even though for the life of her, Alecia couldn't get warm.

She couldn't stop shivering.

CHAPTER 29

Bridget, Tuesday, May 12, 2015

"I'll be honest with you, Ms. Peterson, Officer Harris." Harper leaned forward, adjusted his glasses on his nose, his mustache twitching. "This video is disturbing, there's no doubt. I'm not convinced it has bearing on the case. On Mr. Winters's case. There's never been a question that Ms. Hamm is a troubled teenager."

"This isn't a video about a troubled teenaged *girl,*" Bridget said, the hair on her neck rising, and Harper's brows furrowed at her tone. "This is a video about a troubled teenage boy. Maybe more than one. There has been bullying at the school. The kids call Lucia a witch. They almost set her on fire."

Harper shook his head. "Then go to the school, Ms. Peterson. Go to Bachman and tell him about it."

"I intend to, but I really think there's something else going on here, that Lucia's disappearance maybe has nothing to do with Nate at all."

Tripp stood stoically behind her—she could feel the heat of him less than a foot away—but he stayed silent. Infuriatingly so. She wanted him to get angry, speak up for his friend, protest Harper's steamroll, despite his job being at stake. She knew he wouldn't, that simply standing there was enough for him, and it should probably have been enough for her.

"You may think that, Ms. Peterson, and I can't even say for sure that you're wrong. But it's simply not compelling enough to chase it down the rabbit hole. Now, what I will do is send it over to Clark Mackey, the other detective here in town, to look into it as a separate case. There's no doubt that the video is disturbing."

"So a rape investigation?" Bridget pressed, and she might have imagined the sharp intake of Tripp's breath behind her, the way he shifted his weight. The way so many men were inherently uncomfortable with the word *rape,* like just saying it invoked some unspoken appraisal of all men. She'd found less bristling among cops, who'd seen the worst of the worst, the dregs of humanity on a daily basis. But she'd found it among the kids. Being a creative writing teacher gave her a sort of latitude not employed by her colleagues. She could plunge the depths of her kids' minds, or as deep as they'd let her in, broach subjects like abuse and rape, consent and sexuality, all under the guise of writing. In previous years, she'd used it to her full capacity, and her desire to understand the new generation was worth the price of an occasional talk with Bachman about *appropriate classroom content,* and concerned parent phone calls.

"I said *maybe,*" Harper stressed. His face slacked, his eyes softened. "I have a teenage niece, do you know that? She's fifteen, lives up north a bit. Social media, Facebook, Twitter, YouTube, Instagram, Yik Yak, Kik, it's all terrifying. I get that. You see it every day, you live with the effects of it day in and out. I understand that, Bridget."

"Then help me. Help them," Bridget said, even though she knew he wouldn't. He couldn't.

"I can't spend my days policing teenage behavior," Harper said. "As much as I'd like to. We have a heroin problem around here, did you know that? I'm tied up in that most days."

"Is this because of who it is? Andrew Evans? Porter Max? The baseball heroes of Mt. Oanoke?"

Harper's face hardened, his eyes narrowed. "Ms. Peterson, I'll pretend you didn't say that. I'm not saying this video isn't incriminating. I just think it's not ironclad proof of a crime. There's no sex, he said on the video himself, 'You called me up here.' There's consensual drinking, that much is obvious. But I can't chase down an underage drinking charge."

"It depends on your definition of consensual. Just because she said yes means she consented?"

"Isn't that what consent is?"

"Not if she's so drunk she's passed out. All she hears is 'say yes' and she says yes."

"Who are you angry at? Who are you fighting for?" Harper asked Bridget quietly, leaning forward.

She thought about this—it was valid question. "I don't know. The truth. I don't think Nate did anything to this girl. He loves his students."

"Maybe that's the problem, do you think?" Harper reached behind him to scratch his back, his armpits wet and yellowed. Bridget realized how hot it was in the station, the sweat trickling down her neck. "I'm done, Bridget. Okay?" He stood up, ending their meeting. "If Lucia walked in here now and reported a rape, I'd have a different answer."

Bridget hiked her purse up onto her arm and pressed her mouth closed, her lips dry, her tongue sour. "And what if she can't?"

"So that's it, then?" Tripp stood next to his truck in the parking lot, the sun bouncing off the gleaming red paint, a blind spot in Bridget's eye.

"Not for me. For you?" Bridget squinted up at him and he looked around the lot, his blond hair reflecting light like his truck. He toed the dirt like a teenager.

"I don't know. I can't go off half-cocked like

you can. I have a job to protect here. You get that, right?"

"Yeah." She did get it, but she felt deflated anyway, the pinprick of disappointment in her gut.

"It's too hot for May," Tripp said, suddenly changing the subject. They'd settled it then, sunk to talking about the weather, the hotness, the sweat. Even the dust seemed wet with humidity. Tripp pointed to the back lot, toward the diner, The 543, the letters blinking. Bridget nodded and they walked, wordless, the gravel kicking up at her feet, and she marveled about their comfort level, how easily they'd slipped into friendship.

Inside the diner, seated, they ordered dessert and coffee, sharing a quarter of an apple pie off the same plate, talking very little while Bridget tried to think of what to do next, but it felt easier than she remembered, being with a man. Tripp didn't press her to talk, like even Alecia did sometimes. Then again, Alecia had known her when Bridget herself avoided silence, filling the hole with endless chatter. Alecia still thought of her as that person. Tripp hardly knew her at all.

"I think I need to talk to Nate. Any idea where he is today?" Bridget asked. "I have to show him the broadcast. He's going to flip, I think."

"Why?"

"Andrew Evans is his golden child. His star baseball player. The Evans family has supported

Nate, one of the only ones who have." They'd been at the original pavilion meeting after the story broke. Bridget remembered the way Mrs. Evans nodded, her head bobbing like a puppet. The way she didn't speak, her teeth working the soft skin of her lip.

"I think he's home. He sleeps a lot when I'm not around. When I'm home, he goes out. I think he avoids me."

"He won't take my calls. I've tried twice. I still don't know what to say to him." She shrugged, pressed her finger to the crumbs on the plate and then stuck it into her mouth, thinking. "I haven't talked much to Alecia, either. A few times. She's coming undone, but I don't know how to fix that."

They finished the pie and the waitress ambled up, her apron sagging below an ample bosom, her hair slicked back into a tight bun. She had a red, wintry face, bursting and shiny. "I know y'all, don't I?" Her neck wobbled as she nodded. "You're that teacher, the one who's friends with Winters. Y'all think he didn't diddle that girl, his student." She spat the last word out like it was a cuss word and Bridget found herself shaking her head. "I saw you at the meeting a few weeks back. And now she's missing. You still think that?" Her apple cheeks huffed with the effort, her fingertips with bright red nails flitting in their direction as she pulled out the pad to write up the bill. "My cousin, she goes to that school.

She's a senior. You know her? Ashlee Williams?"

Bridget nodded. Ashlee was a quiet student, a cheerleader with a clique of friends that was neither cruel nor kind but rather just there. She was rounder than the other cheerleaders, her hair frizzy. She'd always slipped her way into the right crowd, a good student. "I know her. Nice girl, cheerleader, right?"

The waitress nodded and tore off the top sheet, ripping halfway down the page, her nameplate blinking a silvery Misty. "Tell you what, if Winters did that to my cousin, I'd castrate him." She pushed the bill down on the Formica with a thick finger and gave them both a wide smile. "Y'all have a good day now."

Night came, hard and quick, and Bridget's house was dark when she got home, as though the day skipped entirely over twilight and sunset and went right to midnight. She wandered to the kitchen, the pie still on her tongue, not knowing if she was hungry or thirsty, but instead made tea. Her phone trilled from the table, and when she picked it up, there was a waiting text from Tripp: *Sorry again about Misty. Call me tomorrow.*

She texted back: *It's okay. Not your fault. This town . . .*

I know it. I live it, he replied.

Bridget thought about what Harper said, the heroin problem. Lenny, his oil-slick hair and purple bulging arms, pocked with whiteheads and scabs, the veins running lines down his cottony white skin.

She thought about Tripp, the way the hair on his calf tapered to a smooth ankle. How he smelled, clean yet boyish, a hint of saltiness, like jeans left an hour too long in the washer.

What if I wanted to try it? she texted on a whim and then instantly regretted it, biting her lower lip so hard her eyes stung.

Heroin??

She rolled her eyes. *No. Dating. You said I should try it.*

There was two minutes of nothing then, which seemed more telling than any response, and Bridget was typing *never mind, forget I said anything* when the text finally—finally—came back.

You let me know. I'm here for you. She laughed, and it seemed enormously loud in her empty kitchen.

Later, in bed, she pulled the student journals out of her bag. She skipped the pink ones, the brown leather Moleskines, and went right for the black bound with the gold stitching, the outline of a raven on the front, its beak sharp and pointing to the left, the one smooth eye looking toward the horizon. She paged through it, the edges gold and gilded. How could Lucia have afforded such a thing? It was incongruous. When she fanned through the pages, they smelled musty. Old.

The entries were no less erratic than she remembered: drawings of birds, tarot cards and long rambling descriptions of self-readings, bare trees, pencil and a few charcoal sketches, no color whatsoever. Some poetry entries, some written out like love letters. Scraps of thought, raw and quick, like to a lover.

> Don't you just love Nietzsche? I feel like you mock me when I talk about this. I've been obsessed with Our Virtues, the idea that those who are exceptional are hated. The idea that knowledge is self-torture, a quest for knowing a form of the spiritual cruelty. I can hear you saying shut up. But it's true. Everyone wants to pretend we're this upper echelon, but really, we're just part of the food chain. We've usurped our role but only by luck, by chance. I look at Lenny and all I see is how lucky he is, he's so stupid, still an animal, then. I look around and all I see is animals. Stop laughing.
>
> The thing is, you looked at me so strange the first time I said that, like you were seeing me for the first time. No one ever has. I'm not sure that anyone has ever seen me for the first time. I've

been seen forever by everybody as the same person: The bitch, the witch, Lulu (but only from Taylor, always, always Taylor—I'm reminded of the quote about there being some madness in love, but always reason in madness, and with Taylor, I'm not sure that's true, but we'll get to that), the fucking idiot (by Lenny the fucking idiot, of course, who else). But with you I am just me, and everything I say or do is new or surprising and you act like no one has ever said it or done it before, which is utter bullshit, I know, but when I say that you laugh.

I try too hard to make you laugh.

• • •

When we were nine, you bought me a licorice whip from the QB before it became the QB, while it was still sometimes okay that we rode our bikes there and before it smelled like piss and sex. When we were eleven, your mom gave me money for the Bronx Zoo, over fifty dollars, and I'd never seen a bill with a fifty on it, I didn't even know they made them. But then I could go on the class trip instead of sitting in the gym with the fourth-graders. When we were fifteen, maybe sixteen, you gave me your heart— the day you danced in the fountain, remember now?— and said it was forever, but now I'm not so sure.

People change, we both said, but you, you can be cruel and you don't even know it. You can't see your own meanness, it's all a justification. I've never known a time when you didn't own me, when I wasn't yours.

You'll be gone soon, which is sad and good, but mainly only good for you. I'll be here. I'll always, always be here, your Lulu.

Have you ever wanted to just hurt someone? How about me, have you ever wanted to hurt me?

Bridget ran her thumb over the page, a small silver-plated plastic heart taped to the inside. She pried it off the page, the tape coming up slightly fuzzy from the paper, and could see the broken plastic on the back, like it had been attached to something: a pendant or a ring. She gently pulled the tape away: BE FRI.

She could see the other half in her mind: ST ENDS. The two pieces together making a whole heart. A cheesy, cheap novelty.

It was amazing, really. Something so plastic, so fragile could be holding it all together.

CHAPTER 30

Nate, Tuesday, May 12, 2015

When Nate was a kid, his dad, the late, great Bob Winters, was a man of few words. A mill supervisor during the day, but a baseball coach to Nate at every stage of his life, until the day he keeled over on shift while fixing a gasket on the Fourdrinier table. Bob was in maintenance, could tell you just about anything regarding water corrosion and rust, paper making and humidity. One day he just sat right down with his left hand on the still conveyor belt, his right hand clutching a wrench, and went to sleep. They said it was an aneurysm, but all Nate knew for most of his life is that the paper mill killed his father. He didn't feel anything about it, he wasn't angry about it, it was just plain as fact to him. Unlike Vi, who thought the "fumes did him in," never mind how many people told her that the chemical was harmless. She knew, deep down, that the paper mill killed Bob. The thing is, though, Bob wouldn't have said that. He wouldn't have harbored anger about it, that is, if one can harbor anger about their own death. He would have shrugged, the way he always did about everything, and said something vague and mumbling like, *the only thing you can't outrun is your own skin. Not death or taxes or the mail. Just your skin.*

Nate never knew what that meant.

If either Nate or Bob had been deep, pondering kind of men, they might wax philosophical about consequences and how the decisions made in your life either help you or hamper you, but no matter what, they're yours to keep. But Nate wasn't this kind of man. Mostly he thought Bob was simple, and maybe a bit thick in the skull.

Until now.

The phrase came to him in the early morning, the reddish haze, sun behind closed but awake eyelids: *you can't outrun your own skin,* and Nate sat up, heart thudding, and it occurred to him that he was trying—desperately—to do just that.

His hiking boots sat in the corner, mud caked, from his long walks through the forests he'd long forgotten about, his thigh muscles out of practice, straining under the long treks. Hours he'd be out there, sometimes, even in the same section of woods he'd tried to find Lucia in.

He wasn't looking for her, he would have insisted to anyone who found him, and it would have been true. He was mostly just trying to pass the time doing something he remembered enjoying when he was younger. The smell of damp dirt and rotting vegetation was the perfume of childhood, wet and clinging to his skin and erasing troubles with a muddy thumbprint just as easily now as it did then.

He couldn't have explained to anyone how hard it was not to have a purpose, or rather to have your purpose be yanked from you as quickly as a magician's tablecloth, and to still be able-bodied, able-minded, just empty. He couldn't have talked to anyone about how he was shelled, hollowed out in the middle, and wandering, because then people would say *but what about the girl?* Like he was a monster and how dare he think of himself.

But when you're alone, you can't help but think of yourself.

He thought of Alecia, her anger lighting a fire under his skin until he pushed her out of his mind. He thought of Gabe, his warm, smiling little boy, the feel of his arms around Nate's neck, the smell of his hair, slightly damp, slightly sweet, a little boyish smell, a sticky sourness in his neck.

He spent precious little time worrying about Lucia, and he admitted only to himself that he wished he'd never met her, even though for months prior, he'd spent more time than he'd ever admit preoccupied with her. Worrying about her, wondering if she was all right, thinking about her awful, deranged brother, even once following Lenny through the mall, in and out of Rubic, a well-known head shop, to his truck—the one he and Lucia had shared—until he got in and drove away.

Something about the way her mouth would twist when she said certain things, a whisper of a confidence, the shy duck of her head when she admitted anything at all about herself, like she had no right to do so. She stayed later in his classroom than she needed to, her feet propped up comfortably on the desk in front of him, a ratty, secondhand platform heel bouncing, the skin on her thigh rippling so slightly with each bounce, her legs bare. He didn't look too hard at her legs, in fact, avoided looking at them. He did like making her laugh, a high feminine tinging that tickled the back of his brain.

He couldn't have explained all that. She laughed so little, that was all. Her life seemed like such a shabby confusing mess to him that he worked really hard for those laughs.

She'd say these wild things—throwing broad proclamations at him, just to see how he'd juggle them, and it was this reckless flinging of her soul that he found so intriguing. He wasn't even sure what parts of her ramblings were true. *I can walk on my hands. It's true, my mother was in the circus and she taught me before she had to go away. I've been reading Jung, you know he's full of slightly less shit than Nietzsche.* She was like a constantly streaming ticker tape of isolated statements, fact and fiction tangled together, indistinguishable.

And sometimes she'd stay late and perch on the edge of his desk, his arm brushing up against her leg until he moved his chair a few inches away. He was careful to keep the distance, but he can't say he didn't notice. He can't say only now, and only to himself, that she'd tongue-tie him, his throat dry. And then the kiss, the thing that should have ended all their talks and he probably should have blown her off after that, or least discouraged her in earnest, but he didn't. He didn't think about the kiss, the way her fingers sought his skin between the buttons of his shirt, the warmth of her skin, the confusion in her face that he'd turn her away—she'd been so sure he wouldn't. No, he avoided the corner of his own brain where that kiss stayed, wedged between his first blow job (Melissa Kinney, seventeen, on the railroad trestle) and his last sexual encounter before meeting Alecia (in the bathroom at the QB and all he remembered was her legs wrapped around him, her back against the stall door—he couldn't have even told you if it was the men's room or not). It shone there in that corner, bright like the sun, only ever to be examined in periphery.

Then she came back one day like it never happened, asking him, *did you know that Nietzsche died because he saved a horse?* And hanging on his answer like he had any idea what the *hell* she was talking about and they were back, the way they were before the kiss.

She made him feel.

It was this admission that pushed him into the woods, plowing through the underbrush, the thickets stuck to his pants, his legs, the way he plundered the depths of his mind, wondering if what everyone was saying about him was true. Sometimes he'd stop, his hands on his knees, and suck wind, his lungs bursting, and wonder if that was actually the thing. He wasn't guilty of the things people said he was, but he wasn't *not guilty,* either.

Except he didn't kill her.

He was thinking about this, his guilty-but-not-guilty acts, when he saw a flash of something in front of him. A quick but deliberate movement, that of a person, not an animal in the thick, off to the left. He pushed his way through a wild, sticking raspberry bush, his neck suddenly sweating. He hadn't come into the woods to find her. But he hadn't considered what would happen if he did.

Would he call the police again? He stopped, considering. How would it look? What would she say? What would she do?

He heard a loud snap then, and a low rumbling groan.

Tentatively, he called out, "Lucia?" his voice

358

shaking and wobbly. God he was so stupid, everyone would think so. How do you explain to people that growing up in the woods meant the woods became your only safe haven, the sounds of birds and the smell of far-off babbling creeks, the dew condensing on all the green leaves and the late afternoon sunlight filtering through the canopy of branches were things that felt like home, when home wasn't a place he could go. He was safe here.

Except when he wasn't.

Another snap, another voice. He picked up his pace, pushing at the brush in front of him. He arms being scratched by pricker bushes as he pushed into a clearing, then instinctively ducking back.

He expected to see her, her white hair, her black jacket, that pale skin. Instead he saw a man, crouched on the log, a knife in his hand, skimming across something in his lap, the blood running down his shin. An animal. A fish. A process Nate knew on instinct, and if he kept going, behind the man, behind the log, he'd bet he would find a campfire. He was cleaning a fish for dinner.

Nate pushed his back up against the tree, his hands cold, his heart thumping. He peered around the trunk again. The man looked familiar, older, dirty, his head bowed so low Nate couldn't see his face. Nate crouched down, a stick cracking under his boot, and the man's head snapped up, swinging side to side, his eyes almost meeting Nate's, and Nate felt himself suck in his breath. Suddenly, he recognized him.

It was Jimmy Hamm.

He was making a sandwich in Tripp's kitchen when he heard the front door bang shut and Tripp's quick steps cross the living room into the kitchen.

"Hey," Tripp said, pausing in the doorway like he was the guest, and Nate waved back awkwardly. He never knew what to say to Tripp; it had been days since they'd seen each other. The investigation was ongoing, especially now with Lucia missing for a week. Nate hadn't asked about it, and even if he did, Tripp surely wouldn't talk about it, so typically they fell into talking about baseball or something else utterly inane.

Nate hesitated. He wanted to tell Tripp about seeing Jimmy Hamm in the woods. What if Tripp didn't believe him? Wouldn't that drive yet another wedge between them? Nate floating some wild theory about Jimmy out there, just to have Tripp tell his cop buddies. Nate could hear them laughing at his desperation, playing the role of Dr. Richard Kimble—*it was the one-armed man!* The whole thing had a self-serving expedience to it that even Nate couldn't deny.

Yet he couldn't just pretend he didn't see it, either.

In the woods, he had frozen when he recognized Jimmy. He watched him clean the fish, leave the guts in the clearing, and take the filets and the head back out the path the way he came. Nate should have stopped him. Should have called out.

He didn't because being seen in the woods, the same woods that Lucia had disappeared in, didn't look so hot for him, either.

Still. What the fuck was Jimmy Hamm doing cooking fish in the woods when he had a house? Seemingly, a son. A drug addict abusive son, but a son nonetheless. None of it made sense.

"I kind of wanted to talk to you. I think I saw something today." Waving the pack of lunch meat in Tripp's direction, Nate asked, "Dinner?"

"No, I, um, ate a late lunch." He gave Nate a grin, the kind that made Nate stand up straight and reroute his thinking. He looked like the proverbial cat with the canary.

"Oh? A special lunch?" Nate put away the lunch meat and mayo, then grabbed a Miller Lite, kicking the fridge shut with his foot.

"Kind of. With Bridget."

"My Bridget?" The words were out before he could think about them and Tripp turned his head to the side, gave him a weird look.

"Your Bridget?" Tripp asked, his voice edged with a new kind of wariness.

"Well, I just meant the same Bridget we know, that's all," Nate amended, but he felt the prickle down his back. Tripp, with his zillion dates, moving in on Bridget who was still so goddamn broken. "She's not ready for you, stud." It was meant to be a joke, but it came out thinner, a finer point on it than he'd intended.

"What the fuck does that mean?" Tripp's mouth went firm, set at the corners, and Nate felt the zing between them, an electric tether, a blinking danger sign he'd previously been unaware of. But the speed at which it lit up told him, yes, oh yes, it had been there all along. At every card game, every late night at their house, when Tripp would crash and wedge himself between Bridget and Holden, gaining purchase in any hairline crack he could find, his arms flung wide around Alecia and Bridget, giggling like a schoolkid.

"Nothing. It means nothing. It was a joke, that's all," Nate said, backing up, grabbing his sandwich. "There's fifty bucks on the table for groceries this week, okay? I can get you rent money if you need it. No problem." His thoughts zinged back to Jimmy, his head low over his lap, fish scales scattering. "So, about that thing—"

"I don't think it is a joke, not really," Tripp continued, his voice dipping soft and rumbled, the hardness gone. "Alecia, Lucia, Bridget, Jennifer Lawson, Robin Hendricks—remember her?"

Nate shook his head, although he *did* remember her, a mistake, an escape, a transgression—and a mild one at that—but he'd paid for and forgotten about it, pushed to that same cobwebbed corner of his mind. Jennifer Lawson, well, that was hardly fair; she kissed him. He'd stopped her and it was over. He tried not to think of that night. The fight between her and Burt had a fine edge of violence to it: Jenny had thrown a glass, which splintered on the Tempests' tiled kitchen floor. He'd taken her home; she'd cried and he'd held her, a natural instinct, her face pushed into the pocket of his neck. He didn't remember how the kiss had happened.

Tripp continued, "Are they all yours, Winters? Do you think everyone in Mt. Oanoke belongs to you?"

CHAPTER 31

Alecia, Tuesday, May 12, 2015

Alecia wasn't a drinker, not by any stretch. But when Linda arrived Tuesday morning, a headache pulsed behind her eyes and she pinched the bridge of her nose. Monday night she'd been drunk. Maybe enough to earn a barstool at the QB, certainly enough to send her retching into the toilet at three in the morning, Gabe sleeping soundly for once.

Linda screeched into the kitchen, a monolith, tall and foreboding, hustling Gabe into the next room, leaving Alecia alone for the second day of bad parenting in a row.

She checked her phone, saw a waiting text message. *Are you ok?* Then, *I miss you.*

Oh, she forgot. She texted Nate. She scrolled up the conversation: *Do you know Jimmy Hamm is back in town? Came into the bank, drunk, raving like a lunatic.* Then, *seems like weird timing don't you think?* He wrote back, *He's been gone a long time,* which was a maddeningly vague reply. A few minutes later, *I thought I saw him in the woods the other day.*

A sober thought: What was Nate doing in the woods?

He'd written, *Should I tell Tripp? Don't know.*

She wanted Nate to deny everything again; she needed him to do it. But hadn't he denied his guilt a million times? Begged her to believe him, even?

That hat, the COACH thumbed over and muddy flipping down the embankment.

By telling Nate about Jimmy, she'd all but told Nate she believed him. Maybe she did; it was hard to say in the face of so much evidence. She felt the pulse of truth in her heart. Why was he in the woods? Even as she formed the question in her mind, she knew the answer. When Nate was confused or lost or needed time to himself, he took to the trails. He hiked. She never knew him to be more lost than he was right now.

Was she making excuses? Maybe.

His replies were noncommittal and she remembered getting mad about it. *Why does Bridget care more about your innocence than you do?* He hadn't written back other than to say he missed her. Her words were jumbled, misspelled. He even asked her once, *Are you drunk?*

She'd answered him no, but it was a lie, because sometimes the lie was easier.

By the afternoon, she felt better, fresh, showered and clean, teeth brushed. The only remnant of her night was the disjointed text conversation with Nate.

Alecia reviewed it again, decided she hadn't said anything so awful after all. She didn't know what she wanted, but she didn't want Nate to show up on their doorstep, his bag in hand. She wasn't there yet.

Still, Jimmy was back now, which *was* a weird coincidence. And Nate saw him, too; at least he said he did.

The doorbell rang and Alecia answered it.

Bridget held a chocolate cheesecake. "It's all they had. It's a bit much for the heat." After a pause, she asked, "Can I come in?"

Alecia felt a twinge of annoyance, but couldn't pinpoint why.

In the kitchen, she made tea, Gabe at her hip, tugging on her shirt for one thing or another, pointing at water, then cereal. She bagged Kix for him as Bridget watched.

Bridget was good with Gabe, got down on his level, talked to him like a person. Never cared when he didn't talk back, or when he answered her not so much with words but with grunts or pointing. Sometimes he replied, a yes or a no, *what are you drinking, Gabe? Water,* the easy questions.

But she didn't do that today, she didn't talk to Gabe, just stood in the kitchen holding a cheesecake too heavy for the hot day and shifting in her clogs.

"How was school?" Alecia asked, finally rescuing her, taking the cake from her hands and pulling a knife from the woodblock on the counter.

"Oh, you know, weird. The teachers are weird, everyone whispers. Everything is quiet." Bridget settled onto a stool, her mouth twisted in a grimace like she might cry. "I want to show you this." She pulled out her phone and flicked the screen with her fingers, her hands shaky as she slid the device across the counter. Alecia picked it up, the video already playing, loud shaky music, kids screeching in the background, a deep voice behind the camera.

"What is this?"

"A video of a party. Just watch."

The image of a girl, sprawled on the bed, pale flesh flashing, and Alecia drew a breath. "Why are you showing me this?" But Bridget didn't answer and she saw the hand, a thick scar across the top reach out and jostle the girl's breast.

"That's Lucia?" Alecia asked, her tongue hating the taste of her name.

"Yes."

"So why are you showing me this?" Alecia turned her head, handed back the phone. "This only proves what we know. She gets drunk at a party, films herself having sex. Seems like the kind of girl who would sleep with a teacher, or maybe sleep with a teacher, I don't know."

What Alecia really wanted to say was that no one could compete with the young, tight body of an eighteen-year-old, her belly flat and rippled in the right places, not the wrong ones. Her breasts high and perched, milky white, in lace, tumbling out over the top the exact right way, not in a jiggling, wobbling way. That she could understand why Nate would sleep with her, reach for her, that red mouth on his mouth, his neck, his body. She could almost see it, watching that video.

"You're missing the point, she's unconscious." Bridget snapped the phone back, exasperated. "She didn't have sex or sleep with anyone. She was raped here."

"Am I supposed to feel sorry for her?" Alecia gathered her hair behind her head, fanning her neck with her ponytail. God it was so hot.

"As a woman? Yes. I'd think so."

"As a woman whose husband maybe slept with her?" Alecia shot back.

"I don't think so," Bridget said, "I really don't."

"His hat was found in that woods. He went after her. Why would he go after her if he wasn't trying to . . . I don't know. Silence her. Seduce her. *Something.*"

"I can't answer that, but I know —"

"That's the thing, you *don't actually know* anything. No one does!" Alecia had had enough. She was so tired of fighting the undercurrent of their friendship, Bridget firmly taking Nate's side. "What about the Instagram? The credit card receipt? Twice, apparently? The reporter who *saw them making out in the parking lot.*"

"They weren't making out. He hugged her," Bridget protested, but feebly, flimsily, the words sliding around between them. "She's been fucked with at school, and I think Nate knew it, but he won't answer my calls. I'm going over there after this to talk to him."

"Why do you defend him so much? Like you don't even think of taking my side?" The whine came out, petulant, and Alecia could hear it but couldn't stop it. Her voice edged up, she felt the hysteria rising in her chest.

"I just want the truth, Alecia. It's not about sides." Bridget's voice raised to match hers. "God, you're so stubborn. Just see it for a moment. What if Nate is telling the truth, that he was trying to help her?"

"He saved that picture!" Alecia shouted. "I can't ignore that. And listen, I'm here in this goddamn house every single day of my life. He's out there, cavorting with his students, following them on Facebook and Instagram and monitoring their every move, like he's got some kind of

369

savior complex. I just can't take it! Why doesn't he care more about us, this family, than he does some little white-haired weirdo sex bomb on Instagram?"

"He does care about you, Alecia. But you are so wrapped up in Gabe, it's all you care about. For two seconds, can you just think about Nate?"

"Why? He doesn't think about us. You know what? I saw Jennifer Lawson at the Stop & Shop the other day and you know what she said? That Nate kissed her at the Tempest Christmas party."

"The party three years ago?" Bridget held her palm to her forward, eyes tipped toward the ceiling, and laughed. "Three years ago?"

"So what? We were married three years ago! What difference does it make? I've heard this kind of thing before. The student at the Quarry Bar, what was her name? The night Gabe took a header down the steps. I couldn't get in touch with him. My point is, *we are not his priority.* I have no reason to believe him." She shook her head, back and forth, back and forth. "None."

"Jennifer Lawson kissed *him.*" Bridget stood, slapped her palms on the island, her voice a screech. She was practically yelling.

"Why, Bridget, tell me why? Why does the whole world throw themselves at my husband? And I'm supposed to believe he's an innocent bystander? I can't. I can't do it."

Bridget sat, deflated. She shook her head,

cupped her chin in her palm. Alecia felt the burn of tears behind her eyelids, threatening to spill over. She was the monster now?

Bridget looked toward the living room, where Gabe sat entranced by *Mighty Machines,* then toward the window above the sink.

Alecia closed her eyes and let her breathing level out, the anger pulsing under her skin, a slow burn.

After a minute, Bridget spoke. "Nate lets people in, Alecia. It's like a drug, you remember? It's why you fell in love with him. When he looks at you, it's like you're all that matters. He does that to everyone. Holden was addicted to it, loved Nate more than anyone. This is what he does to people. He doesn't mean to do it."

Alecia walked to the sink and turned on the tap, her back to Bridget. She didn't want her to see the tear that slid down her cheek, the sting in her throat as she tried to stop it.

She braced herself against the counter, tired, just so damn tired.

Finally, she said, "But does that make it right?"

CHAPTER 32

Bridget, Wednesday, May 13, 2015

Bridget's classroom overlooked the parking lot, where she could see the news van parked in the fire lane, a photographer and reporter fighting against the wind and rain to stand under the front awning. The heat wave had finally broken and brought furious thunderstorms that had been raging off and on all day. She watched the reporter talk, soundless from where she stood, her mouth moving, her hand gesturing, pointing to the school entrance. Bridget studied her mouth—she wore burgundy lipstick—for any indication she was saying Nate's name and saw none.

It was her break period.

She waited for them to leave, but they didn't, and the reporter moved her hand around in a circle—a retake. No, not now, not ever.

Bridget walked out of her classroom, slamming the door behind her, and down the hall to the front door. She pushed against the release bar and stepped outside, where the reporter rushed her and shoved a microphone in her face.

"Miss, what do you know about the missing student? What about the teacher accused of having an affair with her? Is there a sex-for-grades scandal at Mt. Oanoke high school?"

"No comment. It is a school day, and we are in session. Please, you need to leave the premises."

"Ma'am with all due respect, this a public school. You can't kick us off the property."

"During the school day, this is a no-trespassing zone. I sure as hell can, and if I have to, I'll call the police." Her finger hovered above Tripp's name on her cell phone.

"Just give me a statement and I'd be happy to leave." The woman smiled, wide and gleaming. Capped.

"I'm calling now," Bridget said just as Bachman came up behind her.

"What's the problem here? I'm the principal of this school, and you need to leave now."

"I'm calling the police," Bridget repeated, her finger still hovering, shaking. She pressed the phone against her cheek without dialing. "Officer Harris? We have a situation at the school with a television reporter, can you please send a patrol car? Thank you."

The reporter held up her hands, palms out, buying her bluff. Her eyes swept Bachman and peered around him toward the door. A crowd of students had gathered in the doorway, piling on top of each other, craning to see.

"We'll go," the reporter finally said. "But technically we don't have to. Do you want to give us a statement, Mr. Bachman?" She smiled sweetly at Tad and his neck reddened.

"No comment. Please leave." His voice was low, his teeth clenched. He turned and went back inside, the students stepping out of his way. Bridget remained outside, but heard his directive from the hallway: "No one talks to them, got it? No one." He sliced through the crowd, his arm swinging behind him, the door slamming shut until it was just Bridget who remained, her arms folded across her middle.

"We'll be back, Ms. Peterson." She gave Bridget another dazzling smile.

They knew her name. Of course they did.

The day dragged on, slower than a herd of turtles, and by sixth period, Bridget had her students watch *Dead Poets Society* instead of journaling. She was tired of their thoughts anyway. They'd all gotten in her head: Ashlee smacked and snapped her gum from the back of the room; Josh snorted at texts from, assumedly, Kelsey, who from across the room watched him, sleek as a cat, her legs crossing and uncrossing, her finger working a blond curl into a corkscrew.

Bridget was so sick to death of all of them.

But Taylor was missing.

"Has anyone seen Taylor?" she asked, but they all just looked around and shrugged. Kelsey snapped to attention, her back taut as a rubber band.

Bridget pressed play and dimmed the lights. She sat at her desk and flicked through her emails, all business as usual. Nothing about Nate or Lucia.

She texted Nate, *I'm coming over after school, have to show you something. Please be there. 3:30.*

She waited ten minutes for the reply, just a simple *OK*.

Robin Williams jumped on the desk: *The world looks very different from up here.*

And then: *Most men lead lives of quiet desperation.*

The bell rang and Bridget took her time, packing up her desk, the daily journals, her laptop. She rummaged around in her purse as the students burst out the front door like a canon, looking for the news van, the excitement buzzing on their skin.

She waited until three thirty, knowing she'd be late to Nate's and wanting him to wait for her. She envisioned him there, checking his phone, sighing, looking out the window. Good. Let him wait.

The last of the student cars pulled out and she

pushed open the door into the wet, gray after-noon, the air smelling like earthworms and dirt. The kind of day that reminded you of summer love, hot and thick.

Bridget dumped everything in her trunk and climbed into the driver's seat. On her way out, she cut through the student lot. She saw a lone red truck, parked along the edge. Bridget wound around the outside of the lot, slowed to a crawl next to it. There was a flash of movement inside the cab, in the driver's seat, and a face close to the glass, black hair with thick bangs and red lips parted, eyes closed.

Taylor.

She moved her body, writhing like a snake, the boy inordinately tall, his blond hair grazing the fabric of the roof. His mouth was on her neck, his big hand inside her pink T-shirt, her tan skin shining as she bucked and pulsed against him. He turned his head, his eyes rolled back until all she could see was the whites through the window spotted with drying rain. Bridget hit the gas hard, before he could see her, and the car lurched, her heart in her throat.

Andrew.

"You never answer your phone," Bridget whined, the first thing she said, and she cringed. Nate shook his head.

"For what? I can't stand to talk to anyone."

Nate turned and walked away from her, and Bridget followed dutifully like a dog licking at his heels.

"Nate, why am I doing more work for you than you are for you?" She hopped twice to keep up, his steps long and even toward the back of the house. The house shot straight back, like a railroad car: front door, living room, kitchen—no hallway. Ten long Nate-steps to the kitchen.

She'd been in Tripp's house before, but never without Tripp. It felt weird.

"Where's Tripp?" she asked after Nate didn't answer her.

"Work, until eight or something. I never know. That guy works a lot."

"Well, there aren't a lot of cops." Bridget turned her phone over in her hand, her palms slick.

"There's more crime than I thought." Nate cleared his throat, his hands shoved into his pockets. "Drugs. Overdoses."

"Yeah," Bridget said.

"So what'd you want to show me?"

He'd pulled inside himself, his eyes flatter than she'd ever seen them. She used to think they could all live in those eyes, surviving on the sparkle. He'd given them all life. For whatever time you spent with Nate, you escaped the confines of Mt. Oanoke, the drugs and the mill, the woods and the Stop & Shop. Now he looked like everyone else, a flatness to him that twisted her insides.

"Nate," Bridget said without knowing what she'd say next. He shook his head, *don't*. She raised her phone and opened Periscope. Flicked her fingers across the screen, finding Andrew's profile and *Temp's party;* it was still there, what an idiot.

She pressed play and moved the slider to twenty-seven minutes, the last three minutes of the party. She heard the *heyyyyy baby, wake up.* She swallowed, her tongue dry, tasting like acid, and passed the phone to Nate.

He took it and watched it, expressionless. When it was done—*she said yes, dog,* and that deep, echoing laughter—she imagined Andrew's hand on Lucia's breast, the way he'd cupped Taylor's breast in the car, his big, knuckled hand knobbed and rippled underneath the stretched knit of pink, and swallowed the sick to the back of her mouth.

Something itched in the back of Bridget's brain.

Nate winced, but not enough. He handed it back without saying a word.

"Well?" Bridget asked him finally.

He shrugged, shoved his hand back into his jeans pocket. "Well what?"

"This changes everything, Nate. Something bad is going on at school. Has been. Something that has nothing to do with you. You're being set up for something."

He laughed then, a hollow, scary sound, deep from somewhere inside. "I know that. I'm the only one who believes it."

"Not anymore. I believe it. So does Tripp, maybe. Hard to tell. He can't say much."

Nate laughed again, and Bridget wanted to slap his cheek. She imagined it, the red welt on the side of his face, his eyes open wide in shock.

"Stop laughing, nothing about this is funny."

"Bridget, godddamn it, I get that." He rubbed his jaw and moved past her to the fridge. Popped a beer on the edge of the counter, too comfortable. Too easily. "Alecia texted me last night. Drunk, maybe. Does she miss me?"

He turned away then, his voice breaking. He'd gained weight, maybe ten pounds even in the last three weeks. His back was a soft dough with newly formed love handles.

"I think so," Bridget lied. She opened the fridge, pulled out a beer, and handed it to Nate to open it. She took a long gulp and the fizz felt cold and bubbly in her throat. Nate watched her.

"You and Tripp, what's up with that?" He leaned, casual, against the counter, his eyes moving around the kitchen.

"Nothing." She swallowed and repeated, "Nothing."

"He's always had a thing for you. He's not

a wildcat anymore. I was surprised by that. Remember all his women? He always had women." Nate tipped his head, took a long gulp. "God I was jealous of that guy. I've never even dreamed of that much action."

"He was jealous of you," Bridget blurted. "With Alecia."

"Yeah. Alecia." He let out a bitter *ha* and flicked the empty beer bottle into the recycling can. The glass broke.

He drank it too fast.

"She was so fun, remember? She loved our game nights. They were great." He reached for the refrigerator and Bridget put her hand on his arm. His skin burned hot under her palm. "Anyway, he tell you that? That he was jealous?" He raised his eyebrows. "That's a pretty cozy conversation. You should really think about it with him. I mean it—"

"Nate, listen to me. I want to help you, but you can't spend your whole days at the gym and your nights getting wasted."

"I don't go to the gym, Bridget, look at me." His palm slapped his belly, firm but bigger. His cheeks puffed out.

"Where do you go?" Bridget asked.

"Anywhere, sometimes nowhere at all. But mostly, *anywhere*. The woods. The lookout over the river. Sometimes the mill." He swept his arm wide, knocking over a jarred vanilla musk candle.

"What are you doing?" Bridget righted the candle. "When you go there, what do you do?"

"What does anyone do? I think. I worry. Sometimes I bring a book."

Nate never read a book in his life, she was pretty sure. War books, maybe. Not a novel.

"You read a book." Bridget repeated it, slowly and dumbly. It seemed like a lie. "Nate, what about the video? Help me help you. I want to figure this out. Did you do something to Lucia?"

"Do something?" He cocked his head to the side, his mouth twisting. "Like fuck her?"

"Like kill her." Bridget gnashed her teeth. "She's *missing*, Nate. People think you did something to her. Did you?"

"Do you think that, Bridge?" He came closer and his eyes went dead. Flat again.

She stepped back. "No. But you are so different now. I want to help you. I want to reach you."

"You're the only one, then." He turned around and walked to the back door, his hands on his hips, watching the small, fenced-in backyard. Then, "Wanna hear something crazy? Jimmy's back."

"Jimmy who?" Bridget shook her head, her mind racing through the options and not being able to pick out a *Jimmy*.

"Lucia's father. He left a few months ago. God, I heard he's awful. Spent the day in the drunk tank. I knew him, years ago, when he worked at the mill. He was a bit crazy, but a good guy, I guess. Now . . . this town has changed a lot."

"Do you think he has something to do with Lucia being missing?" Bridget asked, incredulous.

"Maybe? What the hell do I know?" He lifted up a curtain and pushed it off to the side, craning to get a better look at something in the yard. He tapped his skull. "Guy's not exactly right here." He took a deep breath and then said, "I saw him, you know. In the woods. Why, do you think?"

"Did you tell anyone?" Bridget asked.

"No. Who would believe me? I barely believe me. Besides, Harper would just say *why were you in the woods?*"

"Are you sure it was him? We should go to Harper. If you're sure." She eyed him like she didn't quite believe him, either.

Nate shrugged. "Listen. It's a huge forest. Thousands of square miles. It's not a crime to be in there, for anyone. I go to the police and I look like I'm desperate and guilty as hell, right?"

Bridget shrugged. She honestly didn't know. "Okay, Nate, but that video." Bridget took a deep breath, her lungs puffing out her chest. "I think they raped her."

"They did." He turned to face her and he never looked so sad. "I've seen it already."

"You *knew about it?*" Bridget couldn't keep her voice even. But then it clicked, of course he did.

He knew everything they did. He watched them, their lives his own personal play. She pushed her palm against her forehead to stop the spin. "Nate, help me help you, for God's sake—"

"Bridget, she told me about the party. She told me and I didn't believe her." He let out an indistinct sound, like a guttural groan. His fingers went to his lips, tracing the edge with his thumb. His eyes darting, his voice a whispered regret. "I told her that I didn't believe her."

CHAPTER 33

Lucia, April 18, 2015:
Three days before the birds fell

Party at Temp's, the text said. Taylor.

They would go days without talking and Taylor would come back, sickly sweet and sorry. Lucia didn't care: only a few more months and then Taylor was gone. So was everyone else, scattering like leaves in the wind.

Gonna be lit.

She pocketed her phone, the screen cracked and broken. It only worked half the time; she'd gotten it from Walmart and paid for month-to-month data packages with her check from the Goodwill store. She could just pretend she never got it. No way was she going to Temp's house. God, she hated that guy.

She hated all of them. Except Taylor. And Andrew. She didn't think about Andrew.

Come over. Randy from the Goodwill. She wanted to go there less than Temp's.

Taylor had asked her once, her nose wrinkled, *are you dating him? Fucking him?*

No, neither. Well, except that one time. He'd

texted her all the time ever since. Even begged her one, *just one more time, just the tip in.*

It was so fucking desperate. But sometimes it felt nice, to be that wanted.

C'mon, hooker. You're coming w/. Taylor again. *Drinks for days.*

She hadn't heard from Taylor in a week. Why now?

C'mon, we'll Xbox and chill. Randy.

Oh God. Lucia rolled her eyes.

She texted back to Taylor. *You gotta get me.*

OMW. On my way.

She muted her phone.

Taylor brought her clothes. A tank top and jeans, decent ones from Free People. Like a hundred dollars. Lucia changed in the bathroom, running her hands up and down the denim, softer than anything she'd ever felt. The top was thin, a flimsy black, but silky. So hot; Lucia had never worn anything so perfect.

She brushed out her hair, wore it long, worked hair cream into her scalp until it flowed, clean and billowing down her back, her chest, dipping into the cleavage. She slid her fingertips along her scalp, above her neck over the healing scars. She hadn't pulled in days. The pain was dull, like the tip of a safety scissor.

She stripped and quickly put on her red bra, the one with the lace that Randy had bought her from the store. The nicest lingerie she owned, and it had been someone else's first. There was a rip under the right tit, but who would see it besides Randy (he liked to slip his finger into it, called it *easy access*).

You were no one if you were poor in this town. More accurately, you were just like everyone else who didn't matter.

Taylor gave her booties, gray and soft suede, a zipper up the side. She felt like goddamn Cinderella.

"You look ridic," Taylor said, and Lucia laughed in the mirror, her red mouth open. There was a crack there, from when Lenny punched it a year ago. She heard the glass break from her room and rushed out to see the blood all over his hand. A piece of the mirror had fallen out of the middle, weirdly in the shape of a jagged heart.

When she laughed, the spot where the heart used to be fit perfectly into her mouth, and it looked like her face was cracking wide open.

Maybe for the night, she could just be wide open.

It was so loud she couldn't even think. Josh's house was the biggest house she'd ever seen. She'd never been inside.

Andrew handed Lucia and Taylor two cups, his arm around each of them, like they were his. She downed her juice; it tasted like fruit punch Kool-Aid, the kind Jimmy used to make them before everything went bad, when the mill was still open and Lenny was just a kid. They were all just kids. It would be so much fun to be like that again, filled with bright red Kool-Aid. She could feel it there in her blood, right away, pulsing like something alive, all that sugar and sweetness.

She wanted to spin like that time with Taylor in the fountain.

Andrew looked at her, not Taylor. His eyes up and down her face, her body. He smiled.

She wrapped her hands around his arm.

He kissed her neck.

Taylor got them all more drinks, more juice in clear cups.

"Selfie!" Taylor demanded, her face pushed up against Andrew's mouth. Andrew pulled Lucia against him, his body unyielding like a stone wall. She could feel the bones in his shoulder under her fingertips. He was thin, but strong. His eyes sleepy.

"My girls," he said in her ear, his breath sweet, his skin moist, tangy, like cologne and sweat.

Lucia pushed her face against Taylor's, all their lips together, like a three-way kiss.

They all laughed and Andrew leaned his body against hers.

"When'd you get so hot?" he breathed.

Later, the rooms ran together, so many rooms. She was sure she'd never been in so many rooms in her life. She found the bathroom, a full mirror the size of a wall.

She'd hardly ever looked in a mirror that didn't have a crack in it.

She looked. She stood there in the soft bathroom light (so many lights, why did they need pink lights? But God, the pink made her skin look nice) looking in the mirror in the red bra. What had happened to her shirt?

She heard them call her, *Luuuuuuuuuuuuuuuuuu*

"Come upstairs! I'm upstairs!" she yelled out, running her nail along the tear in the red silk.

Back in a bedroom, she didn't know whose, but she assumed Josh. Trophies everywhere. So much gold, was it real?

On the bed, she lay down. Her eyes so tired, the room spun around her.

Sometime later, *Heyyyyyy baby. Wake up babbbbyyyyyy.*

Her stomach roiled, flipped with the sweetness.

There were two Andrews, one Porter.

"She's wild like that."

Lucia smiled, she never wanted to be wild. To be the witch, the weird one with the white hair.

I want to go home now. Can I go home now?

"Say you want it, honey. Say yes."

Yes. I want to go home.

"Say you want it, honey. Say yes."

"Yes." Her voice wasn't her voice, it was like the voice of an alien. Or a monster. She laughed then, spinning, spinning, spinning in her mind. The voice of a *witch*.

Even later, Taylor, somewhere Taylor, *Luuuuuuuuuuuuuuuuuu. Luuuuuuuuuuluuuuuuuuuuu!*

Andrew's face, a bead of sweat there on the side of his nose. His bare skin beneath her hands. Her hips lifted up to his hips.

A pain, sharp and cutting right into her center, a hot knife through butter.

Like she was being split wide open.

CHAPTER 34

Nate, April 20, 2015:
One day before the birds fell

She came to Nate's classroom on a day she hadn't been in school. She looked like hell, her hair pulled low against the nape of her neck. He couldn't lie, he looked out the window nervously when he saw her in the doorway. The parking lot was empty, it was too late in the day, almost six. Alecia would be waiting for him.

He remembered her kiss. He didn't want to do that again.

She looked like she was falling apart. Her sweatshirt, the words Oanoke Paper emblazoned across her chest, the silkscreen flaking off, and he thought of the mica they used to collect in the stream behind his parents' house. The black rock, dark as coal, peeling apart in paper-thin sheets, as light as air in his palm. Her jeans had dirt on the knees, like she'd been kneeling on them.

"Are you okay?"

"Yes. No." She scanned the doorway, hitching her backpack up on her shoulder. "I'm fine. I just . . . I just can't stay here anymore. I need help. I have some money . . . not a lot."

"What's the matter, what are you talking about? You're talking crazy." Nate stood, motioned to the office chair behind his desk, more comfortable than the plastic back chair he usually gave students. She sat and looked up at him. "You have to graduate, Lucia, you'll regret it your whole life. You are weeks away. Nothing can be that bad."

She looked at him like he was crazy. "Yes it can. A lot of things can be that bad, you just don't know about them." She pushed her thumb into the fabric of his armrest, making a divot. "What do you know about things being bad? Your perfect wife? Your son?"

"My son is autistic," he said, and regretted it. It didn't have the effect he'd hoped. Her face crumbled and her chin puckered like she was going to cry. "I'm sorry, I'm trying to find the right thing to say. What's the matter, Lucia, just tell me."

"The thing is, no one will care. I'm not looking for a pity party, it's a fact." She sat up straight, her shoulders back, strung tight like a violin string. Like she might snap.

"Well, I care," Nate said, but then remembered the kiss, the way her fingertips brushed against his skin, his visceral reaction, and it sent his heart racing. *Careful, here.* He heard

Bridget's voice, her admonishment in his head.

She stood up, crossed the room, and stood at the window, her arms across her waist, rocking from side to side, slightly, gently. Something told him to let her be. The sun was setting, the sky streaked with orange and pink, a deep red at the horizon like a warning, tucked behind the billowing Pocono Mountains.

Finally, after minutes, what seemed like hours, she spoke. "I might have been raped."

He was not prepared for that.

"Might have been?" he asked.

"I'm not sure. I can't remember it all. I didn't want it. And . . ." She wouldn't look at him; her hair escaped the ponytail and fell over her eyes. She pushed her palm into the bowl of her belly, low between her hip bones. "I hurt. All over." She shook her head. "Should I go to the police? No one will believe me. Will you come with me?"

"What happened? When?"

"I went to a party at Josh's. I drank something red, but it tasted like nothing. Like sugar. It's possible . . ." Her breathing was ragged, the twilight on her face. "It's possible there was something in it. But, I don't know. Maybe not. Just booze." She wouldn't look at him, just stared out the window, her face in profile. "Then it was my fault, maybe."

"Was it Josh?"

She shook her head. "It's a serious accusation. Could ruin lives. Right?"

Nate nodded, then remembered she wasn't looking at him. "Yes."

"A life more than mine. I could ruin another someone's life. But then again, so could he. If he did it again." She shrugged.

"What about *your* life?" Nate asked.

She let out a laugh, or what sounded like a laugh. "That's not worth all that much." He clucked with his tongue, his hand out to touch her shoulder, and she held up her hand. "No pity, just the truth."

"I can take you to the police. I know a cop," Nate said. "Just tell me what happened."

"It was Andrew. And maybe Porter. He was there, but I don't know if he . . ." Her voice was a whisper; he barely heard her.

His Andrew. He thought of Marnie Evans, her face pinked and gleaming, watching Andrew whip pitches across the plate.

She pulled out her phone, the shitty, slow cheap phone with the cracked screen. She hit play, her fingers flying across the screen like she'd done it a million times. He realized yes, she'd done it a million times.

She moved the slider to the end, the last three minutes, and pressed play, handing it to him. Put her fist between her teeth and waited, watching him with those water-blue eyes.

When it was done, he blinked, the room and the world both a tiny bit darker.

"Are you sure?" he said.

Then, "Were you drunk?" he said. And the worst one, "But you said yes," he said.

CHAPTER 35

Bridget, Thursday, May 14, 2015

Lucia had been missing for one week and two days. If you read the paper, you knew that the statistics on finding a missing person after a week were grim. Bridget had little hope.

But she had some.

First of all, Lucia wasn't most people. And Bridget suspected she'd run away. She was hiding, waiting—for what, Bridget didn't know—but she wasn't being held captive by some kind of Buffalo Bill copycat killer.

This was Bridget's theory, anyway; not that she could tell anyone. They'd all think she was crazy. It was also possible that no one would care. She broached the subject with Jane Blue in the hallway, her voice dropped to a whisper, and Jane shook her head.

"I don't know what to think, but I'll tell you this. I've never been Nate Winters's biggest fan. That guy thinks he owns the school, the town, and everyone in it. He flirts with women, students, and teachers alike. He's a *bro* to everyone, all while subtly putting down the guys like Dale.

He's got Bachman and the superintendent wrapped around his finger, and the parents think he hung the moon in the sky." Jane rocked up on the balls of her feet as she spoke, her small hands wringing in front of her. She was a head shorter than Bridget, her voice low and gravelly, grating on Bridget's ears.

"So do you really think, though, that he killed her?" Bridget pressed, wanting to know what everyone else was saying, since obviously no one was saying it to her. "Is this what everyone thinks?"

"Gone a week? Hard to say. What are the viable alternatives?" Jane shrugged and patted Bridget's arm. "I know you were friends. I won't pretend to understand why. Then again, I'm in the minority. Most people love the guy. I tend to believe he made sure of that."

The last bell rang and Bridget motioned to her classroom. Jane gave a little shrug, just one shoulder lifted, and walked away. Bridget started in the other direction, but Jane called to her.

"You know, it doesn't mean anything but, he knows I don't like him. It drives him nuts."

Bridget turned. "What do you mean?"

"I just mean," Jane put her hands up, searching for the words. "He goes after me every chance he gets. He knows I can't stand him. I roll my eyes or tell him to go chase wind or whatever. Makes no difference. He just laughs and says things like,

'C'mon, Janie Jane. We can be friends.' Says he'll win me over someday. He can't let it lie."

Bridget smiled. It seemed like Nate, and frankly, made Jane look like a bitch. Maybe his intention, maybe not.

She took a step toward Bridget and cocked her head, her eyes narrowed to a slit. "But, don't you think it's a little pathological? That he needs to be liked that much?"

There always seemed to be a cloud over the mill and its hundred feet of stacks poking holes in the sky, even on the brightest day. The faint smell of sulfur hung on the grass blades, the trees. She'd been told that while the mill was in operation, before 2005, the whole town smelled like rotten eggs, and eventually you could tell a shutdown by the odor. Clean air meant trouble at the mill.

Nate explained once that the smell wasn't harmful. It was called TRS—total reduced sulfur—and was the same chemical that was added to natural gas to make it detectable. If you were an Oanoker for life, you learned to like the smell. *Making paper, making money,* they'd say. You could hear the hum and screech of the pulper as you drove up Mill Road. Bridget couldn't imagine it. She sometimes wondered if it was a chemical cloud that hung over the plant, low and thick, like a fog.

She remembered what Dale said about the birds: *arsenic poisoning from the mill.*

Was arsenic a by-product of paper production?

Bridget pushed open the huge steel door, the inside unchanged from the week before. If pressed, she couldn't have explained why she was back, just that she was. She felt like she had a flimsy, tenuous grip on the truth. That she had all the pieces, and still couldn't assemble the puzzle.

Rows and rows of rolled brown paper sat in the room to her left, giving off a moldy smell. The air inside the mill always felt wetter, like somehow it rained on the inside. It was the pulp room, the one they'd been stuck in last week, where the lost, squawking goose waddled his way around.

The pulp room was littered with debris, steel machinery, cranes, and conveyors.

Bridget cleared her throat. "Hello?"

She didn't know whom she was yelling for—it was just a hunch. She didn't even tell Tripp she was coming. She felt stupid for it and certainly couldn't have explained it. Except . . .

This mill was the place Lucia was drawn to the first time she'd run away. If Nate was right, it was the place that ruined her father and her future in one fell swoop the day it closed its doors. Did she know her father was back? Or worse yet, did he have anything to do with his daughter's disappearance?

There was no sign of her, no gas heater. But it had been in the sixties at night and hot as Hades in the day, so that might not mean anything.

The pulper sat in the far corner, twenty feet around, a concrete bathtub sunk into the ground. It contained a tank that went down to basement, fifteen feet deep, with a steel rotor in the middle. Bridget had seen it before.

The mill was a destination in Mt. Oanoke.

Years ago, before they'd known that Holden was sick, Bridget and Holden would come here with Alecia and Nate. Like kids, they brought bottles of Two Buck Chuck and sat in the pulp room throwing rocks into the pulper. Two points for each metal *ting* of the stones bouncing off the rotor. Alecia and Nate snuck off somewhere between the rollers, and later Alecia had told her drunkenly they'd had sex back there, up against a metal spool, a screw digging into the small of her back, her feet braced on the cylinder in front of her.

"It's the angle," she'd giggled, lifting one foot to demonstrate, her hands pushing at her thighs.

Holden and Bridget stayed near the pulper, throwing stones at the rotor and intermittently talking, but mostly each thinking about the things they weren't talking about—the conference, the fingernail, *Watercress 6:30,* and why Holden was being so different. Bridget remembered looking off toward the big rollers, to the sound of Alecia's giggle, and feeling a pang. Wishing she'd had that love, wishing she had someone else. Wishing they'd come back. Nate made things between them all bearable.

Bridget pushed past the conveyor, the rubberized mat that she remembered walking on like a balance beam, drunk on the Chuck, her hands out to her sides, Holden holding one arm and Nate the other and Alecia in the back protesting, *you guys, get down, someone is going to get hurt, we're too adult for this bullshit,* and they'd all laughed, their voices mimicking her. When she hopped off the end and stumbled, her ankle twisting, it was Nate she grabbed, not Holden.

Now, next to the pulper was a new thing. A stepladder. It wasn't there years ago, and she didn't remember it being there a week ago. Bridget pushed past the old control panel, under the pipes that had moved the pulp from the tank to the sheeter. She pressed her hand up against the flat expanse of steel, dusty and rough with rust.

The sun gleamed through the windows, dust sparking and dancing in the air. She'd never been in the mill in this kind of daylight; she'd always come at night.

She stood next to the tank, open on the top, the concrete coming to her chin. With one foot, she tested the stepladder and found it sturdy.

She climbed to the top and looked down. It was empty, the rotor shining, leaves curled around the smooth edges, but the center, around the rotor, smooth and bare. Except for a small black backpack with a rainbow zipper.

Lucia's.

CHAPTER 36

Bridget, Thursday, May 14, 2015

"Lucia!" Bridget's voice echoed off the brick walls, the floor. The inside of the pulper, along the rear wall, contained a maintenance ladder, steel pipe and thin. Bridget wound her way around the concrete casing and tested the ladder. It was about a fifteen-foot drop to the floor, but the ladder felt solid. She dropped her foot down on the first rung, her moccasin slipping, and then caught herself. She climbed down, her throat closed and heart thudding with every creak.

At the bottom, there was a smooth concrete ledge around the rotor that held Lucia's backpack and a small rolled blanket. Bridget picked it up and called *Lucia!* one more time to make sure. She gingerly pulled the zipper open, pawed through contents, all black fabric. She felt a sweatshirt. A few pairs of underwear. She felt dirty pawing through Lucia's most private possessions; her skin crawled. She hoisted the backpack onto her back and climbed the ladder on shaky legs.

Back on solid ground, in better light, she

could see the contents more clearly. Underneath everything, a spiral-bound notebook, a cracked paperback: *Modern and Ancient Philosophy*. She fanned through the paperback. Words so tiny you could barely read them, the warm smell of sweat on aging paper. She put it aside and flipped through the journal. More of the same. Pencil sketches, ramblings about Jung and Nietzsche, letters and poetry. Something fluttered out, beautiful and thin, like a butterfly. Bridget bent down, picked it up. A tarot card.

A crumbling brick steeple, the top aflame. A jagged branch holding a keen one-eyed raven. The falling jester, the twining king. The tower.

She'd only ever drawn it once. Years ago, before she'd met Holden, when Aunt Nadine's husband had run their pickup into a swamp, drowning himself and their pastor, both of them drunker than Cooter Brown off Father Noone's moonshine. Unlike many other cards, it only had one meaning: *impending disaster.*

Bridget's hands shook as she tucked the card into her purse, her mind flashing on the bird's one sharp eye.

With the backpack in one hand, Bridget found her way back outside, the sun fiery above the horizon, twilight looming.

"Lucccccciiiiiiaaaaaaaa!" she yelled again, her voice cracking at the end, her head thick, her pulse beating behind her eyes.

To everyone else, the draw of the mill was the building itself—dark corners and endless industrial hideouts. The floor littered with broken beer bottles, the delicious danger of the pulper, like it could suck you down and just start pulping again, all by itself. Teenage horror stories, fueled by hooch and weed. Plus, it's the place that ruined many of their lives. Before, they had family dinners, blue-collar fathers with short commutes, storefronts without soaped and broken windows. After—well, it was all different after. There was something satisfying about ruining small parts of the place that ruined you.

The dam, though, was too fast, too much. All that water striking the poured concrete wall with enough force to spray upward. In the summer, the discharge feels electric, a zinging through your face and limbs until you're chilled. The fence along the clearing up top had long since fallen away and, maybe five years ago, a boy drowned. A middle-schooler, hanging out with his older brother, went over the edge, his head breaking on the rocks at the bottom. Bridget didn't know the boys or the family, and they moved away shortly after. The kids still talked about it, said you could hear him scream if you stood out by the water long enough.

Everyone said you can still smell the sulfur, feel the burn of chemicals as it mists your skin. Tripp shrugged it off as pure imagination. *Sulfur dissipates,* he said. *No one can actually smell it. The mill has been out of operation for ten years.* Nate had agreed: hydrogen sulfide is harmless at low levels. At high levels, when it can kill you, you can't even smell it anymore.

Bridget swore she could smell it, as thick and noxious as rotten eggs. She followed the smell, the rhythmic pounding of the water in the background; she could feel it in her feet and up her legs. A warning, like a bellow.

The back of the mill had grown over, a single trampled path where people walked, the dirt packed down, the weeds and thistles slapping at her ankles, her calves. The backpack bumped against her back with each step. She paused before the clearing, yelled out *"Lucccciiiaaaaa!"* her voice straining above the whoosh of the water, the birds and the flies and the mosquitoes silenced, and all she could hear was the water, filling her ears and her head and her lungs, that chemical water in her lungs until she couldn't breathe.

The brush cleared right before the bank. The dirt was speckled with black, dusty birds. For a moment, Bridget panicked, eyes swung upward to the sky, looking for the swarm to fall again, and then realized no one had come back here to clean them up.

Where were the buzzards, the crows, the vultures?

Bridget wondered if they avoided the noxious mist like everyone else. She could feel it now, a soft rain on her forearms and her forehead. Just a haze.

In the sun, ten feet straight ahead, right at the bank, a glint of metal caught her eye. Something reflecting the sun at exactly the right angle. Bridget dropped the backpack, dust billowing, and picked up the shining thing, turning it over in her fingertips. A metal heart ring. Half a heart, the etching worn down and soft, like it'd been rubbed with a fingertip. Small enough for a child.

She'd seen it before.

Bridget looked back toward the mill, the parking lot hidden beyond it, then up to the sky.

A lone vulture circled, out over the water. She thought about how you never seemed to see only one, like maybe the rest knew to stay away.

She tucked the ring into her palm, the point of the heart digging into her skin, and crept to the edge of the bank. She looked up at the bird before she looked down to the bottom of the falls, her heart pulsing in her throat, the whoosh in her ears that matched the whoosh of the water.

Bridget saw the white of her hair first—splayed out like an angel, at least twenty, maybe thirty feet below. She floated face-up, arms stretched to the sides, like she'd simply jumped backward and landed that way, the way you fall onto a freshly made bed. Her mouth was open, almost like she was laughing, her skin gray as the rocks. The water lapped at her forehead in a kiss.

She'd been there awhile.

Bridget called to her again, *Lucia!* But it was quieter, halfhearted, and inaudible over the thrumming drone of the water. It didn't matter anymore. She was never going to answer.

CHAPTER 37

Nate, Thursday, May 14, 2015

When Harper and Mackey came back, they banged on Tripp's front door while Tripp was at work, yelling because they didn't care that Tripp had nosy neighbors.

"Come on, Winters, know you're there. Open up, buddy. Time to chat."

When Nate opened the front door, he saw Harper first, leaning a bit to the side, against the door frame, and in the back, Mackey, listlessly picking at his teeth.

"Oh, the dynamic duo. What do you have for me today?" Nate opened the door wide, letting them pass, and Harper raised his eyebrows.

"Just some questions, Winters." They stood in the hall. Mackey folded his arms across his chest. "We think you should come with us this time. Down to the station."

"Am I under arrest? Should I call a lawyer?" Nate asked.

"Do you have a lawyer?" Mackey asked, his voice reedy and nasal.

Nate didn't answer him; he just slid on his

sneakers. The frustration bubbled up into his throat. He had nothing to hide, nothing to fear. He was tired of worrying about everyone, hiding out in the woods, Tripp's living room. The sooner he got this over with, the better.

"No. I don't. Am I under arrest?" Nate persisted.

Mackey and Harper exchanged glances. "Not at this time, Mr. Winters."

Nate hadn't yet been inside the Mt. Oanoke police station. He was surprised to see it was much like any other office; it could have been an insurance office, really. The phones ringing, the clickity-clack of typing, the smell of coffee and something sickly sweet. A birthday cake maybe. In the corner, a blue balloon bobbed.

He was led to an interview room, white and smelling of fresh paint, so fresh you could get high off the fumes. The plastic chairs were high-backed and comfortable. Nothing like he would have expected. Except in Mt. Oanoke, is the interview room really used? He imagined the druggies, tweaking and twitching in the holding cell at county. He might have been the first customer of the brand-new room.

Mackey gave him a bottle of water without asking, something Nate took as a good sign. They were being nice and easy.

"Winters, listen. Chances are, this girl ran

away, got it? But there are some things we need to figure out." Harper started, almost right away, without any preamble. Nate wondered if he went home at night and told his wife, *I think I might be close to breaking this case wide open. Wide open, I tell you.*

"Plus, not for nothing, Winters, but by your own admission you were the last to see her." Mackey. This guy. A second-string detective in a town that barely needs one.

"Right. By my own admission. I called 911 for God's sake. I'm not hiding anything, guys. I didn't sleep with her. I tried to help her. I saw her run into the woods and I called the police." Nate pulled his face down, tried to make it look sympathetic, but then admonished himself, *answer the question you're asked, you idiot.*

Alecia used to tell him that he seemed to spend so much energy pretending to *be* something, that he'd forgotten how to just be. That's what he felt like now, like the walls were closing in, and he was both annoyed that he was here, for he knew he truly didn't do anything, and only a tiny bit fearful of getting into real trouble. Unless he was already in real trouble, but even then it was hard to tell.

"Yep, we got that part, Winters. But here's a thing." Mackey pushed the sides of his hair behind his ears, one then the other, with the flat part of his thumb. "Did you go after her?"

"I answered this already," Nate said, the sweat springing from under his arms. The thing was, he'd already stupidly started this lie. He had to see it through. He'd tell the truth with everything else if he could just get out of this *one little thing.* It was stupid, the lie was for nothing.

"Humor us, Winters," Harper said.

"No. I got out of the car, looked over the guard-rail, called for Lucia to come back. She didn't. I waited maybe five minutes and left."

"You just left her there? Alone in the woods? A girl you claim, in previous interviews, was abused and alone. You just left her there."

"Guys, listen. I was pretty mad at her. I *am* pretty mad at her. My life is a mess and it's largely Lucia's fault. She's telling people we had an affair, which isn't true. I could lose my job, my family, my whole life. So . . . yeah." Nate nodded, going with the lie. He'd just have to win them over another way, the way he did with everyone else.

Harper nodded, rubbing his palm along his jaw. "This. This actually makes sense to me. I'm not sure I would have chased the bitch, either. What do you think, Mack?"

"So that was, what, elevenish? And you say you drove home before midnight?" Mackey asked, ignoring Harper. Harper rolled his eyes in Nate's direction.

"Okay, then tell us about the relationship," Harper said, steamrolling over Mackey.

"There was no relationship." Nate clenched his hand into a fist and then spread his fingers out, stretching his palms. He was starting to itch, his skin buzzing and tight. "I'm a teacher. I also am closer to my students than most teachers. I've been invited over for family dinners more than a handful of times to various kids' houses. I follow a lot of them on social media and keep track of who's fighting with whom, who's sleeping with whom. It makes me a more involved teacher. That's all. I have, in the past, helped Lucia Hamm. I've given her close to $250 to stay at various motels and away from that brother. I've let her hang out in my classroom after school. A lot of kids had my cell phone number, for various reasons. She was one of them. But there was no relationship. No sexual relationship at all. None."

He let the air out of his lungs. That was the first time he'd really said all that to anyone but Alecia. It was the first time anyone had let him get through the whole speech, anyway. Tripp usually cut him off, waving his hand around about propriety, changing the subject to baseball or basketball.

"What about this, though?" Harper asked, casually pushing a printout across the table. Nate glanced at it, his stomach starting to turn.

An email. *Meet me at our hotel. I need you.*

Fuck. Fuckfuckfuckfuckfuck. Yeah, this was real trouble.

"That's not sexual. I see why you think it is but it's not. This was the second time I helped her. 'Our hotel' meant the place we met before. To me, 'I need you' meant 'I need help.'"

"But she didn't say, 'I need help.' She said 'I need you.' These are drastically different things, Nate. You do see that, right?"

"Yeah, but all I can tell you is how it seemed to me. At the time."

"From here, you look pretty stupid to me." Mackey pulled a toothpick from his shirt pocket and stuck it in his teeth, gnawing it. "Why, though, that's the thing we can't figure out. Why would she set you up as you're claiming here?"

"Because I rejected her." He paused then, too long. Thinking about the rape, about her accusation, Andrew, his doubt, even though in the darkest parts of his night, it was the most obvious part of this entire debacle. Except he still didn't know, for sure, what had happened. Was it his place, *really,* to go making that accusation? He thought of Marnie Evans then. Two days ago she'd called him. Almost whispering, like she was sneaking it. *We still want you to help Andrew, Nate. We believe you didn't do anything to that girl.* Her voice hitched, a clucking sound. *She came here before, she wasn't right. Strange girl, you know?*

Harper's grin spread across his face, slowly and disbelieving. "You mean to tell me you think she's accusing you of having an affair and she's now *missing* because you rejected her advances? You turned her down?"

Mackey laughed along with him. "Seriously, son."

Nate hated both of them, the heat flushing his neck, his cheeks.

Mackey leaned forward. "So what time did you say you got home that night, then? The night she ran into the woods? Monday, May fourth?"

"Twelve. Twelve fifteen at the latest." As he said this, he could hear the soft click of detonation, almost feel it under his feet like a trip wire.

"So the problem I have, Winters. Nate," Harper started and scratched the back of his head. "Is someone called your car in. On the side of the road, off Route Six, right where you called it in, flashers on. Your license plate, he was alert enough to write that down considering it was one thirty in the morning."

Boom. Nate felt the bomb go off in his heart, down his legs. There it was. His lie exposed. He'd been waiting for it, really. He'd been a shitty liar his whole life. A decent bullshitter, sure. There was a thread of truth in bullshit. But the second he told a straight-up lie, he started sweating and counting down the minutes until he was outed.

"Also, see, we found your hat." Mackey tossed

a plastic bag onto the table and there was Nate's white COACH hat, smeared with mud, the one he'd lost down the embankment and all but forgotten about since he hadn't been coaching. "A bit far into the woods. More than it would have blown off, say, if you'd just leaned over the embankment like you said."

A one-two punch. Nate swallowed, a thick ball of fear in his throat, his eyes burning.

"So we've caught you in at least one lie. We actually have a few more, but we gotta keep some of it to ourselves. That's how they do it on the *tee-vee* right now, Barney?" Mackey smirked as he looked over at Harper.

Barney Fife. They were mocking him, his thoughts, his attitude, the way he'd assumed they were bumbling cops from Mayberry. Kept him off his guard, easy and buddylike. They were not his pals.

They knew more about investigating than he did about being investigated, which should have been obvious, but for some reason, it wasn't.

Nate sat up, pressed his back against the chair, and crossed his ankle over his knee. "I think I want a lawyer."

Harper rubbed at his eyes, the skin around them thin and pink. "Aw, Nate. C'mon now. Don't get sour on Mack here and lawyer up. We can handle this here, like grown-ups." He shot Mackey a look and Mackey gave him a grin.

"No, I'm serious. I should have asked for a lawyer a long time ago. You guys aren't interested in the truth. You just want to close this case so you can get back to chasing heroin dealers and whatever. I'm not saying another word. I want to call a lawyer." Nate didn't even know who he'd call. Probably start with Bridget. When this was over, he owed her a case of wine. Dozens of roses. Both.

The conference room door opened and a woman scuttled in, her hands flying. Short, helmet-like brown bob, large glasses.

"Detective Harper, Detective Mackey, can you come here a second?" Her voice was breathless and her gaze shot from Harper to Mackey to Nate in a frenzied circle.

"Sure, Stacey. What's the problem?"

"The EMTs were just called out to Oanoke Paper. They found Lucia, sir." Her voice wobbled, tinny and high. "She's dead."

CHAPTER 38

Alecia, Thursday, May 14, 2015

Usually the evenings were Alecia's favorite time of day—after Gabe's bath, when he was clean, smelling like strawberry shampoo, all the moist boyness washed away, the only time his hands were ever clean, his mouth unsticky. Sometimes, but not always, Gabe would curl up, tucked into the U of her body, his back against her belly and if she angled a little bit sideways, he fit just right like they were jigsaw pieces; it seemed that no matter how much he grew, he always fit there perfectly, his knees to his chest, the two of them hip-to-hip. She could push her whole face into his scalp, past the commercial soap, and smell his real Gabeness, the smell of his skin, a little bit like almonds with a sour touch of onions, but in the most delicious way.

And sometimes during these moments, but not always, she thought about how much she loved her son. He'd hold her face in his hands and kiss her nose, because he saw Nate do that once, and Gabe's mind latched onto certain things never to be forgotten. She'd giggle softly and do it back, his thinning cheeks between her palms reminding her of his changing body—growing steadily from chubby, tumbling toddler to strong, lean kid. But his movements were still jerky, like a baby or a toddler. Or the tag on his pajamas suddenly, for no reason at all, itched his skin and he'd cry out, his hand slapping at his neck, his back rubbing against the sofa like a cat in heat, and Alecia instantly would be overcome with exhaustion all over again.

Except tonight he did not do these things. Tonight he sat calmly, his heart a slow thump through his back under Alecia's palm, his head tucked under her chin and when she suggested they watch something else, something besides *Mighty Machines*—because even now, she couldn't resist trying to "stretch him"—he nodded carefully, like he knew she needed it. It sort of broke her heart that he did that sometimes, gave in to his mother's needs, because Alecia knew she should be strong enough to not have needs for Gabe to meet. But if she thought about it too long, her brain swirled around and around, funneling into darkness. She tamped it down, the feeling of inadequacy, and turned on *Golden Girls*, and Gabe laughed in all the right places—only because of the laugh track, he loved the laugh track—but he kept his hand on her cheek the whole time and she wondered if this was how peaceful heaven was.

Still. With her right hand, she kept checking her phone. Clicking the volume up button, to make sure it was on. Checking the missed calls—she could have missed a notification, of course. She felt like one of Nate's students with a boy.

How weird that all of this would bring about a renewal. All this heartache, this uncertainty, the past few months, erased as easily as a hand wiped across a fogged window and suddenly, the picture was clear. Last night had done that. For her. For *them.* That's what Alecia was thinking about when she first heard something. It could have been a shout, or even a car. The sound was sort of indiscriminate, the kind of sound that later, during an interview, a bystander might say, "Well it *could have been a gun,*" and everyone watching television would think, *how could she not know?* It was that kind of sound. Whatever it was must have been alarming, triggering some basic mama-bear instinct, a little buzz in Alecia's belly that said *get up, something is wrong,* because otherwise nothing would have disturbed the perfect Alecia-Gabe jigsaw puzzle on the sofa.

As Alecia made her way to the window, the instinct grew stronger, such that she looked back at Gabe, still focused on the television, on Bea Arthur, throwing some barb at Estelle Getty, and the laugh track tripped and Gabe laughed, his wide hand slapping at his legs, his head tilted back, then forward and Alecia fought the urge to take Gabe and flee out the back door. But something flashed in the window and she almost turned to Gabe, almost told him to go to his room because her stomach pulled, a suction right down the center of her body, until she felt lit up from the inside with danger.

At the window, she lifted the curtain. The front walk was covered with people, bright lights, and news vans, their satellites and wires and antennas glinting in what looked, under the whitest spot-lights, like daylight. People milling about with cameramen, some talking into square-lensed cameras, some jockeying for a better angle, some just standing stupidly, waiting for something, anything, to happen.

Alecia shut the curtain, sagged against the window, and before she had time to think, reconsider, she flung open the door.

"Get the hell away from my house. You are scaring my son!" she yelled into the chaos, and it was hardly the truth. In fact, her freaking out would scare her son more, considering her son didn't even know they were there. They rushed to her door, microphones in her face, shouting into her face, and Alecia panicked and slammed the door. They knocked, a louder sound still, and Gabe found his way to the hallway, his eyes wide at the lights through the window, and asked, "Mommy, what's that?" his finger pointing.

"I have no goddamn clue, Gabe. Go to your room."

Gabe, understanding only that he was now being punished, started to cry. Alecia, her heart in her throat, turned her phone over to call the police and saw that it was already ringing, but she hadn't heard it over the whoosh in her ears.

She clicked "accept" without looking at the caller ID, and before she could even say hello, a voice on the other end said, "Hello? Alecia, are you there?"

She nodded and croaked out a yes. Libby Locking.

"Alecia, have you heard? Have the police talked to you?"

Alecia shook her head again, her eyes on Gabe, who was starting to flap his hands and cry, louder and louder, his head ticking to one side, his ear banging off his shoulder (he had, in the past, done that so hard his ear bled). This is what Alecia was thinking about when Libby continued, "Alecia, listen to me. They found Lucia. She's dead."

Alecia felt the vague dawning that something bad was happening, but couldn't work through it all in time before Libby said the next thing.

"I heard they've arrested Nate."

"When?"

"When did it happen? I don't know. They're saying she died on Wednesday. Which is weird; where has she been all this time?"

"Wednesday?" Alecia's lips felt dry. Cracked. Yesterday. "How do they know it was Wednesday?"

"Her body temperature, is what the paper said. They can tell that I guess. Don't you watch *CSI*?" She paused, the question rhetorical, and Alecia said nothing, her mind blurry and cottony. Then Libby said, "They're saying Nate killed her. Everyone is saying that."

"It wasn't Nate," Alecia said, automatically, calculating. "It wasn't Nate." Her heart, free-falling with relief. "He was with me. Yesterday. All day."

One day: a doctor appointment, lunch, a tentative thawing, dinner and a glass of wine. For one day, her anger had melted off, like butter in the sun.

"With you?" Libby's voice pitched up, a soft cluck on her tongue.

Alecia wondered what would have happened if they hadn't been together. Would she have believed it wasn't him?

CHAPTER 39

Bridget, Thursday, May 14, 2015

Call me, now.

The phone rang only a minute after Bridget texted Tripp, like he was waiting for it.

"Lucia's dead. I'm at the mill." Bridget's teeth clattered together, a ringing in her ears. "Can you come get me?"

"Yes, of course. Are Harper and Mackey there?"

"Yes. Ambulances and cops are everywhere. I found her, Tripp."

"Why did you go there? Alone?"

"I just did, it's fine. Just come."

In her hand, the point of the heart broke the skin, the tip tinged with Bridget's blood. That's how tightly she'd been holding it.

Later, after questioning, statements, and interviews, Bridget's head pounded, her hands shaky, and she needed food.

She and Tripp sat at the diner behind the police station, The 543, the same one they'd sat at not even a full week ago with the same waitress, her thick fingers smoothing down her apron front, Ashlee William's cousin. She watched them with her eyebrows raised, her wide neck wobbling as she talked about them to the cook. He leaned out, looked over the grill at them, and shook his head.

"Nate did not do this thing, Tripp. They asked me in there about Nate's activities, his comings and goings. Did they ask you?"

Tripp nodded slowly, stirring a fistful of sugar packets into his coffee. "They did. He walked in the woods all the time, Bridge. I had to tell them that."

"It looks bad." Their waitress brought over a plate of rheumy eggs. The plate clattered as she tossed it down in front of Bridget. "This is something else. Something worse than Nate. The school, this town. I found that ring. And something about that video."

"It's gone now." Tripp snapped his fingers like he just thought of it. "I looked it up as soon as you called me. He took it down." He fished his phone out of his pocket. "Glad we saved it, right?"

Bridget took it like it was a poisoned thing, a sharp-toothed poisonous snake, pincered between her fingers, and clicked play on the video. She skipped to the end, watched until the hand, dark against the pale backdrop of Lucia's breast, the ethereal *wooooooooooooooooooooowoooo ooooooooooo.* Until her brain itched. Something. Something.

"Tripp. The voice in the back, the *wooooooo-wooooo* that sounds like it's a ghost sound? They're not saying wooooowooooo."

She couldn't be sure. She had to be sure.

She stood, motioned in a circle with her hand, and threw a ten-dollar bill on the table. It would be a small tip. Deservedly so.

Tripp rose, following her, confused, his hands pawing at his wallet to beat her to the bill. She was out the door and in the parking lot, trying to catch her breath, her mind skipping on all the pieces that were right there. So close she could touch. Tripp trotted behind her.

"Bridge, wait up, where are we going?"

"My house." She spun around, her purse clutched between her fingers. "I think I figured it out."

"Here, here." Bridget flipped through the journal, the other notebooks strewn around her dining room in her frantic haste. She found it then and shoved it toward Tripp.

"Look. There. See?"

She said, I'll tell your mama, I know just who you are! You said, Then who are we? Did you really think she was lying? She called you out so fast, Taylor Lawson, she said, and then she looked at me, like she'd never seen me before. Lulu something, she said. You nearly died laughing.

"Taylor called her Lulu. The voice on the recording. It's saying *Luuuuuuuuuuuluuuuuuu* not wooooooooowoooooooo." Bridget felt breathless, jittery. "Do you see it?"

"Yes, gimme a minute, Bridget okay? Let me read it."

His eyes scanned the passage, seemingly forever, and Bridget jiggled her foot, hopping back and forth. She focused on her breathing, on not snatching the journal away from him. Until he looked up at her, done, his eyes a question mark, and she did take it back. She fanned the pages forward then back again. Until she found the second thing.

The ring, or what she now knew was a ring, but before was only the charm, the ring part broken off, the metal heart, worn thin, the BE FRI rubbed smooth. Taped to the pages with scotch tape. She pried the sticky charm off the paper, painstakingly, to avoid tearing the paper.

"Okay. I don't get it."

"It's Taylor. Taylor was there. I don't know when exactly, but that ring? The one in the clearing that I gave the police? This is its counterpart. Do you see now? They fit together. It said BEST FRIENDS."

Tripp nodded. "I do. But do you think Taylor killed her?"

"Yes. No. I don't know. But this isn't as simple as Nate and an affair. I know that."

Bridget asked for his phone and he handed it to her. She watched the video again, trying to make out the voice. Before it seemed disconnected, maybe a series of voices, maybe a boy with a falsetto *wooooowooooooo,* but now, her fingers turning around the sticky charm, rubbing at the embossment, she knew. Without a doubt.

"Taylor was there. The night she was raped, Taylor was there."

And then she thought of Taylor, folded on top of Andrew in his truck, her compact body kicking against his to some internal beat.

Bridget had to wonder: When did they become a couple, before or after the party?

Ironically, Nate would have known.

"I think Taylor killed Lucia. Maybe to keep her quiet. About Andrew."

Tripp nodded like he understood, but then asked, "But why? Why does she want to protect him?"

"Why else?" Bridget fought the urge to pat his cheek. "For love. She loves him."

At the police station, Bridget paced in the small waiting room with three blue vinyl and metal chairs and a glass table. Tripp let himself into the back, looking for Harper.

Bridget tried Nate again; no answer.

She'd marked the pages in the journal with a Post-it note, the ones to show him about Lulu, the video, the counterpart to the ring. She realized, too late, that it's not enough. It's just not enough to string together.

A detective came out, one Bridget had never seen before, not Harper, not Mackey, and she realized that they were sending out their third string. Everything she had would be tossed in a pile to be sifted through later. Evidence to be gathered to support the accusation, not the other way around.

Tripp followed the man and nodded behind him.

"Do they have Nate? Did they arrest Nate?" Bridget asked, and Tripp looked left and right before he finally nodded again. He started to speak, but the detective cut him off.

"I can take a statement, Ms. Peterson. And anything you'd like me to have?" He held his hand out, an expectation without promise. Bridget pulled the journal in tight to her chest.

"I'll come back. I made a mistake, okay?" She backed toward the door, Tripp looking confused behind the detective and shaking his head, mouthing *no,* but Bridget left anyway. Back into the parking lot, Tripp burst through the door after her.

"What are you doing?"

"I don't know. I don't know, but I'm not doing this. I'm not serving Nate up on some kind of platter. I need to figure it all out first. If we give everything over to Harper, who knows what will happen? I haven't read this thing cover to cover. Anything in it will be torn apart, scrutinized, and put back together in any way that supports his agenda."

"Bridget, stop it. That's not what will happen. Besides, I suspect this journal will become evidence regardless."

"Fine, but then I have time."

"Time for what?" Tripp came to her, so close she could smell him, leather and peppermint and something musky. She felt her heart flip, just once. His hand twitched on her elbow.

"I have to talk to Taylor. I'm the only one."

"I'll come with you." He said it automatically, like a statement, not a question.

"No. Stay here. Nate needs you. I'll be back." She was glad she'd brought her own car, glad she insisted on driving separate. She turned, started to walk toward her car.

"Bridget, don't be an idiot. Let me come with you." Tripp followed her, close on her heels.

At the car, before she got in, she hesitated. She turned and looked at Tripp, his face a reflection of both confusion and worry, the lines on his forehead permanent and something she'd never noticed before. In the weirdly dim parking lot—later she'd wonder why the lot at the police station was so dark—he looked older. Almost like an old man.

Bridget remembered this now, this quick pulse of heat, this wanting. She put her hands on his waist, right at the belt of his jeans, leaned up, and pressed her lips against his. Softly, at first, and then a bit more insistent, and he gave a soft cry of surprise. Bridget felt an unusual sort of power surge through her, high on the idea that she was giving him something he'd wanted forever, and admitting to herself that she'd known it.

Then his arms were around her and she didn't know how they got there but they were, and he pulled her against him, his mouth warm and his arms and chest unyielding, his thumbs rubbing at her waist, where her skirt sat. His mouth moved under hers, his tongue slipping between her lips, her body pressing closer, her heart hammering wildly in her chest so she was sure he must be able to feel it.

When she pulled away, the back of her hand against her mouth, she found she was smiling. He held her tight and she had to arch her back to look at him.

"I'm coming with you," he said, but he was smiling.

"You stay here. I'll be fine. I'll call you. She's

a high school girl. She won't say a word to me if you're with me. It's ten o'clock at night. I'm sure her mother is home."

"Call me immediately when you leave," Tripp said, and let her go, openly reluctant about it.

"Of course. Stay here until I get back." Bridget placed her palm against his chest and he moved his hand over it.

"You'll come back?" Tripp asked, his eyebrows raised in surprise.

"To you? Yes," Bridget said, her blood pumping with adrenaline, mixed up with the rush of new love and the idea that she could still have this feeling, could still be this person.

"That's not what I meant," Tripp said, smiling, his head turned to the side, his palm against his chin, his jaw. He looked back at the door, the detective backlit in the hallway, watching them.

"I know. But it's what I meant." She kissed his cheek.

Bridget got into the car and drove away. In the rearview mirror, she could see Tripp watch her go.

The Lawsons' house sat in the same development as the Tempests'. Part of the Mt. Oanoke elite, if there were such a thing. Their house was high on a rise, imposing but sterile, tan brick on the outside, utterly devoid of personality. Not even a potted plant. She wondered what Burt Lawson must pay to be free of Jennifer and Taylor. Seemed like a lot.

Before Bridget could second-guess herself, she rang the doorbell. The house was dark and she suspected either no one was home or everyone was sleeping. The door opened without either a porch light or an interior light being flicked on and Bridget gasped in surprise, Tripp's peppermint taste still zinging on her tongue.

"Mrs. Peterson! Really? What are you doing here?" It was Taylor, her voice lilting and dreamy.

"Taylor, is your mom here?" It was the first question Bridget could think of to ask and it was met with a high laugh, brittle in the quiet night.

"That would be a no, Mrs. Peterson." Bridget could smell the liquor on her breath wafting across the darkened threshold. A giggle, a stumble. Then, bam, like the sun, a porch light.

Taylor's hair was piled high on her head in a messy bun, her ears devoid of dangly earrings, her face white in the fluorescent ecofriendly LED porch light, her eyes black. Bridget almost didn't recognize her. Without her makeup, her thick cat-eyed eyeliner, she looked like a twelve-year-old. Prepubescent, even, gangly legs jutting out from beneath her cotton nightgown.

Taylor opened the door wide and then wandered away into the darkened house. Bridget tentatively stepped inside; it smelled new, cheap, and chemical. A light flipped on from somewhere upstairs and Bridget followed it and Taylor's footsteps up a winding staircase to a gaping hallway and an interior balcony, bumped out above the foyer below. She looked down and saw the front door, the glass and brass swinging chandelier. Below, the ceramic tile floor.

Bridget couldn't be sure because of the dark, but it seemed to be the only furnished room in the house.

Taylor sat in a monstrous plaid armchair under a dim table lamp, the smoke curling from a lit cigarette in her hand. In the far corner perched a dry bar, the clear bottles stacked together, an ice bucket sweating on the glass. The rich were strange.

"My mom hates when I smoke in here," she said. "But she's not here, so . . ." She shrugged then and laughed, a glass jangling with ice and clear liquid. Bridget would have bet it wasn't water. "So, Mrs. Peterson, are you here to talk to me? Or my mom?" She stretched her long skinny doe legs out, flexing her painted toes like a cat.

"You," Bridget said, and wondered briefly if she underestimated her. For some reason, in the dim of the balcony, watching the smoke spiraling from between Taylor's blue glittering fingertips, Bridget felt like Taylor had the upper hand. The sensation, like at the mill, of being driven forward by forces out of her control. "They found Lucia, Taylor. At the mill."

Taylor opened her eyes wide, but there was something black and dead in them. She shook her head.

"I'm not surprised, really. I'm sure Mr. Winters killed her, to shut her up. They were a thing, you know. I knew it, everyone knew it." Her voice changed, as well as her face. Her posture was slung low like a cat, slinking over the rolled arm of the chair, and she gave Bridget a slow, torpid smile. In that second, she seemed both beautiful and deeply malicious and, for a beat, Bridget was afraid.

"Oh? I didn't know it," Bridget said.

"Sure. Andrew saw them once, behind the school. He had his hand down her jeans."

Truth or lie? Lie, Bridget decided.

Taylor shook her head and blew out a cloud of smoke, which filled the space between them. "Andrew said she was a *big* girl, you know, down there. He should know."

Bridget tried to make her face passive. The Taylor she'd known was so different from this girl, this crude, drunk, calculating girl.

"So I'm sure he kinda lost it when the whole thing about Temp's party was about to blow, you know? I think she was losing her mind. She was babbling crazy things. She said Nate loved her. Was gonna leave his wife and that kid for her."

434

Taylor hiccupped, her bun bouncing, the ash from her cigarette scattering onto the plush of the plaid La-Z-Boy. She looked Bridget up and down. "He might leave that cunt of a wife, but he'll never leave that kid."

For a few moments all she could hear was the sound of Taylor's inhale, hold, exhale.

"The thing with Andrew was, well . . . She wanted that. Has wanted it forever. She took everything from me. All the time. And then to say what she said? That he *raped* her? Stupid. He had her on video. She didn't care if she was going to ruin him. Ruin his whole life."

"What about her life, Taylor?" Bridget asked.

"There's only one way out of this town, you know that."

"How's that?" Bridget asked.

"Only a man can get you out. No one knows that better than you, right?" She meant it to jab, to hurt. It didn't.

"Taylor, when I had a man, when he was alive, we lived in this town by choice. We moved here."

"Well, no accounting for taste, I guess." Exhale. "Jennifer says that."

"Does she also say the only way out of this town is with a man?"

"Sure, why not?" A giggle, exhale. Then, softer, "He's my only shot. I'm not going to college on my own. I don't think."

"Why not? Your grades are good. You could get out on your own, Taylor."

"Oh, don't you know? Burt's gone. I mean, he was gone before, but now he's really gone. Skipped town, no one can find him." She snorted. "No more money from him. You think Jennifer's gonna work now? Nah. We're upside down here. Stuck in this house. Look around, do you see any furniture?"

Bridget peered into the empty foyer below. The cavernous living room. The ugly incongruity of the plaid chair. She said nothing, stood with her hand resting lightly against the railing, the cool wood beneath her palm.

"We'll see when I get down there."

"Down where?" Bridget asked, the answer plain.

"Texas."

"Does he know yet? That you're following him?"

"Not yet. We have time before he goes. I'll graduate, get a shit job, and wait for him. It's fine. He's been freaked out. Coach Winters, then Lucia." Her voice pitched downward, like *Lucia* was a dirty word. "It will all be okay now."

"Lucia? Why?" Bridget feigned innocence, her phone in her hand, her thumb scrolling through the apps, looking almost bored while she pressed the button. The phone flashed red, blinking in her hand: record.

Taylor lit one cigarette off the other, clinked her ice cubes. She pushed off the armchair and stumbled to the bar in the corner, dimly illuminated by a night light. She leaned close to the railing and Bridget held her breath, *just one little misstep.* She imagined her flipping, feet over head, into the abyss below, the chandelier swinging gently.

"It was all so fucked up. She was going to just disappear long enough to fuck him up. Get him fired. Ruin his marriage. She was gone too long. That girl was always too dramatic. Always too much." Taylor poured more vodka from the bottle and flopped herself back into the chair. Caught her breath, like it was one big effort.

Finally, "He was mine first, that's all."

"He's not now?" Bridget asked, wondering briefly if she meant Andrew or Nate. Andrew. Definitely Andrew.

"Not with the lies Lucia's been spreading about him. It's all going to shit now. Well, maybe not anymore." She heaved another one of those big breaths, her hands splayed across her chest. "She ruins everything she touches."

Everything you touch. Accusatory, not amorous, then. *You ruin everything you touch.*

"You wrote that note, Taylor," Bridget could hardly breathe. "Who set it on fire?"

Taylor said nothing, just stared over her shoulder at the wall, shaking her head, an indistinct smirk playing on her mouth until her eyes darted away again. "Why? You love Lucia. She's your best friend."

Taylor leaned forward, her face white, her nose scrunched. "That girl. The truth?" She didn't wait for an answer. "I'm glad to be rid of her. She's been nothing but an anchor around my neck. Jennifer always pecking at her, worried about her. It's enough to make anyone sick."

"The thing is, I didn't say she was dead, Taylor," said Bridget, trying to look bored. Taylor watched her keenly.

"What?" She stopped, her eyes at the ceiling, staring at the glittering chandelier, her eyes spinning, blinking, her tongue licking the corner of her mouth. Every time a car passed, its headlights scattered a flickering strobe light around the hall.

"A minute ago, you said Nate killed her. But I never said she was dead. I just said they found her. How'd you know she was killed by anyone?" Bridget asked again.

"You said it. You did." Her eyes flitted around, her mouth working, twitching.

"What if I think *you* killed her?" Bridget whispered, her insides roiling like a careening car, the smoke and the sticky sweet smell of the house burning her eyes, the insides of her mouth, her nose.

"You're hilarious, Mrs. Peterson, really." Her

head lolled to the side. "You can think whatever you want. No one listens to you, you're just the town sad sack."

Taylor snapped to attention then, stood up, unsteady, knees knocking and came toward her. Bridget backed up, the railing right against her back, all that blackness below, and wondered if this is how it was for Lucia, the inkiness about to swallow her.

She grabbed the railing behind her, and in doing so let the phone go. She heard it crack on the floor below, a tinny, hollow sound. It didn't matter, she had the important part. The world had it.

It happened so fast. Before she could think, react, get out of the way, Taylor's arms shot out. Bridget felt herself pinwheel, the wood of the railing against her back.

Right after Taylor pushed her, as she tumbled over the railing, she wondered if Lucia had felt this way.

If she'd felt, for just a second, like she was flying.

She tried to kill me!

The voices were coming from inside her, screaming from her pelvis, her legs.

Then, *miss, I need you to please step outside.*

Then a scream. A slamming door. A siren. Then, finally, blessed silence.

CHAPTER 40

Lucia, Wednesday, May 13, 2015

"Lulu! Lulu!"

Lucia heard her before she saw her and wondered if Taylor would come all the way into the pulp room.

Taylor was afraid of the mill. Even when they'd come here two years ago, maybe more, with Andrew and Porter. Before things got weird, harder, when they'd build a fire and throw stones at the windows, the sound of the break becoming some kind of contest, the loudest raining glass eliciting a rumbled cheer from the boys. Daring each other to go inside. Alone.

Lucia was the only girl not afraid. She'd walked up to the pulper, the rotor shining in the middle, and wonder what it was like when it was bladed. They'd heard a story once about a man working there who'd fallen in, his body sliced to ribbons before they found him. Lucia had told Lenny about it and he'd laughed at her. *It didn't even have blades. It was just a mixer. The real danger was in the chemical they used. If you fell in, your face would slide clean off. Like The Joker.*

Lucia heard the yelp again, a dainty cry, and slid down into a far corner behind the cement wall of the machine. Taylor wouldn't come all the way in.

"Lulu!" Her voice, wobbling and wet, but close. Too close. "I know you're here. I know you. God, you love this fucking place. I'm alone. Come out, okay? I won't tell anyone. I just want to talk to you. The police are all up in our shit, looking for you. Can you hear me?" A scream, followed by a furious rustle, a stomping. Lucia covered her mouth with her hand. A spider. "Fucking spiders. Fine, you know what? Have it your way. I'll just have to find you."

Footsteps away from the pulp room, into the roller room. She kicked a cardboard roll, the hollow *phlump!* of the tube against the stone wall.

Lucia slid out along the side wall and climbed soundlessly through the front window. She edged along the outside of the building until she got around the corner and then ran for the dam, the weeds and grass up to her waist, licking at her bare arms.

It was hot for May.

Lucia didn't have a plan. She didn't always have a plan, but she usually had something in mind, the general outline of what to do next. This time, there was nothing but whiteness. A blank, beautiful whiteness like the foam of the dam flushing out her mind. She stood with her back against the widest oak, a bead of sweat zigzagging down her spine, and waited for the time to pass, for Taylor to get bored and leave.

"Found you, hooker. Knew I would. God, you're so predictable." Taylor shoved at her shoulder, hard, and Lucia was knocked sideways, into the oak, her elbow scratching at the bark.

"Jesus, Taylor, what the fuck are you doing out here?" Lucia rubbed her elbow and looked out at the water, the blackbirds looping around at the crest of the dam.

"See, I should ask you the same thing. You know everyone is looking for you. You're hiding. Why?"

Lucia laughed then, this honk of a laugh that got swallowed by the dam, the loudness of it clouding around them until she could almost feel the spray on her face.

Taylor continued, but stepped toward her, into her space, her mouth twisting, like she'd sucked a sourball. "What's your next move, genius? What's your plan? Just come waltzing back to Mt. Oanoke High like everything is A-OK?"

"No. I don't have a plan. Haven't you ever just wanted to get the fuck away? Like get out?" Lucia pulled her hair down, her skin tingling where it met the root, and she felt the first prick of pain there, like a pin. She wound a small thread around her index finger, just ten hairs maybe, baby stuff, and pulled until it popped and her eyes watered.

Taylor watched her and shook her head, closed her eyes. "Not like this, you freak. Do you know that people think Mr. Winters killed you? You know what else I heard? Mrs. Peterson is all over it. She found that video, she asked Mr. Trevor about it. She's about to be running her mouth around that Andrew killed you. And yet"—she swung her arm wide, her fingertips grazing weeds and sending a swarm of gnats up in a cyclone— "Here you are. This is what you wanted. Right?" She stepped forward again until Lucia stepped back. "Right?"

She felt something inside her pop, like the lid off the seltzer that Lenny used to drink, a fizz and then a rush of bubbling. "I wanted to ruin his life. His happy, perfect little life with his happy, perfect little wife. He's the only person who has ever understood me. He knew me. But he picked Andrew when he had to. I made him choose and he chose Andrew. He chose someone else." Lucia looked out over the river; the blackbirds were back, looping and ducking, four of them now. "You wouldn't get it, not really. You have your mom—"

"My mom fucks anything that moves. So don't go acting like she's the greatest thing. You don't see me out here, framing perfectly innocent people because my mom is a whore—"

"Perfectly innocent? Taylor, what the hell is perfectly innocent about Nate Winters? He's the reason." Lucia felt her voice screech, her fingers seeking the corn silk threads at the back of her head, her face tilting up to the sky. "You'd never get it. He's the reason. They all think he's God. He's like the God of Mt. Oanoke. Andrew, Porter, Josh. They're all this club and no one else matters. And they all take turns building each other up, so high, so tall until they're in this giant ivory tower in the sky and we're all nothing. We're all nothing."

"Are you high? For real, are you high?" Taylor stepped toward her again, her face white with bloodred lips and her eyes flashing.

Something fell then, inside of her. A muscle or a bone, or maybe it was just whatever made people stand up straight, until suddenly, she couldn't. She wanted to crawl down into the dirt, with the bugs and the sulfur water spray, her head lolling into her chest, her body feeling so heavy.

"Are you even fucking listening to me? You've done what you set out to do. You ruined his life. His wife kicked him out. He lost his job. And you know what else? You ruined Andrew's, too. He'll lose that scholarship, wanna bet? Winters was his ticket, his recommendation. So you'll wreck everyone's lives and I'll just stay here, in Mt. Oanoke, forever. I guess taking care of you like I've done my whole life. All because why?"

Lucia had never seen Taylor so angry. She was like a different person. "He didn't believe me. About Andrew. None of you believe me. But he has it on video."

"He has you saying yes on the video. You hooked up with Andrew and Porter that night. Everyone was there. Listen, I could be pissed. I won't be that girl. But you, you're fucking ridiculous."

Fucking ridiculous, Lenny's open slap across her cheek, sharp and quick.

"He let me think I mattered to him. He was interested in what I thought, what I had to say. He got inside my head. Then he threw it all away like I was nothing. Because of Andrew." Lucia pushed past Taylor, but Taylor reached out, her fingers like talons on Lucia's arm.

"You need to come back. Now. Tell everyone what you did. Have you been here the whole time?"

Lucia shook her head. She'd been in the woods for a while, a hunting shack about a mile off Route Six, then she walked through trees, keeping the river to her left, and found her way down to the mill. She figured eventually someone would come looking, but she'd wagered on Mrs. Peterson, and Lucia knew she could outsmart her. She hadn't figured on Taylor. She tried to remember Taylor spinning that day in the mall, that mossy water all up on her long, skinny calves, her mouth parted, glistening, and cotton-candy-glazed eyes up toward the ceiling, her hair flying around her like a cape. Just so happy. It's the last time she remembered them being so happy together.

"Come back with me, Lucia. I'll stay with you." Taylor's voice was high, like a blade through air. Something flashed in her fingertips and she waggled it in front of Lucia's face. The ring. The plasticky, shining heart ring, from that day in the mall. "Do you still love me? Do you trust me?"

Lucia could envision Taylor, taking care of her, almost preening, rallying her troops, her mom. She could see it all happening. She'd stay at Taylor's, they'd come up with a story.

Lucia shook her head.

The plan was to always go back. But now, the light was different, the air. The sky shone brighter. Something.

"Are you with him now?" Lucia couldn't look at her when she asked this and instead watched the dirt.

"Who?" Taylor said, playing dumb.

"Pfft. Who. You know who. The rapist."

"Stop. Saying. That." Taylor's voice changed, a rumble in her throat. "You fucked him and now you're sorry. It is what it is. Doesn't mean he's yours forever."

"I don't want him. I didn't fuck him. I didn't

want it. I wanted to go home. You know that, you were there. Why?" Lucia finally did look up, Taylor's hair flying, the sun behind her shining red through the black. She looked like an angel. "Why does no one believe me?"

"You said yes." Taylor shrugged, cracked her gum. Lucia got a whiff of Juicy Fruit.

"I was barely conscious. I didn't say. . . ." Lucia thought about it. She had watched the video. Just once. On her phone, her feet pulled up on the toilet, crouched in a stall in the janitor's bathroom by the cafeteria. Out in the hall, Minnie, the lunch lady, had latched on to her shoulder. *Why you cryin' girl? You okay?* Lucia hadn't even known she was. "He *broadcast* it, T. Why is this okay with you?"

Taylor laughed. "You know, you've been on me since we were kids. Even my mom feels sorry for you. How many dinners have you eaten at my house? Like all the dinners you've ever eaten in your whole life have been at my house. I tried to bring you with me, to the right crowd, the right friends, the right parties. You still couldn't be normal. You've never just been *normal*. You never were grateful or thankful or anything. And now you're just gonna do this? He's the only one in this town that has anything going for him. And you're just gonna, what? Ruin it? You know he's got a baseball scholarship? Full ride. Nobody gets that shit anymore. Down in Texas, biggest baseball school of the country. Like maybe he'll be a pro one day."

"What, you've got big dreams then? Like he'll take you with him?" Lucia laughed. She couldn't help it. *This fucking town.*

"Why not? Maybe." Taylor shrugged. "But not with you running your mouth all over. Nope. Not that way for sure." Taylor grabbed Lucia's arm then, her knuckles white, tight against her skin. Taylor got close, her breath candy sweet, her face red and shining, her mouth black, open. "Remember that night at the mill? You thought you were special. You thought he didn't kiss everyone. That was years ago, we were practically kids. And now, you *still* think you're special."

"I don't think I'm special. No one thinks I'm special." Lucia tried to pry Taylor's fingers off her arm, but they held strong, like a vise.

"All anyone ever talks about is you. Even Andrew—*where's the witch tonight?*—like they want you around but they hate you, too. Even now, two years later, he's so into you, of all people. You think you're so smart with your philosophy and tarot cards, your artsy drawings. Your stupid druggie brother, your runaway dad. Everyone feels sorry for you. But you're just a freak. And the only one who knows it is me."

Lucia wrenched her arm away and backed up through the clearing. Taylor smiled a little but her eyes went dead in a way Lucia had never seen, her cheeks fevered and hot, and suddenly Lucia was there, right at the edge, the embankment looming behind her like a black shadow. Taylor was still walking toward her, her mouth moving, her words crawling into Lucia, into her mouth and down into her stomach, roiling and rolling until she felt like she was going to throw up.

Taylor stopped right in front of her, blinking, her face twitching. "Maybe everyone would just be happier if you were dead."

Her hands were on Lucia's chest, a single, air-sucking jab, like a punch, and Lucia felt herself flying backward, into the air, the sprinkling water cold on her face, her arms, and for a split second, she felt easy, light.

Free.

Then she started to fall.

CHAPTER 41

Alecia, Friday, May 15, 2015

"She's awake."

Nate stood in the waiting room doorway, a swaggering stance she'd gotten used to over the years, but still somehow seemed to startle her when she saw it: thumbs hooked in his jeans pockets, a lock of blond hair falling over his eyes. Like she'd married a boy.

"And?" Alecia stood, her book falling to the floor, her breath caught in her throat.

"Two broken legs. A few broken ribs. Miraculously, no concussion."

"Okay. I'll be in."

Nate lingered a minute, some unspoken plea caught in his open mouth. Then he left her there.

It was early Friday morning, but there was already a paper at the nurses' station. Alecia touched it with her fingertip, twirling it around to read the headline.

Student Charged in Death of Mt. Oanoke High School Senior

Friday morning, a student at Mt. Oanoke High was charged with the murder of Lucia Hamm, 18, a senior at Mt. Oanoke high who has been missing since May 4, 2015.

Nathan Winters, a teacher at Mt. Oanoke High, was previously suspected in Hamm's disappearance. Winters has been cleared of any involvement in the missing persons case, but is still under investigation for his alleged relationship with Hamm. His job has not been reinstated at this time.

Tad Bachman, the high school principal, had no comment on the case or the status of Winters's teaching position at this time.

"Yeah, I think he slept with that student. It'll all be swept under the rug now," said Rob Minnow, father to junior student Kelsey Minnow. "My daughter will be a senior next year, likely to have him as a teacher. People love him. I've never understood why. Baseball, I guess."

Alecia stopped reading. The early morning light, pink and orange, streaked through the windows, lighting up the waiting room like the inside of a Christmas bulb.

451

What she believed about Nate seemed just as naïve and rose colored.

Did he sleep with a student? No.

Was he attracted to his student? Maybe.

Did he kill her? No.

Anyone else would have kicked him to the curb.

The Wednesday before, the day that ended up inadvertently acting as Nate's alibi, thanks to a well-timed Chinese food receipt that he happened to sign for, she'd felt the first prick of hope. That day at Gabe's doctor's appointment, they told her they were taking him off one of his meds, the one that gave him stomach pains and diarrhea, the one she'd begged them to take him off of for months. Nate had come, for the first time in as long as she could remember. She'd texted him on a whim and he showed up, hesitantly in the waiting room, his thumbs hooked in his jeans pockets.

He'd been patient.

They exchanged a smile over Gabe's head.

It wasn't everything. But it was something. The start of something or the end of something, it was always so hard to tell. Sometimes they looked the same.

She watched Nate with Gabe and realized, with a sudden, sinking clarity, that he did do one thing well that she did not. The thing that Linda had urged her to do: accept. Nate had always been more accepting of Gabe in his weirdness, his messiness, his Gabeness. Nate's impatience came from Alecia more than from his son: the money and energy Alecia insisted they spend trying to fix him. He didn't care about the therapies, the herbal medicines, the diets, and the rituals that made up "living with Gabe." Nate was happier to simply live with Gabe.

Bridget's room was filled with people: Nate and Tripp on one side, Petra on the other, a nurse taking her blood pressure, clicking off the beats with her acrylic nails then flashing big white teeth at them. "All good!"

Both of Bridget's legs were in giant black-and-blue Velcro air casts up to her thighs. Her hair was matted and damp, her face scrubbed clean and shining.

Tripp, closest to the bed, had his hand resting beside Bridget's. Alecia glanced over to Petra, feigning ignorance, and wondered if she noticed. She must. The room vibrated when they looked at each other.

Alecia wondered when it happened.

"Bridget was the hero," Nate said. "If it wasn't for her, well . . ." He'd left the rest unsaid, and Alecia swallowed her shame, looked away. Studied Bridget's chart, the wall, the fire extinguisher instructions.

Bridget talked, filling in the gaps, her voice halting and croaky: Lucia framed Nate for the affair. She'd come onto him and he rejected her. On top of that, Nate questioned the validity of her rape claim (at this, Nate had the decency to look down, ashamed). Petra examined her fingernails the whole time.

She was only supposed to disappear long enough to make Nate sweat it out, get him fired, end his marriage. But she never came back. Taylor went looking for her, they argued, Taylor pushed her over the edge of the embankment. Just like Taylor pushed Bridget.

Taylor, so in love with her best friend's rapist that she killed to protect him. Was everyone really so desperate to leave this place?

Alecia wondered if she actually meant to do it. She imagined a quick flash of anger, the impulse to push her, to shut her up.

"What will happen to Taylor?" Alecia was the only one who asked, and now everyone else looked away; no one had an answer. Bridget had recorded the whole fight in Taylor's hallway, the darkened room catching the voices clearly. She'd sent it, broadcast to the world, on her Periscope account, so even the shattered phone didn't matter.

"And Andrew? The rape?"

Nate shifted in his seat. "I sent a letter to the school. I don't know if it will matter. I told them I couldn't write his recommendation. I told them what he did."

Tripp tapped the bed. "We saved the video, right, Bridge?" He leaned forward.

Bridget nodded, her eyes half closed.

"It might not matter. She's dead. She said yes. It would be hard to prosecute." Tripp sat back, deflated. "He'll lose that scholarship. But he won't pay in any real way." He said it with the confidence of someone who'd learned the hard lessons of the law, first hand, for years.

"Hard, but not impossible," Alecia said, suddenly wanting this, Andrew's lost baseball future not enough. None of it enough.

Nate's hand covered his mouth, his eye twitching. "Can I testify?" he asked, dumbly, trying too hard to save a girl who was long past saving. The offer was for himself, a balm on his guilt.

Alecia turned away, glad, maybe for the first time ever, that Gabe wouldn't be a "normal" boy.

Perhaps Linda had been right. There is nothing so great about normal.

Later, after everyone left and only Alecia remained, they watched *The Price Is Right*. Alecia rested her hand in the same place Tripp had, right next to Bridget's hand. She studied her long, delicate fingers. So thin. She looked like a child, and Alecia had no idea when that had happened.

"So . . . you and Tripp?"

Bridget gave a shrug, didn't take her eyes of the television.

"You have to say *something*," Alecia said, pushing her the way you press your thumb to a recent bruise, just to feel the pain in all its newness.

"Okay." Bridget sighed. "What will you do about Nate?" Now she looked right at Alecia's face, almost defiant, until Alecia felt her heart fill up her chest, the pain quick and sharp, then abating.

Nate.

"I can't make it up to him," Alecia said, holding Bridget's gaze. Watching her friend shake her head, agree with Alecia that no, she couldn't. Could Nate make it up to her?

She recalled the way Nate had behaved at home on Wednesday (how lucky he was that Lucia had been killed on Wednesday, that science could prove it): attentive, gentle, his hands over hers, jumping up to answer the door, quick to sign the credit card receipt, hurrying to get Gabe a cup of milk, her a glass of water, and later, an uncharacteristic glass of wine.

She thought about how quickly she'd adapted to a life with just Gabe, how much lighter the air in the house felt after Nate had left, the cord of muscle between her shoulder blades loose and easy. She felt something else, too, away from Nate. Something new and just born, fresh but raw, stripped bare like skin after a chemical peel: Gabe might be okay. Not the child she'd hoped for, not the person she thought he would be. But he'd still be fine, just as he was. She thought of the soccer ball sticker, peeling and curled in the bottom of her drawer. It would turn yellow and gummy before she'd use it.

Was it up to only her? Would Nate even want to come home?

"He'll come home," Bridget said, reading her mind. She licked her lip, took a sip of the ice water from the cup on her nightstand. "You're everything to him." She looked away then, almost like it made her sad.

Alecia wasn't so sure. She thought of Gabe, tucked into bed; Mandy, the baby-sitter, lying on the couch, tongue lolling out. She thought of Nate letting himself in, watching her sleep. Would he watch her sleep?

Would she always question him?

"I'm going home, Alecia," Bridget said. "To Georgia. Just as soon as I'm better—eight weeks probably."

"Why? The kids love you," Alecia said, but it was a lie. They liked Bridget just fine, but they'd be fine without her, too.

"My mom isn't well, hasn't been for years. I'm missing this time with her. I can't stay here. In this town, the ghost of that girl, I just can't. That mill, that school." Bridget ran her finger along her upper lip. "It's never been good here. Not for me. You see that, right?"

Alecia did see it, but instead she took Bridget's hand in hers. "What about Tripp? Holden's mom?"

Bridget sighed, ran her palm along the top of Alecia's hand. "We'll have the memorial. I'll find a tree. I'm ready. I wasn't before, but I am now. Tripp is . . . Tripp. He's an Oanoke lifer."

Alecia knew and did not say that Nate was, too.

"You know, the birds did this," Bridget said.

Six weeks ago, Alecia would have laughed at her. Bridget with her herbs and her tarot and her instincts.

"If it weren't for them, there would have been no reporter to see Lucia and Nate at that motel. It's like they all fell for a reason. Or a warning. We're all too complacent here, too sleepy, too insular. Like when the mill closed, the town died, too." Bridget continued, her eyes squinting, watching the coil of tubes running from the IV into her arm, a clear liquid dripping. "You know, they never even figured it out, what really did it. Sometimes I wonder . . ." She shook her head, her voice lowered, her fingertips trembling. "If she really was a witch. You know she saw dead blackbirds all the time? I read her journals; she said whenever she saw one, something bad happened. She had this obsession with blackbirds, ravens, crows. What if Lucia did it? What if all this is her fault?"

"She was just a girl, Bridget," Alecia said. "Think of how many times we see birds, on the side of the road, whatever, and pay it no attention. Besides, the birds that fell were starlings, not blackbirds." Alecia pulled her hand out of Bridget's balmy grip, flexed her fingers. "Listen, she was just a girl with a big imagination and no one to love her."

"Except Nate?" Bridget said softly.

That part could have been true. Nate had a flair for the girls in need. Alecia thought of herself, an ice island floating in the warm Carolina sunshine, surrounded by bubbly, sorority giggliness, and he'd reached out and saved her. Took her in, thawed her out with a heat she almost couldn't bear.

And now, somehow they were here again. His humanity would be his downfall, the reason she'd cite later if she left him. The same one she'd cite if she stayed.

"Jimmy. He came back. He loved her, in his own way," Bridget said suddenly, her voice rasping, almost urgent. She was right, it was the only reason he came back. Alecia thought of what Nate had told her that night, with the Chinese food in living room that had felt like a cocoon. *He had a house, why did he stay in the woods?* She imagined the fish, shimmering and bouncing on his knee, the blood on his hands. They had thought it weird, suspicious even. Now, with everything that had happened, only one thing made sense: he was in the woods, looking for his daughter.

Outside the first-floor window, Nate locked his Honda, the *beep-beep* audible through the hospital window. Alecia watched him lope across the parking lot, back to her, back to his old life, like nothing had happened, a bump in his step that hadn't been there for weeks. She watched his long legs, his noticeably bigger paunch, the puff of his face. He might have been whistling.

She'd never know, that's the thing. She'd never know the whole truth, not only what he did but how he felt, what he thought. She'd never know, *for sure,* whom or even why he'd loved. She knew now, and didn't know before, that there were gradients to love. That sometimes saving someone requires giving up everything, including yourself, and some people need that to feel whole.

You never know the deep down truth about anybody, except yourself. And sometimes, not even then.

I'm not a witch, of course not. But anyone can make things happen. It's called magical thinking. The baseball team with their mismatched socks. The way Taylor's grandmother never walked under a ladder or opened an umbrella in the house. The idea that these small rituals keep bad things from happening: a lost game, lost love, lost money. Superstition. The avoidance of bad luck. But what about making things actually happen? It's harder, but possible. And it's not witchcraft. I should know.

No one pays for anything in this town. The mill closes up, everyone out of a job. Good people, or at least people on the razor edge of goodness.

The game will go on, no matter what the coach or his players have done.

I can't be responsible for everyone. I'm nothing if not practical.

But Andrew. Mr. Winters. Taylor. Jimmy, even.

I can make them all pay, even just a little.

It wasn't hard. A tip to the reporter, she was just hanging around anyway. Her phone glued to her hands at the Bean Café, waiting for the birds. Waiting for the DEP. Bored.

Sex for grades. He takes them to Deannie's Motel, up the river.

The part about being in love? That day in Bachman's office? That might have been true. I ask you, how would I know?

The rest was unplanned, see? I'll go back one day. Maybe. It might be fun to just fly away. People around here would talk about that their whole lives.

Remember the witch, they'd say. She just—poof—disappeared. Later the story would change because it sounded better: she disappeared the same day the birds fell.

There's poetry in that. Or magic.

ACKNOWLEDGMENTS

I'm incredibly fortunate to have landed at Atria/ Simon & Schuster, and am forever grateful for Sarah Cantin, Stephanie Mendoza, and Hillary Tisman for making my every writerly dream come true. Thank you doesn't seem like enough to agent extraordinaire, Mark Gottlieb, and all the foreign rights team at Trident Media Group. I'm so lucky it's ridiculous. To all my first readers: Elizabeth Buhmann, my Badass critique team: Aimie, Jamie, Andrea, Theresa, Ella, Orly, and Gwen, you guys are amazing. Also Karen Katchur, Ann Garvin, Amy Impellizzeri, Sonja Yoerg, Amy Nathan, and Kimberly Giarratano. Everything you say is gospel, I swear to God.

To my writer tribe, Tall Poppy Writers, I'd be so lost without you all. Sarah D, you'll be in every acknowledgment forever because without you, I wouldn't ever have written a word. I still have my reindeer fur.

To my family, especially those of you who talk about my books loudly and often, even when not entirely appropriate to do so, you're the best. To Mom and Dottie, who cover kid duty when I have to play author, I'm eternally grateful. Love my village.

Thanks to my dad, the greatest teacher I ever had. Nothing from this book was stolen from his impeccable career.

And finally, to Chip and my girls, who play a constant second fiddle to the muse in my mind and only seem to get really irritated with me when you have to say it a third time. I appreciate your mostly bottomless patience. I love you to the moon and back.

Center Point Large Print
600 Brooks Road / PO Box 1
Thorndike, ME 04986-0001 USA

(207) 568-3717

US & Canada:
1 800 929-9108
www.centerpointlargeprint.com